BARBARA DELINSKY

Flirting
with Pete

A NOVEL

DOUBLEDAY LARGE PRINT HOME LIBRARY EDITION

Scribner
NEW YORK LONDON TORONTO
SYDNEY SINGAPORE

This Large Print Edition, prepared especially for
Doubleday Large Print Home Library, contains
the complete, unabridged text of the original
Publisher's Edition.

SCRIBNER
1230 Avenue of the Americas
New York, NY 10020

SCRIBNER and design are trademarks of
Macmillan Library Reference USA, Inc., used under
license by Simon & Schuster, the publisher of this work.

Manufactured in the United States of America

ISBN 0-7394-3515-9

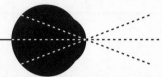

This Large Print Book carries the
Seal of Approval of N.A.V.H.

Acknowledgments

I first came to know Jenny Clyde and her Pete seven years ago. *Flirting with Pete* has been on my mind ever since then, waiting for the right moment to emerge as my book of the year. Now that it has, I realize how precarious publishing can be and how easily this book, which has consumed so much of my heart and soul, might have gone unwritten. That it didn't is as much a result of the tenacity of the story as the endless support of my agent, Amy Berkower. Amy understands Pete, my audience, and me. Her encouragement has made all the difference in the world.

As with most books I write, this one involved a significant amount of research. Helping me with that task were Elizabeth Fisk and my daughter-in-law, Sherrie Selwyn Delinsky. Both are experts in their fields. If there are mistakes herein, I take full responsibility for them. I do try to get things right. On occasion, though, I either misunderstand, unintentionally misstate, or simply assume that I know the answer and therefore don't ask the right question. Connie Unger would not be pleased with me. My apologies to him, and to you.

I thank my editors, Michael Korda and Chuck Adams, for being there for me. I thank the entire Scribner team, from Susan moldow on down, for enthusiasm, creativity, and smarts. I thank my assistant, Wendy Page, for deflecting phone calls so that I might have uninterrupted writing time, and my Webmaster, Claire Marino, for exploring the hidden gardens of Beacon Hill with me and throwing her knowledge of plants into the mix.

My family knows what *Flirting with Pete* means to me. I thank them all—Eric and Jodi, Andrew, and Jeremy and Sherrie—for being excited each time I breathed word of this book. To my husband, Steve, for his forbearance, indulgence, and input, always my thanks and love.

Again, always, still, I thank my readers, who embrace every new book I write, appreciate the differences between them, and incite me to write better and more. You are good folk. I am lucky, indeed.

Flirting
with Pete

Little Falls

The call came at three in the morning. Dan O'Keefe rushed into his uniform and drove out to the Clyde house, not because Darden Clyde demanded it or because it was Dan's job, though both were true, but because he was worried about Jenny.

He should have been used to worrying about Jenny. He had been doing it since signing on as his father's deputy eight years before, when she had been a bruised sixteen-year-old who always kept a distance from her peers and could never quite look you in the eye. He had worried when she was eighteen, when her mother died and her father went to prison, and he had worried in the six years since then, watching her become more and more of a pariah in town. He hadn't done much to help her. So he felt guilt.

That guilt was compounded now. He didn't want Darden out of prison any more than Jenny did, but he hadn't fought against it. So he felt guilty and he worried.

And then there was his shoulder. It always ached when bad things were in store. His father blamed that on his being a lousy football player, but those old injuries were long healed. Tension needled the scars, that was all. The shoulder had burned when Darden Clyde stepped from that bus onto Little Falls dirt at 6:12 the evening before. Now it ached something fierce.

He sped through a drizzle out from the center of town, straight down West Main, past houses so dark he wouldn't have known they were there if he hadn't memorized every inch of the town. A mile out, and the houses grew farther apart. Turning in at the only one with a light, he held the wheel tightly as the

Jeep bounced through puddles down the Clydes' rutted drive. He parked near the kitchen door, which was ajar, took a pair of mud-streaked steps in a single stride, and pulled open the screen.

The kitchen was a tired pine—cabinets, table, and chairs—with pink Formica counters and linoleum so compulsively scrubbed clean as to be the color of flesh, which at that moment was the most human element in the room. Darden sat on the floor at the end of a trail of mud. He was propped against the wall under the phone, looking like a wet rat, with his hair and clothes sodden and gray. His face was streaked with blood. He was cradling his right arm, favoring his entire right side. He raised only his eyes, as if he didn't have more strength than that. Even then, those eyes held evil.

"She ran me down," he charged in an angry growl, "knocked me right out. I was lying in the rain for hours. It took more hours to crawl in here. My hip's killing me."

Dan couldn't have cared less about Darden's hip. He went to the door that led to the hall and listened. The house was dead still. "Where is she?"

"How the hell do I know? That's why I called you. She ran me down with my own friggin' car and took off. That's hit-and-run, theft, and driving without a license."

Dan knew that the Buick was gone. His headlights had lit up the empty garage when he had turned in off the street. But he figured Jenny might have ditched the car somewhere and come back. Yes, she told him she was leaving town and, yes, she mentioned a friend, but no one had ever seen the guy. Alone, Jenny Clyde was shy and insecure. Dan couldn't see her suddenly wandering off after all this time. Easier to see her crouched in the dark on the roof, taking her life in her hands on the rain-slick slate.

He headed that way.

"Hey!" Darden hollered after him. "Where do you think you're goin'?"

Ignoring him, Dan made a fast check of the house. He braced himself against finding the kind of gruesome scene he had found there six years before, but he saw neither Jenny nor any sign of vio-

lence. Other than a wet dress on the bedroom floor and a nest of pillows, quilts,
and newspaper clippings in the attic,
everything was neat. The roof was deserted, as was, mercifully, the ground far
below.

He returned to the kitchen.

"I could a told you she wasn't here,"
Darden groused. "She took my car. Want
me to say it again? *She took my car.* You
have to look out *there.*"

Dan intended to do that. He knew
Jenny wasn't much of a driver. He had
caught her behind the wheel more than
once and had given her a talking-to each
time, but what more could he do? Ticket
her for weaving across the road? Take
away her keys? Haul her in for driving
without a license and send her over to
the county jail to be locked up with
cokeheads and hookers?

What worried him was the possibility
that she'd had an accident. There were
many places around Little Falls where a
car could go off the road and not be seen
for days. He planned to check out those
places. First, though, he wanted Darden
to talk.

He pulled out a chair and sat. The remains of dinner, dried-up beef stew and half-eaten rolls, were still on the kitchen table. An upset bottle reeked of warm spilled beer. "What happened here?"

Darden put his head to the wall. "I told you. She ran me down and left."

"Why?"

"How the hell should *I* know? I was having supper. She said she was leaving. When I tried to stop her, she ran me down." His eyes were cold and hard. "Find her, O'Keefe. That's your job. If you have to charge her, charge her. Just get her back."

"Why? She's twenty-four and the farthest she's ever been from here was visiting you in prison. Maybe it's time."

"The hell it is. It's time she was *here*," the man argued, jabbing a rigid finger at the floor. "She's had six friggin' years—"

"To do what?" the deputy cut in loudly. "Escape? How could she? You busied her here keeping things up the way you wanted, and you told her how much she owed you each time she went to visit, and that's not counting phone calls. I can't *begin* to imagine what you said to her in those."

"She's my daughter. She did what she did because she loves me."

Dan came to his feet. He figured that if he didn't use his legs to get out of there, they'd soon be kicking Darden Clyde. He wasn't one for police brutality—actually he detested it, which was only one of the points he and his father argued about— but he was coming close to it now himself. He was that angry.

"Let's get one thing straight, scumbag," he said. "Jenny did what she did all these years because you scared the living daylights out of her. She should have sold the house after what happened here, but you wouldn't let her. She should have sold it or burned it or just left it and took off. I kept telling her to, but you kept telling her not to. You wanted her tied to those memories, you and your perverted mind. That poor thing suffered for a whole lot more years than you spent in jail, and you're the one to blame." He leaned in, feeling a hatred so raw he could have spit. "So listen to me and listen good. If I find that girl harmed by your hand, you'll wish you died in jail. Got that?"

Darden sputtered dismissively. "You don't have the guts to touch me. Your daddy does, maybe. Not you."

Dan straightened. "And I've had more'n thirty-two years of watching him," he warned, "so don't you underestimate me. If she's harmed, you'll see just how deep my guts run. I got no use for you."

Darden's face said the feeling was mutual. His eyes could have killed.

The deputy rubbed his shoulder. "Did she say where she was going?"

"No."

"Do you have any *idea* where she was going?"

"She mentioned someone named Pete."

"Do you know him?"

"How the fuck would I know him? I haven't even been back here twelve hours!"

"Maybe she met him up at the prison?"

Darden stared at him in silence, and, not for the first time, Dan wished he had pushed the issue of Pete with Jenny. He had let it be, because she had seemed happy enough, and Jenny happy was such a rare thing. Given the turn of events, though, he would have liked to know she had run off with someone good. He would have taken great pleasure in telling Darden that.

"Did she ever mention him to you before?" Dan asked. "Did she ever mention any guy before?"

Darden grunted a no.

"So what'd you say when she told you about him?"

"I told her," Darden snarled, "she wasn't going anywhere."

The deputy was willing to bet he'd said a hell of a lot more than that. "What did she say?"

"She said she was."

"So you went back and forth on it. Was that all?"

"What do you mean, 'was that all'?"

"Did you hit her?"

"I don't hit her. I love her. She's my daughter. I came back here to take care of her."

Oh yeah. Dan knew how *that* worked,

and told Darden so with a look. "Did you touch her?"

"I didn't go *near* her. Go *after* her, O'Keefe. Every minute you sit here asking your blasted questions, she's getting farther away."

That was Dan's point, assuming Jenny was alive and well and escaping Darden like she should have done years before. If that was the case, he wanted to give her as much of a lead as he could.

If she'd been in an accident, though, he needed to find her.

He went to the phone and called the community hospital two towns over for an ambulance to come for Darden. Trusting that the man wasn't going far, he left him sitting alone on the floor, took the flashlight from the Jeep, and went out searching for Jenny on the grounds near the house and in the woods. While he was at it, he looked for something to suggest that a motorcycle had been around. Jenny had said her Pete drove one of those. But Dan came up empty on both counts. So he set off to search for her in the Jeep.

* * * *

By the time the sun rose, he had covered every mile of road in Little Falls, but he hadn't come across the Buick either parked, stalled, or crashed. He stopped at his parents' place to fill in his father, who was too busy standing in front of the radio talking back to Imus to pay Dan much heed, and was quite content to leave the search for Jenny in his hands— which pleased Dan. He knew he would do a better job of it simply because he cared. His father had been the chief of police in Little Falls for nearly forty years; he was bored, blasé, hardened.

Dan was none of those things. Feeling a growing urgency, he returned to the garage that housed the police station and made a handful of calls. Once he had the neighboring police chiefs on alert for the Buick, he headed out again himself.

By his figuring, he was one of only three people in whom Jenny might have confided about her plans to leave town. The other two were Miriam Goodman, who did catering throughout the state from her little kitchen here in town, and the Congregational Church's own Reverend Putty. Dan talked with both. Neither could shed any light on where she might be.

He covered the roads again, in daylight this time, but the end result was the same. So he returned to town for coffee and eggs at the luncheonette. He guessed that if anyone knew anything, he would pick it up there.

The only thing he picked up was the extent of the ill will the townsfolk held toward Darden Clyde. No one seemed pleased that he hadn't suffered a broken hip after all, but only a lot of scrapes and bruises, or that all the while he'd been treated at the emergency room, he had been cursing Dan O'Keefe.

"He says you're aiding and abetting a felon."

"Says you don't know diddly about proper police work."

"Says if you had anything but you-know-what for brains you'd bring in the FBI."

So reported Dan's friends with offense neither intended nor taken. In truth, he listened with only half an ear. Odds and ends of things were nagging at him. His shoulder was tight. His insides were shaky. His worry for Jenny was growing.

He hit the road again, stopping to search every gully and turnoff, thinking that the higher the sun went, the greater the chance that it might throw light on something he hadn't seen on one of his earlier passes. By mid-morning, he still hadn't found a thing.

So he went to the quarry. He had already been there twice that day, but this time he did it just for himself. Pulling into a parking spot at its base, he climbed out of the Jeep. Clear as it was in town, it was foggy here, which was one of the reasons he had come. Fog freed the mind. It blurred truth and allowed for hope. The quarry was a place of dreams under any condition. The thicker the fog, the richer the dream.

His own dream? To do something good. To *do* something good.

Naive as that sounded, it was one of the reasons he had taken the job. A second was that back then he had tried but hadn't found his feet yet as an artist, and he needed the money. A third reason? His mother had begged him to take it, because his father couldn't get anyone else to do the work. Law enforcement in Little Falls was not inspiring. It consisted of delivering truants to school, drunks to jail, and addicts to the treatment center three valleys west. It entailed settling petty spats among the townsfolk and refereeing domestic disputes. It called for cruising the roads of Little Falls for hours on end, letting people think that they were safe.

Were they? It sure felt it right here, right now. Hard to believe evil existed in this place, what with the whisper of water against granite, the rustle of pine needles drying out from the rains, the scurry of creatures in the underbrush, and everything smelling moist and new. Fog left no shadows for demons to lurk in. On a day like this, the quarry had the feel of a church, a waystation on a path to heaven.

It was a fanciful thought—just the kind that his father would call the waste of a big-city college education—but it stuck in Dan's mind. There was something peaceful, even sacred about this place. He felt calmer standing here. Hopeful. Even his shoulder felt better, which was odd given the dampness.

He rubbed the shoulder. Definitely better. He breathed in a lungful of fog and looked around. Definitely hopeful.

How to explain it?

The quarry was a giant ladle, its bottom a granite bowl filled with springwater from high up the mountain, its top the dirt ledge that capped a twenty-foot handle and was a springboard for the town's fancy. Dan walked around the bottom of the bowl, stepping cautiously on granite still wet from last night's rain. He crossed the planked bridge over the runoff of the bowl, which gurgled rapidly downstream, and found himself on the far side, looking off through trees that came and went as the fog drifted, shifted, and bunched.

He had no idea what he was looking for.

Then again, he did. Following a hunch, he left the granite for a narrow path that wove through the trees. His sense of certainty grew as he worked his way over pine needles and tree roots, past snarled evergreen thickets, under overhanging boughs.

Even before he reached it, he knew what he would find. Darden Clyde's old Buick was hidden in the trees in a spot that few in town knew existed. He hadn't dreamed Jenny knew of it. He had underestimated her.

The Buick was empty. He knew that even before he looked. It was part of his certainty, as was the sudden knowledge of what she had done.

He bowed his head. A spasm of sorrow worked its way up from his gut and forced his head back with a moan. It was a minute before the sorrow gave way to guilt, and another minute before the guilt let him move.

Retracing his steps to the granite pool, he picked his watchful way around its edge, but there was no sorrow here. There was nothing heavy or tragic or dark. The air was lighter, brighter. His shoulder felt fine here.

It made no sense, of course. But there it was.

The fog danced over the water in playful little gusts. A thin spot in the mist caught his eye. He followed it from place to place, higher and higher, until his gaze rested on the dirt ledge above. That was when he saw the clothes.

He felt another spasm of guilt, but it didn't paralyze him. Fast now, he went to the far side of the quarry and began to climb. Boulder to boulder he went until he reached the ledge.

He recognized the dress right away as the one Jenny had bought at Miss Jane's and worn to the dance the Friday before. It lay neatly folded next to her under-things and the worn sneakers that had taken her many miles into town and back. Her footprints were small and delicate, which few people thought of Jenny as being because delicacy suggested fragility, which suggested vulnerability, which suggested innocence, which should have inspired protectiveness. But Little Falls hadn't protected Jenny Clyde any more than Dan had. He would live with that knowledge for the rest of his life.

Small, delicate, lonely footprints were the sole markings on dirt that earlier had been washed smooth by the rain. If she had been with a fellow, he hadn't accompanied her here. The map was clear, a trail from the spot where Dan stood, to the one where she had removed her clothes, to the very edge where she had let her heels take her weight while her toes went ahead. Then nothing.

The odds and ends that had nagged at him earlier now fit into a single piece. All the little things Jenny had done that had unsettled him over the past months, even more so over the last few days, made sense. Had he been sharper, he might have seen the emerging picture.

No. Sharpness had nothing to do with it. He hadn't added up the signs in Jenny, because he hadn't wanted to know the sum. Knowing it would have meant acting on it, and he was a party of one in this town, at least where feeling bad for Jenny Clyde was concerned.

He studied the water. It was calm, still, smug in its silence. They would dredge it, but her body might well have drifted downstream in the rush of water that had followed the storm. They would track the shores in case the body had washed up, but most never did. The annals of Little

Falls contained other such suicides, and in none of those had a body ever appeared. According to popular lore, what the quarry swallowed never came back up.

Seeing nothing in the water, Dan ran his eye slowly around the rim of the bowl and into the edge of the woods. The fog played games with him now, creating the semblance of something alive, something human, before clearing and leaving nothing but stone, trees, moss.

Suicide was a sin. Dan couldn't condone what Jenny had done. But he knew how narrow her world had been. Within that narrow world, she had chosen what she had seen to be the lesser of two evils. He couldn't find it in himself to condemn her for that.

Darden Clyde was another matter. It struck Dan that Jenny had exacted the purest form of justice. In killing herself, she had robbed Darden of what he had most perversely wanted. She had left him alone in a hell of his own making.

That pleased Dan. He wanted Darden tormented, and he wanted Jenny free. Though he grieved for her, he felt content. He guessed that was why the ache in his shoulder was gone.

Suddenly tired, he drew in a deep breath. Exhaling, he hooked his hands on the waistband of his trousers. There was work to do. He should call in the report and get help here for the more focused search that would have to be done. But not yet. Not for another minute. There was something about this place, something peaceful, something at odds with the idea that a life had been lost here last night. Dan wanted to think that it was the spirit of Jenny Clyde wafting through the woods—Jenny Clyde free at last, and happy.

Then the fog shifted. A flash of red, far below, caught his eye. He grew alert. The flash of red moved only the smallest bit, but it was enough to get him going.

Unexpectedly, as he hurried back down, he felt a stab of disappointment. He had wanted Jenny to escape. There was no life for her here, not with Darden back.

On the heels of that thought, the germ of another took root. If doing good was what mattered, there was possibility here.

He raced down the boulder trail, sliding part of the way in his rush and not minding the sting in the least. At the bottom, he jogged into the woods toward the spot where the flash of red had appeared. He slowed as he neared, fearing that she would be spooked and would run away. But Jenny Clyde wasn't moving. She was huddled over herself, a pitiful little bundle of shivering flesh with her face buried in her knees and her red hair shockingly vivid against all that pale skin.

As he trotted the last few steps, he removed his jacket. He knelt by her side, covered her, and scooped her up. Without a word, he headed back to the Jeep. Once there, he tucked her inside, curled low enough in the passenger's seat that she would not be seen. Then he slid behind the wheel and drove off.

He took the back road out of town, the one he knew he would have to himself. When Jenny continued to shiver, he turned up the heat. She kept her head buried and didn't say a word. He drove on.

When he was well past the town limits

and into a zone where his car phone reception was strong, he called information, got the number he wanted, and spent three minutes talking with an old college friend, who was perfectly happy to take two hours from work and meet him halfway.

His father would have been livid. "Obstruction of justice!" he would bellow, ever the stickler about following the letter of the law. "You're in big trouble, Dan-O, and so's your friend. Is *this* what I sent you to college for?"

But his father would never know. Nor would anyone else in town. The quarry would be dredged and the streambed searched. The consensus would be that her body had either been carried into the deeper, rougher whitewater of the river and wedged under a bed of rock, or lost to whatever mysterious force ruled the quarry.

The cause didn't matter, only the effect. For all practical purposes, Jenny Clyde was dead.

Chapter One

BOSTON

The memorial service was held in a dark stone church on Boston's Marlboro Street, not far from where Cornelius Unger had lived and worked. It took place on a sunny Wednesday in June, three weeks after the man's death, just as he had instructed. Whatever had occurred before then had been private and small. Casey Ellis had not been invited.

She sat four rows from the back of the church, and a more genteel audience she couldn't imagine. There was no sniffling, no whispering, no sighs or moans or wails. Sorrow was not a factor here. This was a professional gathering, a crowd of men and women wearing the neutral shades of those who would rather see than be seen. These were researchers and therapists, present today because Connie Unger had been an eminent leader in their field for more than forty years. The packed house attested as much to the man's longevity as to his brilliance.

Casey would have bet on the fact that of the several hundred gathered here, she was the only one with an emotional stake, and she included his wife in the count. It was well known that the renowned Dr. Unger kept his spouse in a lovely home on the North Shore, where she did her own thing, while he lived alone in Boston and visited her on the occasional weekend. Connie liked private time. He disliked social gatherings. He had colleagues, not friends, and if he had family in the form of sisters, brothers, nieces, nephews, or cousins, no one knew of them. He had never had children with his wife.

Casey was his daughter by a woman he had never married, a woman to whom he had never said more than a dozen words after their single night together. Since no one here knew about that night or about Casey, to them she was just one more face in the crowd.

On the other hand, she knew quite a few people here, though not thanks to her father. He had never acknowledged her, had never reached out, offered help, opened a door. There had never been child support. Casey's mother hadn't asked for it, and by the time Casey learned the name of her father, she was so heavily into teenage defiance that she wouldn't have approached the man if her life had depended on it.

Elements of that defiance remained. Casey was pleased to sit near the back of the church, just one more colleague taking a long lunch hour. She was pleased to think that her presence here was more than the man deserved. She was pleased to think that she would leave the church and never look back.

Focusing on these things was easier than acknowledging the loss. She had never formally met Cornelius Unger, but as long as he was alive, so too was the hope that one day he would seek her out. With his death, that hope was gone.

Did you ever try to approach him yourself? her friend Brianna had asked. *Did you ever try to confront him? Did you ever send him a letter, an e-mail, a gift?*

The answer was no on all scores. Pride played a part, as did anger, as did loyalty to her mother. And then there was hero worship. Typical of love-hate relationships, in addition to being her nemesis, Cornelius Unger had been her role model for nearly as long as she had known his name. At sixteen she had been curious, but curiosity quickly turned to drive. He taught at Harvard; she had applied there and been rejected. Should she have approached him and told him she had failed on that score?

She subsequently got her degrees from Tufts and Boston College. The latter was a master's in social work—not quite the Ph.D. Cornelius had, but she counseled clients as he did, and now she even had an offer to teach. She didn't know if she would take it, but that was another issue. She loved counseling. She imagined her father had, too, if his dedication meant anything. Over the years she had read virtually everything he had written, attended every open lecture he gave, clipped every review of his work. He saw therapy as a scavenger hunt, with clues hidden in the various "rooms" of one's life. He advocated talk therapy to ferret them out—an irony, since by all reports the man couldn't carry on a social conversation for beans—but he knew the right questions to ask.

That was what therapy was about, he lectured—asking the right questions. Listening, then asking questions that pointed the patient in the right direction so that he could find the answer for himself.

Casey was quite good at that, judging from the growth of her practice. The people she knew here today were her own colleagues. She had studied with them, shared office space, attended workshops, and consulted with them. They respected her as a counselor, enough to make their referrals a significant source of her clientele. These colleagues were oblivious to any connection between her and the deceased.

The warmth of June remained outside on the steps of the church. Inside, the sun's rays were reduced to muted shards of color cast from the stained glass high atop the stone, and the air was comfortably cool, smelling of history as relics of the Revolutionary War did. Casey loved that smell. It gave her the sense of history that her life lacked.

She took comfort in that as one speaker after another filed to the front of the church, but they said nothing Casey didn't already know. Professionally, Connie Unger had been loved. His taciturnity was alternately viewed as shyness or pensiveness, his refusal to attend department parties as a sweet, social awkwardness. At some point in his career, people had taken to protecting him. Casey had often wondered whether his lack of a personal life helped that along. In the absence of friends, his colleagues felt responsible for him.

The service ended and people began to file out of the church; like Casey, they were headed back to work. She smiled at one friend, hitched her chin at another, paused briefly on the front steps to talk with the man who had been her thesis adviser, returned a hug when a passing colleague leaned in. Then she stopped again, this time at the behest of one of her partners.

There were five partners in the group. John Borella was the only psychiatrist. Of the other four, two were Ph.D. therapists. Casey and one other had their master's in social work.

"We have to meet later," the psychiatrist said.

Casey wasn't concerned by the urgency

in his voice. John was a chronic alarmist. "My day is tight," she warned.

"Stuart's gone."

That gave her pause. Stuart Bell was one of the Ph.D. therapists. More important, he paid the office bills.

"What do you mean, 'gone'?" she asked cautiously.

"Gone," John repeated, speaking lower now. "His wife called me a little while ago. She came home from work last night to an empty house—empty drawers, empty closets, empty bank book. I checked his office. Same thing."

Casey was startled. "His files?"

"Gone."

Her startled reaction grew to appalled. "*Our* bank account?"

"Empty."

"Aeyyyy." She felt a touch of panic. "Okay. We'll talk later."

"He has the rent money."

"I know."

"Seven months' worth."

"Yes." Casey had given Stuart a check for her share on the first of each of those seven months. They had learned the week before that the rent hadn't been paid for any of

those months. When confronted, Stuart had
claimed it was a simple oversight, lost in the
mounds of paperwork that had taken over
so much of their time—and they understood, because they all knew how that
went. He had promised to pay it in full.

"It's due next week," John reminded
Casey now.

They would have to come up with the
money. The alternative was eviction. But
Casey couldn't discuss eviction now. She
couldn't even *think* about it with Cornelius
Unger watching and listening. "This isn't the
time or the place, John. Let's talk later."

"Excuse me?" said a slim, gray-haired
gentleman in a navy suit who had come
down the steps of the church as the crowd
thinned. "Miss Ellis?"

As John moved on, Casey turned to the
newcomer.

"I'm Paul Winnig," he said. "I was Dr.
Unger's lawyer. I'm the executor of his estate. Could we talk for a minute?"

She would have asked what the executor
of Dr. Unger's estate wanted with her, if the
lawyer's eyes hadn't answered the question. Yes, he did know who she was.

Surprised by that awareness and quickly

unsettled, she managed, "Uh, of course. Whenever."

"Now would be good."

"Now?" She glanced at her watch and felt a trace of annoyance. She didn't know whether her father kept clients waiting. She did not. "I have an appointment in thirty minutes."

"This will only take five," the lawyer said. With a light hand at her elbow, he gently guided her down the steps and onto a narrow stone path that led around the side of the church.

Casey's heart was beating hard. Before she could even begin to wonder what he had to say, or what she felt about his saying anything at all, the path opened into a small courtyard out of sight of the street. Releasing her elbow, the lawyer gestured her to a wrought-iron bench. When they were both seated, he said, "Dr. Unger left instructions that you should be contacted as soon as the memorial service was done."

"I don't know why," Casey remarked, having recovered a bit of composure. "He had no interest in me at all."

"I believe you're wrong," the lawyer chided. He pulled an envelope from the pocket of his suit jacket. It was a small manila thing the size of an index card, with a clasp at the top.

Casey stared at the envelope.

The lawyer held it up to show her the front. "It has your name on it."

So it did—"Cassandra Ellis," written in the same shaky scrawl she had seen dozens of times in margin notes on the graphs and charts that Connie Unger projected onto screens during lectures.

Cassandra Ellis. Her name, written by her father. It was a first.

Her heart began to rap against her ribs. Her eyes returned to the lawyer's. Apprehensive, not quite knowing what she wanted to find in the envelope but fearing that whatever it was, it wouldn't be there, she gingerly reached out. The envelope was lumpy.

"There's a key inside," Paul Winnig explained. "Dr. Unger left you his townhouse."

Casey frowned, pulled in her chin, regarded the lawyer with doubt. When he nodded, she dropped her eyes to the envelope. Carefully, she unfolded the clasp, raised the small flap, and looked inside. She tipped out a key, then pulled out a piece of paper that had been folded over many times to fit. In the seconds it took to unfold it—several seconds longer than it might have taken had her hands been steadier— her fantasy flared. In those seconds, she imagined a warm little note. It didn't have to be long. It could be as simple as, *You are my daughter, Casey. I've watched you all these years. You've made me proud.*

There was in fact writing on the paper, but the message was succinct. She saw the address of the townhouse. She saw an alarm code. She saw a short list of names beside words like "plumber," "painter," and "electrician." The names of the gardener and the maid had asterisks beside them.

"Dr. Unger would like the gardener and maid retained," the lawyer explained. "In the end it's your choice, but he felt that both were good and that they loved the house as much as he did."

Casey was stunned. There was absolutely nothing of a personal nature on the paper. "He loved the house?" she echoed, hurt, and met the lawyer's gaze. "A house is a thing. Did he ever love *people?*"

Paul Winnig smiled sadly. "In his way."

"What way was that?"

"Silently. Distantly."

"Absently?" Casey charged, torn in that instant, of half a mind to ball up the paper and toss it away. She was angry that her father hadn't said something to her in life, angry that the note contained nothing she longed to read. "What if I don't want his townhouse?"

"If you don't want it, sell it. It's worth three million. That's your legacy, Ms. Ellis."

Casey didn't doubt the value of the house. It sat in a coveted spot in Leeds Court, itself a coveted spot on Beacon Hill. She had been past it many times. In not one of those passes, though, had the idea that she might one day own it ever crossed her mind.

"Have you ever been inside?" the lawyer asked.

"No."

"It's a beautiful place."

"I already have a place."

"You could sell that one."

"And take on a larger mortgage?"

"There's no mortgage here. Dr. Unger owned the townhouse outright."

And he was giving it to Casey? A three-million-dollar home that was all paid for?

There had to be a catch. "Upkeep, then—
heat, air-conditioning. And taxes—property
taxes alone are probably twice my yearly
mortgage payments."

"There's a trust fund for taxes. And for the
household help. There's also parking, two
spaces in back with private access, two on
the Court itself, all paid for. As for heat and
the rest, he had the confidence that you
could handle those yourself."

She certainly could—or could have, if Stuart Bell hadn't absconded with seven
months' rent. "Why?"

"Why what?"

"Why is he doing this? Why such a lavish
gift after nothing all these years?"

"I don't know the answer to that."

"Does his wife know that he's given me
this?"

"Yes."

"And she doesn't object?"

"No. She was never part of the townhouse. She made out very well in his will
without it."

"How long has she known about me?"

"A while."

Casey felt a stab of bitterness. "And she
couldn't call me herself to tell me about his

death? I had to read it in the paper. That didn't feel good."

"I'm sorry."

"Did he order her not to contact me?"

The lawyer sighed, seeming to weary a bit. "I don't know that. Your father was a complicated man. I don't think any of us knew who he was inside. Ruth—his wife— came as close as anyone did, but you know how they lived."

Casey did. She didn't know whether she felt worse for her own mother, who had lost Connie Unger before she ever had him, or for Connie's wife, who once had had him but lost him.

"Seems to me," Casey declared, "that the man was no bargain."

"Maybe not," the lawyer replied and rose. "In any event, the house is yours. Everything's been transferred to your name. I'll have a courier deliver the papers to you tomorrow. I'd suggest you put them in a vault."

Casey remained seated. "I don't have a vault."

"I do. Would you like me to hold them for you?"

"Please."

Winnig pulled a business card from his pocket. "Here's where I am."

Casey took the card. "What about his . . . things? Are they all there?"

"Personal things, yes. He arranged for Emmett Walsh to take over his practice, so the computer, client files, and Rolodex have all gone to him."

A distant little bubble burst. From time to time, it had held a dream. As the dream went, one day Connie would come to respect her as a professional, enough to refer clients to her. Even make her his protégée. *Even* invite her to share his practice, making it a father-daughter group.

The disappointment was brief. The dream, after all, had never received an ounce of encouragement. "Ah," she managed. Still, she didn't rise.

"You look pale," the lawyer said. "Are you all right?"

She nodded. "Just a little startled."

He smiled. "Run over and take a look inside the place. It has a certain charm."

Casey couldn't go that day. She saw clients straight through until eight, at which time she pushed the issue of the townhouse farther back in her mind and joined her partners in the conference room. Cornelius Unger, the epitome of decorum, would have cringed at the scene that ensued. The mood was adversarial from the start. The group had often had internal differences, but those differences were now magnified by crisis.

"Where is Stuart?"

"How the hell do *I* know. I've made a dozen calls."

"We need the police."

"Pu-leeze. This is private. He's a friend."

"*Your* friend. From way back."

"What were we thinking, letting him handle the funds?"

"He did it because none of *us* wanted to do it."

"He's always been perfectly rational, which is more than I can say for some therapists," remarked Renée, Casey's fellow MSW.

"Excuse me," John said, bristling. "I take offense at that."

"It was a joke."

"I don't think so. You and Casey don't always understand that without us, you'd have no validity."

Casey took offense at *that*. "We would have validity."

"And a more pleasant work environment," added Renée.

"Go, then," John dared. "That'll be less office space we have to rent."

"What landlord's going to rent us space?"

"Hey, *we* didn't default on anything," argued the adolescent specialist, Marlene Quinn, needing to absolve herself for being the one closest to the thief. "Stuart signed the lease. His name was the only name there. He's the only one in default."

"He has our money."

"How do we get it back?"

"I don't want to move."

"Can we come up with the money ourselves?"

"Casey worried about money?" John mocked. "You're such a softie, you counsel clients for *free*."

"What I do," Casey argued, "has nothing to do with being a softie and everything to do with needing to give closure, whether insurance agrees or not. Have I ever been late shelling up money for rent?"

"No," Renée answered, "and neither have I. Eviction is unthinkable. I have patients to see."

"Clients," John corrected. "I see patients. You see clients."

"None of us will see anyone if we're evicted," Casey put in. "And this landlord does evict tenants. Remember what he did to the lawyers on the third floor?"

Marlene said, "They landed on their feet, actually got a much better deal in another building."

"Why do we have to be right in Copley Square? If we're willing to move four blocks over, we'd get a better buy."

"*I'm* not working in the South End," declared John.

"How can Stuart have wiped out the account?" Casey asked in disbelief.

"He had the authority to do it. The bank didn't have cause to question it."

"*Why,* then? Is he in debt? Does he gamble? Is his marriage a wreck?"

Renée picked up where Casey left off. "And none of us saw it coming? Insight is our business."

"Well, hell, we're not mind readers," Marlene argued. "We can't be insightful until we've worked with a client enough to break down walls of denial and distrust."

Casey didn't see the analogy to Stuart. "That's not it."

"Yes, it is."

"No," she insisted, forsaking formal theory for good old common sense. "We're human. Stuart served a purpose here, so we saw what we wanted to see."

"Well, that gets us nowhere," said Renée. "We need money fast. How are we going to get it?"

The meeting ended without a resolution. Exhausted, Casey left the office and headed out of Copley Square. She took long strides, breathed deep from the belly, yoga-style, as she went down Boylston Street to Massachusetts Avenue. Turning left, then right, she cut through side streets until she reached the Fenway with its row of brownstones overlooking a ribbon of water and trees.

The yoga breathing helped only marginally. Her tears had long since exhausted themselves, but as many times as she came here to visit, she couldn't be calm. This was not where she wanted to be, here, seeing her mother. If she could change one thing in her life, this was it.

Up five stone steps, she let herself in. With a short wave to the receptionist, she trotted on up two more flights of stairs. She leveled off at the third floor and greeted the nurse on duty. "Hi, Ann. How's she doing?"

Ann Holmes was a motherly type whose calmness suggested she had come to terms with caring for those with severe brain injuries. Caroline Ellis had been in her charge for three years.

Ann waggled a hand. "Not a great day. She had a couple of little seizures this morning. Dr. Jinsji called you, didn't he?"

"Yes, but the message said the Valium helped." The message had also said that the doctor was concerned with the increasing frequency of the seizures, but Casey was more encouraged than concerned. She chose to believe that after so many months of vegetation, seizures were a sign that Caroline was starting to wake up.

"She did get past them," the nurse said. "She's sleeping now."

"I'll be quiet then," Casey whispered.

Going on down the hall to her mother's

room, she slipped inside. The room was lit only faintly by the city lights, though Casey could have found her way without. Aside from the few pieces of medical equipment needed for feeding and hydration, the room wasn't big enough to hold more than a bed, a pair of easy chairs, and a dresser, and since Casey had brought and placed the chairs and dresser herself, she knew where each was. She had also visited Caroline Ellis several times a week for each of the three years since the accident. After so many hours here, walking these floors, staring at these walls, touching this furniture, Casey knew every inch of the space.

In the shadows, she crossed unerringly to the bed and kissed her mother's forehead. Caroline smelled newly bathed. She always did, which was one of the reasons Casey kept her here. Well beyond the fresh flowers placed on the bureau each week, care was given to quality-of-life issues such as personal hygiene, though—like the flowers—that often mattered more to the families of patients than to the patients themselves. This was particularly true for Casey. The Caroline she'd known had mucked out stalls for the animals she owned, yet the only smell Casey had ever associated with her was the light, fresh one of the eucalyptus cream she used. Casey kept a supply of it here, and the nurses applied it liberally. They couldn't prove that it helped Caroline any, but it certainly calmed Casey.

Sitting by Caroline's hip, she took her mother's stiff hand from the sheet, gently unbent her wrist and uncurled her fingers, and pressed them to her own throat. Caroline's eyes were closed. Though she wasn't aware of doing so, her body still followed the circadian sleep and wake cycles.

"Hi, Mom. It's late. I know you're sleeping, but I had to stop by."

"Bad day?" Caroline asked.

"I don't know 'bad.' 'Odd' is more like it. Connie left me the townhouse."

"He what?"

"Left me the townhouse."

"The Beacon Hill townhouse?"

The question evoked a memory. Casey was suddenly sixteen again, just back from an afternoon in Boston. "Beacon Hill?" Caroline had echoed when, in a rebellious little snit, Casey had slung the word at her. Beacon Hill was a landmark that offered many things, but mention of it in the Ellis home brought one thought: Connie Unger. "Did you go to see him?" Caroline had asked. Casey denied it, but her mother was predictably hurt. "He has not been there for you, Casey. He has not been there for either of us, and we've done just fine."

Back then, there had been anger and hurt. What Casey imagined from Caroline now had more to do with bewilderment.

"Why would he leave you the townhouse?"

"Maybe he didn't know what else to do with it."

Caroline didn't respond immediately. Casey knew that she was thinking of the best way to handle the situation. Finally, tactfully, she asked, "How do you feel about it?"

"I don't know. I only found out about it this afternoon."

Casey didn't mention the memorial service. She wasn't sure Caroline would understand why she had gone, didn't want Caroline to think that she had been looking for anything from Connie. Caroline had always been the perfect mother, secure in every regard except that having to do with Casey's father. Given her present situation and the

fact that her life savings had been deci-
mated by medical costs, she would feel
threatened by so lucrative a bequest from
Connie.

Eager to change the subject, Casey
opened her mouth to tell Caroline about the
office crisis. Before a word had come out,
though, she thought twice. Crises came and
went. She didn't need to burden Caroline
with the latest. Caroline's energies were
better spent on recovering.

So she sat quietly for a while, alternately
working those rigid fingers into a semblance
of flexibility and warming them against her
neck. When Caroline was sleeping comfortably, she gently tucked the hand under the
sheet and kissed her mother's cheek.

*"A townhouse means nothing. You're
what counts. You're all the family I have,
Mom. Get better for me?"*

In the darkness, she studied her mother's
face. After a minute, she slipped silently
from the room.

Leaving the Fenway with a deep ache inside, she walked ten minutes in the direction
of the river to the small one-bedroom Back
Bay condo that she had bought two years
before and was still wondering if she could

afford. The issue would be moot if she moved to Providence to teach, but she wasn't up for grappling with that decision tonight. By the time she had gone through the mail and heated a Lean Cuisine, she was wiped out. With a client due at eight the next morning, she went to bed.

She didn't get to Beacon Hill on Thursday, because when she wasn't seeing clients she was rehashing the Stuart thing with Renée, Marlene, and John. Stuart's wife claimed she had no idea where he was, and the bank claimed that there had never at any point *been* seven months' rent in the partnership account. No amount of back-and-forth in their own conference room was productive. The four of them were getting nowhere but under each other's skin.

"Didn't you look at the bank statement?" Marlene asked John.

"Me? Why me? It was Stuart's job."

"But you're the psychiatrist. You're the senior person. *You* were the one who wanted this office."

"Excuse me? I wanted Government Center, not Copley Square."

"How are we going to come up with another twenty-eight thousand?" Casey asked.

"Try thirty-eight. Our landlord tacked on interest, plus he wants the next two months up front."

"We could take out a loan."

"I can't afford another loan."

"Well, then, what's *your* suggestion?"

"Move somewhere smaller."

"How? We still need four offices, a conference room, and space for a bookkeeper."

"The bookkeeper can work at home."

"Which is an invitation for her to steal from us, too?"

Casey left the office at six, so tightly wound that she headed for the Y. She needed yoga far more than she needed to go to Beacon Hill, and when the class was done, she was too relaxed to think of Connie Unger. Desperate for pampering, she treated herself to dinner with two friends from the class, and by the time they had laughed their way through a bottle of Merlot, it was too late to go anywhere but to bed, and there but briefly. She was on the road by six Friday morning, heading for a workshop in Amherst.

It was evening before she returned to her car. When she accessed her messages during the drive home, voice mail from her partners expressed more of the same quibbling, and suddenly she was tired of it. Relocating to Rhode Island to teach would certainly be an escape from the mess.

She didn't answer their calls. The pettiness embarrassed her—and that, even before she considered what Cornelius Unger would have said about such a discordant group. She had failed again, he would say. *He* had never been robbed by a partner.

Of course, he had always practiced alone. And Casey could do that. She probably would if she took the teaching job, because she would only see clients for a few hours a week, and then from space within the university. She certainly couldn't see herself giving up therapy entirely. She loved doing clinical work.

But moving to Providence raised another issue. She didn't know if she wanted to be that far from her mother—which was an irony of the greatest order. Casey had grown up in Providence; Caroline had lived there right up until the accident. During all the time in between, Casey had been desperate for the distance. Caroline was the epitome of home and hearth, everything Casey was not. The closer they lived to each other, the more obvious this became. Casey's career notwithstanding, Caroline was a hard act to follow.

Giving proof to that now, Casey returned home and rather than cleaning out her refrigerator, sorting through the pile of mail growing like mold on the kitchen counter, or even reading a book, she watched reruns of *Buffy the Vampire Slayer* until she fell asleep on the sofa. She got up at midnight and went to bed, but didn't sleep well. If she wasn't fixating on that ugly word "concern," used by the doctor again that day, she was thinking about the teaching position, which was past the point of needing an answer, or the office situation, which was starting to stink, or the fact that she was thirty-four and without roots. Then she thought of the Beacon Hill townhouse that she had so unexpectedly inherited, and a silent nagging began.

She was avoiding the place. She didn't need an esteemed colleague to tell her that.

She was making a statement to this dead father of hers that she resented being acknowledged only when he died and that she didn't *need* his three-million-dollar townhouse. She was keeping him waiting. It was as simple—and as childish—as that.

Saturday morning, she awoke feeling brave. She wanted to think she was also in grownup mode, though she feared that was asking too much. Defying the conventional wisdom that said she was going to an upper-crust part of Boston and ought to dress the part out of respect for her father if nothing else, she left her face utterly naked, put on skimpy running shorts and a cropped singlet, and pulled the length of her strawberry-blond hair through the hole in the back of her rattiest baseball cap. After lacing on well-worn running shoes and grabbing her darkest, trendiest wraparound sunglasses, she set off for Beacon Hill. She had barely gone two blocks when, chagrined, she jogged into a U-turn and ran back home for the forgotten key. Tucking it, her cell phone, and a water bottle into a slim fanny pack, she set off again.

It was a gorgeous morning. At barely nine o'clock, there were nearly as many runners as cars. She ran at a comfortable pace down Commonwealth Avenue under the shade of aged maples and oaks that dominated the center mall. After jogging in place at a red light on Arlington Street, she entered the Public Garden. Indulging herself, she circled the pond, passing swan boats that were just coming to life, parents pushing babies in prams, other children running ahead to toss pebbles into the water. Each plunk brought a crowd of ducks that dispersed as soon as the ducks realized the pebbles weren't peanuts.

When the circle was complete, she continued on to the intersection of Beacon and Charles. On a whim—a final defiant one, a last-ditch effort to thumb her nose at the spirit of Connie—she took the time to run down the whole of Charles Street. Making a right at the end, she ran up Cambridge Street, huffed up Joy Street, and turned onto Pinckney for the downhill trot.

She had always liked Pinckney Street. It had the same brick and brownstone row houses as the rest of the Hill, with the occasional wood frame house tossed in for added charm. It had the same long, narrow alleyways that were brick-paved and walled, the same window boxes filled with flowers, the same shapely grillwork at windows and doors.

By the time she was a good way down the hill, though, her legs had suddenly had enough. From Pinckney, she turned left onto West Cedar, then left again into Leeds Court.

The road was cobblestone. It stayed narrow only long enough to clear the walls of the abutting West Cedar homes, then split into an oval around a center grove of hemlocks and pines.

Breathless and sweaty, Casey jogged past parked cars, glancing at her inheritance with each casual turn. Sandwiched in with its neighbors, the townhouse faced west from the Court's deepest point. Built of wine-colored brick, now ivy-clad, it rose four stories above a subbasement level. The first two stories had tall windows and glossy black shutters; the third-floor windows were gabled; the fourth floor was smaller, a cupola.

Casey had always been intrigued by that fourth floor, such a sweet thing perched atop the gables. She had always imagined it to be a charming little hideaway—and she still did. But her eye didn't linger there for long. There was so much more to see.

Window boxes on the first and second floors were vibrant with pink flowers. A waist-high iron fence enclosed a tiny front yard, each side of which had ground cover of little blue flowers surrounding a tree in white bloom. Dogwood, Casey guessed—but only guessed. She wasn't a tree person, or a flower person, for that matter. She had never had to be, because her mother was the expert. Unwilling to compete, Casey had let flora pass her by. What little she knew of it she had absorbed by osmosis.

If she took a wild guess, she would say that the flowers in the window boxes were sweet William, though she wasn't sure how she came up with the name. Whatever, they were beautiful. They were carefully tended and full, putting to shame the geraniums in the neighbor's window boxes on the left and the pansies in the neighbor's boxes on the right. She assumed that Connie's gardener, who reputedly loved the house, was the one responsible here, and let herself admire his work longer than she might have if she thought Connie had planted the flowers himself.

It was a final stalling tactic. But time was passing. She didn't want to be at this all day. She had other things to do.

Taking water from the fanny pack, she swallowed a mouthful, capped the bottle, returned it. In the process, she found an old stick of Juicy Fruit gum. Not caring that it might be stale, she peeled off the wrapper and folded it into her mouth.

Chomping defiantly, she straightened her shoulders, opened the iron gate, and strode toward the house.

Chapter Two

The walk was paved with bluestone. A side path on the left led to a stairway to the lower level. Walking straight ahead, Casey climbed four stone steps. The front door and its sidelights were made of wood, painted the same glossy black as the shutters. The doorknob, knocker, and kickplate were all of polished brass.

Heart in her mouth right along with the wad of chewing gum, she fit the key into the lock, turned it, and opened the door. She had memorized the entry code, but there was no hum to say that the alarm had been tripped. Aware that it might be a silent one—and loath to set it off and bring in the police—she hurried through a tiny entryway into the foyer.

It was dark inside—dark wood, dark carpet, dark walls. She hated that.

But the air was cool against her heated skin, and that she loved.

Pulling off her sunglasses, she raised her head to better see from under the bill of her cap, and looked frantically around. She found the keypad for the alarm on the wall to her left, but its lights showed a steady green. Either the last person leaving had forgotten to turn on the alarm, or someone was with her in the house.

"Hello?" she called, hooking her sunglasses on the neck of her singlet. Before her, left to right, were a hallway leading back, a stairway leading up, and a pair of doors that were slightly ajar. With her sunglasses off, the place wasn't quite so dark. The foyer and stairs bore Oriental rugs woven in burgundy, olive, cream, and black. The newel post and the banister rising above it were mahogany. The walls were caramel in color. Everything was clean and well kept.

Feeling grubby by comparison, and sweating now from nerves, she wiped beads of perspiration from her nose with the heels of her hands. Tucking the gum in her cheek, she called out another cautious, "Hello?"

Her voice had barely died when she heard

footsteps running up a flight of stairs at the back of the house. They were light—no oversized thug here, and besides, she figured, an intruder would have slipped out the back. This had to be the maid.

Waiting, Casey had barely taken in an oak sideboard flanked by carved wood chairs when a woman ran in from the hall. Her eyes were wide and her face pale. A fireplace poker hung from her hand.

The running should have prepared Casey. A traditional maid in a discreet gray uniform, with dignified gray hair to match, wouldn't run. She might walk briskly, but she would be proper about it.

There was little that was proper about this maid. Granted, her khaki shorts were nowhere near as short as Casey's wisp of nylon, and her polo shirt was clean and pressed, but it was tucked in none too neatly at the waist. She wore white sneakers with crew socks rolled down. Her hair was pulled up from her face into a haphazard ponytail that was nearly as dark as the mahogany banister.

The smoothness of her skin said that she wasn't any older than Casey. Nor, truth be told, did she look any more composed than

Casey felt deep down inside. For all her running, she looked pale and confused, frozen in place.

Casey softened instantly. "Meg Henry?" she asked. That was the name on her list.

The woman nodded. *Girl,* Casey amended, deciding that she wasn't *even* thirty.

"Who are you?" Meg asked in a frightened voice.

"Casey Ellis. Dr. Unger's daughter."

"Whose daughter? Are you Ruth's?"

"No. I'm Caroline's."

Meg swallowed. "I'm sorry. I don't know who Caroline is." Taking a step closer, she peered under the bill of Casey's cap and caught her breath. "Freckles."

"Yes." It was one of the disadvantages of going without makeup. "I have those."

Meg broke into a smile.

Not sure what to make of that, Casey said, "I inherited this place. I was told that you come with it. But it's Saturday." She glanced at the poker. "Did he make you work Saturdays, too?"

Meg put the poker behind her. "I work every day. If I didn't, who would take care of him?"

Casey didn't remind the girl that Connie was gone. There was something fragile about her—a look in the eye, a tilt of the head, the slight hunch of her shoulders. "Didn't he give you any time off?"

Meg nodded. "Whenever I wanted, but I never wanted much. Dr. Unger was a dream to work for." As she said the last, her eyes filled with tears.

A surrogate daughter, Casey instantly thought, noting that Meg was very much her own height and weight. *A surrogate daughter who could clean.*

So Casey would fail him in that, too. Cleaning had never been one of her priorities.

Hands in her back pockets, she drew in a deep breath. She smelled leather. She smelled books. She smelled warm, damp earth. She *really* smelled that. Frowning, she homed in on a planter just behind the newel post. It was filled with Spanish moss and a riot of fern.

Meg followed her gaze, quickly apologetic. "I gave them too much water. Jordan isn't in today, and I'd been thinking all week that they looked dry. He must have watered them yesterday."

Jordan was the gardener—Jordan from Daisy's Mum, according to Casey's list. She assumed that Daisy's Mum was one of the area's chic all-service little flower shops that had cropped up to care for yuppies' plants. Connie Unger wasn't a yuppie, but if Daisy's Mum was good and if Jordan loved the house, who was Casey to argue? Her own brown thumb was another mark against her.

"I mopped up the spill," Meg was saying. "It's just that the soil will smell until it dries out. I'm sorry."

"It's fine," Casey assured her and took another long breath, this one held uncertainly. Totally aside from the surrogate daughter issue, she didn't know what to do with a maid. This was the first one she'd ever had. "I'd like to look around. Why don't you go on back to . . . cleaning the fireplace?"

"I was just about to dust books. Do you know that between the library and the den, there are nine hundred and twenty-three books?"

Casey was impressed. "Sounds like you've dusted those books more than once."

"I have," Meg replied with pride. "There's nothing worse than looking for a particular book, climbing way up, pulling it off the shelf and getting a faceful of dust. That's how it was when I first came to work for Dr. Unger. Mrs. Wheeler was too old to climb up and dust the books. Would you like a cold drink? Dr. Unger always liked iced tea."

"Not me," Casey was happy to declare. "I'm an iced coffee person. But I'm fine for now, thanks." She gestured toward the doors on her right. "I'll just wander." She turned, heard a gasp, looked back.

"Your hair," Meg said. "I couldn't see it from the front. I didn't expect the color."

With a smile and a shrug, Casey went on into the living room. It was a long, narrow room with high ceilings and two distinct halves. The front half held armchairs and love seats in velvet and brocade, side tables in marble and wood, tall lamps with handsome ivory shades, while a grand piano dominated the rear half. Each section had its own Oriental rug, and though there were subtle differences in their design, they leaned heavily on burgundy to match the room's theme. Sheers covered windows that looked out front and back; they were flanked by draperies that flared out over the floor. At the edge of the draperies, catching light from the windows, large Boston ferns spilled from elegant iron stands.

Casey checked the side tables for photographs. She hadn't expected to find any of her, but she might have liked to see ones of Connie's other relatives. Because of his aloof and unsentimental nature, people might assume there were no relatives, but he had to have come from somewhere. If pictures did exist, this would be the place for them—and if not pictures of his relatives, then ones of Connie as a boy. Old sepia prints would have fit a room like this. There were none here, though. Nor were there any on the piano, a handsome thing with its lid raised high.

Handsomeness notwithstanding, she couldn't begin to guess what the asocial Cornelius Unger had done with this room. She didn't imagine that he had come in here often. The furniture seemed unworn and the piano was probably just for show. There were aged oils of forests and fields on the walls, and interesting bowls and candlesticks on the tables, but the room looked to be the work of a decorator. She doubted that anything here held special meaning for the man who had been her father. Forget photographs; there was absolutely *nothing* of a personal nature here.

Backing out of the room, she stood in the foyer for a minute and looked up. If personal was what she was looking for, "up" was where she would find it. The thought of that unsettled her. "Up" was his private space. She didn't know if she was ready to invade that.

Reminding herself that the man was dead helped a bit. Ultimately, though, it was the force of her own curiosity that impelled her to climb the stairs.

The banister was smooth and polished; if her father had touched it, his fingerprints surely had been wiped away. The landing at the top of the stairs was softened by large pots filled with plants. A room stood on either side of the landing; another staircase led up from its middle.

Cautious, she approached the room on the left and looked inside. Done in shades of blue ranging from powder to navy, it had a large four-poster bed, a desk and chair, a fireplace, and an upholstered love seat. She might have liked the room—blue was her color—if it hadn't felt so abandoned. Not even the cascading baskets of ivy that hung in front of the windows changed that. At the back was a bathroom. After a quick peek inside at plush blue towels, wallpaper that added apricot tones to the blue, and a powder blue robe—all of which looked brand new—she returned to the hall.

The opposite room was his. She sensed it as she approached, saw it in the more worn look of the carpet at one end. The door was only barely ajar. Feeling like an intruder now, she pushed it a bit and peered around the doorjamb. The light was bright from windows front and back, but it fell on an interior that was decidedly dark. She stayed only long enough to make out potted trees by the windows, a heavy sleigh bed, a sitting area, a pair of dressers, and the bathroom door. Ducking back out and feeling instantly safer, she turned away and climbed to the next floor.

There were no plants on this landing, but rather a single oil painting of a woodland scene, yet another staircase, and two closed doors. Opening one, she found a guest bedroom done in lilac—twin beds, a dresser, a love seat. The room's main order of business, though, was storage. Cartons and storage bins filled most of the space.

She found more of the same across the hall in a room done in beige. Since the beds here were bunked, there was even more storage space, and it was used.

Casey was mildly daunted by the sheer number of boxes. Connie's active files had been given to a colleague, but she suspected that an impressive number of books and papers remained here. The woman who had idolized him as a professional wondered whether he had left instructions for bequeathing his papers to a library. The woman who was dying to know the man himself wondered if there were personal items mixed in.

She would look. She would have to. Even if she weren't curious, she couldn't sell the place until all of this was disposed of one way or another.

Closing the door of the second room, she mounted the final staircase. Steeper than the others, it led to the cupola that she had admired from the street.

Here was a totally different feel, a small but open space with a domed roof, exposed rafters, light oak beams, and glass front and back. She looked out over the front of Leeds Court for a minute, before turning around to the back of the house. Behind a trio of potted ficus trees, a single sofa gazed out through glass sliders at a deck. The sliders were open; screens covered the space. Crossing the bare wood, she eased one screen aside and stepped out. The deck couldn't have been more than twelve feet by twelve feet. It was floored with cedar planks and fenced in by a waist-high wall of the same. Plants and flowers were in abundance in long earthenware pots and in ceramic bowls glazed multiple shades of green. In their midst was one sad patio chair.

Casey was struck by the loneliness of it.

Chasing away a chill, she focused on the view. Treetops spread beneath her; neighboring decks lay on either side. Ahead, colored lime by trees, deep green by ivies, and reds and pinks by flowers and patio umbrellas, a succession of rooftops climbed east up Beacon Hill.

A man stood on one. When her eye reached him, he waved. She smiled and waved back, then turned and faced her own house.

Her own house. That's what it was—for a short time, at least. The deck had potential and would surely increase the resale value. Add a grill, a table and chairs, and a handful of standing torches, and she couldn't think of a better spot for a party. Of course, Connie hadn't been a partyer. That was one of the many ways in which they differed.

She did have his hair, though Meg Henry couldn't possibly know that. The man had died at seventy-five, and for the last fifteen of those years, what little hair he'd had was white. For a long time before that, though, it had a blond sheen to it, and, way back, even before that, according to Casey's mother, it had been Casey's own strawberry blond.

Casey also had Connie's blue eyes. But she had her mother's eyesight, which was perfect. So, while Casey had never worn glasses, Connie wore thick ones that had muted the impact of his blues and made them look less like hers as well.

Inside again now, she started down the stairs. The closed doors on the third floor were a challenge indeed. She wondered if there were pictures of a young Connie in the boxes stored there. She wondered if there were pictures of long-lost relatives or of the farm in Maine where he'd grown up. His official biography offered little more information than the state and the date. She knew about a farm because it was one of the few things her mother had ever shared—and that, done only to explain comparing the man's social grace to that of a donkey.

Caroline Ellis wasn't a bitter woman. The only times she had expressed her opinion of Connie was when Casey pushed her to it—and then, yes, she was biased, as she had a right to be. The man had loved her and left her, not so much denying that a relationship had taken place as seeming oblivious of it. Caroline had never asked for his help, but she would have been grateful if it had been offered. Once Casey was grown and self-supporting, Caroline had had no use for the man.

Casey had grudges of her own. But there was a blood connection between Connie and her. That primal link justified her curiosity.

She found it interesting that these boxes were packed up and hidden away behind closed doors in a place where anyone could pass by without seeing them. Some men of Connie's stature would want to advertise their treasures, but that wasn't him. He might be self-absorbed and myopic, but he wasn't arrogant. She had to give him that.

Then again, it was possible that he was the only one who ever climbed these stairs. Between the sofa behind its little wall of potted trees and the single chair outside, the place was the perfect spot for a lonely man to look out at a world he couldn't access.

That said, Casey refused to feel sympathy for him. If Cornelius Unger had been lonely, she decided as she headed downstairs, he had no one but himself to blame. He'd had a wife whom he ignored. He'd had colleagues who might have been friends as well, had he given them the slightest encouragement. He'd had a daughter who would have come running at the first invitation, and *that* was the truth, much as she hated to admit it. She might resent him, but she would have been there in a minute had he called.

Feeling a great sadness, she trotted down again to the second floor. If Connie had been a different kind of man, she might have imagined that he had done up the blue bedroom for her. The only way he could have known blue was her color, though, was if he had given her a look now and again.

Skeptical of *that,* she continued on down to the front foyer. Taking the hall on the left, she found the kitchen through an archway at the end. In stark contrast to the living room, it was open and bright, with white walls, white tile floors, and cabinets and tables of oak. The work area faced the back of the house, with sink and cabinets built around mullioned windows that were cranked open now, letting in a light breeze. An eating area sat before tall windows that looked over the front-yard trees.

The table was round, with four captain's chairs comfortably spaced. The chairs had cushions done in a large green and white check, a pattern that was repeated in café curtains, a basket filled with napkins, and a toaster cover.

Casey was more comfortable in this room than in the others, although she guessed that it in part had to do with the smell of fresh coffee in a pot on the work island. Spotting a mug tree, she dropped her gum in a basket under the sink and poured herself a cup of the brew. She took several sips as she stood at the front window, looking out over the large rings of the café curtains. She imagined her father had often stood like this, half hidden here as he was on the attic sofa, wanting to see the world without being seen.

On impulse, she pushed the rings to either side, opening the curtains wide.

Satisfied to have put her first tiny mark on the place, she left the kitchen with her coffee and headed downstairs. Watercolor seascapes hung one after another on the cream-colored walls of the stairwell; the paintings were gentle and appealing. Casey admired them until she caught the artist's name in the corner: *Ruth Unger.* Connie's wife. Out of loyalty to her own mother, she turned away.

Reaching the ground floor, she found a door on her right. Sensing that she was entering Connie's professional space, she carefully tested the knob, cautiously turned it, and peered into a small reception area where patients would have waited until Connie called them in. One door led directly outside; it was locked and bolted. Another, at the opposite end of the room, led to Connie's office.

Not quite ready for that yet, Casey went

back through the hall to the room on the other side of the stairs. The door here was open. This was the den. It was a cozy place, barely half the depth of the house, with only a shallow pair of windows high on the front. There was a sheltered feel, thanks to walls of dark green, lots of deep furniture, throw pillows, and a crocheted afghan. Intermingled with shelves of books were a television and a music system.

Just then, head bowed, Meg came down the hall carrying cleaning supplies. She was nearly even with Casey when she looked up and jumped in alarm. Several moments passed before she returned from wherever her mind had been. Then her gaze fell to the mug Casey held, and she looked crushed. "You took coffee before I could ice it."

Casey smiled. "I cooled off, so hot was fine. The coffee is wonderful."

Meg's face was transformed by the compliment. "I'm glad! Can I get you anything else?"

"No, thanks. I'm all set."

"I really didn't know he had a daughter. You don't look any older than me, but he was *so* much older." Her brows rose in fear; they were tinged the same auburn as her hair. "I mean, I'm not—I'm not criticizing him."

"I know that," Casey said gently. "I'm thirty-four. He was forty-one when I was born."

Transformed again, Meg beamed. "I'm thirty-one. I was born in August. I'm a Leo. What're you?"

"Sagittarius."

"That's *such* a good time of year. I used to make Thanksgiving dinner for Dr. Unger. I mean, he had other Thanksgiving dinners, but we always had a nice one here."

"With his wife?"

"No. Just him. We always did it the night before, because he went up to see Ruth on the holiday itself. I always call her Ruth. She told me to. Why didn't he have Thanksgiving with you?"

"We weren't close," Casey said quietly.

"Were you with your mother?"

"And friends. There were always lots of us without families."

"That's me," Meg said with a false brightness. "No family but Dr. Unger." Her brightness crumbled. "He was a kind man." Her chin trembled. "I miss him."

"Maybe you'll tell me more about him

sometime." In fact, Casey thought that was an excellent idea. If a scavenger hunt of Connie's life was the game, Meg Henry definitely held a clue or two.

Lips pressed together, Meg nodded. Still struggling with emotion, she continued through the room and went up the stairs.

Watching her, it occurred to Casey that the grief she saw in Meg might well be the greatest that had been felt for the man, which was a *totally* sad state of affairs at the end of one's life. Casey herself might have felt sorry for Connie if there hadn't been anger to balance it out.

Taking a breath, she sipped her coffee and turned back to the den.

This was a place of relaxation. Everything about the room told her that, yet, for the life of her, she couldn't picture Connie here. He was a formal man. Never once had she seen him without a shirt and tie. But he couldn't have worn those in here. One didn't wear a shirt and tie while watching *Toy Story* or *The Last of the Mohicans* or *Sleepless in Seattle,* and those were but three of the diverse collection of videos and DVDs on his shelves. Similarly diverse was his collection of books. Mixed in with aged leather volumes was a comprehensive group of popular novels and recent works of nonfiction, all with their spines creased or dust jackets frayed. Connie had read these books. Casey shuddered to think that he had kept abreast of the world beyond his immediate life by reading books and watching movies.

Music was something else. There was a similarly used look to the LPs in the cabinet under the stereo components, but this collection was one-dimensional, fully in keeping with the elegant formality of the grand piano upstairs. Clearly, he had been a classical buff.

Casey had never in her life played either the piano or an LP. Nor was classical music her preference. She liked bluegrass.

So there was another strike against father and daughter as a compatible pair. Hair and eyes notwithstanding, they were clearly two very different people—not the least indication of which being Casey's preference for openness and fresh air. She guessed that if his office was in the subbasement as this room was, she would find it confining.

On a wave of bravado, she returned to the hall. At the end was a direct door to the office. She opened it, slipped inside, closed it.

Pulse racing, she leaned back against the door and looked around. She half expected Connie to be there, waiting, watching.

He wasn't, of course. The office was empty. Easily the widest room in the house, it stretched all the way from one side of the building to the other. Like much of the rest of the house, it was done in dark colors and fabrics. She saw lots of wood, and shelves on every wall. Some of the shelves had cabinets built into their lower half; others went unbroken from ceiling to the floor. She caught the faint scent of wood smoke; a fireplace was nestled into the wall of bookshelves behind her, the poker now back in place with other tools on an iron rack.

On her left stood a large desk with a tall leather chair behind it. A not so large conference table stood on the right, surrounded by six wood chairs with corduroy seats. In the middle of the room was a sitting area, with a long sofa on one side, a pair of large chairs on the other side, and a square coffee table in between. The sofa and chairs were upholstered a dark plaid and, along with the coffee table, sat on a needlepoint carpet of equally dark reds, navies, and greens, but Casey's eye didn't linger there.

Inviting as the grouping was, she looked over it to a pair of French doors that stood open. But she didn't linger at the doors either, handsome though they were. Her gaze went right on out through them, drawn by a vision of sun, flowers, and woods.

When understanding hit her, she caught her breath. But if the gesture was a subconscious attempt to hold back, she failed. It was love at first sight. She was lost.

Chapter Three

Later, Casey might suspect that she simply had been swept away by the sun that dappled the garden, as compared to the dark of the office. Or that what she loved was that the garden was so *not* like her image of Connie. Or that having grown up with a mother who loved everything to do with the outdoors, the garden felt like home.

Whatever, she was drawn inexorably there. Slipping through the screen door, she passed under a pergola onto a path of large stones. Mossy earth lay between them in what would be shade come afternoon, but the sun was high now, and it lit not only the path, but a large bed of flowers on her right. She saw varieties of whites grouped together, as well as varieties of pinks; beyond these were a cluster of purples and blues.

A patio sat on her left before a pair of birches that branched wide and thick above trunks of peeling white bark. A stylish steel table with a glass top, circled by three chairs, stood in the middle of the stone floor, and in the middle of the glass top was a potted hyacinth of a purple-blue hue.

Leaning close, she breathed in its scent. Then she straightened, turned, smiled. She wasn't supposed to like what belonged to Connie, but she couldn't help herself.

The garden was surprisingly large, matching the width of the house at the start but steadily opening the deeper it went. Three tiers followed the rise of the hill. The first, where she now stood, was the most cultivated. Up a railroad-tie step to the second tier, the stone path climbed through more casual plantings—an assortment of flowering shrubs, a bubbling fountain, a pair of maples and an oak.

The third tier was pure woodland. Here the path ambled upward past ground cover and evergreen shrubs, and hemlocks. Filling one of the back corners, as Casey assumed it had done for many score years, was a towering chestnut tree. Its trunk rose limbless until it reached the sun, where it spread into a crown of spring leaves and pink flowers. At the base of the chestnut sat a rustic wood bench.

In the other back corner of the garden, a potting shed stood flush against the tall wood fence that marked the rear of the garden. Halfway between the chestnut and the shed was a door. Curious, Casey approached, unbolted it, and lifted the latch. Outside, as the lawyer had promised, was a brick-paved space large enough for two cars to park.

Relocking the door, she wound her way back down through the garden. At the patio, she slipped into a chair, held her coffee to her middle, and marveled at everything around her. The garden was a gem—bright, beautifully cared for, smartly designed. Leafy trees veiled her view of the surrounding townhouses and theirs of her, yet there was no stifling sensation. The side walls of the garden were built of stone and covered with ivy. The smells were of healthy plants and soil. The air was pleasantly warm. She saw a pair of finches duck under one of the maples and slip through the bars of a cage that encircled a hanging tube of seed. They pecked for a bit and had barely flown off when another pair swooped in.

Casey raised her face to the sun. Closing her eyes, she drank in its warmth. She breathed deeply, enjoying one quiet moment, then another and another. The angst of the office crisis faded, right along with the gripes she had with her father, the fear she felt for her mother, and the loneliness that sometimes kept her awake in the night. Here in the garden, she found an unexpected peace.

Setting her fanny pack on the table, she slid lower in her seat and basked in the sun. She lifted her head for the occasional drink of coffee, but she was far more interested in listening to the stir of the trees, the chatter of birds as they flew in and out, the bubble of the fountain. This was an enchanted spot, justification in and of itself for the price of the townhouse. Casey might not know viburnum from vinca, but she knew that city gardens didn't get better than this.

The screen door slid open. She raised her head just as Meg emerged from the house with a tray. She carried it right to the table where Casey sat and began to unload goodies.

Getting a whiff of something tantalizing,

Casey sat straighter. "Oh my. Those croissants smell fresh. Did you make them?"

"My friend Summer did," Meg replied. "She owns the bakery down at the corner. I stop there every day on my way here. I'm sure you know the place," she said, aiming a thumb toward Charles Street. "I mean, you've come here before, haven't you?"

"Actually, no."

"Not at night, when I wasn't here?"

"No."

Meg's face was a kaleidoscope of emotions—changing from surprise to puzzlement to embarrassment in the wink of an eye. Seeming just as quickly to realize that she wouldn't figure it out, she turned back to the tray of food. "I did make this," she said as she pulled the cover off an omelet. "It has cheese, mushroom, and tomato. I'd have added onions, only Dr. Unger didn't much care for onions."

Neither did Casey. "But I see chives."

"Just a few," Meg quickly admitted, "but they're totally fresh, and they're organic." As she talked, she set Casey's coffee cup aside, poured an iced cup from a carafe, and neatly arranged sugar and cream. "We grow them over there by the shed. Jordan put in an herb patch that has chives and parsley and basil and sage and thyme. Dr. Unger never minded chives."

Casey didn't know if she would. But the omelet looked delicious, and she was suddenly starved. Putting a green-and-white-checked napkin on her lap, she began to eat. Meg stayed only long enough to see her started, then went back into the house. Casey didn't stop eating until the entire omelet, one and a half croissants, and a glass of orange juice were gone.

Feeling decidedly pampered, she lowered herself to the warm stone and stretched out in the sun, pulled her cap over her face, and let the food digest. She hadn't intended to fall asleep any more than she had expected to eat a huge breakfast, but by the time she woke up, the sun was higher, the table was cleared, and a fresh glass of iced coffee had been left.

Shaking off grogginess, she sat up and looked around. Hers? *So* hard to believe. The question, of course, was what to do with it.

Meg came out. She looked a bit neater now, as if she had done some fixing of her hair, her shirt, her socks. Her eyes were eager. "I was thinking I would make chicken salad for lunch. I do it with cranberries and walnuts. It's really good."

"Oh, I don't know if I can stay that long." When Meg looked bewildered, she added, "I have my own place in Back Bay."

"Won't you be moving in here now? There's *so* much space, with the bedrooms and the office and the garden and the den. I could help make room for your things— you know, clean out his dresser. Oh, but you'd probably want to do that yourself. But you just tell me. I'll do whatever you want— I mean, really, anything."

Casey figured that if anyone was going to touch the contents of Connie's dresser, it should be his wife. "Has Mrs. Unger been by?"

"Yes. But she didn't take anything away."

"Not even personal photographs?" That would explain their absence.

"I never saw any photographs."

"Maybe they're in the storage boxes on the third floor."

Meg spun around at the sound of a distant buzz. Then she laughed at herself. "Just the drier. I'm rewashing the bedding from the master bedroom, so it'll be fresh. It's yours now."

Casey wanted to say that she had her own bedroom, but Meg left before she could get the words out, and it was probably just as well. The girl would be nervous if she thought Casey was considering selling the place.

Hearing a quiet rattling—the vibration of her cell phone on the patio table—Casey pulled it from the fanny pack, flipped it open, and glanced at the caller's number. "Hello, Brianna," she sang, feeling suddenly light-headed. She and Brianna Faire had roomed together in both college and graduate school. Taking different jobs after graduation rather than setting up shop together had been a conscious decision.

Brianna remained Casey's closest friend. She had been a lifeline in recent years, filling the void where family might have been. The knowledge that she was on the other end of the line now made Casey feel more herself, which surely explained her excitement.

Intuitive as ever, Brianna asked a curious, "What's up?"

"You have to see something. Are you busy?"

"Just woke up. It was a late night."

"Partying?"

"Arguing."

"Oh dear."

Brianna sighed. "Same old same old. He wants me to be something I'm not. But he's gone now, off to Philly for the weekend. Cheer me up. What do I have to see?"

"I'm going to give you an address. It's on Beacon Hill. How quickly can you get here?"

Brianna was the only person Casey had ever told about her connection to Cornelius Unger. Now she was silent a second too long before asking a cautious, "Are we talking Leeds Court?"

"The same." Casey had driven her past the house more than once. "Do you remember how to get here?"

"With my eyes closed. Do I have to dress up?"

Casey smiled. "Dress down. I literally ran over."

"Give me twenty minutes."

* * *

"Yours?" Brianna asked as they stood side by side at the front gate, looking up at the house.

"Apparently."

"How *cool!*"

"That's one word for it," Casey mused. "Another is pathetic. I'd have been happier with a phone call before he died. Or a letter. A letter would have been nice."

"He wasn't the type, Casey. You knew that."

"I did. But there was always a part of me that said he was just so bashful or shy or . . . or *something* . . . that he didn't know *how* to do it. I always had a little bit of hope that he'd find a way."

"Maybe this is his way."

"The grand gesture?"

"I'm serious," Brianna said. "This is his house. It's him."

An iron gate rattled halfway around the Court. They looked that way just as a man came through. He was in his thirties, tall, and finely sheathed in a multicolored racing shirt and black biking shorts. As they watched, he reached back to lift a shiny yellow racing bike up and over the gate.

"Oh my," Casey whispered. She wasn't referring to the bike.

Brianna leaned close to whisper back, "Who is *he?*"

"Beats me, but he is very nicely built."

The man was straddling his bike as he strapped on his helmet. Settling a tight butt on the seat, he fit his first shoe to its clip and was about to push off when he saw them. Dismounting again, he walked his bike over and smiled.

"If you're looking to buy this house," he warned, "I have to tell you there's a ghost in there. His name is Angus, and he lives in the master bedroom."

"Is that so?" Casey asked with a smile.

"I'm told, but then there are ghost stories about most of these houses. *Are* you looking to buy?"

"That depends," said Brianna. "Would you recommend the neighborhood?"

He considered the question. "It's getting better. Getting younger, slowly, as the old guard dies off."

Casey tossed her head toward Connie's house. "Was he old guard?"

"From the looks of him, he was. Personally, I never talked with the guy. He kept to himself, wasn't outgoing, if you know what I mean. It'd be neat to get fresh blood in here. Are you two related?"

It wasn't the first time they'd been asked that. Brianna was dark-haired to Casey's light, but they were the same height, had the same build, and often, like now, dressed alike.

"Friends," Brianna said.

"We roomed together in college," Casey explained. "I'm the one looking at the house. She's along for the ride." Lest he misunderstand the relationship, she added, "She has a boyfriend."

"With whom she's on the offs," Brianna said quickly, "and *she*"—she pointed a thumb at Casey—"has *two* in tow."

"Wrong," Casey told her. "Dylan's just a guy pal, and Ollie's done." She looked at her neighbor. "What's a nice guy like you doing in a stuffy old place like this?"

He grinned. "Thought I hit it big in investment banking, so my wife and I moved in. Now that the market has stalled, we're expecting a child. I guess I like being mortgaged to the hilt."

Brianna hung her head. "He has a wife."

Casey sighed. "The good ones always do. When is your wife due?"

"August. She was biking with me until the doctor nixed it. If you have other questions about the street, though, ring our bell. She's Emily, and she'd love to talk. I'm Jeff, and I need to bike."

Lifting a finger to his sleek helmet, he re-clipped his shoe and pushed off. Wisely, he held his backside off the seat while the bike bounced over cobblestones. He sat only when he turned the corner onto West Cedar. Seconds later, he was out of sight.

Not one to pine over a lost cause, Casey steered Brianna up the walk. "Come. You have to see this place."

They walked through the living room, then went up the stairs, explored the guest bed-room—"Your colors," Brianna remarked in passing—and did no more than peek into Connie's room. They opened and closed the doors of the third-floor rooms, admired the roof deck, and looked at the kitchen. If Bri-anna noticed that the paintings on the stairs leading down to the lower level were by Connie's wife, she was wise enough not to comment. They peeked in at the den, then the office, but the latter was simply a prelude to the garden. Like Casey, Brianna was instantly drawn there. The sun had moved enough to touch the seat of the wood bench under the chestnut tree, so that was where they sat. The spot was as private as any room inside.

Brianna studied the house. "That is wisteria on your pergola. It's beautiful. The whole place is beautiful."

Casey drew up her knees and wrapped her arms around them. She didn't look at the house, but kept her eyes in the garden. The greenery soothed her. "I wish the timing were better. So much else is going on in my life right now."

"Have you decided whether to accept the teaching position?"

"No."

"When do they need to know?"

"Last week."

"Is it your mom that's holding you back?"

"Partly. I could move her to Providence. If she was there, her friends might visit her more. I didn't like the facility I saw, though. The one here is better."

"But you always wanted to teach."

Casey did look at the house then. She imagined Connie was standing at the window, looking out, saying the same thing, but in a scolding way. "Relocation is a problem, and it's not just my mom. It's my practice. It's my friends."

"Is Oliver really done?"

Casey crinkled her nose. "Yeah. Maybe I'm crazy. He's a nice guy."

"Last week he was a 'great' guy."

"Well, I really wanted him to be, but he isn't. I mean, some woman will think he is, but me? No. We're at different places. He's already there—has the law practice, the BMW, the house in the suburbs."

"And the kids."

"Yup, every other weekend, but I love the kids, they're great, they're really fun and interesting and spontaneous."

"Sounds like you like them more than you like Ollie."

"I do, which is why it's over between him and me, before the kids get hurt."

"How about Dylan? Truly just a pal?"

Casey rocked a little. "Yeah. Zero chemistry." Considering the discussion over, she inhaled deeply. "These flowers smell so good. The whole garden's a gem."

"Makes moving to Providence more difficult."

"Not because of this," she said; she refused to let Connie be the one to hold her back. Any one of her other qualms about moving was far more compelling. "I can sell this."

"It's the kind of place that you used to dream of owning. Why would you sell it?"

"Because it was his."

"That's why you should keep it."

"If I keep it, I invite him to judge every little thing I do."

Brianna could analyze feelings and thoughts as well as the next clinician. What Casey loved about her, though, was that she was first and foremost down-to-earth. So now she said, "Casey, he's dead."

"Technically," Casey agreed. "Spiritually, not so. In my mind he's all over this townhouse."

"Is it him, or the ghost that lives in the master bedroom?"

"Angus? Good name for a ghost, but no. I'm talking about Connie. He's there in the broadest sense of the word."

"Well, I didn't see it. The place is nearly as impersonal as your condo."

"Excuse me? My condo isn't impersonal. My stuff is all over the place."

"Mess doesn't mean personal. Mess simply means that you aren't neat, and that isn't what I'm talking about. Your walls are bare. Your bookshelves are filled with professional books. Your refrigerator contains absolutely nothing that would give a clue about you or your friends."

"My bulletin board is filled with personal pictures."

"Tacked on. Taped on. Balanced precariously on one another, like you don't know if they'll stay or not and you don't really care. You've been talking about putting up drapes since you bought the place, but you haven't shopped for them once."

"Drapes are expensive. I'm strapped just paying the mortgage. If I sell this place, I can pay the mortage ten times over."

That awesome fact silenced them both. In the ensuing quiet, the city sounds emerged. Traffic thrummed over Beacon Hill from the highways, rocked by a siren, the honk of a horn. A chopper flew over the State House. A bus grunted and grumbled down Beacon Street.

It was all there, but distant. Casey felt removed from the outside world. Here in the garden, the smells were of clean earth, budding flowers, and water trickling over time-worn stone. As for the siren, the honk, the grunt and the grumble, they were softened by the rustle of leaves when a gray squirrel ran up the nearby oak toward the bird feeder hanging there. Dashing out on a limb, it dropped headfirst down the cage surrounding the tube of seed. When it couldn't squeeze through the bars, it tried to gnaw its way through one bar, then a second and a third. In time it gave up, leapt to the ground, and ran off.

"Does it feel discouraged?" Casey mused. "Does it feel confused? Does it feel like a failure in its parents' eyes? No. It just . . . goes . . . on. I think I'd like to be a squirrel."

"No, you wouldn't. I saw one mashed on the street on my way here. That happened because it lacked the brains to look both ways." Brianna slid her a wry grin. "Not that you always look both ways either." The grin faded. "Will you mention this to Caroline?"

Casey felt the gnawing inside that thought of her mother always caused. "I already have. She didn't bat an eyelash."

"Oh, Casey."

"I'm serious. I thought it might get her going—you know, fire her up to look me in the eye and say something perfectly reasonable and totally guilt-inducing." She met Brianna's gaze. "Not a word."

Brianna didn't say a word, either. She might have said, *Of course not. She's as close to being brain dead as a person can be without actually* being *brain dead.* But Casey didn't want to hear that. They had argued about it more than once. Casey clung to the belief that Caroline heard something, felt something, thought something. Medical science said that the likelihood of it was slim. Still, there were brain waves. They were weak. But they were there.

"Would she be happy about this, Brianna?" Casey asked.

"Yes. Caroline adores you. She wants the very best for you. She'd be thrilled that you've come into this."

Casey wanted to believe it, but she had her doubts. She felt like a traitor just sitting here in Connie's garden.

Feeling the weight of that thought, she slipped down to the bare earth. From all fours, she sat back on her heels, then gently lowered her upper body until it rested on her thighs. Her forehead touched the ground. Letting her arms trail beside her, palms up, she closed her eyes and drew in a long, slow breath.

The earth smelled rich. It felt moist against her forehead. Taking one deep belly breath after another, she focused on clearing her mind. She focused on releasing the worry, focused on relaxing, focused on the positive force of the energy her body created.

"Does that help?" Brianna asked from somewhere above.

Casey focused on the primordial coolness of the earth. She breathed slowly and deeply. "Mmm."

"Is that your phone rattling on the table?"

"Ignore it," she murmured between more of those same slow, even breaths. After a minute, she rolled her head from side to side, gently stretching her neck.

"It's still shaking," Brianna advised in a voice that moved toward the offending sound.

"Take a message," Casey instructed. Her mother wasn't going anywhere. The doctors were alarmists. Her friends could wait, she didn't want to talk to Oliver or Dylan, and her clients didn't call on her cell phone.

"Hello?. . . No, this is Brianna. Who . . . Oh, hi, John. Casey can't come to the phone. . . . No, she'll be a while. . . . I'm sure you *wouldn't* be calling if it wasn't important, but she can't talk right now."

Casey released a breath. Pushing her upper body erect, she put out a hand just as Brianna returned with the phone. When she put it to her ear, she said, "I hope this is good."

"I think it is," John informed her airily. "I've made a decision. I'm leaving the group."

Casey's spine stiffened. "Leaving the group for what?"

"Walter Ambrose and Gillian Bosch. They have an office ready for me. A receptionist is already calling my patients about the change."

"What about us? What about our group? What about the *rent*?"

"The way I see it, I paid my rent every month. If Stuart chose to keep it, that's the landlord's problem. Let *him* go after Stuart, and as for the group, it's not working for me anymore. I'm outta here, Casey. I have a practice and a reputation."

"So do I," Casey said.

"I have better things to do than bicker with you ladies."

"So do *I*," Casey insisted.

"I'm gone."

"So am I," Casey fairly cried, and she didn't back down. Swept along by indignation from one condescending dig too many, she told John her plans as they popped into her head. It was only when her thumb ended the call that she raised wide eyes to her friend in an expression that said, What have I done?

Chapter Four

Casey didn't say a thing. She simply held her breath and looked at Brianna.

It was a long moment before Brianna said, "Not that you always look both ways either."

"Okay," Casey admitted, reasoning aloud, "I'm flying by the seat of my pants here, but it isn't so crazy, is it? I have an office inside all set to go. There's a waiting room with its own entrance. There's zero rent."

"You just said you were going to sell."

"That was before John bailed out. Without him, there's no group." As she said it, reality hit. "We'd have to find another psychiatrist, because a group practice needs at least one, and that'd mean getting word out and interviewing candidates, but even before that comes the question of whether I want to stay with Marlene and Renée. And then there's the issue of finding a new place, because there's no way we can come up with the back rent, especially now that John is washing his hands of the whole thing. He's right; the rest of us did pay our rent. Stuart signed the lease; Stuart collected our money; Stuart pocketed it and rode off into the sunset. If the landlord goes after any-one, it'll be him. So maybe I should be wor-ried that something terrible has happened to him, but he and I never clicked. Now I un-derstand why. He's abandoned his wife, about whom I *do* worry, but Stuart? We're talking a snake, here. He's off somewhere, living on my hard-earned money. Well, I have an ongoing practice, and I need a place to see clients." She looked toward the office. "Can you imagine meeting with clients in there, looking out, and seeing this? It would be totally therapeutic."

"It's your father's."

"Was. He's dead. You pointed that out."

"Right, and when I did, you said that in your mind he isn't."

Casey took a deep breath. "Well, I'll just have to work on that. And you and I both know that the best way to do that is to con-front it. Confront him. Beard the lion in his den. And here's his den."

"Will you sell your condo?"

"I don't know. I haven't thought that far. I mean, we're not necessarily talking a permanent decision. Staying here could be a totally temporary thing."

"How temporary? Providence can't wait very long."

"Things happen for a reason," Casey said as she lifted the phone. "If I go to the effort of setting up shop here, calling clients, starting over even for a little while, maybe I'm saying that I'm meant to be in Boston. Maybe my mother will wake up. Maybe Mr. Right lives here on the Hill and will see me if I hang out on the roof deck long enough. Maybe I want a clinical practice more than I want to teach." She pulled up a number with her thumb and made the call. "If that's so, maybe Stuart's disappearance and John's defection were in the cards all along." With expectant eyes on Brianna, she waited for the friend she was calling to answer.

"Hi, there," said the voice on the answering machine. "It's Joy. You got me at a bad time, so just leave a message and I'll return your call."

At the beep, Casey said, "It's me, and I'm sorry you're not free, because plan A is for you to be right here, right now with Bria and me. Since you're not home, we go to plan B. I'm throwing a move-the-office party tomorrow morning, and I need you there. We'll be packing up Copley Square and moving to Beacon Hill, and the prize at the end is brunch in the Garden of Eden. So be at my office at nine tomorrow morning. I know it's early, but, trust me, it'll be fun. See ya then." She was smiling when she ended the call, and quickly pulled another number from those programmed into her phone.

"Brunch?" Brianna asked.

Casey made the call. "Um-hmm." She put the phone to her ear.

"Your maid?"

Casey nodded. "You should taste her omelets." A movement at the office door caught her eye. "Here. Look."

Meg emerged with another tray. If the point was impressing Brianna, her timing couldn't have been better.

"Hi, Darryl," Casey said when the phone was picked up. "You're the man I need."

"Is this a romantic proposition?"

"If it were, your wife would kill me." Standing to get a closer look at the goodies on the tray as Meg approached, Casey said into the phone, "I need you both for tomor-row morning. Actually, I need your pickup truck." She explained about moving as the tray settled on the patio table and two places were set. "Jenna will be delighted. She hated my group from the start." Jenna, Darryl's wife, had gone to grad school with Casey, Brianna, and Joy. "So it's fitting she be there when I make the break. And there's a treat at the end—brunch in a Beacon Hill garden." The plates now held the chicken salad that Meg had mentioned earlier. It looked spectacular. "You're gonna *love* this, Darryl. Hey, I have to run. It'll be fun. Can you make it?"

"Wouldn't miss it," Darryl promised.

Ending the call, Casey focused on the table. The chicken salad was mounded on a bed of Bibb lettuce and was accompanied by cantaloupe crescents, carrot and raisin salad, and crusty bread with dipping oil. As if that weren't enough, Meg was filling two glasses from a pitcher.

"Tell me that's fresh lemonade," Casey ventured.

Meg beamed. "It is. Dr. Unger liked fresh lemonade second to iced tea."

Casey was saved from reacting to that by Brianna, who said, "I *love* fresh lemonade."

So did Casey. She also happened to be thirsty. After taking a long drink from one of the glasses, she turned to Meg. "Here's a question. If I were to have a dozen people over tomorrow between eleven and twelve, could you make us brunch?"

Meg's eyes lit with childlike enthusiasm. "I could. I used to work with a chef. We did brunch all the time. Twelve people is easy as pie. What would you like?"

Casey and Brianna exchanged anticipatory looks. "Pie," Brianna echoed, "as in quiche?"

"I can do quiche," replied Meg.

"Omelet, croissant, and brioche," Casey put in.

"That's easy."

"Mimosas. Lemonade. Soda. Coffee."

"I already have makings for those in the house."

"And salad. Chicken salad?"

"Since you're having chicken now," Meg offered, "why not do ham salad and lobster salad tomorrow?"

"Lobster salad," Brianna breathed.

"My absolute favorite," Casey said, raising both hands. "Done," she told Meg. That decided, she sat down at the table like a lady, unfolded another of those delightfully homey green-and-white napkins, and gestured for Brianna to join her.

There ended up being fourteen for brunch on Sunday morning, again under clear skies and a warm sun. Meg had set up a serving table in the garden, covered it with a cloth, and laid out on the cloth every one of the dishes of food they had discussed the day before. They hadn't discussed dessert. For that, she served Italian pastries from the North End. Casey's guests were duly snowed.

They ate well, and deservedly so after a frenzied few hours packing up Casey's office and trucking boxes to Beacon Hill. Since Casey hadn't touched Connie's drawers, the only boxes they unpacked were the ones containing files, which fit neatly into the space previously emptied by Connie's colleague. The rest of the boxes were stacked in the hall. Once Casey's computer, which held her schedule, case notes, and billing information, was put on the side of the desk and connected to the Web by Evan, her computer-whiz friend, she was all set to go—or might have been, had her friends left.

But they lingered. They helped themselves to another iced coffee, nibbled another pizzelle, stretched out on the ground following the shift of the sun, and relaxed. They stayed as long as they could, ignoring the demands of their own lives until the latest possible minute. Then, a few at a time, and only reluctantly, they drifted off.

By mid-afternoon, there was quiet at last. The garden had been cleaned of all signs of the party. Meg was gone. Casey sat on the wood bench under the chestnut tree, with Brianna on her left and Joy on her right, and they stayed there until they, too, had to leave. Alone then in her woodland garden, she looked around in a stupor that had nothing to do with one mimosa too many.

A short week before, she wouldn't have imagined this scene even in her wildest dreams. Yes, the property was a huge responsibility, foisted on her without so much as a "please" by a man who hadn't had the time of day for her once in thirty-four years. But she did love this garden. With its shelter of trees, its vibrant flowers and shady paths, its birds, its squirrels, and its fountain, it was an oasis. Her appreciation of the rest of the house was intellectual. Here in the garden, there was a visceral connection.

That thought brought a wave of guilt.

Casey set off a short time later to see her mother. Beacon Hill to the Fenway wasn't far as the crow flew, but far longer with traffic and a stop at her Back Bay condo to change clothes. In the forty minutes the whole process took, her mind wandered all the way to Providence.

She had made that trip from Providence to Boston and back so many times over the years that she could do it in her sleep. From thirteen on, she and her friends had taken the train. They walked around the Common, had lunch at Copley Place, window-shopped on Newbury Street. Casey had her ears pierced in a store on Boylston when she was fifteen, and when she was sixteen and learned that her biological father lived in Boston, she discovered Beacon Hill.

By then she had her driver's license, and so began the trip her mind made now, modified only as Caroline moved from one house to the next. Casey's first memories were of a brick Federal in Providence's upscale Blackstone area. Caroline had nearly bankrupted herself buying the place, but as a single mother in need of both income and flexibility, she had settled on selling real estate, and a nice home was part of the image. She struggled for a dozen years, as much with the house as the career. Finally throwing in the towel, she bought a Victorian with an acre of land on the outskirts of the city, and put her artistic talent to work weaving small household goods. One table loom became four. A large floor loom joined those, then a second when she hired an assistant to help weave the fabric she designed. The detached garage became a studio, but even that was quickly outgrown, and, by then, Caroline's sights had broadened. She bought a sheep farm another little bit farther out and set herself up to grow, spin, and dye the wool that she wove.

At the time of the accident, she still had a few sheep. By then, though, her main interest was Angora rabbits. She kept them in special quarters that she built at the back of the house, with heat and air-conditioning controlled for constancy. She cleaned their cages every two days, brushed them every four days, limited their treats to once every seven days. She fed them a diet rich in protein, with timothy hay for roughage, and fresh water. In exchange, her rabbits produced fine, sweet-smelling wool for harvest four times a year. Their wool was in high demand both raw and spun.

Waiting in Boston traffic now, Casey mentally relived the turn off the rural road at the hand-painted mailbox that had marked Caroline's drive. Sheep grazed in fields that were level and open; the grass would be newly green this time of year, the trees fresh with spring leaves. Approaching the farmhouse, all was pretty and pastoral, no doubt about that.

Casey couldn't help but make comparisons. The visceral connection she felt in the Beacon Hill garden? She had never felt anything like that on her mother's farm. The place had been as earthy and natural as Caroline, as straightforward, down-home, and blunt. Everything had been up-front. What you saw was what you got.

But Casey liked layers. She liked complexity. The therapist in her liked peeling back the skin that covered a personality, place, or event. Her mother's farm had been lovely to visit, but it had never held her interest for long.

The guilt compounded, Casey squeezed her little red Miata into a parking space several doors down from the nursing home. She wore a white wrap blouse with black slacks and high-heeled sandals; her hair was tacked back in a wide barrette. Slinging a leather bag over her shoulder, she climbed the steps and let herself in.

There were other visitors now. She knew them all by face, if not name, and greeted them quietly. Climbing the two flights to the third floor, she waved at the Sunday desk nurse and continued down the hall.

It was one of those days. She never knew quite what caused it, whether it was the way the sun tripped through the window, the way the nurse had angled Caroline's head, or something that came from inside this shell that the doctors claimed held nothing of substance, but the cruelty of what fate had dealt her mother kept Casey at the door for a minute.

Caroline looked beautiful. Barely fifty-five,

she had long and incredibly thick hair that the years had turned a striking silver, but the color didn't add a day to her looks. Her skin was smooth, if pale. What few facial lines she had were from an easy expressiveness. She smiled often.

Or used to, Casey corrected her thought, because there was no expression now. Caroline's features were as vacant as they had been every other time Casey had seen her in the last three years. Had her eyes been open wide rather than half so, the hazel in them would have exuded warmth. Had she been talking, her lips would have been moist. Had she been engrossed in conversation, she might have sat forward with her chin on her palm and those hazel eyes enrapt.

Caroline had been twenty and a senior in college taking an advanced psychology course taught by Connie when Casey was conceived. Casey imagined Connie had been taken with her mother's looks— though in truth she had no idea who had caught whose eye and how the affair had actually come about. Caroline had never talked about it, and Casey, for all her defiance, had never had the heart to ask. Her birth had changed Caroline's life forever. Had it not been for that one-night stand, who knew where Caroline would be now? She might have gone on in school for an advanced degree of her own. She might have had the freedom to pursue her love of art and gone on to either teach or write. She might have become a renowned textile artist and traveled the world. Unencumbered by single parenthood, she might have married and had a whole houseful of children with a man who paid the bills without her having to worry.

One thing was certain: she wouldn't be in this hospital bed. Caroline had been crossing a street in Boston, in town to visit Casey, when she'd been hit by a car. The trauma of the impact had injured her brain and left her without oxygen long enough to compound the damage. Though she breathed on her own, followed the customary waking and sleeping cycles, and made the occasional reflexive movements, she gave no sign of processing anything of an intelligent nature. She was dependent on artificial feeding and hydration to live.

Had Casey not existed and that trip not

been made, Caroline would be alive and well.

Refusing to believe that she wouldn't ever be her old self again, Casey left the door and came forward. "Hi, Mom." She kissed her, took her hand, and perched in her usual spot on the side of the bed.

"Hi, sweetie," Caroline said in obvious pleasure, as welcoming as always.

Back in Providence, she would have been barefoot, wearing an oversized shirt whose tails flapped out to the sides, and faded jeans that showed her slimness. If she had just come from a shower, she would waft in with that fresh eucalyptus scent, wrapping damp hair around a hand and deftly tacking it to the top of her head with a bamboo knitting needle.

Yes, she knitted, too. Not only did she grow her Angora rabbits, harvest their wool, spin it, dye it, and weave it, but she made sweaters. And mittens and scarves. She was dying to knit for a grandchild. She told Casey that on a regular basis.

"I'm glad you're here," she said now. "I am in such a mood to cook. Can I make us a mutton stew?"

Casey felt a bottoming out. "Oh no. Rambo?"

Caroline teared up. "He died peacefully. I was with him. He lived a long life."

She was rationalizing. Rambo had been a favorite among her sheep. She would miss him, Casey knew. "I'm sorry, Mom."

Caroline brushed the back of her hand under her nose. "Well. He's gone. Somewhere up there, he's happy. I want to celebrate that."

Casey didn't. They had been through this before, in other years, with other sheep.

"I know," Caroline preempted her reply, "you absolutely can't see how I can eat something I've loved, but that's the way of nature, sweetie. It's an honor for an animal like Rambo not only to produce wool during his lifetime, but to produce food when his life is done. I would love it if you would share that with me."

"Any other day I would," Casey offered, "but I'm a little pressed for time now."

"Chops, then. They're quick."

"I just want to share some news."

Caroline's eyes opened wide. "Good news?"

Good news, in Mom-speak, meant a man.

Caroline wanted a son-in-law nearly as much as she wanted grandchildren.

Casey worked Caroline's fingers until they were open, and laced her own through them. *"I think it's good news. I'm leaving the practice."*

Caroline drew back in surprise. "Wow. Why?"

"Money clashes, personality clashes, and it isn't just me. The group has fallen apart. We're all making other arrangements."

"Just when you've built a solid practice?"

"My practice won't go away. My clients will follow me."

"Where?"

"I have a new office."

There was a pause, then an intuitive, "You're talking about Connie's townhouse, aren't you?"

"It's a remarkable place, Mom. Four floors' worth, plus a cupola, a garden, and parking." She wouldn't mention the maid and the gardener. Given that Caroline had performed all of those chores herself even when she was bone tired, it would have been pouring salt on the wound.

"Four floors, with the cupola, a garden, and parking on Beacon Hill?" Caroline

asked, now in her realtor tone. "That has to be worth two million."

"The lawyer guesses three."

"Have you had it appraised?"

"Not yet. That townhouse is my office right now. I can't put it on the market until I have another place to see clients."

"How long will that take?"

"I don't know."

"Don't wait long, Casey. The market's strong now, but there's no guarantee what it will be like next month or next year. The up-keep for a place like that has to be mega. What kind of mortgage did he have?"

"None."

Caroline was momentarily taken aback. "Well, that's something, I guess." She recovered quickly. "But it's all the more reason to put the house on the market. That much money invested will give you an unbelievable nest egg. I certainly can't give you one like it. My farm isn't worth but a fraction of that. If you sell the house and invest the money, you'll be able to rent prime office space on the dividends alone."

Casey knew that.

"Will you do it?" Caroline asked.

Casey had never been good at lying. "At some point."

"Soon?" Caroline pleaded.

"What if I decide to keep the place awhile?"

Caroline bit on her lower lip. She looked at Casey, then at the floor. When she raised her eyes again, they were haunted. "I'd hate that."

Casey's heart sank. Caroline was being honest, and for that she was thankful, but it didn't ease Casey's guilt. "Okay, Mom. There's an analogy here. Remember what you just said about Rambo?"

"I loved Rambo," Caroline argued, smart enough to know where Casey was headed. "He gave and gave and gave all his life."

"But he's gone now, and you have mutton in the fridge—and you're right, in the most primitive hunting-and-gathering scenario, Rambo was born to be eaten. And why not? He's dead. Well, so is Connie. Just as Rambo's body is yours, Connie's town-house is mine. I can do what I want there, whether it's scrawling graffiti on the walls, being rude to the neighbors, or throwing parties that would make the man turn over in his grave." She softened. "There are posi-

tives, too. I can use the place to my advantage. I need an office, and now that I'm set up there—"

"You're already there?" Caroline asked in alarm. "Are you living there?"

"No."

"Are you planning to?"

"I don't know. But the place is gorgeous, Mom. Come with me and see it?"

Caroline drew in a slow breath. "I don't think I can do that."

"Why not? He's gone."

"It's not that, sweetie. It's me. I'm getting tired."

"Of course you are," Casey argued. "You're tired of this room, tired of this bed. Those seizures are a sign, Mom. They say things are healing inside. You'll be waking up soon."

Caroline held her breath for an instant, then asked quietly, "What if I don't?"

"You will," Casey insisted. "You have to. We have things to do, you and me—mother-daughter things."

"Cassandra," Caroline chided, "you were never one for those things."

"Maybe not before. But I am now. You're

part of my life. That's why I need you to come see this townhouse with me."

"Sorry, sweetie. I have pride."

"This is more about practicality than pride. I need an office. The townhouse has an office."

Caroline pressed fingertips to her lips. She didn't need to speak. Her eyes expressed ample sadness. Finally, she dropped her hand and sighed. "If practicality was all that mattered, you'd put the house on the market, take the money, and run. But you've always been obsessed with the man."

"Not obsessed."

"Fascinated, then. You went into his line of work. You set up shop in his city. You bought a condo ten minutes from his home. Did he ever refer you a client? Did he ever invite you to his place? You set yourself up for failure, and that's what you got. You failed to get his attention."

"But I did get it," Casey said. "He left me his townhouse."

"He certainly did. He didn't ask if you wanted it, didn't ask what you'd do with it, just dumped the thing on you. He had no time for you when he was alive, but now that

he's dead, he wants you to clean out his closets."

Casey wasn't thinking about closets. "You have to see the garden, Mom."

"I have my own garden." She did, indeed. No small herb patch for Caroline Ellis. She grew lettuce. She grew green beans, zucchini, and broccoli. She grew tomatoes.

"This one's different," Casey insisted.

"Oh, sweetie. It's always different. But that's not enough. You deserve more."

"I'd say," Casey wagered, "that a three-million-dollar townhouse is something."

"Will it give you stability?"

Casey hung her head. This was another discussion they'd had before. Sighing, she looked up again. "You want me to have a husband and kids, and so do I, but that's not the issue right now. I didn't ask for the townhouse, Mom. I was ready to bury the man and move on. Then he left me this thing, and it's opened a whole new realm of possibilities—and problems."

"Really," Caroline confirmed.

"I want your help with it."

"My advice is to sell. That's the best I can do."

"I want you to see it."

Caroline's eyes held hers. Slowly, she shook her head.

"It's a house, Mom—mortar and bricks. Why are you so threatened by it?"

Raising a hand, Caroline gave Casey a warning look. *Don't you analyze me,* it said.

Casey backed down, but only from sounding like a therapist. As a daughter, she said, "This has nothing to do with love. I love you. You raised me. You sacrificed for me. It's just that I've never known anything at all about him. You won't talk—"

"I can't," Caroline broke in. "I don't have anything to say. The man didn't open up to anyone."

"He must have said something . . . before . . . after . . . I mean, you and he . . ."

"Slept together? He barely talked." Caroline shot her a dry look. "Haven't you ever been attracted to the dark, silent type? Connie wasn't dark, but he was surely silent. Silence creates a mystery, and that holds appeal. Every woman thinks she'll be the one to break through. Well, I didn't. So I failed."

"You got me."

"You know what I mean."

"And you know what I mean, too," Casey insisted, because she was desperate for *her mother's understanding. "You couldn't break through. Other people couldn't break through. But I have a chance."*

"He's dead."

"His house isn't. Maybe it has stories to tell. Look at it this way. When I have kids, they'll carry half my genes, which are really your genes and his genes. They'll know you and love you, and what they don't see for themselves, I'll be able to tell them. Wouldn't it be nice if I have a little to say about him, too?"

Caroline thought about that for a minute. Then, ever the mother who wanted more for her child than she'd had herself, she smiled. "Promise me the husband comes first?"

Sitting in the car parked along the Fenway with her mother's feelings fresh in her mind, Casey put in a call to the realtor who had handled her condo purchase. The line rang on the other end; a recorded voice invited her to leave a message. She took a breath to do it, hesitated, and disconnected the call. How to say that she suddenly owned a townhouse on Beacon Hill and wished to sell it? One didn't choose tiny condos over townhouses on Beacon Hill. The realtor would think she had lost her mind. An in-person phone call would be better than a message. Casey would try another time. Caroline was right; there was definite merit to the idea of selling the house, investing the money, and leaving Connie behind. It was what he deserved.

First, though, Casey had to explore the place, learn what she could about Connie, satisfy herself that there was nothing else of interest. More immediately, she had to notify her clients of the office change.

With that in mind, she drove straight to the townhouse. Parking out front, she unlocked the door and let herself in. She had one aberrant thought as she ran down the stairs—that if she stayed here for long, she would have to replace Ruth Unger's paintings. But she returned to focus as soon as she entered the office, pulled up the client list on her computer, and began making calls. When she opened the doors to the garden, she told herself it was for the sake of letting in the evening air. When she wandered outside between calls, she told herself it was to stretch her legs. As soon as she had finished leaving messages for Monday's and Tuesday's clients, though, she shut down the computer, set aside the phone, and gave up any attempt to resist.

Evening in the garden was special. Mushroom lamps lit the path; floods hidden behind shrubs spread a soft spray on the trees. There were no birds or squirrels now, but the fountain continued to trickle. Low sounds came from neighbors' windows. Someone was barbecuing—steak, from the smell of it.

Stretching out on the wood bench under the chestnut, she looked up. More stars were visible than she usually saw in the city. She wondered whether the night was simply that clear, or whether it was the power of suggestion. This garden was a magical place. Closing her eyes, though, brought the real treat. Between the smells of evergreens, of flowers whose names she didn't know but whose scents she loved, of earth and of grilled steak, and the whisper of the evening breeze through the branches of her trees, she was totally sated.

It was that visceral something again, she realized. Had she believed in reincarnation, she might have thought she had been a wood nymph once. She felt totally at home in this garden.

She awoke curled in a ball on her side. It was two in the morning, and she was chilled. Appalled to have fallen asleep there on the bench—and for so *long*—she went inside to turn off the lights, set the alarm, and go home. It was dark enough on the stairs so that she didn't have to confront Ruth's art, but by the time she reached the kitchen, something else had hit her. She chose to call it fatigue.

Continuing up to the guest bedroom, she undressed, washed up, and put on the pale blue robe that had been hanging in the bathroom with its tie so neatly bowed. It was brand new, never worn. In her drowsy state, she pretended that it had been bought with her in mind and been waiting for her all this time. It was definitely her color.

Back in the bedroom, she went to close the door because, after all, Connie's bedroom was right down the hall. Yes, he was dead. She knew that. But something of him remained in that room. Angus the ghost?

She thought not. All kidding aside, she didn't believe in ghosts. But there was definitely a presence there.

Deciding that she didn't want to sleep on this floor at all, she went back down two flights to the den. Yes, Connie was here, too, but there was also a coziness. Curling up on the sofa, she covered her feet with the crocheted afghan, arranged a pillow under her head, and went back to sleep.

She woke up before five with the day's early light and was immediately disoriented. By the time she realized where she was, she couldn't have possibly fallen back to sleep. Rising from the sofa, she stood for a minute in the middle of the room trying to decide where to go, what to do, how to feel. Waking up in her father's home was something she'd never done in her life. It was abnormal.

She needed normal. Coffee was normal.

So she went upstairs to the kitchen and brewed a pot. While she waited for it to finish, she looked out the back window at the garden, but darkness lingered there. Though the eastern sky was growing brighter by the minute, the sun hadn't risen high enough to spill over onto her side of the hill.

Filling a moss green mug with coffee, she went back down the stairs, this time going to the office. Her computer was there. Her Rolodex was there. Normally on a Monday morning, once the hour was reasonable, she would be working with those two and the phone, if not arguing with insurance companies on a client's behalf, then doing time sheets for billing, which was why she never scheduled a client on Monday before ten. Her first one today was at eleven, and she had to return to her condo for clothes and be back here before then. But it was only five. She had plenty of time.

Warmed by the coffee, she looked around the office for signs of her father. The only things bearing his name were a pair of diplomas on the wall, but they didn't tell her anything she didn't already know. There were several original botanical prints, framed simply, but while they were beautiful, the only thing they marked was Connie's ability to purchase them.

That was it for accolades. A visitor to the office would never know that the man who had lived and worked here had been an icon in his field, that he had received innumerable honors in the course of his career, or that he had been published many times over. Scanning the shelves of books, she couldn't find any of his—and she would have recognized them on sight. She owned every last one.

She did spot several of the same reference books that she owned. They were de rigueur for a therapist's office—precisely the thing, she realized, that a father would pass to a son or daughter entering his field. Setting her mug on the desk, she took down one of the books and opened it, fancying that she might find an inscription, *To Casey, from your father, with my love and best wishes for a successful career.* She would have been satisfied even without the love part. But the flyleaf was bare.

She tried a second book and found a second bare flyleaf. Same with a third.

Disappointed, she studied the shelves of books. Those most readily accessible from the desk were more focused on psychoanalysis than the ones Casey preferred. In a fit of pique, she pulled off the loftiest of the bunch and exiled them to distant slots.

Handful by handful, she did the same with the rest until two prime shelves were completely purged. Then she searched the boxes stacked in the hall until she found her own favorite books. In no time, she had them in the place of honor, neatly arranged.

The reorganization made the shelves look warmer, she decided. Encouraged, she turned her attention to the desk. It was an oversized mahogany affair with three drawers down each side and a shallow pencil drawer in the middle. The chair was leather, large also, with a high back. She sat in it, testing, first forward and back, then left and right. Swiveling left again, she opened the top drawer on that side and found pads of lined yellow paper. The second drawer held a stapler and staples, boxes of lead pencils and red pencils, boxes of paper clips, a microcassette recorder, and a packet of tapes.

She held the recorder in her hand much as he must have done, and turned it on, hoping to hear his voice, but the tape was blank.

Replacing it, she closed the drawer and opened the bottom one. The metal brackets said that it had once held hanging files. It was empty now, but wouldn't be for long. In no time, she filled it with files of her own. She did the same with the bottom right drawer. The drawer above it held Connie's stationery, both a formal letterhead with the Harvard insignia that he was entitled to use as a member of the faculty, and his personal stationery. The latter was ivory with black block letters. CORNELIUS B. UNGER.

She had no idea what the B stood for. She had asked a number of people over the years, but no one else knew, either.

Stationery offered a golden opportunity. Had Casey been in Connie's shoes, leaving her home and its contents to a child she'd never known, she would have left a note here.

Both piles were neatly arranged, but neither of the top sheets had the slightest markings on them.

Disheartened, she closed that drawer, opened the one above it, and found half a dozen small mesh boxes. One held elastic bands, another erasers, a third Post-it pads. The rest brimmed with Callard & Bowser butterscotch candy.

The candies gave Casey a start. She loved butterscotch candies—had been a chain eater in grad school, so much so that she had cracked several molars because of her habit of biting rather than sucking. So she wasn't very good at proper candy eating either, but Connie couldn't have known that. She might have imagined he had filled the little boxes with her in mind, if, given all else, it hadn't been improbable.

She reached for a candy, thought twice, pulled her hand back.

Closing that drawer, she opened the shallow center one. Half a dozen Bic pens lay in a slim pen tray—and that did her heart good. She hated Bic pens, never *ever* used them. The pen she used was a Mont Blanc. It had been a gift from her mother.

Feeling redeemed, comforted to think she had thwarted Connie in this one thing, at least, she opened the drawer farther. Behind the pen tray lay a wooden ruler, and behind that a manila envelope.

When she pulled it out, her pulse quickened. A "C" was scrawled on the front, definitely by his hand. C was for Cornelius, but she didn't know why he would have put his own initial on the front. C was also for Casey.

Heart pounding, she unfolded the clasp, opened the envelope, and pulled out a wad of typed papers that were held together by a binder clip. *Flirting with Pete,* she read front and center, and beneath it, in smaller letters, *A Journal.*

Flirting with Pete. A Journal.

Casey flipped through the papers under the top one. They were double-spaced, full sheets, each one numbered. She returned to the first.

Flirting with Pete. A Journal.

C was for Casey. The same something that told her that was true drove her on.

Removing the binder, she laid the papers on the desk, turned the cover sheet aside, and began to read.

Chapter Five

Little Falls

The Friday morning fog was so thick that Jenny Clyde couldn't see much more than a smear of scrub grass to her right, a swath of rutted road to her left, and the scuffed rubber tips of her own worn sneakers taking her steadily on into town. Drifting left, she saw less grass than road. Left a little more, and the grass disappeared.

Holding steady in the middle of the road, she focused straight ahead, blotting out all but the mottled gray of the tar and the hovering white mist. Fog was a late summer staple in Little Falls. Wedged in a gully between two high peaks, the town got caught

in the war between warm days and cool
nights. Jenny had always imagined clouds
caught in that war just hit the slopes, slid
down to the bottom, and lay there helpless and spent.

Not that she minded the fog. It let her
pretend that the town was protective, forgiving, and kind. It buffered her from the
cold hard facts of her life.

A car approached, a muted hum at
first, then a gargle that grew more distinct the closer it came. Jenny didn't
budge from the middle of the road. The
gargle became a rough sputter. She
walked on. It came louder and nearer . . .
louder and nearer . . . louder and
nearer . . . louder and nearer . . .

At the very last minute, she trotted out
of harm's way.

Tugging her baseball cap lower, she
tucked in her chin, slipped her hands in
her jeans pockets, and did her best to
shrink from sight. But Merle Little saw
her. He saw her at much the same spot
most every day, as he drove home for
mid-morning coffee with his wife.

"Keep out of the road, MaryBeth
Clyde!" he bellowed through the car

window, seconds before he was swallowed back up by the fog.

Jenny raised her head. "Hey, Mr. Little," she might have said had he slowed, "how are you today?"

"Fair to middlin'," old Merle might have answered had he been a more compassionate sort, "and you, Jenny? My, but you're looking pretty today."

She might have smiled sweetly or blushed. She might have even thanked him for the compliment and pretended it was earned. She certainly would have waved when he drove off, because that was the friendly thing to do to someone you had known all your life—someone whose family had founded the town—someone who lived right on your very own street, even if he resented that fact and wished it were otherwise.

She walked on. The Booths' mongrels barked, though she couldn't see them through the fog. Nor could she see the rusted hinge on the Johnsons' front gate up ahead, or the flowers blooming in the Farinas' yard, but she knew those things were there. She could hear the first and smell the last.

"Shhhhh," she might have warned whatever children she'd had. "Keep your voices low. Old man Farina has a temper. It won't do any good to rile him up."

"But he can't come after us, Mama," one of the children might have pointed out, "he can't *walk*."

"He can so," another might have argued. "He has canes. He hit Joey Battle with one, even after Deputy Dan told him not to do it. How come he did that, Mama, after Deputy Dan said no?"

Because some people are bad, Jenny might have answered if she'd had children, and all the while she would have been hugging the baby to her hip—a sweet, silk-haired powdery little girl, so warm, so clingy with the love and need Jenny craved that Jenny would have been hard put to set her down for so much as a nap. *Some people don't care what's the law and what isn't. Some people don't listen to Deputy Dan, not to one word.*

The fog shifted to give a glimpse of September-green birch leaves and peeling white bark. In another two weeks, those leaves would turn yellow. By then, Jenny mused, she might be gone.

As the fog closed in again, she imagined a different town beyond it. She imagined something like New York City, with tall buildings, long avenues, and no one knowing where she'd come from, who she'd been, or what she'd done, and if not New York, then someplace in Wyoming, with the kind of wide-open spaces that went on and on and on. She could get lost there, too. First, though, she had to escape Little Falls.

She drifted left again, closing her eyes now, timing the slap of her sneakers on the tar to the whap-whap-whap of Essie Bunch's rag rug against the veranda rail just beyond the fog. She moved left again, then left even more, until she guessed she was in the middle of the road, and on she walked. Her mind's eye counted satellite dishes, her ear caught Sally Jessy Raphael's voice coming from the Websters' open window, *The Price Is Right* from the Cleegs', QVC from Myra Ellenbogen's. The nearer she got to town, the closer the houses were to each other. She heard muffled voices, the flap of a flag on its pole, the buzz of a saw making firewood for the cool September nights ahead.

The sounds were very real. Yet when she opened her eyes, the swirl of the fog suggested something unearthly—like the Pearly Gates, which was a dream if ever there was one. Jenny Clyde wasn't going to heaven, that was for sure.

Another car materialized deep in the fog. Its engine was smoother, newer, more intent. The crackle of its tires on the broken pavement suggested a slower speed. This car was cruising. She knew the sound of it. This car belonged to Dan O'Keefe.

Jenny continued on down the middle of the road a little longer . . . a little longer . . . a little longer . . . a little longer . . .

She jogged to the side seconds before the Jeep emerged from the fog. Not surprisingly, it came abreast of her and drew to a stop.

"Jenny Clyde," the deputy scolded, "I saw you there."

She shrugged and focused on the tail of the Jeep. The fog played around it, little white imps first on the fender, then the window, then the roof rack.

"You take chances when you do that," he went on in a voice that held a genuine concern she didn't often hear. He didn't get that caring from his father. Edmund O'Keefe was hard. Maybe he *had* to be hard, being police chief and all. But Dan was different. "One day someone won't see you," he said.

"I move away in time."

"Sure you do, because you know just who's driving which car and how fast he'll be coming, but one day there'll be a car you don't expect. You'll wait just a little too long and—wham!—it'll toss you right up in the air, and Lord knows where you'll land. Listen up, Jenny Clyde. You're playing Russian roulette, here."

"No," Jenny said factually, "if I was playing Russian roulette, I'd cover my ears."

"God in heaven, don't even *think* of doing that," he scolded. He rubbed his shoulder. "So. This is the week."

Her shrug was lopsided this time. One shoulder refused to go along with the nonchalance that the rest of her tried to express.

"Are you okay with it?" he asked.

Fixing her eyes on the ground, she smiled. "Why wouldn't I be? He's my father."

"Why doesn't that make me feel better?"

She tried to think positively. "I'm looking forward to seeing him. I kept the house up, just like he asked, so everything's the way it was when he left. I mean, I did some things, like get a new furnace when the old one couldn't be fixed and rebuilt the roof where the big oak fell, but I didn't have any choice about those changes, and, anyway, I got his permission, so he won't be mad." Darden Clyde mad was a nightmare. Jenny knew.

"It's been six years," Dan remarked.

Six years, two months, and fourteen days, Jenny thought.

"And you're all right with his coming back?"

"Fine." What else could she say?

"Are you sure?"

She wasn't sure at all, but her choices

sucked. When she let herself think about them, she got sick to her stomach, and her mind started fighting with itself—stay, run, stay, run—until her bones locked, just locked in place. So she didn't often think about those choices. It was easier to look into the fog and think happier thoughts.

"I'm going to the dance tonight," she told the deputy.

"Are you, now? Well, that's a good idea. You haven't been to a town dance in years."

"I'm buying a new dress to wear."

"Another good idea."

"At Miss Jane's. Something pretty. I do know how to dance."

"I'll bet you do, Jenny."

She took a step toward the Jeep, raked her upper lip with her teeth, focused on the spot where a prominent vein on the underside of the deputy's forearm hit the lowered window, and murmured, "He doesn't know I've been using the name Jenny. I don't think he'd like it. I mean, it's my middle name and all, but he liked MaryBeth, that being my mother's name—" which was precisely why she hated it, why the sound of it brought a sharp pang to her stomach. But a sharp pang was better than what she would suffer if she made Darden mad. "So maybe you could go back to calling me Mary-Beth from now on, just in case?"

When Dan didn't answer, she dared a glance at his face. What she saw there did nothing for her peace of mind. He knew a whole lot more than most about what had happened to send Darden away six years, two months, and fourteen days ago, and what he didn't know for sure, he had guessed.

She shook her head in a second's pleading, then averted her eyes.

"Jenny fits you better," he said.

His gentleness made her want to cry. Instead, she just shrugged, both shoulders this time.

"Jenny—MaryBeth—you really ought to get out of town before he comes back."

She dug the side of her sneaker into the cracked tar at the road's edge.

"Take a new name and start a new life someplace far away from here. I understood why you didn't do it back then, being just eighteen and having no one to help, but you're twenty-four now. You have work experience. There are restaurants all over the place that'd be glad to hire as trusty a waitress as you. He'd never be able to find you. You need to get away. He's a mean man, Jenny."

Dan wasn't saying anything Jenny hadn't told herself hundreds of times, *thousands* of times. The security she had felt when her father had first gone away had dwindled to nothing over the past few weeks. She was a bundle of nerves, when she let herself think about it.

So she didn't. Instead, resuming her trek through the fog into town, she thought about the dress she was going to buy. It had been hanging in Miss Jane's window for most of the summer, looking right out at her in a way that said, *I was made for you, Jenny Clyde.* With tiny flowers on a burgundy background, it had short sleeves, a scoop neck, and an empire waist. It hit mid-calf on the mannequin. If it hit the same length on Jenny, it would cover the scars on her legs. If not, she could wear dark tights.

She might wear dark tights anyway.

Meg Ryan had worn dark tights with a nearly identical dress in a picture Jenny had seen. Not that Jenny had Meg Ryan's looks, her smile, or her spunk. Not that Jenny could *bear* having people stare at her, like they stared at Meg Ryan. Jenny was a most, most, most private person.

Tonight, though, things were going to happen. Tonight, she was going to meet someone as handsome as the Sexiest Man Alive. He would be passing through town on his way to a place where he had a good job and a fine home, and he was going to fall for her so hard he would be begging her to run away with him before the week was done, and she would. She wouldn't give it a second thought. He was the one she had been waiting for all this time.

As she turned the corner onto Main Street, the fog thinned to reveal the awnings that, in the name of urban renewal, the town had voted to install the March before. They were deep green with large white letters marking, in order, the hardware store, drugstore, newspaper office, five-and-dime, and bakery on one side of the street, and the grocery store, garden center, luncheonette, ice-cream store, and dress shop on the other.

Jenny didn't know about urban renewal. She didn't know what effect awnings would have if everything else stayed the same. The cars that were parked angled-in were the same cars that parked in the same spots at the same time each morning. The same people shopped in the same stores. The same people sat on the same wood benches. The same people stared at her when she passed by.

Jenny couldn't make them stop staring, but she didn't have to watch them do it. Lowering her head enough for the bill of her cap to shield her face, she put her hands in her pockets and walked on. She hadn't expected hellos, and she didn't get any. When she reached Miss Jane's, she slid her dress an anticipatory look and slipped into the store.

Miss Jane was a small woman with a large voice. Whatever difficulty she was having pushing and pulling at large sheets of tissue paper in her attempt to wrap what looked like a sizable purchase by Blanche Dunlap, she made up for in booming chatter.

". . . so she drove down to Concord and bought those dishes *full price*. Now I can understand a dress"—this said with love—"but *dishes*? Dishes are covered with stew, bloody steaks, *liver,* for heaven's sake, and, after that, with *leavings,* of which there will be plenty, since the girl can't cook worth a dime. I'm worried, I tell you—" At which point she caught sight of Jenny. Everything about her stilled. Then she nodded. "Mary-Beth."

"Hello," Jenny said with what she hoped was a pleasant look. She stayed by the door, alternating glances at each face and the floor, until both women turned back to the goods being wrapped. In the ensuing rustle of tissue, she tried to think of something to say, but the only thought she had was that it was just as well that few of the townsfolk ever called her Jenny. There was less to change now. It was safer.

And then she didn't have anything to say, because the dressing room curtain parted and Blanche's daughter, Maura, came out. "I need help, Ma." She was twisting around, fiddling with the strap that went over her shoulder. It was connected to a baby carrier that hung lopsided on her front.

Jenny had gone to school with Maura. Though they had never been the best of friends, Jenny shot her a smile. "Hi, Maura."

Maura looked up in surprise. From Jenny, she glanced at her mother, then at Miss Jane. Moving closer to her mother, she jiggled the strap. "Hi, MaryBeth. Gee, I haven't seen you in ages. How've you been?"

"Fine. Is that your new baby?"

"Uh-huh."

The baby was a couple of lumps in the carrier. Jenny took a step forward—all she dared—and craned her neck. She couldn't see much. "What is it?"

"A boy. What's the trouble here, Ma? Something's crooked. Is my dress almost wrapped? I'm late."

Miss Jane was working more quickly now, bagging the tissue-wrapped bundles. Blanche was concentrating on the carrier straps. Maura was covering the baby's little bald head with a hat.

Jenny felt an achy hollow inside. After a lifetime of being eyed warily, nervously sidestepped, and deliberately avoided, she should have been used to it. But the hope that things would change never left her. She still dreamed of the day when the townsfolk would greet her with the same warmth they showed toward each other.

The dream was fast becoming a prayer. Darden Clyde was coming back. She needed help.

Blanche made a show of finishing with the strap. The carrier seemed as crooked as before, but Maura was hurriedly divvying up the bundles while she and her mother thanked Miss Jane with quick smiles and knowing looks. The smiles were stiff by the time they reached Jenny. She moved aside to let them pass.

"I'm *really* late," Maura said. "Take care, MaryBeth."

Jenny had barely raised a hand to wave, when the door closed behind them. She caught her fingers together and gave herself a minute to let the aching hollowness pass.

"May I help you, MaryBeth?" Miss Jane asked politely.

Jenny turned to the dress in the window. "I'd like to buy that."

"What?"

Jenny hitched her chin toward the dress. "I've been looking at it all summer. I'd like to wear it to the dance tonight."

"Tonight? That dress? Oh dear, I'm afraid you can't. That dress is sold."

Jenny's heart fell. "Why is it still in the window if it's sold?"

"Well, *that* one isn't, but I doubt it's your size. The one that would be your size is already sold."

Looking at the dress from the back, Jenny could see where it had been pinned to fit the mannequin. But the mannequin was skinny. Jenny was only slim. It might fit. "Could I try it on?"

"You could for color and style, but it would be a waste of your time. I couldn't possibly get the right size here in time for the dance. Actually, I doubt I could get the right size at all. This dress was part of the summer line. Everything coming in now is for fall and winter."

Jenny had been thinking about the dance for weeks. For just as long, she had been picturing herself in this dress. She went to the window and touched the fabric. It was as soft as she had imagined. "You do alterations, don't you?"

"Alterations, yes. Recuttings, no. This dress will be ridiculously big on you, MaryBeth."

"It's Jenny," Jenny said softly, defiantly, because something told her that Miss Jane would call her MaryBeth to her dying day and be no threat at all when it came to Jenny's father. "May I try it on, please?"

One look at the three-paneled mirror at the far end of the dressing room and Jenny nearly lost her nerve. But she wanted that dress. So, turning away, she put a toe to each heel and removed her sneakers. She slipped off her hat and, still with her back to the mirror, refastened the elastic band around her hair. She was trying to work loose strands into the mass when, looking pinched, Miss Jane joined her with the dress.

Jenny reached for it. But rather than handing it over or hanging it on a hook,

Miss Jane slid her arms inside, from hem to neckline, and waited.

Jenny hadn't expected an audience. No one had seen her without clothes in more than six years, two months, and fourteen days. Having Miss Jane see her was nearly as bad as the mirror seeing her. But it couldn't be helped. She had a feeling Miss Jane wouldn't let the dress go without a fight, and Jenny had a point to make.

So she hurried out of her jeans and tee shirt and took refuge inside the dress before either of them could see much. While she busied herself smoothing the front, Miss Jane did up the buttons in back, tugged at the shoulders, and brushed at the sleeves.

"Well," the woman conceded with a sigh, "it isn't as big as I thought it would be, but I still don't think it's quite right. The waist is too high."

Jenny looked down. "Isn't this where it's supposed to be?"

"Well, it is. Maybe the problem is with the sleeves. They don't look comfortable."

Jenny moved her arms. "They feel fine."

Miss Jane put a worried hand to her chin. She shook her head. "The neckline's wrong. Someone with freckles like yours needs a higher neckline. And then there's the color. Quite frankly, it clashes with your hair."

"Quite frankly," Jenny said, "everything clashes with my hair, but I still need a dress for the dance."

"Perhaps one of the others would do."

Jenny touched the folds that fell so gently from the waist that Miss Jane claimed was too high. "But I like this one."

"You know, dear, people come to me because they respect my opinion. They trust that if they try on a dress and it doesn't look right, I'll tell them. Everyone in town has seen this dress in my window. They'll know where you bought it. They'll think that I didn't do right by you. I wouldn't want that."

Jenny ran the tips of her fingers along the neckline that lay so peacefully against her freckles. "I'll tell them. I'll say I bought it against your recommendation. I'll say I insisted."

"Look in the mirror, MaryBeth," Miss Jane said with exasperation. "It just isn't *you*."

Jenny imagined that she was wearing dark tights and pumps. She imagined that she was newly bathed and sweet smelling, with her hair brushed, her cheeks blushed, and her eyelashes darkened. Holding all that in mind, ready to superimpose it on her image, she turned to the mirror and slowly raised her eyes.

She caught her breath in delight. The dress was beautiful. It was just long enough, just sweet enough, just colorful enough. It was the most stylish thing she had ever worn, and it fit just fine.

Miss Jane might be right: the dress might not be Jenny. But it was what she wanted to be, which, given the hopes she had for the night, was enough.

Chapter Six

Jenny was in high spirits as she walked the two miles from her house to the VFW hall where the dance was being held. It didn't matter that her toes pinched in the too-small suede pumps her boss had lent her, or that none of the cars that passed her stopped to give her a ride. They didn't recognize her, that was why, looking as nice as she did.

And she *did* look nice. She had checked. She had to untape only three things from the mirror—a matchbook cover from Lisa Pearsall's engagement party, an autographed PUT MOONY IN THE STATE HOUSE bumper sticker, and the printed menu from Helen and Avery Phippen's golden anniversary bash—to have room enough to see her face. The rest of her had been reflected in the frosty glass panel on her front door. The image there had been dark and a little vague, but nice—far nicer than she had looked in a while.

The VFW hall came into sight. The glow from inside pierced the dusk, scattering yellow shards of light across the parking lot, where laughter and shouted greetings rang out above the slam of the car doors.

Jenny slowed to watch the stream of townsfolk climbing the steps and crossing the porch. Those who knew how to bake carried foil-covered goodies. Jenny herself had made a batch of the lemon crescents for which Miriam's catering service, Neat Eats, was known. Their weight in her hand was a commitment. It meant she couldn't turn back. There would be no watching the dance from behind the chestnut tree this time. This time she was going inside.

Carefully balancing her foil pack on one hand, she knelt to brush dust from Miriam's shoes with the other. When she straightened, she was horrified to see dust on the hem of her dress. Quickly, she brushed at that, too. When her hand came away filthy, she batted it clean against the back of the dress, where no one would see it. She took a deep breath.

Then she thought of her hair. Letting out the breath, she whisked a hand around her head to check for strands that might have escaped both mousse and French braid, but there were none. She patted down the sides for good measure. She took another breath for courage, but paused again, this time to press the pads of her fingers to the bridge of her nose, and a good thing she did. She found small beads of sweat there. She didn't know if they were a result of walking or nerves, but she was careful to blot them without smudging her makeup. What little of that she had used was crucial, especially there on her nose. Blotchy red freckles scared men off.

She searched the faces before her, looking for one that was new, but all were familiar.

Her stomach was jumping with nerves. She put a hand there, took another breath, and forced herself forward.

Within seconds, she had joined the people climbing the steps. To her relief, no one seemed to notice her. She might have been one of them, so seamless was their chatter.

Once inside, she glanced around quickly. Miriam had told her to go straight to the refreshment table, so she hurried over, took the foil off her crescents, and set them down at the dessert end. That done, she turned to face the dance floor. Not much was happening there, and she felt awkward just standing, so she turned back to the table and surveyed the food. There were three plates each of brownies and oatmeal cookies, two plates each of chocolate chip and fork-scored peanut butter cookies, and a random assortment of carrot cakes, mini cheesecakes, and gingerbread squares. In the middle of the table, past the desserts, were chips, dips, and popcorn. Drinks were at the far end.

"This is an effective arrangement," she said, aiming her words at the women behind the table, but when she dared glance their way, none seemed to have heard. Eyeing the food again, she said more loudly, "Whoever set this up did an excellent job. Miriam and I arrange our buffet tables exactly like this."

When she looked up this time, two of the women were looking right back at her. She smiled. "It's very good."

They seemed uneasy. No, not uneasy, she decided. Confused.

So she helped them out. "I'm Mary-Beth Clyde. I know I look different. It's the dress." That said, she further eased their discomfort by turning away.

The band was playing something light, but people weren't yet dancing. They were milling around, more pairs of legs than Jenny could count. She saw denim ones and khaki ones. She saw bare ones. The ones that pleased her most were those covered by dark stockings like hers. They were being worn by stylish women, by *popular* women. That boded well.

"Good crowd," she said, turning back to the dessert ladies. Then, "Do you need any help?"

"No, thank you."

"We're fine."

Jenny nodded and moved off to stand by the wall in a break between chairs. It was a spot with a view, which she put to good use. People continued to stream through the door. She skimmed their faces, then looked again at those already inside. The whole town appeared to have turned out to celebrate summer's end.

She remembered it being that way all those years ago, too. She had been twelve then, and had come with her parents, but they hadn't been a happy threesome, what with her father furious at her mother for not having bought Jenny a new dress, and her mother furious at her for needing one.

She had a new dress now, and it was a beauty. Smiling, she raised her eyes to the stage. The song had ended. The band-leader—Christ Community's own Reverend George Putty—waved his arms in the air, then held them high with only his forefingers counting time. Jenny jumped when cymbals and drums burst into a fanfare. Her heart had barely recovered when Reverend Putty began bouncing on the balls of his feet. Seconds later, the band broke into something fast and loud and totally different, Jenny wagered, from anything ever heard within the cold stone walls of Reverend Putty's church.

The crowd cheered and moved with the beat.

Jenny tapped her toe. She clapped in time to the music for a minute. She folded her arms over her chest, then, recalling an article on body language in *Cosmo,* uncrossed them and let them fall.

Caught up in the mood of the crowd, she was smiling when her eyes met those of Dan O'Keefe, who was watching her from across the room. He touched a finger to the cap he wasn't wearing. She sent him a nod in time to the music and looked off again, always, for that new face. A new man would notice her, look at her as no one else here could. He would talk to her. He would ask her to dance. And the whole town would see.

Wouldn't *that* be nice.

She ran a glance around the perimeter of the room before focusing on the front door. She wished he would come. Yes, she was impatient, but she had a right to be. It had taken courage to come here, weeks of changing her mind, going back and forth, until she realized that she had no other choice. It was now or never. Once her father was home, there would be no dances for her, no men, no hope.

And tonight she looked good, really good.

Her breath caught. Someone stood in the shadows just beyond the door. He lingered there . . . not rushing in . . . perhaps looking around . . . scoping things out. She drew herself taller, moistened her lips, and waited, waited, waited for him to step into the light.

At last he did. But it was only Bart Gillis. Late forties. Potbellied. Married, with five kids and no job.

She sighed. The night was young. There was time.

As the minutes passed, Little Falls boogied through song after song. Couples filled the dance floor, young and old, same sex, other sex, sibling with sibling, parent with child. If the dancers were good, fine; if they had no idea what they were doing, that was fine, too. As for Jenny, she wasn't making a fool of *her*self. She shifted from foot to foot to ease the pressure on her toes, and waited for the right dance to come.

And there it was. The band struck up a country tune and a line formed. Jenny knew the dance. She had practiced it in front of her TV and could do it as well as anyone else. Most important, no partner was needed.

As she started forward, she saw friends falling into place beside friends, lovers beside lovers beside sisters and aunts and even pesky little boys showing off their stuff in a flurry of flying elbows and butts, a sight to see—and incredibly, before Jenny could stop staring and join in, the moment had passed.

She returned to her spot by the wall and promised herself to be faster next time.

When the band slid into "Blue Moon," the crowd that had been bopping around the floor yielded to couples dancing slowly, romantically, cheek to cheek, just as Jenny had done at home so many times with her pillow as a partner and the sweetest of dreams. She kept her eyes down, watching only the slide of shoes and the intimate brush of legs, feeling more awkward and alone by the minute.

A small, familiar face entered her lowered line of sight. The skin was the color of alabaster overlaid with fiery red freckles that accompanied a riotous head of flaming red hair, all of which endeared her to this child and he to her—if the sly slip of his small hand into hers was any indication. It was always this way when he saw her. They were pals.

Joey Battle was his name, and though his family made a point to deny it, Jenny was convinced that somehow, somewhere, they were distantly related. Only three people she knew had quite that same coloring—her mother, herself, and Joey. Had the child been older, Jenny might have imagined that he was her biological brother, adopted out at birth. But Joey was barely five; Jenny's mother had been dead two years when he was born.

Holding tight to her hand, he slipped into the narrow space between her and the chair. She knelt beside him and asked, "Hey, Joey, what's up?"

"Mama's looking for me," he whispered.

"Something wrong?"

"She says I can't stay past nine. But no one else is leaving. I don't see why I gotta be the first one to bed."

Because your mama's got the hots for your daddy's brother, Jenny thought. She had heard the rumors. Hard not to, standing at any cash register in town. Not that she was surprised. She had gone to school with Selena Battle. She had seen the girl in action. Selena had three kids by three different men and looked to be working on a fourth. She wasn't about to let Joey get in the way.

"Maybe your mama feels you need the sleep, what with starting kindergarten and all."

"But that's not for three whole days, so why do I hafta go to bed *now*?"

"Joey Battle, where you been?" His mother grabbed a handful of his tee shirt and pulled him out of hiding. She shot Jenny a nervous look. "Hi, MaryBeth. Has he been botherin' you?" By Joey's ear, she hissed, "What are you *doin'* here with her?

She has better things to do than baby-sit you."

"I don't mind—" Jenny started to say, but Selena was already dragging Joey off; the big clock over the stage read nine.

Jenny looked at that clock and tried not to worry. There hadn't been any new faces arriving in a while, although that didn't really mean anything, she supposed. He was late, that was all. She figured work had delayed him, or traffic on the interstate. She imagined he might even have found himself at the last minute without a clean shirt—and she could just see him rushing one from the washer to the dryer, then pressing it—or trying to, because he wasn't very good at ironing. No, he really needed someone like Jenny to iron his shirts.

She was expert at ironing shirts.

Guessing that he would be a while longer, she let up on smiling and gave the muscles of her face a rest. Around her, people were doing the same for their feet. Anita Silva had fallen into the chair on Jenny's right and was turned away to talk with Bethany Carr. All Jenny could see of Johnny Watts, talking with his wife on her left, were his wide shoulders and back.

Jenny leaned against the wall. She alternately stepped out of one shoe, then the other, and did her best to look winded from dancing and grateful for the break, just like everyone else.

"Pick your partners, ladies," Reverend Putty called, and women throughout the hall reached for their men and led them onto the floor.

Pick someone, Jenny told herself, quickly looking around the room. *Anyone,* she told herself, but, for the life of her, she didn't see a man she wanted to dance with, certainly no one within reach, let alone one who would actually accept if she asked. After a minute she felt foolish for even looking.

So she touched her throat in an indication of thirst and slipped along the edge of the dance floor toward the refreshment table. The wait there was a long one. Each time her turn came, someone more thirsty pushed in ahead of her, but it wasn't worth making a scene. When she finally had her cider, she took it to a new nook on the opposite side of the hall. She sipped from the cup. She alternately tapped her toe, rapped her hand against her thigh, and nodded in time to the music.

She had barely finished her drink when lines formed for the Electric Slide. Quickly, before losing her nerve, she crossed the floor and fell into step with the others, and if her heart was beating double time, no one knew, because the Electric Slide was her dance. Her body knew its moves. She didn't have to give them a second thought. Before she could begin to see who was or wasn't looking at her and with what degree of distrust, she was moving back and forth across the floor in perfect step with everyone else.

Relaxing for the very first time in days, her body caught the beat. Arms, legs, hips—she moved with ease, and what fun it was! She didn't think about her hair or her freckles or her father. She shot grins at Reverend Putty and at the people beside her. Incredibly, they grinned back. In that instant, she was everything she had never been in Little Falls: she was pretty, she was happy, she was part of the crowd.

She danced until the very last note had been played, then cheered as the others did. All too quickly the line broke up into smaller clusters that drifted off. Clinging to the moment, Jenny raised her hands and clapped for the band. But her applause was lonely this time. Everyone else had moved on.

Feeling flushed, she made for the door. A wave of refreshingly cool air hit her the instant she stepped out on the porch. She fanned herself with a hand, considered her options, finally found a free spot, and perched on the old wood rail.

"Hey, MaryBeth."

She looked around. Dudley Wright III stood not four feet away. He was tall, thin, and still adolescent looking, though she figured him to be twenty-six, what with his being two years ahead of her in school.

In any case, he was not the man of Jenny's dreams.

What he was, was a reporter for the local weekly newspaper founded by his grandfather and currently published by his father. Everyone knew that Dudley III wanted to be editor in chief by the time he was thirty, but that the promotion was dependent on his showing the doggedness, imagination, and writing skill that his grandfather, Dudley Senior—retired but still calling the shots—deemed necessary for carrying on the family tradition.

On occasion, Jenny had wondered at the kind of pressure poor Dudley lived under. This wasn't one of those occasions. Given that the Wrights approached the Clydes for one reason and one reason alone, she was on guard.

He came closer. "I saw you dancing. You looked happy. Was it the dance or knowing Darden's getting out?"

Jenny touched her neck and found escaped strands of hair clinging there. She pushed them back into her braid. "It's real warm in there."

"Tuesday's the big day. Right?"

She didn't want to think about it. Not tonight.

"How do you feel about it? What's it been—five years?"

She figured he knew it had been six years, not five. She figured he had been talking with his father about it. His father had covered the case from arrest to trial to conviction. She figured they decided it was Dudley III's turn now.

She searched the night for her chestnut tree, found it, wished she were there.

"He got out early," Dudley remarked.

"They give time off for good behavior."

"Still. He was convicted of murder."

"Involuntary manslaughter," she corrected.

"I wonder what it's like, knowing you've taken a life."

"You could ask him," she said, though she knew full well that if Dudley Wright III came to the house, Darden would slam the door in his face. Darden was a private man. He claimed prison had been a relief, after being raped by the press.

"So, what'll he do when he gets back?" Dudley asked. "He has to work, doesn't he? Isn't that a condition of parole?"

"He has a moving business."

"Had," Dudley was good enough to remind her. "After all this time, his contacts will have dried up, not to mention the truck. Will it still run?"

Jenny didn't want to talk about this. She really didn't. She imagined being out by her tree, leaning against it in the dark of night, talking to someone who cared. The man she waited for had more caring in his baby finger than Dudley Wright III had in his whole knobby body.

"I have to tell you," he warned as if he was doing her a favor, "people are worried. They aren't sure how they'll like having an ex-con in town. Does it worry you that he might not fit in?"

"He never did," she said, but distractedly. She could have sworn she saw movement at her tree. Someone was there.

"Being independent is one thing," Dudley argued, "being ostracized is another. How will your father take to that? Has he thought this whole thing out?"

A car swung out of the parking lot. As its headlights arced around, they lit a man standing by the chestnut tree, watching the goings-on. A local taking a break from the dance? Jenny didn't think so. None of the locals were that tall. None were wearing a leather jacket and boots shiny enough to reflect the headlights of a car. None carried a motorcycle helmet.

"Has he thought about what it'll mean to return to a place where everyone knows where he's been and why?" Dudley asked.

Jenny was beside herself with excitement. She was trying to decide whether to stay where she was and let the stranger come to her or approach him herself, when Dudley broke into her thoughts with a sharp reminder. "MaryBeth?"

"Excuse me?"

"I asked if Darden knows the drawbacks of returning to the scene of the crime."

She frowned. "What?"

"Some folks think he should relocate, just start over somewhere else."

Jenny thought the same thing, but she knew it wouldn't happen. Darden had made that clear the last time she had gone to see him. Little Falls was his home, he said. He had a right to come back, he said, and he didn't give a good goddamn whether the town liked it or not. Let them put up with something *they* didn't like for a change, he said.

"Bad things happened to him here," Dudley went on. "Maybe he shouldn't come back."

"Is that what people are saying?"

"Some. Well, lots."

"You, too?"

"I'm a journalist. I can't take a stand."

Jenny had no use for cowards. Deciding that he wasn't worth another second of her time, she looked back at her tree. But whatever aura had alerted her to the motorcyclist's presence before was gone. She cupped her hands around her eyes to block out the sidelight and sharpen her vision. Still she couldn't see him.

It was Dudley's fault. He had seen Dudley with her and thought she was taken.

"Does Darden scare you?" Dudley asked.

She shot him an angry look. "Why should he? Why are you asking me these things? What do you want from me?"

"An interview. People want to know how you feel about Darden getting out of prison and coming back here. They want to know what he's planning to do. They want to know what *you* plan to do once he's back. They're curious, and they're worried, and you're the only one who can give them an inside look. This is the biggest story around here since the day Merle's cousin showed up married to a stripper. It's front-page stuff."

Jenny shook her head firmly. The curiosity of the townsfolk wasn't her problem. Their *worries* weren't her problem. She had problems enough of her own. An interview on the front page? Good God, that was the last thing she wanted. Darden would *kill* her.

"Please leave," she said, because it struck her that it wasn't too late. The man by the chestnut tree might simply have backed into the woods. If he saw Dudley walking away, he might come out again.

"You can help them understand what it's like," Dudley insisted.

"No one can understand," she snapped, though she knew it was a waste of breath to try to talk to him. Nothing Dudley Wright said or did or wrote could change the facts of her life.

She slipped off the rail.

"Are you saying it's very bad?" he asked.

She turned and began to walk down the porch.

"I'll pay you, MaryBeth."

She didn't know whether to spit in his eye or pray for a hole to open and swallow her up. Everyone on the whole long porch was watching her.

"Don't you owe it to the town?" he called.

Head held high, jaw set, she dared those watching to speak as she swung around the stair post and ran down the steps. Crossing the yard and the driveway, she went straight to her tree. Its back side was familiar and dark. She leaned against it until her anger waned, then longer, because anger wasn't her only problem. There was embarrassment, too. She shouldn't have run off, not in front of everyone. That made it harder to go back.

But she had to. There wouldn't be another night like this one before Darden returned. It was her last chance. She *had* to go inside again.

She pushed away from the tree and

looked back at the porch. The music had changed several times, so the crowd there was different now from the one that had witnessed her flight. Dudley was nowhere in sight.

Lips blotted together. A hand to her hair. Fingerpads to her freckles. Damp palms smoothing her dress.

She took a breath, thought of her dreams, and returned to the dance.

Two hours passed. Jenny watched the goings-on from the left side of the hall, from the right side of the hall, from the refreshment table, from the steps near the stage. She smiled. She nodded to the beat. She tried to look approachable.

The only one who looked at her was Dan O'Keefe in his watchful way, and the only one who approached was Miriam as she breathlessly Hully-Gullied her way by. "Are your feet okay?" the woman asked in one go-round, and in another, "Why aren't you *dancing*?" In the last, it was, "Are we on for tomorrow morning at ten?" She was swept past by the line before Jenny could answer.

As the evening wound down, the music slowed to mostly cheek-to-cheek numbers. With each family that called it a night, each group of friends, each couple, Jenny felt more frightened. This was supposed to have been her night. She was running out of time.

She stayed until the very last song had been played, until Reverend Putty had clapped for the band himself and said, "Thank you, good night, and God bless you all," until the last of the dancers filed out the door, and the dance committee was stashing trash in bags, wiping down tables, and folding up chairs. Only then did she leave.

The porch was empty. Just a handful of cars remained in the parking lot. She went down the steps and stood for a minute in the drive, staring sadly at the chestnut tree. Then she started down the road.

The night was moonless and dark as pitch. Fog hovered in the treetops, a heavy curtain waiting to fall and end the show. *Do it already,* Jenny cried. As she walked toward home, she told herself that tonight's failure wasn't the end of the world. But her heart wasn't buying it; it felt heavy as lead.

So much for new dresses. So much for makeup and mousse. So much for borrowing Miriam's shoes and enduring hours of crunched-up toes just because the shoes finished the look.

Stopping, she removed the shoes and continued in her stockinged feet. The freedom felt so good that, moments later, she stopped and peeled off her pantyhose. She tossed them into the woods and walked on. Seconds later, she tore apart her French braid.

Her stride became long and defiant. She indulged her feet by walking in the cool grass for a bit, then left the grass for the middle of the road, and there she stayed. She had nothing to lose, nothing at all.

A car came from behind and honked. She took her time moving over, and then she didn't go far. The car passed by riding on the shoulder of the road, and the driver pelted her with a hail of shouted insults. Seconds later it was sucked into the thickening mist.

Dan O'Keefe neither honked nor

shouted insults. He pulled up ahead of her and waited for her to reach him. "Climb in."

Jenny noticed the way the Jeep's head-lights speared the fog, and thought of Luke Skywalker's lightsaber. "I'm okay."

"A chill's coming along with the fog. You'll get sick, and I'll have to answer to Darden for it. Come on, Jenny. I'll drive you home."

But she wasn't ready to be home yet. Once there, the disappointment of the night would close in. She wasn't ready for that.

"You sure?" the deputy asked.

"Yes."

He sighed, rubbed his shoulder, waited. When she didn't budge, he said, "Well, I offered." Shifting into gear, he drove off.

Jenny watched the fog eat his taillights. Then she sat down in the middle of the road and dared another car to come.

None did. And sitting there, just sitting there with everything bare but what was covered by her dress—and that not very thick—she did feel the damp and the chill. So she pushed herself to her feet, found a strip of softer, warmer dirt on the shoulder of the road, and set off.

She hadn't gone far when a motorcycle broke through the mist from behind and passed her, then quickly downshifted and slowed. Coming to a full stop, it idled at the edge of a cotton-batting arc of light. Its driver balanced a booted foot on the road and looked back. After a minute, he took off his helmet.

Jenny barely breathed.

Chapter Seven

"Jenny barely breathed."

Casey read the line again, then grabbed the manila envelope and reached inside for more pages. When she felt nothing, she opened it wide and looked. The envelope was empty—no cover letter, no business card, no little memo that might give her a hint of what the story she had just read was and why it was there, no directive at all, just the scrawled letter "C" on the front that could have been C for Casey, C for Cornelius, or C for a mediocre grade on an English paper.

Casey would have given the paper an A. What it might have lacked in sophistication of prose, it more than made up for in content. She had surely been drawn in. Sitting here now, she most urgently wanted to know whether the guy on the motorcycle was good or bad, whether he would take Jenny away before her father returned and, if not, what was going to happen to Jenny— and that was before she began listing questions she had about Jenny and her father. The therapist in her had sensed despair; she wondered whether Connie had, too— whether Jenny was perhaps a client of his, which led Casey to a whole *other* set of questions. Totally aside from content, she wanted to know who had written these pages, what they were doing in Connie's desk when everything else remotely sensitive had been removed, and whether they had been deliberately put there for her to find.

But there were no answers. She was left high and dry on all counts.

Annoyed, she pushed back in the chair and pulled the center desk drawer out as far as it would go. There was nothing else way back there, no random sheets of paper or half-used pads. The drawer was empty except for the pens and pencils in the tray at the front, and this manila envelope that had been behind that.

C was for Casey. She felt it in her gut.

Or maybe she just wanted to feel it.

Dismissing that thought, she began to hunt for more of the story. She groped in the far back of the other drawers in the desk to make sure that she hadn't missed another envelope the first time around. When she found nothing, she turned around and systematically searched the cabinets built in under the bookshelves behind her. She had simply assumed they were empty when she and her friends had dropped in her files. Now she pulled out each drawer, and checked under and behind the folders.

Finding nothing, she tried the cabinets they hadn't touched.

Empty.

Standing back, she scanned the bookshelves one by one for an envelope sticking up behind or between books. Frustrated, she turned to study other spots in the office where a journal might be hidden.

In passing, her eye caught on the garden. It was filled with morning light now, a lime glow on greenery that suggested another warm June day. Needing to be a part of it, she opened the French doors and was immediately lured outside by the scent of the woods. She was about to push back the screen when a movement at the back of the garden stopped her. It was the iron latch on the door, rising.

The door opened, and a man slipped inside. He was tall, with shoulders that looked absurdly wide—until Casey realized that he was carrying something. He had reached the potting shed when she identified the "something" as a case of flower flats.

The gardener.

Casey didn't move.

Kneeling by the potting shed, he eased the case of flats to the ground. Rising again, he uncoiled the green garden hose that was hooked on the side of the shed and connected it to a sprinkler. Once a light spray was arcing toward the prettiest of the flowers, he went back out the door. She caught glimpses of him pulling and tugging at the open hatchback of a dusty Jeep. He reappeared with two bags of loam on his shoulder and yet another under an arm. Setting all three against the shed, he went inside.

The gardener.

The *gorgeous* gardener, Casey amended when the man emerged laden with tools, because he was definitely that. He had dark hair, broad shoulders even without the flats, a tapering torso, and long legs. He wore a black tee shirt with a rip on one sleeve, jeans that were faded at strategic spots and spattered with dirt at others, and work boots that were barely laced in a cocky show of neglect. His forearms were bare and ropy, his hands strong. She guessed that he was a year or two older than she was.

Go out and introduce yourself, Casey thought. *You're the new lady of the manor, and he is one of your staff.*

Still she didn't move—or thought she didn't, but something tipped him off. He looked up with wide-set eyes, seeming alarmed at first, remaining startled even after many seconds had passed. She had time to note the dark shadow of a beard before he acknowledged her with a brief nod and returned to his work.

Casey had never been a shrinking violet where men were concerned. Sliding the screen open, she walked blithely up the garden path—through the first tier, up the railroad-tie step, halfway through the less-manicured middle tier—before she paused to wonder if it was wise. Barefoot and wearing not a stitch under the robe, she looked as if she had just tumbled out of bed. It wasn't the best way to greet a stranger, much less a disreputable-looking one who was also in your employ.

But she couldn't turn back. He was watching her again. And, besides, she *loved* disreputable-looking men.

"Hi," she said as she crossed the third and last tier. "I'm Casey Ellis. You must be Jordan."

He was even more compelling close up. As deep brown as his eyes, his hair was short enough to show flat ears, long enough—and mussed enough—to look as if he had just rolled out of bed himself. His skin around that beard shadow had the start of a tan, a reddish-bronze on his nose and cheeks. Fine lines fanned out from the corners of his eyes.

Those lines made her rethink his age. If she was thirty-four, she guessed that he was nearing forty, and it wasn't only the crow's-feet. Those brown eyes were wise. They had a startling clarity and depth. Fixed on her as they were, their touch was almost a physical thing.

"I'm Dr. Unger's daughter," she announced.

He nodded.

"I've inherited this place."

"The lawyer told me that," he said in a deep voice. "I didn't expect the resemblance."

"Do you really see it?"

He nodded again. His eyes scanned her face for a minute, then fell along the lapel of the robe all the way down to her bare feet. "I didn't know you'd moved in."

"I haven't. I just fell asleep here last night and never made it home. I have to go back soon to change clothes. I'm seeing a client at eleven." She looked at the flowers he was about to plant. Some were pink, some were purple, some were white. All were small. "Are those begonias?"

"Impatiens."

"They look a little . . ."

"Sparse? They won't be in a couple of weeks. Impatiens grow quickly."

"Ah. That tells you how much I know about plants. What're the ones out front?"

"Sweet William in the boxes. Myrtle on the ground. The trees are dogwood."

She grinned, recalling the guesses she'd made. "Not bad. I was two for three. Impatiens I just don't know."

"Then you don't care where I put them?"

Care? He could plant them in the kitchen sink, as long as she could watch. "Put them where they'll grow best."

He pointed the trowel toward the middle tier. "Impatiens like shade. We usually put them down there by the trees."

"We?"

"Dr. Unger and I."

"Did he garden?" she asked. Realizing how odd the question probably sounded, she explained, "I didn't know him." Flippantly she added, "I was the product of a one-night stand."

The gardener held her gaze with eyes that were male and very aware.

"Totally irrelevant," she hastened to add, "but it does stop the rest of the questions. So I have some for you. How often do you come?"

He didn't blink. There might have been a tiny movement at the corner of his mouth. Before she could react—she hadn't intended a double entendre and was slow to find words, much less recover from the meaning in those eyes—he said a mild, "Mondays, Wednesdays, and Fridays."

She nodded and struggled to think of a

follow-up. "Always at this time of day?" she finally asked.

"Either early or late."

She knew what early was. "What's late?"

"Five or six in the evening. Watering's best done away from the noon sun. When I'm planting, like today, I need three hours. Once the planting's done, two suffice. In winter, one hour twice a week is enough."

"What's to do out here in winter?"

"Not much," he said, "but the plants inside still need tending."

She nodded again and smiled. Absently, she held the neck of her robe together. "They're all beautiful. He must have liked plants."

"Yes."

"They're in every room."

"Except the office. He didn't want to risk my barging in there when he was with a client."

Neither would Casey. She would lose her concentration entirely.

"So tell me when I shouldn't go in the house," Jordan said.

"Oh, it isn't a problem. I can work around you."

"Then you're not seeing clients here?"

"I am." She paused. Apparently, he knew more about her than just the fact of her inheriting the townhouse from Connie. "Did the lawyer say I was a therapist?"

Again, the gardener held her gaze without blinking. "Your father mentioned it once."

"He did?" That was interesting. "Did he say anything else?"

"No. Should he have?"

She smiled. "Of course not." She didn't say anything more about Connie. It would have been inappropriate to involve the gardener in personal issues. Not that he looked like a gardener, with those wise eyes, and he also didn't talk like a local. Despite the roughness of his looks, he was nothing like the hired hands her mother had used around the barn.

She rocked back on her heels and hitched her chin toward the carpet of green leaves under the chestnut tree. "What're those plants?"

"Pachysandra."

"And the ones climbing the shed here?"

"Clematis. Another couple weeks, and it'll bloom. The flowers are pink."

"Ah." She shifted her gaze to the shrubs near the hemlocks. "What're those?"

"The broad ones are junipers. The taller ones are yews."

Looking down a tier, she focused on pretty white flowers nestling among green leaves under the oak. "And those?"

"Trillium. It's a spring blooming bulb. Does well under deciduous trees."

Lips pressed together, she nodded and glanced at the house. Seconds later, she looked back at Jordan, who was still—disconcertingly—looking at her. "Do you have the time?" she inquired politely.

He checked his watch. It was a sports watch on a ratty black band. "Seven thirty-five."

She was impressed. He had picked up flats of impatiens, along with who knew what else for other clients, and was already at work. "You're an early riser."

"There's nothing keeping me in bed." He held her gaze for a final few seconds before returning to the impatiens.

Not so much dismissed as simply finding herself without a comeback, Casey headed off, back down the path. The stones were cool against her feet. She walked faster the closer she got to the house, trotting the last few steps. Once inside the office, she pulled the screen closed.

She did not look back at the gardener. Intending to go upstairs for more coffee and then to dress, she crossed the office. At the door, though, she did an about-face and returned to the desk. If the gardener had free rein of the house—and it was an alluring idea—a measure of prudence was in order. Gathering the typed sheets of the journal, she replaced the binder clip and was in the process of slipping them into their manila envelope when something stopped her. Pulling them back out, she set them on the desk, facedown this time so that what had stopped her could be seen. On the back of the last sheet, written in pencil, almost light enough to be missed, was Connie's scrawled note. It was brief but pointed: *How to help? She's kin.*

That changed everything. If Jenny was "kin," it didn't matter whether C was for Connie or for Casey. Anyone who was kin to Connie was kin to Casey.

That changed *everything.*

Stepping back from the desk, she faced

the shelves of books again. There was more to the journal. There had to be. But where?

She went shelf by shelf, book by book, but there was nothing that remotely resembled an envelope like the one on the desk. Meg had dusted here, but if she had found something, she would surely have left it. Casey didn't think she was bold enough to clean things out and dispose of random papers.

She moved to the side shelves and studied those with the same care. When she found nothing, she went into the den. There were bookshelves here, too. Again, she stood before each, raising her eyes higher and higher, moving from one shelf to the next. Realizing that she needed to push books aside, pull some out, and look behind, she glanced around for a chair to stand on, but everything here was large and too heavy to move.

Not so in the office. The desk chair was on casters.

She was returning for it when something she had seen earlier registered. It took her a minute, standing with her hands on her hips in front of the side shelves, before she spotted what she wanted. Without the protrusion of cabinets to stand on, she pulled the chair over and stepped up with care. Holding the edge of a shelf for balance, she reached as high as she could and grasped several books. She felt the desk chair slide out a smidgen and shifted her weight accordingly. She was in the process of lowering both the books and herself when the screen door opened fast.

"You're going to fall," Jordan warned.

She could hear him approaching. "No. Don't touch. I'm fine." Seconds later, she managed to get a hand on the arm of the chair and lower herself the rest of the way. It wasn't a particularly graceful move, certainly not ladylike, but she did it herself. That was important to her.

Smoothly, holding the books in one hand and her robe closed with the other, she got her feet out from under her, lowered them to the ground, and stood. Jordan was taller than she, so much that she had to look up. Her smile was broad enough—triumphant enough—to compensate for it.

"There," she said. "That wasn't so bad." She held up the books. "And I got what I wanted. This must be my day." Mustering as much dignity as she could under the circumstances, she slipped around the gardener and headed up the stairs.

Little Falls was in the atlas all right—once in Minnesota, once in New York, and once in New Jersey.

Sitting at the kitchen table, where Jordan wouldn't see her, Casey located each on the map. She immediately ruled out New Jersey; the Little Falls there was too close to metropolitan areas to be as rural as Jenny Clyde's Little Falls. The ones in Minnesota and New York were possibilities, since they were more remote. She guessed there were others as well, places where the population of the town was so small that it didn't appear on the map, and then there were hamlets that weren't quite towns. Little Falls could be a pocket of South Hadley Falls in Massachusetts, River Falls in Wisconsin, or Idaho Falls in Idaho. It could be a corner of Great Falls in either Montana or South Carolina. Or it could be a name that was made up by the author of the journal for the sake of privacy.

The Sierra Club publications that she'd taken down with the atlas focused on northern New England, but she checked the index anyway. When she came up with a blank, she refilled her coffee and went to the window.

Jordan was still down there, visible between the boughs of the trees, planting impatiens. He was working between the flats and a bag of loam, alternately sitting back on his heels and leaning forward. For a tall man, he seemed perfectly comfortable on the ground. He seemed perfectly comfortable with his plants, period.

She admired that. Gardeners, carpenters, outdoorsmen—she appreciated people who could use their bodies that way. They didn't have to run for the sake of exercise or do yoga to relieve stress. She envied them the simplicity of their lives.

He glanced up in her direction. She might have shrunk back to keep from being seen. Instead, she raised the mug in a small salute, and sipped the hot brew. She could look if she wanted. She was the boss.

She was still watching Jordan when the garden door opened again and Meg came through. She talked with him for a minute, shot a surprised look at the house, then hurried in, but not through the office. Casey watched her disappear into a corner of the garden. Seconds later, there was the slam of a door, then footsteps running up the stairs.

Casey waited at the top until Meg was in sight. "How did you get in?" she called down.

"The service entrance," Meg said as she ran up the rest of the way. "It's on the side. I'm sorry. I didn't know you were staying over. I'd have come earlier. I picked up fresh bread. Can I make you something for breakfast?"

Casey shook her head. When Meg's face fell, she turned the headshake into a nod. "I would adore the following: one egg over easy, cooked with very little fat; one slice of toast, dry; and more coffee. How's that?"

Meg beamed. "Easy as pie," she said and set off.

Casey went up to the bedroom for her clothes, fully planning to wait to shower when she got back to her condo. But the bathroom was too tempting—everything new, everything clean, everything just begging to be used. She found soap. She found shampoo. She found body lotion. She even found a toothbrush and toothpaste in its own little travel pack.

Twenty minutes later, all scrubbed and clean, albeit in yesterday's clothes, she left the bedroom. She was about to go downstairs when she heard a low murmur coming from Connie's bedroom. She paused, listened. She crept to the door and was trying to make out words when the murmuring stopped.

Seconds later, Meg emerged and smiled. "Just cleaning up after the night. You look beautiful. I have breakfast ready for you. Would you like to eat in the kitchen? Or on the patio? Dr. Unger always had breakfast outside in weather like this. Jordan certainly doesn't mind. He'll just work right along. You can sit there and read the newspaper. It was out front. I brought it in with me."

"I have a better idea," Casey said. "I need to check something on the Web. Can you bring breakfast down to the office?"

While she ate, Casey searched for information on Little Falls. She found references to those she had already discovered, but none of them felt right to her. Connie was from

Maine; he claimed Jenny Clyde was kin. Casey searched through information on Maine, but found no reference to a Little Falls. She found Island Falls, Lisbon Falls, Kezar Falls, and Livermore Falls. In theory, Little Falls could be a hamlet of any one of them. She tried a second search engine, then a third, but came up with nothing definitive, and by then she was out of time.

Back at her condo, she put on makeup, secured her hair in a marginally professional twist, and changed into a pair of linen slacks and a silk blouse. She was halfway out the door again when she returned for running gear. As an afterthought, she dropped makeup and a change of clothes into the gym bag. Then she returned to her car.

Jordan's Jeep was gone when she drove down the narrow alley and pulled in at the back garden door. She didn't have time to feel disappointment, though, because as soon as she was down through the garden and into the house, her first client arrived.

There was no dwelling on thoughts of Little Falls then. Nor could she dwell on the oddness of seeing clients in what had been her father's office. There was a flicker of thought from time to time—the image of a little girl playing grown-up sitting behind this very big desk—but the truth was, she was with her clients mostly in the sitting area, a far more relaxed place to be.

She saw clients at eleven, twelve, and one—spending fifty minutes with each and ten minutes entering notes. Between two and two-thirty, she nibbled on a sandwich while she made phone calls. Then came another four clients.

The first of those was Joyce Lewellen. Casey had always liked Joyce. She was a precise woman, and while she did make a tailored appearance and liked her life neatly shaped, she fell far short of being obsessive-compulsive. She communicated well and was insightful enough to easily identify a problem. Casey had always suspected that Joyce used their sessions simply to air her thoughts to an unbiased ear.

Joyce was in her early forties. Eighteen months before, her husband had died of complications from what should have been a routine hernia operation. Unable to accept his death, much less explain it to their children, Joyce had needed to find someone at fault. She had gone the route of a medical malpractice suit. Her case wasn't strong; she'd had to talk with three lawyers before finding one who would represent her.

Casey had seen her weekly for several months at one stretch. Joyce's major issue was anger. It was keeping her up at night, distracting her during the day, making her a one-issue woman. Her therapy had been focused on letting go of the anger.

"It's been a while," Casey said when they were seated opposite each other, Joyce on the sofa, Casey in a chair.

"Four months," Joyce acknowledged. She was outwardly composed; the only sign of tension was her hands, which were tightly clenched in her lap. "I've been okay. So have the girls. They're back doing their usual stuff—soccer, scouts, ballet. They'll be starting summer camp in another week."

"And you? Are you working?"

Joyce had designed store windows prior to her marriage. She had done some freelancing after the girls started school, but had let that go when Norman died. Casey and she had discussed her returning to work if not for the money, which she could use, then for its therapeutic value.

Now she wrinkled her nose. "No. I've

wanted to be available for anything the lawyer needed. I know, I know. You said that was only keeping the anger alive, but I can't help myself. I need to do this for Norman. But I've been okay with it, really I have. The lawyer's working. My anger's under control."

"Are you going out with friends again?"

"Well, for lunch. Not evenings yet."

"You're still wearing black."

"It seemed appropriate while the lawsuit went on. Last month, there was a hearing before a judge. Both sides presented affidavits and legal briefs. The other side filed for a summary judgment, claiming that we could not prove the case to a jury. The judge's decision is due at the end of the week."

"How do you feel about that?"

"I'm a basket case," Joyce said in a high voice. "That's why I'm here. Yes, I need the money, but it's more than that. It's the principle of the thing. Norman shouldn't have died. He has two little girls who miss him. He'll never see them become teenagers or get married or have kids. And me, I depended on him. We were supposed to grow old together. Now we can't. Someone ought to pay for that."

Casey heard the same old anger. Back at the start, they had talked about bad things happening to good people. Joyce hadn't accepted it then, any more than she was accepting it now.

"Our chances of winning aren't good," Joyce went on. "My lawyer said it when I first hired him, and he said it again at the end of the hearing. There were things that the judge did and questions he asked that didn't bode well for our cause. So what am I going to do? What if he rules against us? I mean, this doesn't have to be the end. We could take the case to an appeals court. But my lawyer won't do that. He says we have to abide by the judge's decision now, and maybe he's right. There are times when I feel so *sick* of all this that I just want it over. Then I get a second wind and I want to win; I just *do.*"

"If you do win, what then?"

"I'll have proven something. I'll be able to put all this behind me and move on."

"And if you don't win?"

Joyce was slower in answering. "I don't know. That's what's making me nervous. We keep talking about anger, you and me. But what do I do with the anger if there's no one left to blame?"

Three client sessions later, Casey was still thinking of Joyce's words. It had been easy to sustain anger while Connie had been alive; as long as he was living and breathing, he could pick up the phone, send her an e-mail or mail her a note, even pass her a message through an intermediary. Now that he was dead, those avenues were gone. And her anger?

Heading for the garden now, she couldn't sustain it. She tried. She thought of moving the patio table and chairs to another spot, simply to do what *she* wanted. Three steps out from under the pergola, though, and she couldn't think of a better spot for the table than where it already was.

The garden was a black hole when it came to negative thoughts, sucking them right in, making them vanish.

The sky was overcast, the air more humid, but the place didn't suffer for the absence of sun. If anything, the diffuse light gave it a plusher feel. The trees were delineated from each other by color, rather than the texture of their boughs. The flowers were muted, the stones softer.

The instant she unclipped her hair from the wide barrette that had kept it contained, it began to curl and swell. Combing her fingers through sped the process. She lifted the mass and closed her eyes, only to open them seconds later when, with the slide of the screen door and the patter of footsteps, Meg emerged from the house. She carried a bottle of wine and a plate filled with mini skewers of grilled beef and veggies. Casey was wondering how she was going to make a dent in the pile when company arrived to help.

"Just took a chance you'd be here," Brianna explained gaily as she quickly dug in. "I could get used to this."

Casey was thinking she could, too.

"So what's it like, practicing where he practiced?" Brianna asked.

Setting a cleaned skewer aside, Casey sat back in the patio chair with her wine and tried to process her feelings. "Very, very weird. I kept thinking, What are you *doing* here, Casey? He wrote at this desk. He talked on this phone. The ideas that came out of this office are read all over the world. And now all that's left here is little old me."

"What's wrong with little old you?"

"I can't begin to do what he did. I identified with my one-o'clock client. She's a really bright, really successful entrepreneur—owns three upscale restaurants that have absolutely taken off—but she suffers from a severe impostor complex."

"What's it from?"

"Her father owned a deli. Her mother kept house. They thought she was throwing her life away going to culinary school. They warned her against buying the first restaurant, said she was getting in over her head when she opened the second, and when she opened the third, they took her out of their will."

"Why?"

"They said that she was reckless and that they didn't want her squandering their hard-earned savings. So here she is, solidly in the black, doing better each year, and still she feels like those restaurants are a deck of cards on the verge of collapse. Her parents see her that way. It's been ingrained in her."

"But that's not your story. Connie never told you you weren't any good."

"Not in words," Casey said, rubbing the rim of the wineglass against her lips.

"Would he have left you this place, knowing you'd practice here, if he thought you were a lousy therapist?"

Casey shrugged. She had no idea what Connie had thought about her, good *or* bad.

"You have a *great* practice, Casey. Joy and I took the easy way out, going in-house." Joy worked for the state, Brianna for a rehab center.

"I wouldn't call what you do easy."

"But we don't have to worry about getting clients. They're always there. You *do* have to worry, and look at the practice you've built. Give me a rundown on today's list."

Casey could count on Brianna to boost her morale. "Two phobias, the low self-esteem, three adjustment disorders, and one panic attack."

"Yours or hers?"

"Hers. She couldn't find the townhouse. She panics when things don't fall just perfectly into place, and begins to imagine all sorts of things."

"Like?"

"Her husband's voice. He has abused her verbally for so many years that she actually hears him yelling at her. It sends her into a tizzy."

"Has she reached the stage where she knows that he isn't really there?" Brianna asked.

"Intellectually, yes. Emotionally, no. There are times when she's paralyzed by it."

"Should she leave him?"

"Yes—if the issue were simply her own personal development. But it's more complex than that. They have four children still at home, and the only career she knows is being a homemaker. She considers him her employer. If she quits, where does she go, what does she do, what happens to the kids? No, she won't leave him. The best I can do is to help her gain perspective—stand back, evaluate what she does well, learn to deal with the things that he says. She really does hear his voice."

Brianna was suspiciously silent. She sipped her wine, looked momentarily pensive. Then, quietly, she asked, "How's your mom?"

Casey sent her a sidelong glance. "Speaking of hearing a voice."

"Do you still?"

"In my way."

"Casey," Brianna scolded softly.

"I know. If she's in the persistent vegetative state that the doctors claim, she doesn't hear, doesn't think, doesn't know. But I feel her there, Bria. I swear I do. I know what she's thinking."

"Is there any improvement?"

"She had another seizure today. The doctor says she's failing."

"How do you feel about that?"

"I should be relieved. What she's living can't be called a life."

"So what *are* you feeling?"

"If she's failing, I know it's for the best. I don't cry anymore. After three years, I'm all cried out. I don't even start shaking like I did then, I'm so used to seeing her this way."

"So what are you feeling?" Brianna persisted.

"Devastated," Casey said with a hand on the ache in her chest.

Over three painful years, Casey had learned that the best way to deal with the devastation was to fill her mind with other things.

She was fine when she was with clients, when it was her job to feel *their* thoughts. She was fine when she was doing yoga, running, or playing with friends.

That evening, though, after Brianna left, she had only thoughts of Connie and *Flirting with Pete* for distraction. If the manuscript was part of a scavenger hunt, she was more than game.

She went through the den inch by inch. She didn't find anything remotely related to the journal, but she did find Connie's personal files—bank statements, canceled checks, income tax returns. They were in plastic bins in lower cabinets, neatly labeled and consecutively arranged. Sorting through, she learned that he wrote his checks by hand, that he paid his bills promptly, supported public radio and television, and gave large amounts of money each year to naturalist causes in Maine.

He had been born in Maine. He still had a *thing* for Maine. Casey bet that Little Falls was there, fictitious or not.

She sorted through those Maine receipts, hunting for a reference to the town. She sorted through brochures on which he had filled out applications for hikes, canoe trips, bird-watching expeditions, and mountain-climbing adventures. A few looked as though they had never been sent—actually, quite a few, some even with uncanceled checks stapled to the top. Others must have been sent, because there were letters confirming receipt. She read through them all. Nowhere was there any reference to Little Falls.

By the time she had put everything back in its place, she was too tired to return to the condo. With a client coming at eight the next morning, it didn't make sense.

This time, she went straight to the guest bedroom. Connie was still right down the hall, but after going through his bills and realizing the size of the responsibility he had left her, she was feeling brash. After all, she reasoned, since she was the one—not some ghost—who would be paying those bills now, she had a right to bed down wherever she pleased.

She fell asleep thinking about safe, practical, physical things like heating, air-conditioning, roofers, house painters, and exterminators—but came awake at midnight with a start, sure that she had heard a noise. She sat up in bed and looked around. The room was lit by gaslights from the Court. She could see quite well.

She saw nothing.

Holding her breath, she listened. The city was sleeping, snoring softly outside her window. She didn't hear anything in the room. She didn't hear anything in the hall.

Telling herself that her imagination had gotten away from her while she slept, she lay back down and closed her eyes. Seconds later, though, she was up again, this time slipping out of bed. Pulling on the robe, she crept to the door and listened. She had left it half open, and half open it was.

Of course, that didn't mean anything. Ghosts walked *through* doors.

But she didn't believe in ghosts.

Slipping out into the hall, she held herself very still and listened. She heard a hum from somewhere deep in the house, but it was a mechanical sound, nothing eerie or odd. Tiptoeing to Connie's door, she listened. And she did hear something. The sound was very soft. She couldn't define it.

As always, the door was ajar. Without touching it, she peered inside, but she couldn't see much.

She wasn't going in. She wasn't that

brave. Assuring herself that there was a perfectly rational explanation for the sound she heard and that Meg would give it to her in the morning, she backed off. That was when she saw the eyes.

Chapter Eight

Casey didn't linger. In a flash she returned to her own room and shut the door tight.

She had imagined the eyes. No psychosis here, simply the power of suggestion. Her neighbor had mentioned a ghost, so a ghost was what she saw. It was not a whole lot different, really, from carrying on a conversation with her mother. The doctors claimed that Caroline hadn't talked in three years, and who was Casey to argue? If she heard a voice, she imagined it.

Of course, she heard Caroline's voice because she wanted to hear it, which was not the case with a ghost.

So, was it the strangeness of the house that got her imagination going? Or the fact that the room at the end of the hall had been her father's and a part of her did want him to be there, after he'd invited her into his house?

Very quietly, she got back in bed. She didn't take off the robe—*she* wasn't having any imaginary ghost see *her* in the nude—but lay on her back in the middle of the bed—lay very still with her hands laced at her waist and her eye on the door.

There was no movement. There was no sound. She watched and listened for an hour before finally falling asleep, but she slept uneasily, awakening often to listen and watch. When daylight finally arrived, she was feeling more perturbed at herself than anything else.

Taking a yellow singlet and shorts from her gym bag, she hurriedly pulled them on and stretched a scrunchie around her hair. She gave a moment's thought to the night sounds she'd heard when she opened the door to her room—and she did glance at that narrow strip of darkness where Connie's door was open. But she made it to the stairs without mishap. From there, it was a straight shot down, through the front hall, past Ruth's paintings—keeping her eyes on the stairs—through the office, and out to the garden.

Emerging from under the pergola, she felt instant comfort. Dawn in the garden was fresh, even on another warm day. The air was sweet with . . . lilacs, she smelled lilacs. This scent drew her to a pair of bushes on her right. Lavish purple clusters in leafy green bouquets rose behind the cultivated flowers. She smiled, closed her eyes, savored the scent.

Minutes later, soothed by the flowers in a kind of spiritual foreplay, she staked out a spot in the garden's wooded section and lowered herself to the ground. She had the routine down pat, fifteen minutes moving through the postures of the sun salutation, focusing on her breathing as much as she did on fluidity and stretch. She relaxed one part of her body after another, concentrated—really concentrated—on letting go of the tension brought on by scary little thoughts, like ghosts, bombing as a therapist in Connie's office, and Caroline dying and leaving her alone in the world. Drawing positive energy into her system with each complete breath, she felt the release of tightness in her neck, her back, her belly and legs. When her mind began to wander, she dragged it right back. Again and again, she drew in deep belly breaths and exhaled slowly and completely.

She went through the cycle of poses three times, and when finished she felt infinitely more relaxed. As always, she saved the best for last. Using the trunk of the old chestnut for backup, she fit the top of her head to the ground, clasped her fingers behind it for support, and slowly lifted the rest of her body—hips, then legs, then feet—until she was perfectly balanced and still.

Inversion was restorative. She always felt it, but never more so than after a restless night. The force of gravity pulling her body in a different direction gave the flow of her blood a refreshing jolt. It made her body tingle, her skin breathe, her breasts rise. Like cool water slapped on cheeks burning with fever, it woke her up.

Viewed upside down, the garden was a revised world of color and shape. There were no ghosts here. Everything was geometric and solid—not the least of which being the man who suddenly, silently, appeared before her. He had come in from the back gate while she was lost in deep breathing and concentration, but he was as real as the junipers and yews that formed a backdrop for his upside-down form.

At least, she thought he was real.

Then she changed her mind. Tuesday wasn't his day. She simply wanted him there—wanted him to see how athletic she was, how attractive she was in her workout yellows. She wanted to tease him, wanted to feel power in the teasing to counter the lack of power she felt when it came to her parents. She wanted him there for the male-female thing. His presence added pleasure to the garden, an Adam to her Eve.

Imagining Jordan wasn't so much the power of suggestion as the power of wishful thinking. The gardener was a cool guy to conjure up—and intriguing upside down. He was solid as brass this way, what with the weight of his body resting on shoulders that were amply broad to support it. They were handsome shoulders, she decided. Not bulked up. Just leanly muscled. She could see this, because in her mind he wore a tank top. It was black, stuck loosely into low-slung jeans that were in turn stuck into half-laced work boots. She knew that the jeans and boots were for protection as he gardened, but she guessed they would make him warm. The flush on his cheeks suggested that. But then there were those brown eyes, steady as the chestnut behind her. And that dark brown bed-head hair. Viewing it upside down, she fancied he was planted right here in her father's garden, rooted to the spot by that hair. But then, she guessed that he would be firmly rooted no matter where he stood—he was that hardy a guy.

The image moved. It was a subtle move, the shift of weight to one hip, but it was real enough to jar her.

She swayed and began to totter.

He started forward, extending an arm.

"No no no," she cautioned quickly. Without the weight of gravity, her voice was higher than normal. "Don't touch." She steadied herself. "I'm fine." She concentrated, took a leveling breath, refocused.

He was still there.

"This isn't Wednesday," she said in that higher than normal voice. She didn't usually sway, didn't usually totter. Her yoga instructor was amazed at how long she could stand on her head. As shows went, this was definitely not her best.

"The impatiens need water," he said.

It was a reasonable enough explanation, though it raised another question. "My father had every modern convenience in the house. Why not an automatic sprinkling system out here?"

"No need. He had me."

"Having you stop by to water flowers is neither time- nor cost-effective."

Jordan lifted one of those broad shoulders in what Casey's mind correctly translated into a shrug. "Doesn't bother me."

"You like watering."

"I like watering."

"But to come all this way . . ."

"The shop's not far."

"Ah." She had been thinking about his home. She couldn't imagine he lived here on the hill. Even the smallest apartments here were way too expensive. "How long have you been doing his garden for him?"

"Seven years."

"And before you?"

"No one. The place was nothing but overgrown grass and weeds."

"And wonderfully aged hemlocks, maples, birches, and oaks," she reminded him sweetly.

He was quiet for a minute, before granting, "Yes. There were those."

"What about those shrubs one tier

down—the ones with the buds about to burst? They look pretty old."

"The big ones are rhododendron, the little ones azalea, and no, we brought them in."

"Who did the landscape design?" She was holding herself well now, even starting to get used to her voice.

"Me."

"Through Daisy's Mum?"

"Yes."

"Do you have a degree in landscape design?"

"No. I just know plants."

"Did he?"

"Who?"

"My father. We established that he loved them. Did he know them?"

"He knew what he liked."

"And you took it from there."

There was a pause, then a curious, "Does that bother you?"

It was the type of question that Brianna would have asked her, the kind that might have brought an approving nod from Connie, because it was definitely the right question. And the answer? Yes, it bothered Casey. Call it envy or jealousy. Call it resentment. It seemed to her that her father's employees had his confidence and respect, even his affection, while his daughter went without.

But she couldn't blame the gardener. He was obviously good at what he did. "You've produced an incredible garden," she said. "But you never did tell me if he did any of the gardening himself."

"Your father? He pitched in from time to time."

"So he . . . just . . . liked doing it, too?"

"No. It was his way of thanking me for helping him out with other things."

"What things?"

"Things. Moving stuff. Carrying stuff up the stairs."

"What kind of stuff did you carry?"

"Files. Whenever he closed a case, he put the file in a special drawer. When the drawer got filled, he moved the contents upstairs."

"To the spare bedrooms? Those boxes can't all be filled with files."

"There are books."

"More books? Omigod."

"And letters. Professional correspondence."

"Anything personal?"

"Those'd be in boxes with m-e printed on top."

Connie's me-files. If there was more of the journal to be read, it would be there. Casey's thoughts flew up to those carton-filled bedrooms so quickly that she swayed again.

Again, the gardener reached out.

"Don't touch," she cautioned as she had before. She pulled her mind back down. "I'm fine."

She had barely steadied herself when he asked, "Do you have a problem with that?"

"With what?"

"Touching. Your father did. He didn't like to be touched. If there was the brush of an arm or a hand, it was accidental. He kept a physical distance from anyone who was near."

Casey had always sensed that, but she had always seen Connie in professional situations where physical distance was appropriate. Working in and around the house was different. She might have asked Jordan more about it, if she hadn't been bothered by his first question. Her own image was at issue here. She felt compelled to set him straight. "No. I don't have a problem with touching."

"Then with the hired hand? That was the third time you've told me not to touch."

The third time. Ah, yes. Once in the office the evening before, twice now.

"No," she replied patiently. "I have a thing about being self-reliant. I wasn't about to fall off that chair, and I'm not about to fall now." As if to prove her point, she slowly bent her knees. Hands flanking her shoulders, she carefully curled her body forward, lowering her legs until her feet touched the ground. Refusing to be rushed despite the view of her backside that he surely had, she slowly raised her head and reacclimated herself to being upright. When she felt confident she wouldn't topple, she took a final breath, rose to standing, and turned.

The gardener was tall, far more so than five-foot-four Casey. She compensated by tipping up her chin and looking him in the eye. "Some men think women are fragile. I'm not."

He seemed mildly amused.

No, she realized. He seemed mildly *aroused*. Those dark eyes held a definite flicker of appreciation.

Incited by it—and, truth be told, by a sudden, fanciful recollection of D. H. Lawrence's passionate Lady Chatterley and her virile groundskeeper—Casey walked right up close to him. "As for touching," she said, sliding an arm around his waist, "I like it a lot." Holding his gaze, daring him to be the one to step away, she pressed a palm up his chest, over his shoulder, down his arm, over his wrist. Her fingers sifted through his, caught up by them for a brief moment. "I *love* touching," she said softly. "I've never had a problem with it, and as for your being a hired hand, I grew up eating dinner with hired hands. I shared an apartment with one in college and lost my virginity to another." She shouldn't have said that, because the moment was suddenly hot—that flicker in his eyes had grown into something beyond the clasp of his hand, something that licked at the touchpoints of their bodies—and mention of sex didn't help. Rushing to tamp down the heat on her end without moving away, because not only was he lovely to touch but he smelled like pure man, she said, "No, no problem with hired hands. Yes, a problem with ghosts. What do you know about Angus?"

Jordan was silent as he looked down at her. His eyes were an even richer, deeper brown, his cheeks more ruddy. Casey felt the movement of his chest, barely an inch from hers and less steady than before. It was a heady sensation.

Then she realized that the chest movement was suppressed laughter.

Pulling her hand free of his, she stepped quickly back. With some indignation, she asked, "Is Angus a joke?"

"No," he said, though the corner of his mouth did twitch. "He's a cat."

"A *cat.*"

"Haven't you met him?"

Eyes in the dark, a soft padding across the floor in the night, a sound that could as well have been purring as the flutter of a ghost's breath. And Meg's murmurs. Of course. Casey should have guessed.

Feeling the fool, she frowned. "No, I have not met him. No one told me about a cat."

"If it's a problem, I'll take him."

She wasn't having any part of that. "If he comes with the house, he's mine."

"Angus and I get along great."

"He and I may, too." There could be one

problem. "Is he always in the master bed-room?"

Jordan's mouth lost its humor. "During the day, yes. He may wander around at night, but since Connie died, he doesn't go far. He's waiting for his friend to return."

Casey felt a pang. "That's the saddest thing." She started toward the house, then stopped and looked back at Jordan. "Will he resent me?"

"I don't know."

"Does he scratch and snarl?"

"Never has."

She raised her brows, pressed her lips to-gether, stepped back, gave the gardener a might-as-well-check-it-out look, and set off. Cutting back through the office, she went up one flight, then a second. Her pace flagged when she reached the bedroom landing. Turning toward Connie's room, she approached with caution. Not a ghost, but a cat; not a ghost, but a cat—she kept telling herself that, but still her heart rapped against her ribs. When she was a good three feet away, she sat down on the carpet and folded her legs.

She knew cats. Her mother had always kept them in the barn. Two were there at the time of the accident. Casey would have taken them to live with her if one of Caroline's weavers hadn't begged to do it. The woman had a big house, a big heart, and a big void in her life, having lost her husband of thirty years out of the blue the year before. How could Casey say no? Her own house was small, her heart was preoccupied with Caroline, and she was already used to ignoring the little void inside—which wasn't to say that she hadn't thought of kidnapping those cats. She might have liked the company at night. More, though, she might have liked to tell Caroline that she was caring for the cats herself. Caroline would have approved.

"Angus," she called softly and scooted a little closer. "Are you there, Angus?" She waited, listened, heard absolutely nothing. It occurred to her that the cat was probably sound asleep somewhere deep in the room, and that her time—of which there wasn't a great deal left before she had to shower and dress—was better spent exploring Connie's me-cartons. But the journal was a story, perhaps real, perhaps not, but not immediate in any event. The cat, however, was alive. It was here, waiting for

Connie, as it had been doing for nearly four weeks. Casey needed to let it know that she could take care of it, too.

"An-gus," she coaxed, inching closer. Connie's cat, now hers? Sight unseen, she felt possessive of it. "Come say hello, pretty kitty," she sang, because she hadn't ever met a cat that wasn't pretty, hadn't ever met one that didn't like being praised.

Scooting up another little bit brought her within arm's reach of the door. Leaning forward, she peered through the few inches of opening. When she imagined she saw eyes, she drew back. *Not a ghost, Casey. A cat,* she reminded herself. Reaching forward, she opened the door a bit.

The eyes were there, definitely not imagined. They sat two feet into the room and glowed out at her from a shadowed patch. With daylight filtering in behind, the animal was silhouetted. Casey saw the outline of ears angling up from the corners of its head, but little else.

Waiting for his friend to return. Her heart melted. She might resent Connie Unger for many things, not the least of them making her feel unwanted, unloved, and unfit for the job of being his daughter. But she didn't resent his leaving her a cat. A cat was as close as she could get to having a living, breathing part of him. A cat was more important than a townhouse. She could do a cat. She could do it very well.

She extended a hand toward the eyes. "Oh, Angus, I am so sorry. I'm not Connie, but I do love cats. I'd be *very* happy to take care of you." She slid forward another little bit, which brought her as close to the threshold as she dared go. She kept her hand out, inviting the cat to sniff it. "Come say hello, big guy," she coaxed gently.

"How do you know he's big?" asked Jordan as he came up the stairs.

"Big eyes, big ears, big cat," Casey said and tacked on a prudent, "Yes?" After all, Jordan knew the cat. Jordan also knew the garden. He *also* knew the house. Casey might have fixated on the unfairness of a stranger knowing everything she didn't, if she hadn't been thinking of something she did know. She knew that despite his outward scruffiness, this man smelled of soap, that when she had run her hand over his chest she had felt soft hair under his shirt, that even this early in the day his body was warm. These things were embedded in her brain and, with his approach, became wedged in her throat.

"Yes," he confirmed as he rounded the newel post.

She let herself enjoy the sight of him for a minute, then, like a good girl, returned to the cat. "How old is he?"

"Eight. He has lots of years left. Connie took good care of him." Squatting down beside Casey, he called gently, "Hey, Angus. Come on out here. I'm your buddy." He made a ticking sound with his tongue.

"Does he have food and litter in there?" Casey whispered.

"Everything he needs. Cats are pretty self-contained." He went forward on one knee and opened the door a bit more. "Come on out here, Angus. She won't bite."

Able to really see the cat now, Casey sighed in delight. "He's beautiful." Largely gray, with bold white and black markings, he had a square muzzle, a pug nose, and a bib of fur that fanned out over his chest. He was looking right up at Jordan with large, green eyes—large, green, *beseechful* eyes that might have suggested unhappiness, confusion, or fear.

"He's a Maine Coon, isn't he?" Casey asked.

"Yes." Jordan reached for the cat, but the cat drew back. "Hey," he scolded in a raspy voice. "What's that about? You know me. I'm your pal."

Angus knew that. The look he gave Jordan said as much. *You may be my pal,* it said as the cat turned wary eyes on Casey, *but who in the devil is she?*

"She's Connie's daughter. She's okay."

Angus did not look appeased.

"I wouldn't have pegged Connie for an animal person," Casey mused. He had always seemed too formal.

"Cats. That's all. Actually, Angus is all. Dr. Unger wasn't wild about other animals, not even other cats, and the feeling was mutual. The only lap Angus'd ever sit on was Dr. Unger's."

"And Connie allowed it?" Casey asked, surprised as she looked up at Jordan.

He met her gaze. "You mean, the touching thing? I guess that only applied to people. He was an old softie when it came to Angus."

"Why?"

"Why did he love Angus?"

"Why didn't he love people?"

Jordan shrugged.

A shrug didn't do it for Casey, and while this man surely knew more about mulch than he did about the human mind, he was all she had at the moment. "Did he ever drop a hint—you know, suggest that his father beat him? Or that he grew up with people who couldn't bear to be touched? Or that he was sexually abused?"

The gardener slid her a dry look. "If that was the case, he clearly overcame some of it, since he sired you."

"One night. That's all he was with my mother. And what he had with his wife isn't what I'd call a marriage."

"They seemed happy enough together. Besides, who's to say she wasn't the one who wanted to live apart?"

"If that was so," Casey suggested, "maybe it was because he wouldn't touch her. I'd think that would drive a woman crazy after a while."

"Not all women are like you."

She drew back. "Excuse me?"

"Not all women define themselves in terms of sex."

"I don't do that."

"What was that down in the garden about?"

"Making a point that I'm different from my father," she informed him. "I like being with people. I like touching people. My greatest dream is to wake up each and every morning with a warm body beside me, and I'm not talking about a dog or a cat." She couldn't believe she'd said that—couldn't even believe it was true—but the damage was done. She hurried on. "I can't begin to fathom what made my father not want that. I've had dysfunctional clients. I've had socially dysfunctional ones and sexually dysfunctional ones, but only a handful were as solitary as Connie Unger appears to have been. He was abnormal. Brilliant. But abnormal."

"And you're normal," Jordan observed. "Brilliant, too?"

She held his gaze. "No. I couldn't have gotten a Ph.D. if my life depended on it. I struggled through high school, struggled through college, and I sure didn't set the academic world on fire in graduate school. But I'm a very good therapist." With that reminder, she glanced at her watch. "Oh God." She scrambled to her feet. "I have to get going." She remembered the cat. Her eyes flew to the door, but he was gone. She looked questioningly at Jordan.

"Back inside," he said. "Waiting."

Again, Casey melted. "That's *so* sad." She went right up to the threshold. "Angus? I'll be back."

"You could go in and see him."

She could. But she wasn't ready. "Maybe later."

"You're not afraid of a cat, are you?"

Casey gave him a look that said she was not, and started across the landing toward her room. She was barely halfway there when she suddenly turned. Jordan had just risen. "Those cartons upstairs—the personal ones. Are they arranged any particular way?"

"Like how?"

"Chronologically?"

"I don't know."

"You helped him move stuff up there."

"I didn't examine the contents. That's not my place. I'm just the gardener."

Casey had the absurd notion that he was more. Not knowing if it was true and, if so, what it meant, she felt threatened. "If you're just the gardener, what're you doing up here?" She didn't see a watering can, didn't see pruning shears or a mister. "Shouldn't you be down with the tulips?"

"We don't have tulips."

"Pansies, then."

"Viburnum, agapanthus, gardenia, verbena, lupine, aquilegia, heliotrope. No pansies."

"All those?"

"For starters."

"Well then, you have your work cut out for you, don't you."

He stared at her for a minute. Then, holding both hands up, he sauntered toward the stairs. "The cat's yours. Do what you want."

What Casey wanted was to divide the morning between exploring the cartons Connie had stored and coaxing Angus out of his room. Once she was dressed, though, she had to review her notes on the day's clients. She did that while she ate the breakfast that Meg insisted on making, and once she was done eating, she had phone calls to make. She had to give her new office address to clients scheduled for Wednesday and Thursday, to her bookkeeper, to the service providers with whom she most often worked, and to a psychiatrist who would prescribe medication for her clients now that John was out of the loop. Once she had done all that, her first client arrived, and then she didn't have time to think about either Angus or Connie's cartons. When she was with a client, she was focused.

She was more comfortable in the office today—which wasn't to say that she helped herself to a butterscotch candy, though she did consider it. Callard & Bowsers were good. She could have used the sugar pick-me-up a time or two. But they were Connie's candies. And the comfort today came from making the office her own.

She did that by spreading out her papers, pushing them around, leaving them slightly askew. Connie would have hated that. But she wasn't Connie. She wasn't compulsively neat. Organized, yes. She knew what was in each group of papers. But they were *her* papers, and they sat beside *her* computer, with *her* books on the shelves immediately behind. And these were *her* clients. She owed them her total attention.

So she thought only of them until the last one was gone. By then it was six, and she was mentally spent. Needing quiet time, she had Meg fix a tall iced coffee and took it out to the garden.

The air was heavy with heat and humidity.

Jordan was pruning the shrubs.

She was startled to find him there. This was still Tuesday, and he was no longer watering impatiens. She wanted to say something smart, but she was too tired. Taking her drink to the patio table, she sank into a chair and watched him work.

He was showing the wear and tear of the day. His hair was damp, his jaw stubbled, his jeans dirty at the knees and the seat. Sweat made his tank top inky and gave a sheen to his skin.

She thought to ask if he wanted a cold drink. But he wasn't a guest at her cocktail party.

Though he didn't look at her, she knew that he knew she was there—and there she stayed, relaxing as she watched him, feeling a lazy warmth inside.

He took his time, cutting back one branch, then a second. Tossing the cuttings aside, he stood back, studied the shrub, went forward and made another two or three snips. He wiped a forearm over his brow. Minutes later, he ran the back of his hand over the bridge of his nose. His hair was spiky and wet. His shoulders gleamed around a scar or two. He was hot.

She did feel sorry for him and was indeed about to ask if he wanted a drink when he dropped his pruning shears and whipped his tank top up over his head. He mopped his face with it, tossed it aside, retrieved the shears, and returned to work, but it was only a matter of minutes before he dropped the shears again. This time, he reached for the garden hose—which had been trickling water into the shrub bed—held it over his head, put his face back, and let water flow from there, on down his torso and into his jeans.

It was a stunning show. Casey barely breathed, not wanting to miss a moment. His throat was strong, his Adam's apple just protrusive enough. His chest was leanly muscled and dusted with hair. His torso tapered, firm without being skinny. His jeans rested low enough on his hips to expose an arrow of hair and the hint of a navel, but just a hint. Watching the trickle of water over all of that, she was entranced.

And he knew it. She could tell, because he didn't look at her once. She had seen heat in his eyes that morning. He was playing it cool now. Nor did that other obvious sign give him away, since he was amply endowed to begin with. But she did want him to be aroused. It wouldn't be right for her to be so attracted to him and for him not to feel the same fire.

Unrequited lust did happen, of course. Poor Dylan was attracted to her, and she felt nothing.

And *that,* she decided in a moment of wryness, was because she'd been saving it all up for her father's gardener. The chemistry was here in force. Her body hummed with it. She couldn't remember ever feeling so physically drawn to a man. Watching him work was a pleasure approaching sin.

When he was done watering himself, he looped the hose into the center of the shrub and went back to his pruning, and still she watched. She didn't move other than to sip her iced coffee—simply sat there and admired his body as he bent and straightened, turned, trimmed, and tossed.

As the minutes passed, though, her pleasure began to fade, replaced by something darker that had come on like thunder in the heat. She knew loneliness when she felt it;

she had lived with it a long time, had felt a greater intensity of late. Now, coming on the tail of intense desire, it was stronger and sadder—and she wasn't prepared. When her eyes filled with tears, she couldn't do a thing to stop them. Nor could she leave. She didn't know whether it was the suddenness of the emotion she felt or the fatigue of the day, but something held her in her seat. Mortified, she pressed her fingers to her upper lip.

The movement drew Jordan's eye. He stared at her, frowned, started forward.

Not knowing what else to do, she bent over, buried her face in her knees, and cried softly. She wanted to stop, wanted it desperately because this wasn't at all the side of herself that she wanted to show to Jordan. But other wants were so great that they overrode this small one.

She wanted to *be* with someone. She wanted family. She wanted to be loved.

Jordan surely wasn't the one. Physical attraction did *not* a relationship make. At that moment, though, consumed as she was with loneliness, she would have given anything for him to hold her, hold her so tightly that the loneliness just burst and drifted away.

Though her head was down, she knew from the nearness of his voice that he was right in front of her, hunkering down.

"Can I do anything?" he asked with such gentleness that she ached all the more.

What could he possibly do? He couldn't make Caroline wake up or bring Connie back from the dead, and she couldn't begin to tell him the story of her life. He wasn't her therapist. He wasn't even a friend.

So she shook her head no.

She had barely stopped shaking it when she felt a touch, so light at first that she might have imagined it, then firmer. It was his hand, fingers and palm covering her hair, conveying surprising solace. For that minute, at least, she wasn't completely alone.

She didn't move, didn't want to dislodge that hand. Gradually her tears slowed. Aside from the occasional hiccup of breath, she grew calm.

"I'll finish up here tomorrow," he said in that same gentle voice. Seconds later, the hand left her head.

She didn't look up. She was too embarrassed. Rather, she listened while he cleaned up his things, carried them back to the shed, then went out the garden door. She heard him start his car, but it was several minutes after that before he drove off. Only then did she straighten, wipe her eyes with the heels of her hands, and return to the house.

Twenty minutes later, the doorbell rang. Casey had soaked her eyes with a cool cloth and repaired her makeup, so that she was feeling more like herself. Even then, she would have let Meg get the door. But Meg had left for the day.

She went down the front stairs and peeked through the sidelight. A dark-haired, dark-skinned woman stood there. She wore an overblouse and tights, carried a bunch of papers in one arm, and had the most beautiful skin Casey had ever seen—the most beautiful skin and the most prominent belly, though the rest of her was elegantly slim.

Casey opened the door with a cautious smile.

The smile she got in return was far more easy. "I'm Emily Eisner, come to welcome you to the neighborhood. You met my husband, Jeff, the other day. We live here on the Court"—she gestured—"four doors down."

"I remember Jeff. He did say you were very pregnant, but he didn't say you were very beautiful, too."

"Bet he didn't say I was black, either," Emily said with a forthrightness Casey instantly loved. "That gives people a shock. I think I'm the first one of my kind living here on the Court in an upstairs capacity, if you get my drift."

Casey did. She held out a hand. "I'm Casey Ellis. I'm pleased to meet you."

"Likewise," Emily said, returning a warm clasp. Her smile faded. "Jeff didn't know you were related to Dr. Unger. He isn't privvy to the gossip of the household help. My condolences."

"Thank you. But I didn't really know him."

"No matter. He was your father. A loss is a loss. And I know you've just moved in and that you have plenty to do, but I wanted to return these." She held out the papers—books, Casey could see now. "It's music. Dr. Unger and I used to exchange. These are his."

Casey took the pile. "You play the piano?"

"Not as well as him. I've taken lessons,

but never had much time to play until now. Actually, I think I'd have gone crazy with boredom if it hadn't been for the piano. I'm used to working, but we figured we wanted a baby more than the income. I've had two miscarriages in three years, so we're being extra cautious with this one."

Casey stood back. "Will you come in and sit?"

"Oh no," Emily said and grinned. "I'm *loving* standing." Again, the grin faded. "I just wanted you to know that I'll miss your father. He didn't mix much with people on the Court. I was one of the few who ever knocked on his door. I heard him playing one day and couldn't resist."

"I didn't know he played until I saw the baby grand. And you say he was good?"

Emily's smile was thoughtful now. "He was . . . precise. He didn't have a natural ear, couldn't pick up a sheet of music and just play. He had to work at everything, had to study and practice and practice and practice, but he got good results."

"Did he take lessons?"

"Not that I knew of."

"Never?"

"That's what he said, which makes it all the more remarkable. I mean, he was accomplished. He could have easily played in a chamber group, but I don't think anyone other than Meg and me ever heard him play. It was like, for him, this was something totally personal."

"He was shy," Casey said. For the first time, it wasn't a criticism but an observation, and an empathetic one at that.

"Very. We never talked much, just played."

"You said that you and he exchanged. Does he have anything of yours?"

"A few books"—she gestured in dismissal—"but I can get them another time."

Casey waved Emily in with greater determination this time. "Where would they be?"

"In the piano bench. He kept all of it there."

"Well then, that's easy enough," Casey said as she led Emily through the foyer and into the living room. At its far end, in the shadow of the piano, sat the bench. It was of the same rich wood as the piano, and had a tapestry seat. It hadn't even occurred to Casey that it opened.

Actually, the greater surprise, she decided, was that it *closed,* given the three piles of music stacked in it side by side. Making the fit even more snug was the large manila envelope that was taped to the underside of the lid.

Chapter Nine

Little Falls

With one booted foot on the road and his helmet held against his thigh, the motorcyclist called across the clearing, "It's kinda late to be walking alone." His voice was low, rough.

Jenny didn't move.

"Cold, too," he added. "Where's your ride?"

"I, uh, he left."

He gave the fog a squint. "Any chance of someone else coming by?"

She shook her head.

"Then you'd better climb on." He hitched his bottom forward a notch.

Jenny couldn't do much more than stare. She recognized the jacket and boots. And the helmet. She saw now that he wore jeans, and had a jaw full of stubble. His hair was as black as the jacket, boots, and bike. And up close, he looked bigger, even dangerous.

Darden would hate him for being larger and younger than he was. He would feel threatened.

Jenny pinched herself inside her elbow. This was no dream; the hurt was real; the sexy man on the motorcycle remained. She flew across the clearing before he could take back his offer of a ride.

The question was how best to mount the motorcycle. She had never done it before, and the way she was dressed didn't help. After weighing the options, she tucked up a knee and slid it over the saddle and down. A tug and a push on her dress, and she was settled.

"Not bad," he remarked. She imagined he sounded amused.

"Thank you."

"Put this on." He took her shoes in trade for his helmet.

"What'll you wear?"

"Nothing."

"But—"

"If we crash and you die, I'll have to live with the guilt. Better we should crash and I die."

Jenny could identify with that thought, all right. She knew about guilt—did she ever. But she wasn't dwelling on it now, what with the helmet settling over her face, all warm and male-scented, and then his hands—large, able hands—catching her behind the knees and pulling her tight against him. She was trying to recover from that, when his foot left the ground and they shot forward, headed into the fog.

Her heart flew to her throat. She clutched fistfuls of his jacket at his sides, her fists scrabbling for more to hold on to with each tilt of the bike, moving forward little by little until the only thing that made sense was to wrap her arms around him and hold on for dear life. She was terrified, but had he stopped and offered to let her off, she would have refused. This was too good to let go.

Then the bike slowed. He touched his boot down when it stopped. She was preparing to resist, thinking that she vasn't getting off no matter what, when she felt the shift of his body, heard the rasp of a zipper and the slither of leather. He handed his jacket back. "Better put this on. You're shaking from the cold."

So she was, though it could as easily have been from the dampness, or from fear, or from relief or even exhilaration. Maybe especially exhilaration. Only after she slipped into the jacket, which was way too big but, oh, so warm, did she notice his plain cotton shirt.

"What about you?" she asked.

"I have heat to spare." He revved the engine. The motorcycle took off with a spray of gravel and a rising growl.

Jenny held him more easily now. He had no beer belly at all, but a stomach that was washboard hard and golden warm where her palms touched.

She wondered where he was from. She wondered where he was headed and if he could stay, and if he could stay, then for how long.

They reached a fork in the road. She pointed the way, then pointed again when another turn came. By this time, fear was no longer a factor. She felt his control of the bike, and she relaxed. The night rushing by blurred the ugly details of her life. The only things in focus were the man, his bike, and a sense of something unbelievably good about to happen. They sailed down the last stretch to her house with such ease that Jenny just knew that all this was fated to be.

When he pulled into the drive and stopped at the side door she always used, she took off the helmet and shook out her hair. But she made no move to dismount.

"This it?" he asked.

"Yes."

He twisted his upper body and peered at her, straining to make out her features in the thin porch light. "Is anyone home?"

She shifted her gaze. It fell on the foggy outline of the garage that housed Darden's old Buick. "Uh, yes."

"I won't hurt you," he said more gently. "I was just wondering why you aren't getting off. If the house is empty and that makes you nervous, I'll walk you in."

"No." She felt silly. "No need." But she liked wearing his jacket. She liked the feel of his thighs pressed inside hers. She didn't want him to leave.

Slipping off the bike, she said quickly, "Want to come in?"

He stared at her for a minute, then shook his head. "I'm not the kind of guy you want in your house for long."

She looked away. It was a gentle rejection. But gentle was new for her, so she looked back. "Why not?"

"I'm just not."

"*Why* not?"

He sighed. "Because I'm just passing through. Guys just passing through act without thinking. They get lonely. And when they're lonely, they get selfish. Me, I'm selfish, lonely or not." Another headshake. "I wouldn't risk it if I were you."

But Jenny had no choice. No choice at all.

"Where are you from?" she asked, trying her best to sound casual, like she was just making conversation, like she did this kind of thing all the time. She didn't want him to know she was desperate. That would scare him off.

Besides, she wanted to know the answer. He wasn't from these parts—she could tell that by the way he talked. And the way he looked—all that dark mystery. She couldn't keep her eyes off him.

"Born?" he asked. "Out west."

"Oh? Where?"

"Wyoming. Just south of Montana."

She couldn't believe it! She had dreamed of going to Wyoming just south of Montana. Horses, cattle, buffalo. Wide open spaces. Friendly people willing to live and let live.

"I haven't been there in a while," he said.

"Do you have family there?"

"Do I ever."

She couldn't *believe* it. Her *dream*. "Lots of family?"

"I'll say." He gazed off into the dark. "Lots of family, lots of responsibility, lots of guilt. Like I say. I haven't been there in a while."

"So where've you been?"

"Here and there."

"Those places aren't on my map."

He made a sound that might have been a laugh had he opened his mouth.

"So, where?" she prodded. She had already said more to him than to probably

any other one person in a whole month,
and he wasn't walking away, wasn't looking at her like she was dirt.

"Atlanta, Washington, New York,
Toronto."

"What were you doing in those
places?"

"Proving I was as smart as the next
guy."

"Are you?"

"Oh, yeah."

"So what are you doing here?"

He looked straight at her. "Tryin' to
figure out why bein' so smart isn't
makin' me happy."

"Have you got the answer yet?"

"Nope. I'm still lookin'."

She watched his eyes, saw something
welcoming in them. "Are you hungry?"

"Tired, too. I've been riding since
dawn."

"I can fix you food."

"That'd mean my going inside. I already told you. It isn't a good idea."

"Lonely and selfish."

"Yup."

"What does that mean?"

"Guess."

"I don't know."

It was a minute before he said, "You don't, do you?"

She shook her head.

"I saw you at the dance tonight. Did you know that?"

She nodded.

"Well, I didn't see anyone else. I couldn't. Not once I saw you."

Jenny didn't believe him. "You must've seen Melanie Harper. She was out on the steps. You know, blond hair—" She gestured big breasts.

"Blond isn't as exciting as red."

Jenny touched her hair, ready to argue, but the look on his face told her not to. So she smiled, then laughed. Then she covered her face with a hand.

He took the hand down. "You're very striking."

Again she would have argued, had he not been looking at her like he meant every word, and then he looked at her breasts—just for a moment, but the look was deliberate.

"It's the dress," she said.

He shook his head. "So I'd better not come inside. It's been too long since I've had home cookin'." His voice was rough again, a drawl to match her image of Wyoming just south of Montana.

She forgot all about hair and breasts. "Home cooking is my *specialty*. I have a catering service." It was a small lie, just one word wrong. "I'm doing a luncheon tomorrow and just happen to have homemade meatballs in the fridge. I could cook them right up."

"Homemade meatballs?"

"Skewered with pepper, onion, and eggplant."

He made a small moaning sound. "If I eat 'em, what'll you serve tomorrow?"

"I have so many I could give you *dozens* and they wouldn't be missed."

He looked to be seriously considering her offer.

"Please," she said, trying her best not to sound desperate, but he was so good-looking, just the man she'd been hoping to meet tonight, and he seemed to like her.

She pinched her inner elbow again and felt the pain. Still not dreaming. And yes, he *did* like her. She could tell by the way he looked at her. He made it easy to return the look for a change. He had to stay. If he left now, she would die.

"Okay," he said. "Just to eat. If it's not too much trouble."

She turned from the cycle and went up the back steps and into the kitchen without a backward glance. Since she still had his jacket and helmet, she knew he would follow. She set the helmet on the counter and went to the refrigerator. Four trays of skewered meatballs were inside. She took two out and lit the broiler.

The back door closed. Her breath caught when she turned. It had been years since a man had been in her kitchen, and this one was even taller than she'd thought. He had to be six four. And rock solid. He was also gorgeous—maybe not movie-star perfect like Tom Cruise or Brad Pitt, but better than anything she had ever seen around Little Falls. Plus, he had been all over the country, and in her eyes, that made him seem even larger.

She swallowed and tried to think of something to say. She dashed a look around the kitchen, but nothing inspired her.

He helped her out. "Your kitchen's very clean."

She cleared her throat. "I always clean after I cook. I did the meatballs this afternoon. And lemon crescents, for the dance." She wished she had some of those to give him, but they had vanished suspiciously soon after she had put them on the refreshment table. So maybe those old biddies *had* tossed them out. That was their loss. This man would have eaten every last crumb.

"What's your name?" she asked.

"Pete."

Pete. She liked it. It sounded real. "Mine's Jenny."

"That wasn't what the guy on the porch called you."

She took a short breath. "You heard that?" And how much else?

"Only the end. He was being a pest. Another minute of his yammering, and I'd have been over to shut his mouth for him."

Jenny blushed. No one had ever defended her before. He was so perfect she couldn't stand it, so tall and handsome that her eyes didn't know what to do.

They tried to skitter off, but lingered on his chest. "Oh my. Your shirt is wet. Want a dry one? My father has a whole closetful." Dry, and pressed so nicely. But, *crazy Jenny,* Pete wouldn't want a pressed shirt. Maybe in the city. But not in Wyoming just south of Montana. And not here. The one he was wearing was chambray, she saw that now. It was butter soft, not pressed at all.

She wanted to touch it again, as she had while they were riding, but feared he would think her too forward. Instead, she pointed toward the hall. "The bathroom's out there. On your right. Want a beer?"

"Sure." He disappeared into the hall.

Jenny slipped the pans into the oven and left the door ajar. Heat rose. She stepped away and put her palms to her cheeks. They were hot on their own, beet red, she figured. Not that she cared, not tonight.

I didn't see anyone else. I couldn't. Not once I saw you.

She tried to keep calm, but she felt all bubbly inside, bubbly and brimming and so near to exploding with excitement that she was practically dancing as she opened the fridge. Four six-packs of Sam Adams stood there, bought at Darden's order in anticipation of his return. She didn't figure he would miss one bottle. If he did, she would tell him where it had gone, and if he had a problem with that, he could take it up with Pete.

Pete wouldn't put up with his crap— not Pete, whose return came at that very moment, announced by confident boot-steps and a smoky baritone. "I'm impressed. From the looks of that mirror, you're a popular lady."

His appearance startled her all over again. Now it was the fresh-washed look around his eyes and the finger-comb marks in that thick, dark hair. He kept getting better and better.

"Lots of parties," he said. "You must have a pack of friends."

She gave him Miriam's stock line. "Friends come from nowhere when you're the one making the food." She handed him the bottle of Sam Adams.

He took it by the neck, but didn't rush to take a drink, just held it and looked at her. "A catering business, huh?"

Tell him the truth. "Neat Eats."

"Cute name. How long have you had it?"

The truth, Jenny. "I've been working"— she searched the ceiling—"ohhh, five years." No lie there. She had been a year late graduating high school on account of her mother dying and all. Dan had set her up with Miriam right after that. "We started with local things. Then people from outside started calling. Now we sometimes drive two or three hours. We did a party in Salem. That's down by Boston."

He skimmed her kitchen. "You don't do all that cooking here, do you?"

"Oh, no. We have a big place in town. And cars and a van," she tacked on, because he had to be wondering. "I keep this kitchen old-fashioned on purpose. It's a reminder of my roots. I learned to cook here." She didn't know why she'd said *that*. Okay, it was the truth. But it wasn't something she liked remembering.

He looked pleased. "It's a refreshing woman who admits to cooking these days. You're one of the few I've met who'll do it, besides my sisters. You'd like them."

Jenny would; of course she would. She had always wanted a sister and would have been happy with just one. Pete had even *more.*

"I'll bet you have a book of old family recipes," he said.

"No. Most everything was passed word of mouth." She heard the yelling clearly, like her mother was standing right there, not gone for years. *For God's sake, Mary-Beth, it doesn't take brains. Just cut up whatever we have, throw it in the fry pan with eggs and butter, and you got a meal.*

Jenny fought a choking sensation. "What's Wyoming like?"

"Big and open."

She took an easier breath. "How many in your family?"

"At last count? Three grandparents, two parents, five siblings, four siblings-in-law, and eleven nieces and nephews. How about you?"

"None."

"None?"

"My parents are dead." *Shame on you, Jenny!* "No. That's not true." She studied her hands. "My father's alive. But he's been gone a while."

"Whose things are on the coat tree?"

In the front hall. She had forgotten. Darden's two jackets, his raincoat, and, underneath, his boots, all looking clean and fresh because they *were* clean and fresh. She had taken them from the garage and aired them and brushed them and put them on the coat tree a week ago so Darden would think they had been there all along, the way he wanted them.

She heard a sizzle.

"Oh Lord," she gasped. She wheeled around and opened the oven. The meatballs were more than ready. She set them on the stovetop and grabbed a plate and a fork.

"Can I help?"

She shook her head and pointed him into a chair. Seconds later, she set down the piled-high plate.

He ate every last bit of that, plus seconds and thirds—not that he crammed it in. He had manners. When he paused, it was to say how good the food was.

Jenny was content to sit and watch him

eat, to smile when he looked at her, to
refill his empty plate, and all the while
she kept pinching that inner elbow, because she had never had good fortune
like this before and she wanted, so
wanted it to be real.

"That was the best meal I've had in
years," Pete said when he finally pushed
back in his chair. He glanced at the pans.
"I ate every last meatball. Are you sure I
haven't messed you up for tomorrow?"

"We won't even miss them," Jenny said
and took his dish to the sink. She soaped
it and rinsed it, and was setting it on the
rack to drain dry when he called her
name. She looked around. He was frowning at the backs of her legs. She swished
her dress lower. "What?"

"What are those marks?"

"Oh, nothing. An accident when I was
little." She brightened. "Want to see
something?"

"Sure."

She led him into the hall and up the
stairs. They had to pass through her bedroom, but that couldn't be helped. So she
acted normal, like she had men in her
bedroom all the time, and it did look

that way, what with the big bed and silk sheets that Darden had bought her. Those had just come out of storage, too.

She glanced back at Pete for reassurance. Then she opened the closet door, pushed aside the old quilt that hung in the way, and lowered the attic ladder. From the top, it was a short way over rough planking to the front gable. The window went up easily. Lord knew, she opened it often enough. She sat on the sill and swung her legs out.

"Jenny, what are you doing?" Pete asked from behind her.

She straightened her body and slid.

"My *God,* Jenny—"

Her bare heels caught the gutter with practiced ease. She inched sideways until she had cleared the gable and reached the open slope of the roof, then went farther to make room for Pete.

"Jenny," he warned from the window, just as Dan O'Keefe did every time someone saw her on the roof and reported it to him.

She grinned. "Look at this view, will you? Isn't it *wild*?"

One long leg came out. A boot heel caught the gutter. "I see fog."

"Wait. The fog shifts."

Another leg came out and straightened. He joined her with no effort at all, and propped himself up on his elbows, just like her.

The fog shifted then. "It looks like a little toy town," he said. "Tell me what's where."

She pointed. "The even line of lights is the center of town. Odd little ones are side streets. Over there? That's the school. And there? The library. And the church steeple."

"What's that?" He was pointing off to the east.

"The quarry. A hundred years ago they were cutting granite. When they finished, the big hollow just filled up with water, so the town had a place to swim. Legend says in order for a marriage to be blessed, the proposal has to be made there. Me, all I want is a midnight swim, moon and stars and all. The lights you see are taillights. People park just back of the rim."

"To swim?"

"Not likely."

He gave her a knowing grin that made her stomach flutter. "Ah-ha. Lovers. So. Ever been up there yourself?"

"Dozens of times," she said nonchalantly, like she was popular. Then she thought of the Selena Battles of the town, who really *had* been there dozens of times. She didn't want Pete thinking she was like them. So she confessed. "I lied. I was only there a couple of times." She paused and added a quiet, "To swim. In the daytime."

He smiled at her then, a big, bright, toothy smile that tugged every heart-string inside her. "I'm glad," he said.

She loved hearing that. She wanted him to like her in the worst way. And since he smiled when she told the truth, she said, "And I lied about being a caterer. I work for one. I don't own the business."

"But you cook."

"Yes."

"And serve and clean and do everything else your boss does."

She nodded.

"So you're a caterer," he concluded.

"And anyway"—he looked out over the town—"you don't need to own a business when you own this view."

"Yes," she said with a smug smile. "I do own this view." She had known he would understand. That was why she had brought him up here. She crossed her ankles, took a deep breath, one that stretched her lungs for the first time in ages, and enjoyed the moment. "They say it's dangerous coming up here. That I could slip. But I'm not afraid. Besides, I'm a somebody here. It's my view. I can look at it or close my eyes or even turn around. I can do what I want. Up here, I'm the one who decides."

"Most people call that power," Pete said.

Jenny said, "I call it freedom."

"Like being way, way up in the hills above the ranch with firm ground underfoot and unlimited sky and stars and moon. Kind of like your quarry without water. You'd like it there."

She would. But the freedom would be different if she were there with Pete. Like it was different up here with him now.

Less solitary. More complete. The freedom to be *and* the freedom to enjoy.

"Stay the night," she whispered. When his eyes found hers, she added a quick, "Just to sleep. You said you were tired. I have the room."

"I'd be imposing."

"No."

"You barely know me."

"I know enough."

She slid over him—*shocking heaven!* the heat and hardness of his body under hers—and eased back into the attic. But he was the one who went down the ladder first, then held the old quilt aside to see her safely back into her room.

She settled him in the spare room and returned to her own. Leaving the door open, she took off the dress that had done such a fine job that evening and carefully hung it up. She put on her nightgown and slipped into bed, imagining him sleeping down the hall.

But the silk sheets grated, so she climbed back out, wide awake now. Her eye landed on the magazine open on the chair. She picked it up and, turning page after page, revisited Jeffrey City, Sho-

shoni, Casper, and Cheyenne. In time, she closed the magazine and put it on the shelf.

The night was still. Standing in the middle of the floor, she listened for his heartbeat. But her own was too loud, reflecting a clamoring inside. In the past it would have been from fear and distaste, but tonight it was from something new and wondrous.

She drew the nightgown over her head. She touched the pads of her fingers to the shallow between her breasts. Her eyes closed. Her head fell back. She imagined that Pete saw her, that he loved her, and with the imagining came such an inner fullness that she nearly cried.

But she didn't want to do that. She didn't want to wake him. So she took out the old quilt he had touched and, still naked, wrapped it around her from top to toe. Then she stretched out on the floor and settled her head on that padded pillow of hope.

Chapter Ten

Jenny woke with pillow lines on her cheek and the knowledge that Pete was gone.

"Well, what did you *expect?*" she asked the reflection in the mirror through a mouthful of toothpaste froth. "Why would he stay with you when he can get anyone he wants, and they're ten times prettier and smarter and cleaner?" She spat into the sink. "You're lucky he stayed as long as he did!" She rinsed her mouth, then did it a second time, and a third time, because the sick taste of dread was back.

Three days to go. *Do something, Jenny.* But what?

She scrubbed the already clean bathroom. She scrubbed the already clean kitchen. She emptied the hall closet, shook everything out, then put it all back.

Finally, wearing the pale blue polo shirt, walking shorts, high socks, and sneakers that were Neat Eats' uniform for casual events, she took the pans of meatball skewers from the fridge and packed them in Miriam's insulated case. Hiking the case to her shoulder, she set off for town.

The fog was lighter than usual. She hadn't gone far when Merle Little's Fairlane sputtered past. She kept her eyes on the side of the road so as not to see the greeting that wasn't forthcoming, but the Booths' mongrels greeted her, all right. She was barely abreast of the house when they lit off the porch and hurtled across the grass in full bark. There was no befriending them. She had tried hundreds of times. She imagined that they knew everything about her and, being dogs, were simply less restrained in their dislike than a human would be.

"Oh hush," she grumbled in passing and looked ahead down the road. The Johnsons' front gate creaked, and beyond that came a treat. As the fog lifted, she could see the Farinas' flowers glowing in their yard.

Jenny loved flowers. The best—*the best*—days were when florists for their catered affairs left discards by the door. Sometimes the blooms were past saving. Other times, when Jenny reached them early enough, she had a bouquet to take home. They turned her kitchen into a place of dreams.

The Farinas' flowers were beautiful, bed after bed of different colors and shapes and heights that changed by season. Jenny couldn't say that she loved the spring pinks better than the summer reds and blues or the yellows and purples of fall. There they were now—marigolds and her favorite black-eyed Susans.

She gasped and nearly dropped her bag of food when old man Farina rose straight up from behind the asters. "Think you could do any better?" he challenged. "Well, you couldn't. Summer's been so dry *everythin's* wilted." He jabbed a cane her way. "So don't go lookin' down your nose at *me*, little lady. You don't have one *bit* of color in that whole yard of yours. It's a disgrace. Whole *thing's* a disgrace."

Ignoring him, she focused on the birches on the far side of the road and walked on. At least the birches couldn't talk back. Nor could they make her dreams come true, though Lord knew she had asked. She had written wish after wish on bits of curly birch bark and thrown them into the fire, but not one of her wishes had come true.

Still, she loved birches. On days like this their trunks looked like pearls.

Or leather.

She squinted. A jacket? Boots? Were they there? She searched the dark slots between trees, searched the road.

Nothing.

So who's gonna save you now, Jenny Clyde?

She didn't know. Didn't know. Didn't *know.*

She trudged on past Essie Bunch, past television sounds, past lawnmower sounds. A block away from Neat Eats' kitchen, Dan O'Keefe pulled up. "I just got a call from John Millis. He'll be Darden's parole officer. He wanted to know about you."

Her stomach knotted. Doubling over, she set her pack on the curb, knelt beside it, and fiddled with the zipper. "What about me?"

"He wondered if you worked and, if you did, whether you'd be quitting when Darden gets back."

"Why would I quit?"

"To help Darden get the business going again. Darden must've told them you would."

She remembered what Dudley Wright had said. "He may not get it going so fast."

"Then you'll stay on with Miriam?"

She had to. She didn't want to work with Darden. She didn't want to see Darden, hear Darden, smell Darden. She didn't want to be anywhere *near* Darden. "I'm asking her for more hours. To keep me busy, y'know?"

It was her next-to-last hope, her last hope being that someone like Pete would take her to a place Darden couldn't reach. Darden's return was her punishment. He had endured his, now it was her turn.

Before Dan could start in again, saying

things she already knew but couldn't change, she stood, hoisted the pack, and set off.

"Oh, Jenny, I wish I could," Miriam said when Jenny finally drummed up the nerve to ask. They were forty minutes into the fifty-minute drive home from the luncheon. The rest of the staff—three others—had gone in a separate car. She and Miriam were alone in the van. The ride had been silent up to that point. "But I suppose it's good you mentioned this. I didn't know how to raise it myself."

Jenny didn't like the way Miriam wasn't looking at her.

"I'm winding down Neat Eats."

Jenny figured she must have heard wrong. She held very still, wishing to make the words go away.

"I haven't booked anything past the end of the month," Miriam went on. "I'm closing shop."

The message was the same, but unthinkable. "You can't close."

"That's what I kept telling myself—I'm

happy here, I'm getting good jobs, I'm making money—so I gave myself another month, then another month, but I'm at the point where it's put up or shut up."

"What is?"

"Y'know my brother, the one with the restaurant in Seattle? He's been asking me to come out there and be chef for him, and I've been telling him I couldn't leave here, but now he's going to have to close if he doesn't do something drastic, and I'm the only drastic thing he has, y'know?"

Jenny didn't know. All she knew was that she worked for Neat Eats, and if it closed, she'd be out of a job. With Darden coming home.

She felt like she was going to be sick. She swallowed once, then again.

Miriam darted her nervous looks. "No one in town knows yet. I was going to tell you all in another week. That'll give you time to get new jobs. I know the timing's bad for you, Jenny, but I don't see any way around it."

Jenny scrambled for reasons. "Weren't my meatballs any good?"

"Your meatballs were great. This has nothing to do with you."

"It was the mint dish, wasn't it?" It had slipped right out of her hand.

"The mint dish—the toothpick cup— the creamer filled way past overflowing— you had a bad day today. I think I know why."

Jenny put the heel of her hand to her stomach. "I'm a little nervous."

"You shouldn't be. He's your father. He wouldn't lift a hand to you. Besides, it's not like this'll be the first time you've seen him."

True. Jenny went to visit him every month. It was a long, hot, sick bus trip that she would have gladly made for the rest of her life if only they would have kept Darden that long.

She turned to Miriam, pleading now. "His coming back won't change a thing. I'll be as dependable as ever. I promise. I just need more work."

"What about him? Can't he work, too?"

"It's not the money. It's keeping busy." Neat Eats was one of the few good things in her life. "Take more jobs, Miriam. I'll work harder. You don't even have to pay me for the extra time."

Miriam gave a tight laugh. "Jenny, this doesn't have anything to do with you."

"Then Darden. It has to do with him, doesn't it? You're scared of what'll happen when he gets back. But he won't hurt you. He's not a murderer."

"Jenny." She said her name with a sigh and eyes glued to the road. "Please. Don't make this harder than it needs to be. You'll find another job."

"Where?"

"Why not waitress at the inn over in Tabor?"

Jenny shook her head. A job like that was worlds away from what she did for Miriam. Miriam kept her in the background mostly, and even when she was actually serving food, it was different. The menu was set. There wasn't individual ordering. She rarely needed to speak to guests.

But waitressing in a restaurant would mean juggling a million different meals for a million different people who had a million different ways of telling you that you stunk. Waitressing like that meant looking people in the eye. It meant being out there, unprotected.

"There's no bus to Tabor," she said.

"Maybe your father would drive you."

Oh, he would. He would love the intimacy of the car trip coming and going, would love being involved in her life that way. He would also love scaring off any friends she might make, just like before. She would go mad.

Miriam must have sensed her aversion, because she said, "Then try the bakery here in town. Annie's getting more pregnant by the day. Mark'll need someone to fill in."

Jenny gripped the handhold on the door and looked out the window. Mark Atkins wouldn't hire her, especially not once Darden was back.

"Jenny?" Miriam was darting looks at her arm. "What's that red mark? You didn't burn yourself, did you?"

Jenny rubbed the bruise on the inside of her elbow. She couldn't say that it came from pinching herself. Miriam would think she was crazy. So she said, "I must have caught it on something."

"Today? While you were working?"

"No. Last night."

"Phew. I was worried. Job-related injuries are the last thing I need when I'm
trying to wrap things up. Employers get
sued for the most absurd things nowa-
days. Not that you'd do that." She slowed
the van as they entered the center of Little Falls, and took her first left. After
pulling up under Neat Eats' awning, she
turned to Jenny. "So. Three o'clock tomorrow afternoon? No food. Just you.
Wearing what you have on now, but
washed. Right?"

During the walk home, Jenny tried to relax. She concentrated—left foot, right
foot, left foot, right foot. She walked
evenly—left foot, right foot, left foot,
right foot. She held herself erect—left
foot, right foot, left foot, right foot. She
pushed her worries from mind, then did
it again when they tried to return. She
did absolutely everything that the magazine had said would calm her—left foot,
right foot, left foot, right foot. Still, her
stomach felt like Jell-O when she

climbed the side stairs and let herself into the house.

Then she saw the flowers. They stood on the kitchen table in the deep blue springwater bottle she had taken from a trash can at the Bicentennial Bash. There were three black-eyed Susans. She *loved* black-eyed Susans.

She looked around, ran from kitchen to hall to parlor to hall to kitchen, but there was no sign of him.

Then she heard the motorcycle. She ran to the door to see him pull up at the steps, but he didn't dismount. Only the helmet came off. He looked unsure.

"I keep leaving and coming back, leaving and coming back," he said. "If I had any sense I'd have been through the next state by now." He searched her face. "Didn't get past the next county."

Ask him why, Jenny told herself, then changed her mind because she didn't want him to even think about why he had felt he had to leave.

She needed him to stay.

Ask how he is. Ask how he slept. Ask if he ran into traffic, or when he ate last, or if he's hungry. Ask him in, for God's sake.

"I brought you flowers," he said. "I looked at roses and lilies, but the black-eyed Susans were the best. Maybe it's the country boy in me."

They're beautiful, she thought but was afraid to say it aloud, afraid to say *anything* aloud lest he vanish again.

He was biting the corner of his mouth. "I keep thinking about you. You're different from other women I've known. That makes you interesting. It started with your hair. I've never seen hair like that. Or freckles."

"They're awful."

"They're beautiful!"

"No."

"*Yes.* And there's more. I've never met a woman—not since I left home, and that was a lifetime ago—never met a woman who'd take her life in her hands to climb up on a roof for the sheer joy of owning the view."

"People here think I'm crazy."

"If being crazy means you think for yourself, I'm all for it. I've known a lot of people who do just what's expected of them, and they've been boring as hell. You're an individual. You look out for yourself, instead of sitting back and needing others to do for you. That's what I hated most back home."

Jenny wanted to hear more. "What did you hate most?"

He smiled, shook his head. "You first. Why do you live alone?"

She took a careful breath. "Who would I live with?"

"A husband."

"There's no husband." There never would be as long as Darden lived. He had sworn it. He had sworn that the only thing keeping him alive in prison was the thought of coming home to her. He had said she owed it to him, and maybe he was right. But it was *sick, sick, sick.*

"Where's your father?"

"Up north."

"That his truck behind the garage?" She nodded. "His Buick inside the garage?" She nodded again. "Why don't you drive it?"

"I don't have my license."

"Why not?"

"There was lots going on, and I just kind of forgot. But it's okay. I can walk everywhere in town, and there are buses that go most other places. So what did you hate most at home?"

"How did your mother die?"

She couldn't answer. "What did you hate most at home?"

He gave in. "People who were leaners."

"It's a luxury, leaning. Nice, sometimes."

"Sometimes, but not all the time. You have to *do* things in life." He pulled in a breath. "Not that I'm one to talk."

"Why not?"

"Well, look at me, riding around, halfway between here and there, without the guts to *do* what I have to do."

"What's that?"

"Go home." He gave her a startled smile, teeth white amid all that dark stubble. "Weird. I don't usually tell people my faults, but you just pull it out of me."

She got scared. "I don't mean to. It's nothing, really. I'll forget what you said, and you don't have to say anything more. I wasn't trying to be nosy, it's just that you're here and you're interesting, too, and it's been the longest time since anyone's talked to me like this—"

She stopped short, unable to believe what she'd said. Now he would *know* how pathetic and lonely and desperate she was.

But he was smiling. "Make you a deal?"

She was afraid to hope. "What kind?"

"Another home-cooked meal in exchange for anything your heart desires."

"I don't think you should offer that."

"Why not?"

"I might accept."

He considered that. He studied the helmet for a while. He climbed off the motorcycle, set the helmet on the seat, and kept his back to her for another minute. Then he turned and came toward her.

She had her hand on the screen. When he reached toward it, her heart leapt into her throat. He touched a knuckle to her palm and brushed it lightly through the wire mesh. Watching the small movement, he said, "The offer stands. There's nothing you can ask that I don't have it in me to give, at least today. I can't tell what'll be tomorrow or the day after that. I'm not good at long-term promises. You're the one who ought to be thinking twice. I said that before. My record is lousy. I have a way of disappearing when the going gets rocky. People damn me for that."

"Then here's your chance at redemption," she said, but lost the ability to say anything more when his eyes climbed the screen and caught hers—warm, inviting eyes like she had never seen before, sending heat tumbling down her face to her throat to her chest, caressing her heart for a bit before landing in her belly.

He looked at her mouth. "Dangerous," he whispered. "Do you know what I want?"

He wanted sex. Sex with a man like Pete would be breathtakingly beautiful.

She opened the screen. He stepped through and stood before her, so tall that she had to look up, so broad that she felt sheltered. She was all hot inside, hot and trembly, just like the magazines said she would feel when the man was right.

He was going to kiss her. She knew it. And she was suddenly scared, afraid that the good feelings would die. But she needed him. He was all she had left. He was her only, only hope of escape.

His mouth touched hers. She stiffened

against the smothering, but it didn't come. No smothering, no sickness, no terror. Just gentleness and lightness and—this was new—wanting more.

But he was bent on whispering—kissing, sucking, nibbling, all in whispers. He didn't ask a thing in return, which was good. Jenny couldn't have produced, if her life had depended on it. She was too taken with the newness of what she felt to do a thing but stand there, lock-kneed, with her eyes closed, her head back, her lips parted.

She was wondering what else in those magazines was true, when he released her and took a breath. He drew himself up to his full height. He let his head loll back and took another breath.

Jenny steadied herself against the wall with her chin tucked low and waited for him to say something dark and mean. When it didn't come, she dared a look. He was smiling.

"See?" he said. "That was interesting. And we're still dressed."

She swallowed. He was so cool. She had to get him to stay. "We don't have to be."

He just smiled and brushed his thumb over her freckles. "There's time."

Jenny's heart positively melted. Pete was everything she had always dreamed a man could be. She thought of pinching herself to make sure he was real, but how could such a large physical presence *not* be real? Looking up at him, feeling the caring in his smile, she knew for the first time what it meant to be in love and want to give and give and give to a man. Unfortunately, her assets were slim.

"Do you like chicken fajitas?" she asked.

"I love chicken fajitas."

"I made them for a party, but I made too many, so there's lots in the freezer. They'll fry up nice, unless you'd rather have little beef Wellingtons—"

"Chicken fajitas."

She smiled. "Good choice."

"Do that again, that little smile."

"What little smile?"

"That one. It lights you up."

"Makes my freckles pop, more likely."

"Makes you look happy."

She was happy.

Then the phone rang and she froze.

Nothing good came from phone calls to Jenny. Ever.

She wanted to let it ring, but if it was Darden, there would be *no end* to his questions about where she'd been and what she'd been doing and why she hadn't been at the phone.

"Hello?"

"It's Dan. I got a problem here, Mary-Beth. Old Nick Farina's raisin' a ruckus, something about your stealing flowers from him. Now, I know there's an explanation, only he wasn't listening to me. He kept telling me I had to drive over there and look into the charge. He says you stole black-eyed Susans from his yard. Did you?"

"Why would I do that?"

"That's what I asked him. There are black-eyed Susans growing wild all over the place. He swears he saw you picking three big ones right there in his yard."

"I was on the road. There's no other way to come home from work but past his house."

"I told him that." Dan sighed. "I'll tell him I talked with you, okay, but be pre-

pared. He's apt to give you the what-all
when you go past there tomorrow."

Jenny thanked him for the warning and
hung up the phone. She turned around
and caught her breath, then gave Pete a
big smile, because he was still there. That
made her happy again. "Want a beer
while I cook?"

"Sure."

She took a Sam Adams from the
fridge—another bottle would never be
missed—and passed it to him. Then she
opened the freezer. In no time she had
the makings for fajitas sizzling in a big
iron skillet and salsa bubbling in a
saucepan and tortillas heating in the
oven, and she didn't drop a thing, because she wasn't nervous. Pete was like
no one she had ever known. While she
cooked, he sat peacefully, just watching
her, like there was pleasure in that alone.
He didn't make her self-conscious. He
didn't ask her questions she didn't want
to answer, didn't swear or threaten re-
venge. He kept offering to help her cook,
and she kept refusing, and it got so they
were laughing about it, but the laughing
was easy, too. The laughing was *wonderful!*

She suddenly realized that she felt relaxed, for her a new sensation.

They had finished eating and were sitting across from each other, letting the
food settle, when she started feeling shy
about the choice she had to make. What
did her heart desire in exchange for a
meal? She couldn't begin to choose.

So she asked, "Why did you say you
were selfish?" When he frowned, she said,
"Last night. When I invited you in. You
said you were selfish, lonely or not."

It was a minute before he responded. "I
haven't been nice."

"To your family?"

He looked pained. "I was the oldest of
the kids. The whole time I was growing
up I had more responsibility than the
others. My dad dumped it on me, said I
had to set an example for the younger
ones. I hated it. So when I had a chance
to go to college, I took it and went as far
away as I could. I figured the others
could learn to do the work, just like I'd
had to. And they did. Only there were
some troubles along the way, and I didn't
help. I got great at not returning calls."

"Why?" Jenny asked. She couldn't take

her eyes off him, kept studying him. She liked the way he flexed a hand, strong but no threat. Same with the forearm beneath his rolled-up sleeve—strong but no threat. Even the way his brows drew together indicated wisdom.

"For a while I was just plain angry," he said. "I was convinced I'd earned the right to a little freedom. I didn't want to hear their worries and be drawn in. I didn't want to say no or feel guilty when I did. I didn't want to have to have the answers. Now I really don't have the answers. I'm, like, paralyzed."

"Like you want to go back, but you can't get yourself to do it."

"Exactly."

"Like you know what you have to do. You've listed all the reasons, and other people have, too, but still you can't leave."

"Yeah!"

"Like out of all the choices you have only one makes sense, but to make that one choice is so much harder."

He seemed amazed. "You understand."

Oh, she did. She knew about paralysis, and about deceit and guilt.

"How did your mother die?" he asked.

"An accident."

"Were you and she close?"

Jenny shook her head. "I wasn't the boy she wanted. She had one before me, but he died when he was little. I was supposed to replace him, only I came out a girl. She never liked me."

"I don't believe it."

"It's true, and for more reasons than that."

"What reasons?"

But Jenny had already said too much. She looked at her hands. "I have nothing to give you."

Pete drew her eyes back up with a laugh. "You make a mean fajita," he said. He planted his elbows on the table, warmed the chill from her with his eyes—long, dark lashes to die for—and gave her a crooked grin that made her melt. "So, what'll it be? What's your heart's desire?"

To stay here, right here, right now. To frame the look on your face and hang it on the mirror over all those party invitations I stole. To freeze-dry this moment and put it away for the time when . . . the time when . . .

"A ride," she said. "There's a twisty road up in the mountains. Nebanonic Trail. It takes your breath when you're going fast."

"You've done it before?"

"No." Darden wouldn't take her when she was little, and there had been no one to take her later. But she heard what the kids said in town, and many times she had dreamed of going there.

Pete slapped his hands on the table and rose. "Let's go."

Chapter Eleven

Two hours later, Jenny still wasn't ready to go inside. Back at her house, she lay in a tent of drooping pine boughs in the night-dark backyard, and relived the exhilaration of Nebanonic Trail. All the things she had heard over the years were true. The Trail was as scary as it was breathtakingly exciting. On Pete's motorcycle, it had been *unbelievable*—twenty minutes of leaning into one curve after another, of hugging Pete while the wind whipped and the fog teased and the night held its secrets until the very, very, very last minute, when the bike swerved into a turn or lunged into a dip. The whole time she had felt alive and free and daring.

If they had crashed, she would have died happy.

The boughs parted, and Pete appeared. He had to bend over to enter, but rather than straightening once he was inside, he settled on the ground, cross-legged like her. Their knees touched.

Dark as it was, she saw his grin and grinned back. She knew hers was a silly grin, and that her hair was sticking up every which way from the wind, but Pete didn't seem to mind. If he had, he could have left, could have said something like, "Well, you've had your heart's desire, now it's time I moved on," but he hadn't.

She wanted to thank him for that, and for taking her out on the Trail, so she offered a bit of herself. "This is my special place. I spent hours hiding here when I was little."

"Hiding?"

"My mother hit me when she was angry. She was angry a lot. I hid here until she cooled off."

"She made the scars on your legs, didn't she?" Pete asked.

Jenny took a deep breath and said, "She used her father's walking stick. It had a

brass band around the bottom and
screws holding the band on."

"And she hit you with it? What kind of
mother would do that?"

"I made her angry."

"Okay, so she could have yelled. But to
make you bleed? To permanently scar
your legs? Someone should have stopped
her. Surely someone noticed."

"I wore long pants. Or high socks."

"Then your father. He must have
known. Why didn't he stop her?"

"He had a moving business. Sometimes he was gone for four or five days."

"He never saw your legs?"

"Well, he did. But it was like he let her
get away with it because he felt guilty."

"About what?"

Jenny's strength dwindled. She tucked
up her legs, put her chin on her knees,
and shook her head.

Pete took her hand and held it dan-
gling between them. With each little
swing, the past faded . . . more . . . more.
It helped that she had his fingers to con-
centrate on. They were blunt tipped,
lean, and so real that other things became real, too. Like the size of him and

his sturdiness. Like the clean, windy way he smelled. Like the warmth of his skin, the fuzzy tingles in her tummy, and, deeper, a wanting.

She had never felt that wanting before—or the curiosity that came with it, a curiosity about physical things about Pete. Like whether he had hair on his chest, or how dark his nipples were, or whether there were beauty marks on his back. She should have been repulsed by such thoughts, but she wasn't. Instead, she wondered if he was wondering the same kinds of things about her. He wasn't calm, not to hear his breathing. But was it sexual longing? Or a deeper something? Or was she imagining the whole thing? She still didn't know why a man like Pete would want her.

But there he was, moving closer, touching her neck, her throat, the vee of her polo shirt, and she was suddenly on her knees, holding tight to his shoulders, wanting something she couldn't put a phrase to, because its meaning was so new.

"Tell me," he whispered. His hands hovered over her breasts. She felt herself swelling toward him, but she couldn't quite reach—deliberately, maybe, because breasts hurt during sex—which didn't explain why she ached to feel Pete's hands on her, didn't explain it at all.

Feeling confused but driven, she cried, "You can do what you want, anything, it's really okay, I won't mind."

What he did was to slide his arms around her and draw her close, then hold her, just hold her, until she was feeling less frantic. Then he took her down to the ground. She felt the weight of his body on her breasts and belly, even between her legs for too brief an instant to threaten, before he rolled sideways and tucked her under his arm.

No threat, no force, just a caring hold. She let out a shaky breath and snuggled closer. The achy feeling inside eased. Pleasure took its place, and then, when the warmth of him penetrated, contentment followed. She began to smile.

"Ahhhh, Jenny," he said in a gritty way, "why didn't we meet at another time?"

"Because I needed you now," she answered and listened to the sounds of the night. "Do you believe in God?"

"Sometimes. Why?"

"I remember going to church when I was little and looking at the minister's robes. I imagined God wore robes like those. So I'd hide in here and pretend I was under His skirts. It was a safe feeling. I feel that now, too. Like we're sealed off from the world. Like the ugliness can't reach us. Know what I mean?"

Pete slept in the spare room again—after walking her into the house and saying something about no one telling *him* chivalry wasn't alive and well.

She could have lived without his chivalry. When she was in his arms, the world became a place of possibility and hope. She would have liked to spend the night there. Just being held.

Instead, she lay again on the old quilt on the floor of her room. She couldn't get herself to lie on the bed, not on those disgusting silk sheets, not with Pete in the house. She would have felt dirty. And anyway, she wasn't tired. She lay down, sat up, lay down again, rolled over, sat up. She crept to her door and listened, crept down the hall to Pete's door and listened. When she heard sleep-breathing, she slipped inside and flattened herself to the wall.

He lay on his belly. One arm was under the pillow, the other hung to the floor. His hand was slack. His shoulders were wide, his skin smooth and glossy above the shadow of hair under his arm. His torso tapered to a lean waist and hips. He wore no underwear. There was just the sheet, bunched low, covering legs that were long and muscular, meandering swells in the otherwise flat landscape of her life.

She tiptoed closer. When he didn't wake, she moved closer still, until she could see the details of his ear, the swell of his Adam's apple, the wrinkled back of his elbow. And suddenly she felt full. Like her insides had sponged up gallons of emotion. Like she was ready to burst.

Shaking with the feeling, but quiet as could be, she lowered herself to the braided rug and curled up next to where he slept. She didn't want to burst. That would mean losing what was inside, and she wasn't ready to let it go. So she hugged herself and closed her eyes and counted Pete's breaths until they put her to sleep.

She slept late and was feeling logy when the telephone rang. She had been making tea to wake herself up, but the sound of the phone accomplished that.

It was 8:35. She knew who was calling. So did her stomach, which rolled into a bumpy, jumpy grind.

Don't answer it, Jenny. But she had to. *He'll be home in two days. Can't it wait?* He had been locked up for six years—for her. *So what? Don't answer.*

"Hello?"

"Hi, baby."

She swallowed hard. That flat voice alone—flat, greasy, smarmy—made her sick. "Hi, Daddy."

"How's my girl? Gettin' excited?"

Tell him no. Tell him you won't be here when he gets home. Tell him you're going away. "I did everything you asked," she said. It wasn't true, but she needed something to say.

"Your mama's stuff is gone?"

"Yes." Small lie. Awful job. It would be done by the time he got home.

"Everything out of the drawers?"

"Yes." Tomorrow. She would do it then.

"It don't do no good to have reminders. We're starting over, baby. All that other business is behind us now."

Jenny hung over the sink, trying to breathe through her nose.

"Not that we didn't love her," Darden said, "but she was too jealous for her own good. Jealous and mean. Hey, we can say that. We paid for her death. So now the good times start. Two more nights here, then I'm home. They're saying it'll be after lunch on Tuesday before they get the papers right. Can you believe it, fuckin' dumb bureaucrats," he muttered. "But it's okay, it's okay. It means you can sleep a little longer, take your time getting dressed, doing your hair. You're wearing it down for me, aren't you? You know I love it that way."

"I can't go," she blurted out.

The flat voice hardened. "What?"

"I can't come get you. I have to work."

"Your old man's getting out of the can, and you have to *work?* Seems to me I'm reason enough to take the day off."

Jenny was shaking all over, but what was one more little lie when the alternative was so vile? "There's a big lunch, big as any we've done. It's at a place in the mountains that's owned by someone to do with the governor, and people are coming from all over, in private jets, in helicopters even. Miriam needs me."

"Christ, *I* need you. I've been rotting in here for your sake. So who're you gonna choose, Miriam or me?"

She was close to tears. He always made it as hard as possible. "I'm not *choosing* between you and her. Working just makes more sense. If I could drive there, that'd be one thing, but I can't. I'll be done with work in time to meet you at the bus stop in town."

"Not there. *Here,* MaryBeth."

"I *can't,* Daddy," she pleaded, then had an idea. "Daddy, listen. If I do this big job for Miriam, she won't argue when I tell her I can't work after that, so I'll be able to spend more time with you."

That quieted him. "You're not working the rest of the week?"

"No."

"I suppose that's okay."

"Well, maybe not. I mean, I'll probably be in the way. You'll be wanting to go off seeing people you haven't seen all these years—" She stopped without his saying a word. He didn't have to tell her how silly her talk was. There was no one he wanted to see, no one but her.

In the voice she most detested, the one that said he wasn't taking backtalk this time around, he said, "I want you waiting at that bus stop, wearing that flowered dress I had the catalog send, and I want your hair all washed and curly and soft. It must be down past your waist by now. I'll measure it when we get home, right against your skin, so you keep that skin soft under that pretty dress, and you be right there to meet the bus, y'hear?"

Jenny barely got the phone back on the hook before she threw up the little bit that was in her stomach, and even when that was gone she kept gagging. She threw water on her face. She rubbed water on her neck. She poured it into her mouth and rinsed and rinsed and rinsed. By then she was crying, big sobs that shook the whole of her, because there were only two days left and she was sick and scared and—and *angry* that *she* wasn't the one sent to jail or killed right there on the living room floor, because it wasn't fair, everything she had in her head, and it was only getting *worse*. She didn't care that he said he had done it for her; he had done it for *himself,* and now he was taking his pound of flesh, and if she tried to stop him he would remind her, bring it all right back until she started to cry, so he could hold her and run his fingers through her hair—

Grabbing the kitchen shears from the drawer, she took a handful of her hated red hair and hacked, took a second handful and hacked again, then again and again until hideous red curls were spattered on the counter, the floor, the kitchen table.

"Hey hey hey," said Pete in a voice that was deep and resonant and worried. "Jenny, Jenny, what are you doing?" He pried the shears from her hand. "Good Lord, Jenny, what's wrong?" He tipped up her face and stared into her eyes.

"I hate this hair! It's *disgusting!"*

His thumbs brushed her tears. "Aw no."

"I mean it. I *hate* it. I swear I'd rather be bald!"

He shook his head slowly, deliberately. "No you wouldn't."

"I *would*. You don't understand! That was my father on the phone. He's coming home Tuesday. Know where he's been? Prison. For six years. Know what for? Murder. Know whose? My *mother's!"* Her insides fell away, just as they had during the trial. This was the first time she had said it as bluntly since then, and the horror of it was awful. Nothing had changed, nothing at all.

Only something had. She hadn't just told the walls; she had told Pete. Now he knew what the rest of the town knew, and why they had shunned her all these years. She waited for him to back up, waited for the look of disgust that was sure to come, and if not disgust, pity, and if not pity, fear.

But he didn't back up and the look that came over his face held such a caring kind of pain that she started to cry.

"Oh Jenny," he whispered, and drew her against him. "I'm sorry."

She cried harder. He pressed her head to his chest, then moved his hands over her back to clutch her closer. She burrowed in, letting his arms stave off the world. As the tears poured out of her, so did the worst of her dark thoughts. In their place came something warmer and brighter. It gave her strength.

"He loves my hair long," she said between hiccups. "He runs his fingers through it. It makes me sick to my stomach."

"Do you hate him?"

"Yes—no," she cried. "What can I *say?* He scares me. He does that to people. He *controls* people. Before he went away, he let it be known that anyone who hurt me would be sorry. That anyone who *touched* me would be sorry." She looked up at Pete. "So people are civil, but they don't come close. You're taking your chances by being here."

He brushed away the last of her tears so

that she could see his crooked smile. "About time, I'd say." The smile grew gentler. His eyes went to her hair. He craned his neck this way and that. "Y'know, it's not bad. Not bad at all. I can see your face more without so much hair. You may be on to something." He took the shears. "Can I even it up a little?"

He cut for several minutes, moving around her. Then, bending his knees so that they were on eye level, he took her chin and turned her head from side to side. "Not bad at all," he said with a grin. "You go shower. I'll clean up here." He turned her in the direction of the hallway and sent her off.

Miriam did a double take when Jenny appeared by the open back door of Neat Eats' van. Her mouth opened, closed, opened again. "Jenny?"

Jenny touched her hair. She had felt confident looking at it back home, but that confidence had been shaken by the stares coming her way during the walk into town. Now she was thinking the same thing those staring people had thought: Darden was going to kill her.

"I wanted a change," she told Miriam.

"You sure got one," Miriam said. She slid her trays onto shelves in the van, wiped her hands on the towel tucked into her belt, and took Jenny by the arm. "Let me even it off, at least."

"Oh, not a problem, Pete did it."

"Pete? Pete who?"

Jenny wasn't sure she should have said anything. But it was out. "He's a friend," she said, and felt a touch of pride so new that her cheeks went pink. She fingered the latch on the door. "You don't know him. He isn't from around here."

"Where's he from?"

"Out west."

"How'd you meet him?"

"Oh, just by accident, after the dance Friday night. Big, tall guy, leather jacket, boots. Maybe you saw him?" She dared a glance at Miriam, who looked puzzled.

"No. I'd have noticed someone like that."

"He was outside. Maybe that's why you didn't see him."

"I was outside, too. Leather jacket and

boots? I'd definitely have noticed someone like that."

"Well, he wasn't there the whole time.
He kind of came and went. Maybe he
was behind a tree at a time when you
might have seen him, so you *didn't* see
him. He rides a motorcycle."

"Ah-ha," Miriam said with sudden
playfulness. "The plot thickens. What's he
doing here?"

"Oh, just passing through."

"And he's staying with you? Why, Jenny,
you little devil."

"It's all completely proper," Jenny said
before she realized that Miriam was teasing. Embarrassed then, she shrugged.

"Pete, huh? And he cut your hair?"

"I cut it. He just evened it off."

"Well, then," Miriam said, "I'll just
even it a bit more."

Jenny thought her hair was fine, but
Miriam was her boss, and a neat and
steady person if ever there was one. Besides, Jenny couldn't risk annoying her
by saying no.

"There," Miriam said a short time
later. "It was really only the back."

It hadn't felt like only the back to

Jenny, who was slightly appalled at the length of a few of the pieces of hair that lay on the floor. But Miriam was using the comb now, trying this and that, fluffing Jenny's hair up, actually smiling. "It really does look nice. More sophisticated. Not so overpowering." She turned Jenny to the mirror.

Jenny touched the ends that curled forward under her jaw, and the side part that replaced her usual center one. *More sophisticated.* She liked the sound of that. She liked the look of it, too. She might have called it a sleek bob, were it not for the curls.

Then curls and all fell prey to Miriam's hands, quickly tacked back into the knot she claimed was hygienic. Long after severity took over, though, Jenny clung to the earlier image. *More sophisticated.* She liked that, indeed.

Darden was going to hate it. But not Pete. She smiled. Pete was going to *love* it. She couldn't wait to show him.

She couldn't wait to see him, period. Even now, remembering, she felt the warmth she had experienced when he had walked her to the door and sent her off into town.

"Sure you don't want a ride?" he had asked.

She nodded. She didn't want people asking who he was and why he was with her. She didn't want them reporting back to Darden, not until she knew what she was going to say. "I need time to think. I have to decide what to do."

He had taken her face then, as he seemed to like to do, framed it with his hands like blinders on a horse, blocking out everything else but him. "How can I help?"

She had sworn she wouldn't beg, but the facts of her life lurked just beyond the touch of his hands. So she said, "Don't leave. Stay a little longer. Be here when I get home."

He kissed her on the mouth, on her nose, and on her eyes, which she had closed. Without the distraction of sight, his voice was richer. "I'll be here. Hurry back."

* * *

Jenny worked quickly. She ran the last of the trays from the kitchen to the van, then from the van into the house where the barbecue was being held, and into the backyard where the grills were set up. She ran from table to table around the pool, setting out cocktail napkins and candles. She ran drinks from the kitchen to the far end of the buffet table, ran baskets of rolls and trays of condiments to the middle of the table, ran paper plates and napkins and plastic utensils to the end of the table nearest the grills.

"Slow down," Miriam said at one point, but Jenny couldn't get herself to do it. She figured that the sooner she got things done, the sooner she would be back home with Pete.

Unfortunately, her hands weren't as good at rushing as her feet were. She had to rearrange napkins when Miriam said they looked messy, had to mop up a whole two-liter bottle of Mountain Dew when it slipped from her grasp, had to return an entire tray of twice-baked potatoes to the kitchen when she set it too close to the table's edge and it fell.

"Jenny," Miriam whispered, because

the guests had arrived by then, "relax. There's no rush. Stay *calm*."

Jenny was more deliberate after that. She concentrated on each task Miriam set her to, and would have done fine if the event's hostess hadn't homed in on her to do a dozen little chores. If it wasn't "The gentleman in the green blazer needs A.1. sauce," it was "A glass of *tap* water for the woman in blue over there," or "I want salt and pepper on *every* table," or "Fill the baby's bottle with milk from the refrigerator and warm it a little, not much, just a little. You know how to test it, don't you?"

Jenny did the best she could, but with both Miriam and her client making demands, she couldn't help falling behind, and when she rushed to catch up, she made mistakes. So she had a bad day. One bad day wasn't so awful. The food was still good. And anyway, what did it matter if the affair wasn't perfect, if Miriam was closing down anyway?

None of that made her feel any better, though, when Miriam took her aside after their return and said, "Listen, Jenny, I want you to take the next few days off. I think you're distracted."

"I'm fine. Really."

"Well, it's not coming over that way. Take time off until Darden is back and settled in. You'll feel better then."

"But I have to work," Jenny insisted and began wiping down the long stainless-steel table. "He wants me to work. He'll be upset if I don't. Take my word for it. It's *better* if I work."

Miriam caught her hand and forced her to stop. "Not for me. Look. I have only two bookings this week anyway, and they're small. AnneMarie and Tyler are working them. You need to spend time with your father, or looking for another job."

"I won't get one."

"Yes, you will. I'll give you a great recommendation."

Jenny knew that even a recommendation from the *pope* wouldn't help. People didn't want her around. It didn't matter whether it was because of her hair or her freckles or her name, she didn't fit in like other people did. She couldn't talk easily, or smile easily, especially with new people, who would surely take one look in her eyes and see the truth of what she was.

Miriam had been special. But Miriam was leaving.

"You can work the DeWitt wedding next Sunday. Okay?"

Jenny nodded. She gave the table a dull swipe and hung the cloth by the sink. Then she let herself out into the fast-falling night and set off for home, and she refused, absolutely *refused* to think about all that might happen before she saw Miriam again, but the thought came anyway—not only came, but multiplied, then crowded in on her with such intensity that her legs began to wobble. She hadn't gone a block when she had to sit down on the curb.

She hugged her knees. She put her cheek down and squinted, making Main Street a blur of light and dark that might have been London, or Paris, or Wyoming just south of Montana, and she thought about Pete.

She started to rise, but sat right back down. She didn't know if it was better to stay here and imagine he was waiting for her at home, or to get there and find out he had left. He had said he would stay, but that was before he'd had a chance to think about what she had told him. Now that he knew some of the truth, he was probably gone. And she didn't blame him. She was bad news, *bad* news.

She pulled the pins from her hair and shoved them one by one into the ground, pounding them down with the heel of her hand. She stopped only when a small figure slid down to the curb and a small hand touched her leg.

She managed a smile. "Hey, Joey Battle, what's up?"

"Nothin'." His skin glowed pale, almost bluish, with freckles as iridescent in the night as she knew her own must be. "Who made you get *your* haircut?" he asked.

"Me." She tried to lift his backward baseball hat and take a look at his hair, but he held the plastic band firm on his forehead.

"Mine looks *dumb*," he told her. "She chopped it all off 'cause she says it was getting too hard to comb. Well, I'm wearin' this hat to school, I don't care *what* she says. She says your daddy's coming home. That he killed your mama. Did he?"

Jenny pressed her knees together and tucked her elbows into her middle.

"Did he?" Joey prodded.

"No."

"Then why's he in jail?"

"Because the jury said he did it."

"Why?"

"Because he said he did it."

"So did he?"

"No."

"Joey? Joey Battle, where are you?"

Quick as a flash, Joey flew down the street. Jenny turned her back, hunched her shoulders, and ducked her head so Selena wouldn't see her and know where Joey had been. She waited until the sound of scampering footsteps tapered off and died. Then, with her shoulders still hunched and her stomach in knots, she set off for home.

Left, right, left, right. She walked evenly, setting one foot in front of the other, and tried to walk tall, like the magazine instructed, only her shoulders wouldn't go back, and when she tried to clear her mind of worry, Darden's face barged right in—Darden and no job and no long hair and no escape—

She broke into a run, arms pumping, hair coming alive in the lowering mist, and didn't let up until a stitch in her side slowed her down, but even then she didn't stop. She had to know if Pete was waiting for her. Had to know. He was the only bright thing left for her.

By the time she got home, she was frantic. She ran through the shrouding mist, up the side steps, and into the kitchen. He wasn't there. She ran through the hall, room to room through an encroaching chill—first floor, second floor, every nook, every closet, even under the beds in case he was playing a joke, though she knew he wasn't cruel that way.

Breathing hard, she drove her hands into her hair. If he was gone, that was the end of it. No comfort, no warmth, no last shot at the kind of happiness other people had. If he was gone, her dreams were dead.

Shaking with cold dread, she wrapped her arms over her head, scrunched her eyes shut, and took a breath from the deepest, most wretched part of her.

Then her eyes opened wide on an image of the pine tent out back. Whirling around, she raced from the room and into a large human shape.

Chapter Twelve

BOSTON

Casey was shaking as she put the last page of the manuscript facedown on the pile. A small part of her reaction was from the abrupt appearance of that large human shape, but the better part came from the idea that Jenny's father had gone to prison for killing her mother. Casey had never treated a client who was connected to a murder. Death, yes. She often helped clients adjust to the death of a parent, a spouse, or a close friend. But murder was a different can of worms. It involved a level of violence that Casey had never experienced. Her parents had never fought; they had never *talked*. As odd as that was—as many times as she had attached various psychotherapeutic terms to their particular form of dysfunctionality—she figured that leading separate lives was preferable to the sort of hatred that led to murder.

But Connie had written that Jenny was kin. That made this particular murder personal.

No. Casey stopped herself. What Connie had actually written was, *she's* kin. For all Casey knew, "she" referred to someone who had written the journal as a piece of fiction, and "how to help" referred to getting it published. Casey couldn't help with that.

Nor, though, could she turn her back on Jenny Clyde. Jenny's world was closing in. Her desperation was growing. Casey had to know what had happened to her.

Something told her that Jenny was real. But something else felt odd—something in the part she'd just read. She couldn't put her finger on what it was.

Already on edge, she jumped at the sound of the phone. It was a muted ring that came from the kitchen. There was no phone here in the living room, which was where she had been since Emily Eisner's departure. Nor was there a clock here, though she guessed it to be nearly ten. Meg was gone for the night, and Casey's friends didn't usually call this late.

Uneasy, she set the journal pages aside, ran out and through the hall to the kitchen, and snatched up the phone.

Ten minutes later, after a speedy drive through mercifully mild traffic, Casey ran up the stairs of the nursing home, through the door, and on up to the third floor. Her mother's doctor was at the desk there, waiting for her as he updated Caroline's chart.

Her heart pounding, Casey stopped short. The doctor was dark-haired and slight, a quiet, formal man. Though she knew that the formality was as much a cultural as a personality trait, she guessed that it served to protect him from personal involvement. Few of his patients recovered. They might linger as Caroline was doing, but in time nearly all of them died.

Casey eyed him with caution.

He gave a small smile meant to reassure. "She's all right. It went on longer this time, but she came through it herself."

Casey sagged in relief. Two years before, when Caroline had been vegetative long enough for the odds of recovery to be slim, Casey had signed orders that resuscitative measures were not to be taken. She had consulted with other doctors before taking that step, had talked with the minister in Providence who knew Caroline, had argued the pros and cons with Caroline's friends. Intellectually, Casey continued to stand behind these orders. She wasn't sure, though, what her emotions would be if Caroline died when she might have been saved.

"If she came through it herself," Casey told the doctor now, "I think that means something. She isn't any more ready to die than I am to let her go."

The doctor's smile grew sad. He remained quiet.

Casey crossed the short distance between them. She did respect this man. Otherwise, she would have taken Caroline from his care long before. "Tell me what you're thinking," she invited.

"We've been through this before, you and I."

"With infections." There had been a handful of those over the years. "Not with seizures. Seizures are new."

"Yes, they are."

She didn't like the way he was looking at her. "You think she's trying to die?"

He moved an eyebrow in a shrug. "That's often the case."

"Why didn't she, then?"

"By definition, a persistent vegetative state is one in which what the patient's body does has nothing to do with intelligent life. Vegetative functions continue to work. Same with reflexive responses. Those reflexive responses were likely behind your mother coming out of this particular series of seizures."

"Series?"

"Yes."

"More than one?" Casey asked, disconcerted.

"Three, four, five small ones in the last hour."

"But small ones. And she pulled through. I *do* think that means something." She turned to go to Caroline's room, but turned back. As always, she felt a seesawing between the mind and the heart. Casey accepted that there might be a discrepancy between what she *wanted* to be the case and what *was* the case.

She folded her arms. "If you're right," she asked softly, "what happens now?"

"Perhaps nothing. She could get past this

bump and stay as she is a while longer. You've read the case studies."

Casey had, indeed. She had learned about Karen Ann Quinlan, Nancy Cruzan, and dozens of others who had lived for years with artificially provided food and drink. She knew how medical bills piled up. She knew of the toll taken on the families of those in a prolonged vegetative state.

She had her own way of coping. It was actually a perversion of her father's scavenger-hunt theory. He believed that self-knowledge came with opening doors to all of the rooms in one's life. She didn't agree with the "all" part. She was a totally functional woman. She was professionally successful, personally active, well adjusted, rational, and happy. If the contents of one room in her house were filled with pain, and there was absolutely nothing she could do to change that, she entered that room when she had to, but otherwise kept the door closed.

She visited Caroline often. When she was here, she was entirely involved. When she left, she closed the door behind her. It didn't always stay shut, but when worries seeped out, she did her best to contain them again.

Was that cold and unfeeling? Perhaps. But she didn't know what else to do. The pain, the frustration, the helplessness of thinking about Caroline all day, every day, for more than a thousand days and counting, would have destroyed her.

Right now, though, she was here, and she was curious. "If you're right, and my mother is trying to die, won't she try it again?"

"Possibly."

"With seizures?"

"Not necessarily. I've had patients who experience an episode of status epilepticus—a period of continual seizures—but get through it and then never have another seizure. Different things can signal a change in condition. Patients in a persistent vegetative state generally exhibit circadian sleep and wake cycles. Your mother does. We can get her to react to a glaring light when she's awake but not when she's asleep. One of the signs of approaching death could be a change in this reaction. She could spend more time sleeping and be harder to rouse. This would suggest a change in her metabolism. Her limbs could grow cooler, which would suggest a change in her circulation. If her autonomic functions begin to falter, oral secretions may collect at the back of the throat, which would make her breathing louder and more labored."

"Swell," Casey remarked.

"But she isn't suffering," the doctor said with more feeling than he had showed to that point. Clearly, his concern in explaining the situation was Casey. "You have to keep that in mind. She does not feel pain. She does not feel any sensation at all. Her brain is functioning at too low a level for that."

"Then again," Casey pointed out, "if what is happening to her now is the first step in a reawakening, she could begin to feel pain."

"We'll know if that happens. Even if she can't speak, we'll know, and if not me, then the nurses. I never fail to be awed by their instincts. They are always the first to know when a patient is getting ready to make a move."

Make a move. He meant die. Casey had heard that from nurses and the family members of patients right here on this floor, and more than once. Nurses did know, which was why she had no intention of asking them now. She didn't want to know the answer.

So she nodded to the doctor in silent thanks, pointed down the hall, and set off.

All was peaceful and dim in Caroline's room. If there had been a disturbance that night, the only evidence of it was the Valium drip hanging from the IV pole by the head of the bed. Caroline was propped on her side, held there by two well-placed pillows.

Kissing her cheek, Casey came away with the scent of eucalyptus. It was familiar and soothing. She chose to see it as a sign of life.

"Hi, Mom," she whispered. "So. I'm told there was a little excitement in here."

She took Caroline's hand, but it didn't feel any cooler. She studied her face, but, eyes closed, it was as restful as usual. She listened to her breathing, but heard no laboring.

"Just keeping them on their toes with those seizures?" She smiled. "That is typical of you. Like letting me learn the hard way to check the gas gauge on the car." Sixteen, newly licensed, and driving locally, hence in no danger but that of frustration, Casey had run out of gas on the one day when Caroline hadn't said a word in reminder. "But I don't blame you. We're paying a lot for you to be here. Okay." She corrected herself. "It's not us, not directly. But still, you put the money in all those years when your health was perfect. You deserve the best now."

Gently, she worked Caroline's wrist back and forth. "Speaking of the best," she continued, still whispering, "I think we should plan a trip. You always wanted to go to Spain. I think we should do it." When Caroline remained silent, she said, "It doesn't have to be for a while. We could do it next spring or summer, or even the summer after that. I could book the trip"—she had actually done that the year before—"and we can cancel if we change our minds"—which was what she'd had to do then. "Actually, maybe we shouldn't do it in the summer at all. Spring or fall might be better in terms of the crowds. What do you think, Mom? Something to look forward to?"

"Will I be well enough?"

"Of course."

"To walk around for hours? That's what one does on a sight-seeing trip. Remember when we went to Washington, D.C.? The whole time, you complained that your feet were killing you."

Casey recalled it with chagrin. "I was in seventh grade. I didn't want to be in Washington with my mother. I wanted to be with my friends, all of whom were going to D.C. with the school group, but you wouldn't let me do that."

"Because I wanted us to be together, Casey. You were growing up too fast, and I knew you'd be with your friends more and more. Besides, I didn't trust that there wouldn't be mischief if you went with your friends."

Casey didn't call her on that. There had often been mischief when Casey was with her friends, and, as often as not, she was the ringleader. She loved a party with an ill-gotten keg, loved the idea of being under-age at an X-rated movie, loved the idea of dyeing her hair green to match the uniforms worn by the high school basketball team that year when it made the state championships.

"I loved pushing the envelope," she said now, "but you know what that was about. I was testing. Always testing. I had to know that you loved me, green hair and all. Besides, what fun would adolescence be if the adolescent didn't drive her parents up a tree?"

"Ah-ha. That was a Freudian slip, my dear. You said 'parents,' in the plural. That, in a nutshell, is what much of your misbehavior was about. You had no father. You resented me for not providing one."

"I didn't want you to provide one. I wanted my real one."

Caroline didn't have a rebuttal. There was nothing she could say that she hadn't already said—and Casey might have agreed, if things hadn't changed on her own end.

She spoke aloud. "You always said you didn't know what made him tick. But he's dead now, and I have his townhouse. It can tell you about him."

Caroline remained silent.

"Did you know that he played the piano? Or that he spent hours sitting alone up on the roof deck? Or that his best friend was a cat? I think he was a lonely person. I mean, all those years when I resented him for ignoring me, I was probably happier with my life than he was with his."

Caroline remained still.

"He died suddenly," Casey blurted out,

wondering if she could evoke some kind of reaction. "It was a massive heart attack."

There had been moments in the last three years when, typical of patients in her condition, Caroline had made small movements of her head, hand, or mouth, but there was nothing now. She didn't blink or wince or moan.

"Maybe that's better than this lingering of mine," Casey imagined her saying.

"You're not lingering. You're healing."

Caroline drifted off to sleep—at least, that was what Casey chose to think. Otherwise, she would have argued with her mother. If Caroline was feeling self-pity, Casey wanted no part of it. Self-pity accomplished *nothing*. She wanted Caroline well.

Feeling emotional again, she whispered, "Gotta go, Mom." She kissed Caroline's hand and set it carefully on the sheet. "I'll be back real soon. We'll talk more then." She rose. "About Spain." She revised the thought. "If Spain's too much, we'll do Hawaii. It's a long flight, but once we're there, we can veg for a week. No exertion at all. No sight-seeing. Just sun and sand and piña coladas, so if you're not feeling one hundred percent, that's okay. Hey. If the long flight worries you, we can do the same thing in Costa Rica. There's an incredible luxury resort there. I'll get the name of it, okay?"

Back at the townhouse, Casey slept soundly from midnight to five, but once she woke up, there was no returning to sleep. She couldn't even lie in bed. Her mind was speeding along too many urgent paths.

First thing, she pulled on running gear, caught her hair up and pulled it through the back of her cap, and set off in a steady rain to check up on her mom. She knew she would have gotten a call if Caroline had worsened. She might also have phoned the nursing home for an update and saved herself the trip. But she was uneasy, which was unusual for her. She wanted to see firsthand that Caroline was well. Running to the Fenway and back meant that she got a workout at the same time, which made sense.

Caroline seemed fine. She was positioned differently from how she had been the night before, and while Casey wanted to think she had moved on her own, she knew better. The nurses turned her every few hours.

She was on her back now, having breakfast. A feeding tube hung from the IV pole, letting gravity carry nutrients directly into her stomach.

Casey's own stomach lurched. She didn't know why. She had seen this before, more times than she could count, so it wasn't revulsion or dismay or even surprise. After the initial shock of it three years before, she had come to take these meals for granted.

But something had changed. The doctor thought Caroline was trying to die, and Casey couldn't shake the thought of that possibility. It left her feeling empty and alone, left her thinking about the closeness she and her mother should have had as adults, left her unutterably sad. She wanted to relegate this shadowy version of Caroline to her room, but the door wouldn't stay shut. Casey was desperate for her mother to open intelligent eyes, to speak, to smile.

She didn't stay long. She was too wet and too scared. After standing by Caroline's bed for the briefest minute, she retraced her steps and went back out into the rain.

Oppressively heavy and warm, the weather fit her mood. She ran hard and fast, letting raindrops mix with sweat and tears until her legs screamed. Only then did she slow to a saner pace. It took her more reasonably through the Public Garden, down Charles and up Chestnut to the alley that led to her car.

The Miata wasn't alone. Jordan's Jeep was beside it.

Panting from the run, Casey bent over, put her hands on her knees, and struggled to catch her breath. Rain dripped from the bill of her cap, from the trees, from the sky. She straightened, tipped her head back, and let the rain wash her face.

Her breathing steadied, but the emptiness lingered. Hungry? She probably was, but she couldn't think of eating. The hollow inside went way beyond food.

She didn't have to use her key on the latch. Jordan had left it open. Slipping through, she relatched the door, but it was a minute before she spotted him. He was off on the left past the potting shed, half hidden under hemlocks whose lowest limbs cleared his head by barely a foot. Though he was sheltered there, it looked as if he hadn't been under cover for long. His hair was spiked with rain, his tank top and shorts generously spattered.

Today the tank top was gray. He stood with a hand on one shoulder, his arm angling up across his chest. The other arm hung by his side. The shorts were dark and loose, and hit mid-thigh. Below them, his legs were well formed, very straight.

There was nothing casual about him. With his eyes on her, dark and wide, he looked alarmed.

No, Casey decided, not alarmed. Apprehensive.

No, she decided, not apprehensive. Expectant.

Suddenly, all of the doors in the house of her life closed except one. That door was open and inviting. Jordan was vibrantly masculine. The chemistry between them was strong. She had felt its pull from the start, and it had only grown.

He was her father's gardener. That should have stopped her, but it didn't. Actually, the fact of what he was made him all the more appealing. In that instant, turning her back on helplessness and grief, she couldn't think of anything better than having a grand time for herself at Connie's expense.

Then she stopped thinking of Connie, too, because the tug at her insides was stronger than even that. Holding Jordan's gaze, she crossed the garden to where he stood.

"Is everything okay?" he asked, as if he had known where she was.

She didn't answer, simply brought her body to his, linking her hand to the one that hung by his side. She didn't doubt for a minute that he felt what she did. She knew. She just knew. When she lifted her face, his hand was right there to remove her hat, long fingers cupping her head. His mouth met hers without an ounce of timidity.

Casey gave herself up to the moment. She didn't think, didn't analyze or fantasize. She focused on pure sensation—the heat of his mouth when he deepened the kiss, the simmer of his tongue in long lonely spots. She felt a melting inside when he began to stroke her breasts, felt a greater satisfaction—and need—when he pulled off her singlet and used his hands, then his mouth there, and suddenly she was desperate for the totality of it. She touched every part of him she could, pushed clothing aside and touched more.

Somewhere in the midst of it she heard his voice, low and hoarse. "Is there a reason we shouldn't do this—boyfriend, birth control, whatever?"

She couldn't think of a thing, not with her insides aching so badly and the sensation of solidity and fullness that his body offered. It was all she could do to peel off her wet shorts while he did his, and the rush was worth it. Jordan inside her was the ultimate sensation. Yes, there was solidity and fullness, but there was also wholeness.

Later, she would recall the shifting of positions, back and forth and around, but that was a thought and at the moment she was into sensation. That sensation of wholeness altered her need, changing the urge to *do* to the urge to *be*. It slowed her, suspended her so that she hung there in the glory of his possession, in the richness of ragged breathing and rain on foliage, the solidity of a muscled body and the scrape of a beard, the scent of wet man and trees and earth. Just as with yoga breathing she stretched beyond the norm, so, too, now she opened more and more, opened without restraint, offering every part of her to his hands, his limbs, his mouth, tongue, and sex, until her body erupted in orgasm. The sensation of it was deeper and richer than she had imagined possible.

Contentment. That was the first concrete thought she had. Sitting there on Jordan's lap as he sat against the tree—not caring or knowing how they came to that particular pose—she was utterly content.

Her arms looped his neck. Her forehead rested against his stubbled cheek. She drew in one breath after the other, gradually longer and more steady. He remained inside her through those lengthening minutes, no longer erect but very much there.

When she finally took a deeper breath and lifted her head, he was looking at her. His eyes held more of the same richness that she had felt so strongly, but the force of it frightened her now. She didn't know this man. She had never before had sex as impulsively. She didn't regret it; she felt too good. But he was truly an unknown.

Not wanting to deal with that reality, not wanting anything to put a damper on the pleasure she had felt, and sensing he wanted to speak, she covered his mouth with her fingertips. She didn't know what he might say, but she didn't want words at all. She let her eyes tell him that, and she felt him concede. Only then did she remove her hand and ease off him. Standing up, she pulled on her clothes as quickly as she could, though she was slowed by their wetness and the dirt that clung to her skin. He stayed where he was, watching her with increasing laziness, either perfectly comfortable in his nakedness or just exhausted from the sex.

Whatever, his scrutiny was a turn-on. She made herself presentable, made ready to leave the cover of the hemlocks, even backed off toward the path. Then she stopped, reversed direction, and returned to straddle his legs. Lowering herself to his lap again, she slid her fingers into his hair and held his head for a final kiss. It lingered, at the same time heady and content. She might have stayed there a while longer, might even have taken her clothes off again for the sheer pleasure of being naked against him. But Meg would be coming soon. And Casey had clients to see. And she didn't want him to think she was in his thrall.

With a final peck, she used his shoulders for leverage, pushed herself up, and went to the edge of the hemlock cover. Without looking back, she took a quick breath and raced off into the rain toward the house.

Dripping wet and streaked with dirt, she went to the service entrance which was cleverly hidden away in the corner, camouflaged by ivy. She had barely put her key to the lock there, though, when she withdrew the key, tipped up her chin, and went around to the office door. She wanted Connie to see how she looked and know what she'd done.

Opening the screen, she released the lock and entered the office. She couldn't quite get herself to muck up the carpet, though, so she walked around it, on the wood floor.

If Connie was appalled, he didn't let on. The wood didn't so much as creak. Nor did she feel even a hint of ghostly outrage as she went gingerly across the room. She did feel guilt leaving wet footprints on the floor, though. So she pried off her running shoes and socks, ran up to the laundry room off the kitchen, and left them to dry. On a whim, she left her shirt and shorts there, too, and ran naked up to her room.

She wasn't ready to shower yet, though. Her body still hummed of Jordan. Wrapping herself in a towel, she left the bedroom and went down the hall. Feeling bold and defiant, she pushed Connie's door open wide. She didn't quite cross the threshold, but for the first time she took a long look.

The room was really quite handsome. It wasn't cluttered with furniture, but the pieces that were there were large and strong.

Angus sat in the middle of the carpet, watching her, waiting; suddenly, boldness and defiance seemed silly. As always, seeing the cat, she melted. The poor guy was lonely. He wanted someone to love him, just as she did.

"Poor Angus." Holding the towel closed, she crouched down and held out a hand. "Come here, big guy. Come over here, and let me give you a good morning scratch." Angus stared at her with unblinking green eyes. She made a clicking sound as Jordan had done. She wiggled her fingers. She wished she had a kitty treat to offer and vowed to find out if Meg kept any in the pantry. "Come here, sweet kitty," she whispered and inched forward until her toes bumped the threshold.

She remained crouched low to the ground, holding the towel closed, eyes locked with the cat's until curiosity got the

best of her, and she looked around. Behind
Angus was the bed. Beside the bed was a
nightstand. What she had initially labeled a
pair of dressers were actually a pair of armoires standing on opposite sides of the
room. The sitting area consisted of a leather
sofa and an overstuffed chair. Both looked
decidedly worn.

She wondered if they had come from an
earlier time in Connie's life. Maybe she
could trace their origin. That would be interesting.

Actually, the whole room was interesting,
a gold mine of possibility in the scavenger
hunt for who Connie was. If she wanted to
find a personal journal or an address book,
exploring these closets and drawers was a
no-brainer.

But not yet. She had to explore the cartons upstairs first.

That was the plan. Before she got to the
boxes, though, she had to drive to the
condo and come back with more clothes,
see a day's worth of clients, and handle a
raft of administrative chores, all of which
demanded her full attention.

She welcomed that. She didn't want her
mind wandering to Caroline, because she

had absolutely no control over what would happen there. Nor did she want to think about Jordan, oddly, for much the same reason. Her body had taken over down in the garden. She hadn't had any say.

Should she have done what she did? Of course not. But prudence had never played a strong role in her life.

It helped that Jordan was gone by the time she finished showering. Had he been wandering through the house tending the indoor plants while it rained, she might have had trouble clearing her mind of what had just happened under the hemlocks.

The only other person in the house now, though, was Meg. On impulse, Casey asked her to come along to the condo. After the fact, she realized that what little space she had in the small Miata was better saved for clothes, but Meg had lit up so with the invitation, that she didn't have the heart to rescind it.

Meg's enthusiasm proved to be a godsend in keeping Casey distracted. She loved the small elevator that took them to Casey's condo, loved Casey's tiny galley kitchen, loved the cinder blocks that raised Casey's bed off the floor. She *loved* Casey's clothes, marveling over a silk blouse, a pair of linen pants, a pair of high-heeled sandals. At one point, when Casey stood at the closet trying to decide what to take, Meg pulled out a pair of linen overalls.

"These are *gor*-geous," she said breathlessly.

Casey smiled. "They're yours."

"Mine?"

"I haven't worn them in years. They looked neglected, which was why your hand went right to them. They spoke to you, Meg." She took out the overalls and handed them to Meg, who was grateful and so clearly touched that Casey gave her other things as well—a lace camisole, a tank top to wear under the overalls, three different hair scrunchies.

Meg immediately put one of the scrunchies around her ponytail. Casey thought it was perfect, and told her so. Though the compliment came from the heart, what she got in return, in addition to pleasure, was devotion. Meg couldn't do enough for her—carrying things down to the car, packing the trunk, then sitting in the passenger's seat during the ride home with her lap piled high—and *then* insisting that she would unpack, iron what needed ironing, and put everything into Casey's room in an organized fashion.

Casey wasn't used to being waited on. By the time they returned to Beacon Hill, though, her first client was about to arrive, so she took Meg up on her offer.

Letting go of that chore was heaven. Clearing her mind of Jordan, of Caroline, of Connie, even of Angus, she focused so intently on work that she was totally sharp. Some days she struggled to find the right questions to ask; other days she didn't ask questions at all, but just listened. This day she was inspired.

Her ten o'clock client was suffering from postpartum depression. Casey had previously focused on the client's disdain for her mother, who had apparently grown heavier, more unkempt, and less interesting with each of the six children she had borne. Today, Casey asked what the client's father had said about her mother's deterioration. Bingo. The father had not been kind. There had been verbal abuse, emotional neglect, and infidelity. Casey's client was terrified of suffering her mother's fate, now that she was a mother herself.

Casey's twelve o'clock was a woman much her own age who had held three different jobs and done well in each until a promotion was imminent, at which point she committed a blunder that killed the promotion. She was sabotaging herself. She admitted that. She freely discussed her fear of piling more responsibility onto a life that already included juggling children, a household, and a career. This day, Casey asked about her husband—not what he did for a living, because they had been over that, but what his chances of advancement were and what he earned. It turned out that the client's income already matched that of her husband, that she would earn more than he did if she was promoted, and that she had already felt her husband's resentment that her career might outshine his.

Casey's three o'clock, a woman in her seventies, had been emotionally paralyzed since the death of her husband. Through four previous sessions, she had described how much she missed him, how competent and caring he was, how dominant he had been. Casey had assumed that the woman was intimidated by the thought of taking care of herself. Today, though, broaching a subject they had only discussed in passing, she asked about the woman's children. There were three, all consumed by their own lives—and the floodgate of panic that Casey's question opened suggested that the woman was doing what she felt was necessary to get their attention and involve them more in her life.

Three breakthroughs in one day was something. Casey didn't know whether her insights had to do with physical contentment, because that did linger. Much as she tried not to think about Jordan, a move here or there brought a twinge in her thigh muscles or the awareness of tenderness in her breasts.

Then again, her inspiration could have come from Connie whispering hints in her ear. He might have been shocked by what she had done with Jordan, but she did like to think he would have approved of what she had done with her clients.

She rewarded herself with a single butterscotch candy. She took off the wrapper, dropped it in the wastebasket under the desk just as Connie must have done, and popped the candy into her mouth. She sucked it until it was little more than a thin bar. Then, thinking that a man as compulsively neat as Connie probably sucked his until there was absolutely nothing left, she bit hers apart, chewed the pieces, and swallowed.

It was a good end to a good workday, which was why she was feeling buoyant when Brianna arrived. They went right out to the garden; how not to, when it was so lush? Though the rain had stopped, the air remained humid and thick, intensifying the scent of hemlock, lilac, and earth. Meg was gone for the day, but she had left behind a tray of grilled salmon focaccia sandwiches. Brianna carried the tray; Casey carried a towel and soda cans.

Casey toweled off the patio table and two chairs so that Brianna could set down the tray, but Brianna was distracted. She was looking at the flowers, wearing an expression that said she saw not a one.

"Bria?"

Brianna's eyes snapped to hers.

"Want to put the tray down?"

Brianna did, then sank into a chair.

Casey sat down across from her. "Tell me what's wrong."

Brianna eyed her glumly. "I need to end this."

Casey knew she was talking about Jamie. There had been one too many little barbs of late. The pattern was starting to feel familiar. "Why?" she asked, popping the top on a can of Coke and passing it to Brianna.

"He wants me to be something I'm not."

"So you say. He thinks you should be in private practice. For the money?"

"No. He knows I could end up earning less than I am now. He's not greedy for money, just for me. He wants my time. He wants my company when he travels for business."

"Some women would die for that."

"Would you? Of course not. You have a life. You have a career. You value your independence. So do I, but Jamie, bless him, wants a corporate wife."

"Has he said that?"

"Not in as many words, but he's thinking it, I know he is. Casey, he talks about kids. *Kids.* And we aren't even engaged."

"Whose fault is that?" Casey asked.

"I hate men."

"You do not."

"Why do they try to rearrange our lives? I

mean, look what Stuart did to you. Stole your money, broke up the group, made you all move. Any news there?"

Casey shook her head. "Marlene called before. No one's heard a word."

"Not even his wife?"

"She says not. If she vanishes next week, we'll be suspicious. The police are investigating, but theft of twenty-eight thousand dollars is low on their list. I doubt they'll find him."

"What about your money?"

"Gone. Short of tracking him down myself, there's nothing I can do. I have to let it go." She thought of Joyce Lewellen, and tried to apply the lesson to herself. "I can be as angry as I want, but to what end?"

Brianna didn't answer. She was suddenly more alert, looking past her toward the back of the garden. "What is that?" she whispered.

Jordan had let himself in and was stacking bags of mulch against the potting shed wall.

"My gardener," Casey whispered back. If she was going to tell anyone about him, Brianna would be the one, but the timing wasn't right—not for Brianna, in the middle of this particular discussion, and not for Casey. She could feel a flush climbing her body, which said that making love with him hadn't lessened her desire at all, but other than that, she didn't know *what* to make of the man.

Sparing them the briefest nod, he went back out to the Jeep for more mulch.

"He is *something*," Brianna whispered.

"Well, he is a good gardener."

"You don't think he's hot?"

"He's Connie's gardener."

"Is he married?"

"No." At least, she didn't think so. Hadn't he asked *her* if there was a reason they shouldn't make love, like a *boyfriend*? It followed that *he* had no reason they shouldn't make love.

"How old is he?" Brianna asked.

"I dunno—late thirties, early forties?"

"Where does he live?"

"Beats me," Casey replied, now with a touch of pique. She didn't need Brianna's questions. They only reminded her of all she didn't know about this man.

"I'd like to hire him."

"Marry Jamie, and you can."

Brianna grew defensive. "Should I agree to marry a guy who isn't right for me?"

"Are you sure that he isn't? Would he change his mind about loving you if you refuse to leave your job?"

"No. But I feel like I'm being rushed."

"*Rushed.* Brianna, you've been with him for nearly two years. It's not like you're seventeen. You're both thirty-four. If the relationship's right, you ought to know it by now."

Jordan went out the garden door. The latch fell into place.

"Jamie's a really nice guy," Casey coaxed. "He's good-looking. He's sexy. He's worked for the same company for—how long now?"

"Twelve years," Brianna droned. "He went there right from college, and he'll stay there until they give him a gold watch and boot him out."

"It's a good company."

"Good. But not great."

"Brianna."

"He has no ambition, Casey. I mean, there he is telling *me* to change jobs, when he wouldn't dream of doing it himself. He says there's stability where he is. He says he can climb all the way to VP."

"Can he?"

She lifted one shoulder in a half-shrug. "Probably."

Casey picked up a sandwich. She had to open her mouth wide to get it around the bread, salmon, sprouts, lettuce, and whatever else was in it, but the mix in her mouth was wonderful. She chewed and swallowed. Then she put the sandwich on a napkin and said, "By all objective standards, Jamie's a fabulous guy. He's clearly in love with you. I thought you loved him, too. Suddenly now you're getting nervous—like you did with Rick, and before that with Michael, and before that with Sean."

Brianna didn't argue, simply looked at her, waiting.

"Jamie's the best of them," Casey went on. "He's really a good guy. Comes from a good family, graduated from good schools, works for a good company. So the company's good but not great? Great companies have been known to topple without warning. Good companies are often more stable. So." The million-dollar question, no shot in the dark because Casey knew Brianna's history. "What would your dad say about Jamie?" Brianna's father had been the CEO of a *great* company.

"He'd say Jamie could do better."

"Your dad's been dead a dozen years. The world was a different place back then."

"Still, I respect his opinion. He didn't get to where he was by being shy and restrained."

"Jamie isn't shy or restrained."

"Why are you pushing Jamie?"

"Because," Casey said, "I know you as well as anyone does, and I think that if any man can make you happy and keep you that way for the next fifty years, it's him. Really, Bria. When it comes to compatibility with you, on a scale of ten, I'd give him a nine point five."

"I want a ten."

"That's perfection."

"Why not aim high?"

"Perfection does not exist. Men have faults, just like we do. You want the perfect guy? The perfect guy isn't *real.*"

The words were barely out when Casey's mind flew to Jenny Clyde's Pete, and in that instant, she put her finger on what bothered her about the guy. He was too good to be true.

That would suggest the journal was either a work of fiction, or a true story with high exaggeration.

Which was it?

She didn't know. All she knew was that if *Flirting with Pete* was something her father wanted her to pursue, she had to do it.

Chapter Thirteen

Casey didn't mention the journal to Brianna. She was afraid that Brianna might say it was fiction, which wasn't what Casey wanted to hear. She wanted it to be real. She wanted to have a relative named Jenny who needed her help. She wanted this Jenny to be a link to Connie's family.

Finding Jenny was the problem. Casey couldn't seem to locate Little Falls. She needed more information—for starters, the name of the town where Connie had grown up.

Ruth would know, if anyone did. But Casey wasn't ready to seek her out, any more than she was ready to explore Connie's bedroom. Foolish? Perhaps. But the issue was emotional, and emotional issues were stubborn ones. Besides, Casey wasn't out of other options.

One was Emmett Walsh, the psychotherapist who had taken over Connie's active cases and had possession of Connie's computer, his files, and his Rolodex. Casey found his number in the Boston phone book and punched it in. Before it had even rung on the other end, though, she decided that an in-person introduction might be more productive, and she disconnected the call. Quickly, before she could change her mind, she twisted her hair into a backknot, grabbed a key, and went out the door.

She knew where Emmett Walsh lived. She had taken a course he taught; one of the sessions had been held at his house. He lived on the flat of the hill, barely a five-minute walk away.

Though a gentle ocean breeze had kicked up, a lingering mugginess kept the air moist. Leeds Court was ringed with cars still wet from the rain, and the cobblestones were slick and shiny. Sun broke through a scurry of clouds, setting sparkle to droplets on trees, flowers, and stoops, and the charm of it struck her. Setting off down the walk, she alternately felt like a guest who was awed to be visiting such an idyllic place, or an impostor.

Did she belong here? She had no idea.

She reached the narrowed part of the Court just as a neighbor turned in from the street. He wore a suit, carried a briefcase, and put on a smile when he saw her. "How're you doin'?" he asked as he passed.

His name was Gregory Dunn. He and his wife lived on the east side of the Court. He was a prominent lawyer in town, photographed often and well. If he was fazed at the sight of a new face on the Court, he didn't let on. Could be a guest, Casey would wonder if she were in his shoes. Could be a thief. Could be Connie Unger's daughter, come to claim her inheritance. Connie Unger's daughter? I didn't *know* Connie Unger had a daughter. She was never here in his life. I wonder why.

Turning onto West Cedar, she walked down to Chestnut and waited at the traffic light. People passed in a steady stream, taking advantage of the two hours of daylight that remained in this summer solstice week. Crossing Charles, she continued on to Brimmer. Emmett Walsh's house was the only one on the block made of wood.

There were no steps here, no front lawn. The door was flush with a very narrow sidewalk. She rang the bell, praying that in her moment of boldness the man would be home.

His wife answered the door. She worked in the archives at the university, and was old enough and serious enough to look the part.

Casey smiled. "I hope I'm not interrupting your dinner. I'm Cassandra Ellis. My father was Cornelius Unger. Is Dr. Walsh at home?"

The woman stared. "I didn't know Connie had a daughter."

"I did," said the man who came up behind her. Clothes hung loosely from his tall and lanky frame. "The lawyer told me about you when I asked what would happen to the townhouse. I can see the resemblance to Connie—same hair, same eyes, same intensity."

Intensity. Casey wouldn't normally choose that word to describe herself. But right now she did feel an intensity inside. To offset it, she quipped, "But you didn't pick up on the resemblance when I took your OCD class."

"You took that?" He was clearly pleased. "No. I didn't pick up on it, but I wasn't looking for it then."

It was the polite answer, Casey knew. He couldn't possibly remember her. She had studied under him nearly ten years before, and even if it had been only two years, he taught hundreds of students each semester, and had been teaching for more semesters than Casey had been alive.

"But I do see it now," Emmett went on. "I knew Connie when he was your age. I actually knew him even before that. We went to college together. Bet you didn't know that?" He stepped aside to let his wife escape, then resumed. "And graduate school. I was actually surprised that he passed his active cases to another old guy like me. Not that there were many cases. Neither of us has anywhere near as many patients as we used to, and most of those are longtimers who pay in cash. Insurance balks when you go on for years. I have to tell you one thing, though: that makes it easy when you want to slow down. You don't have to terminate patients. You let HMOs do it for you. But you didn't come here for a lecture. Would you like to come in?"

"I would. But if this is a bad time . . . ?"

He checked his watch. It had a large face and a worn band, and looked like the kind that had to be wound by hand. "I have a few minutes to spare before dinner. I'd invite you to join us, but, quite frankly, I don't recommend it. We're having leftovers of a meal that wasn't particularly appetizing to start with. I have to tell you one thing—getting old isn't fun. When you have to tailor a diet to deal with diabetes, high blood pressure, and irritable bowel syndrome, the food stinks." He stepped aside and waved her in. "Come. We'll talk about Connie. That's what you want, isn't it? The lawyer told me more than he probably should have, but I have a way of asking questions, so *of course* I wanted to know about this daughter of my colleague. Did you ever actually meet Connie? Shake hands? Say hello?" He led her into the parlor and gestured her to a seat.

"No," Casey said. She took an armchair with an upholstered seat and caned back. "I attended lectures he gave. Sometimes, afterward, I'd stand nearby and watch him talk with other people. He knew I was there, but he never invited me over, so I never went. Did he ever tell you about me?"

"Never."

"What was *wrong* with him?"

"Wrong?"

"Clinically. You knew him. Diagnose him for me, please."

Emmett sat back on the divan. "I can't do that," he said, "and not out of loyalty. I did know him, probably as well as any of us psychos," he said wryly, "but that wasn't saying much. He was a quiet person. He didn't talk about himself. He looked and listened. He asked questions. He was the perfect kind of friend to have, especially for someone like me. I do talk a lot, in case you hadn't noticed."

Casey had. She figured that Emmett Walsh had said more in two minutes at his front door than Connie Unger had said in five years at his.

"So Connie and I were a good pair," Emmett went on. "There was no competing for the mike, so to speak. He was never a challenge, never a threat, never a demand. He made it clear from the start that he preferred not talking about himself, so our friendship developed on those terms. He was definitely shy. But was that an inborn trait or learned behavior? I don't know." He shot her a crooked smile. "Maybe that says something about my skills as a therapist—or lack thereof—but you have to draw lines sometimes. Connie was Connie; *why* he was Connie was buried deep enough inside so that it never came out by chance. I didn't feel it was my job to analyze him, so I never did ask the right questions, and then he became pretty famous and was put up there on a pedestal, and understanding his inner workings became moot. I can tell you one thing—he valued our relationship. All these years later, if I had a question and left him a message, he'd call me back within a couple of hours. Did we ever play golf together? No. He wasn't a golfer. Once or twice I'd get tickets to a show and call him up, but he didn't like going to the theater. Didn't like going to movies either."

But he did like watching them. Casey had seen his collection. "Was he agoraphobic?"

"Of course not. He was out in the public all the time."

"That was his professional time. He could be functional there and dysfunctional at home—different states of mind in the different rooms of his life."

Emmett smiled. Dipping his head, he said quietly, "That's very good."

Casey hadn't come for compliments, but

she was pleased. "You know that I'm a therapist?"

"Yes. Winnig told me. Did you enter the field because of him?"

"Of course," she admitted. "But I do like people. I've always been good with them. I'm fascinated by what makes them tick."

"When it comes to Connie, though," Emmett surmised, "it isn't objective curiosity."

"No. He was my father. I have no idea why he refused to acknowledge me. I really would like to know."

"I'm afraid there isn't much I can say."

"Do you know where he grew up?"

Emmett nodded. "A little place in Maine."

"Named?"

Emmett gave her a crooked smile. "A little place in Maine. You wouldn't have heard of it."

Casey smiled back. "Try me."

Emmett chuckled. "That's all I know. I was quoting Connie. 'A little place in Maine. You wouldn't have heard of it.' "

"And you didn't push?"

"No," Emmett said without apology. "It was obvious he didn't want to say, and there was no reason we had to know."

Casey tried another angle. "Did he ever mention having siblings?"

"No. Not a word about any. When we were in college, he used to mention his mother, but I assume she's been dead a while."

"Did you ever meet her? At graduation, maybe?"

"No. She didn't come. Actually, *he* didn't come. Back then, it wasn't the big ceremony it is today. A good part of the class just picked up their diplomas at the dean's office, and that was that."

"Did he ever mention a town called Little Falls?"

Emmett flattened his mouth, squinted, thought for a minute. "No."

"Did he ever mention a man named Darden Clyde?"

Emmett thought again, shook his head again.

"What about Jenny Clyde?"

"No."

"MaryBeth Clyde?"

"No."

"Would any of those names be in his case files?"

"I can tell you that easily enough," Em-

mett said, pushing himself up from the divan. "Stay here. I'll be right back." And he
was. Barely a minute later, he returned with
an album tucked under his arm and Connie's Rolodex in his hand. "Clyde. C-L." He
began flipping cards. "Cardozo. Chapman.
Cole. Curry. Sorry, no Clyde."

"Might he have listed them under their
first names?"

"Why would he do that?"

"If they were relatives of his."

Emmett raised his shoulders and shook
his head, but all the while he was flipping
cards again. "No Darden." He flipped more.
"No Jenny." And more. "No MaryBeth."

Casey took another tack. "Did you find
anything in his case files that had to do with
a journal called *Flirting with Pete?*"

"A journal?"

"Journal, memoir, book?"

"*Flirting with Pete?* No. Who's Pete?"

"I don't know," she wailed softly, with a
desperation that was only half in jest.

"*Emmett?*" came a call from the back of
the house.

Emmett called back, "Be right there."
Raising bushy brows, he whispered a conspiratorial, "I have pictures."

Casey's heart skipped a beat. "Pictures of Connie?"

"In college. Want to see?"

"Very much." She switched to sit on the divan by Emmett's elbow and waited eagerly while he thumbed through pages. She imagined snapshots of grinning friends, faces stuck into the camera lens, party shots, perhaps an embarrassing photo or two—which were the kinds of snapshots she and her friends would have of themselves. When Emmett finally flattened a page and pointed at one faded black-and-white, then a second and a third, she saw that his collection was quite different from hers. The faces here were sober, the poses straight, the bodies clothed. Most were group shots of young men sitting at a table or gathered in front of a window. The closest they came to looking like they were partying were the beer steins they held.

Emmett began to sing in a wavering voice. *"Oh, fill the steins of dear old Maine— shout till the rafters ri-ing—stand and drink a toast once again—let every loyal Maine man sing."* He met Casey's questioning gaze. " 'The Maine Stein Song.' It's from the University of Maine. Connie used to sing it to us after we'd gotten a drink or two or three in him. It's the closest he ever came to sharing a part of his past."

Casey was fascinated by the college-age Connie. He had been very good-looking, with light-colored straight hair, a pleasant smile, and wire-rimmed glasses. Though slighter of build than the others, he was dressed as they were. He stood on the far right in the lineup.

Actually, it was like that in all of the snapshots, she realized, turning back a page to check two others. He was never in the middle, always just there on the end. He did look shy. But there was more, a look that was at the same time tentative and hopeful, like he wanted to be with his friends but didn't dare get any closer lest he be asked to leave.

Casey wondered if he felt like an impostor, too, and, if so, why. "He didn't go to the University of Maine," she pointed out.

"His father did," Emmett said. "Actually, that's not quite right. His father *worked* there. He was a janitor."

Casey caught her breath. "A janitor? And Connie went to Harvard? His father must have been so proud."

"He died before Connie was accepted. I don't think they got along."

"Emmett?"

"Coming!" Emmett yelled back with less patience now. Carefully, he removed one of the photographs from the little black corners that held it on the page, and offered it to Casey. "This is the best one, I think." Connie was one of only three men in the shot. "That's me in the middle. The fellow on the left is Bill Reinhertz. He passed on a while back."

Casey took the photograph. It was indeed the best one—more close-up than the others, showing a youthful face, hair fallen casually across a brow, glasses angled less obtrusively. Connie looked kind here. She had always wanted him to be kind.

Emmett closed the album. "Are you keeping the house?"

It was a minute before the question registered, before Casey could raise her eyes from the snapshot. "The house? I don't know."

"If you want to sell, I have a buyer. He'll pay full price. He's loved the place for years."

"You?"

"Oh, no. It's my stockbroker. *I* can't afford anything like that."

"How could Connie?" Casey asked. She knew that the price would have been far less when Connie had bought it thirty years ago. But everything was relative.

"Textbooks, my dear," Emmett said. *"Unger's Intro to Psych* has been the standard text for twenty years. Do you know the kinds of royalties accruing from that kind of thing? My guess is you'll come into some of that royalty money yourself. Didn't the lawyer mention it?"

Casey shook her head.

"Well, who knows then. It could be that he left the royalty money to Ruth. Have you met her, by the way?"

"No."

"She's quite a painter."

Casey could agree with that, though begrudgingly. She passed those paintings every time she went up or down the stairs. There were layers to them, skillfully applied to create varied moods of the sea.

But it wasn't Ruth's painting talent that intrigued her. "What was their marriage like?"

"I believe it was actually quite normal, with the exception of having separate homes, but I can understand why they did it, knowing how quiet Connie was. Ruth is far more social. She likes having people in. She lives in Rockport, which is a fabulous place to visit on a Sunday afternoon. I've often thought that Connie married her to help him out with people, but then found that the strain was just too much."

"Emmett."

Emmett shot a peeved glance at the door. "I can tell you one thing," he muttered under his breath. "There are times when I think Connie had the right idea."

Casey walked for a while. She was acutely aware of Connie's picture in her pocket. From time to time, she took it out and studied it. When she settled onto a bench in the Public Garden, she did it again. This time, when she put it back in her pocket she took her cell phone out in its place. She punched in the number of the nurses' station on her mother's floor, and was quickly talking with Ann Holmes.

"How is she?"

"About the same," Ann replied quietly.

"There haven't been any more seizures. She had a brief problem with neck spasm—"

"*Neck* spasm." That was new. Casey bent her head and pressed her fingertips to her brow.

"It's not an unusual thing," the nurse explained, "but it's probably just as well that you weren't here. The sound that results isn't a comforting one. Her breathing was labored for a while, but it's back to normal now."

That was some relief. Caroline couldn't recover with physical complications piling up. "Neck spasm," Casey repeated. "Why neck spasm?"

"It's like any other muscle spasm. The cause could be one of a number of things. Likely it's related to circulation. When there's a slowing-down, this kind of thing can happen."

A slowing-down. That didn't bode well. "Could there have been anything deliberate in the movement?"

"I'd like to say that she seemed more aware, Casey, but she didn't. Not at any point."

Casey squeezed her eyes shut for a last few seconds. Then she sighed. "Okay. I'll be there tomorrow. You'll call if there's any change?"

"You know I will."

Heart aching, Casey ended the call. The hole inside her pulled and tugged as she tucked the phone into her pocket alongside the photo of Connie. Hugging her middle, she sat back on the bench, crossed her ankles, and watched the people pass. Some were in pairs, very much self-absorbed. Others were in groups and likewise preoccupied. Those who were alone walked faster, clearly heading somewhere.

For a minute, watching the stream and not knowing a one of them, Casey felt invisible. She thought of Connie sitting in his chair up on the roof deck, looking out at occupants of other roof decks as they gathered, cooked out, partied. Casey had many friends in the world, but, in that instant, she was as alone as he must have felt.

Then she saw Jordan. He stood with his back to an iron railing some thirty feet away. He, too, was alone, and he was looking at her.

At least, she thought it was Jordan. This man had the same dark hair, same wide brown eyes, same tall, tapering body, but aside from sinful good looks, there was nothing remotely disreputable about him now. He was clean-shaven; his hair looked damp and freshly combed. He wore clean khaki shorts and a collarless navy jersey that had three buttons, unbuttoned. His bare legs were long and tanned. He wore Birkenstocks.

Was it Jordan? Of course it was Jordan. Her insides wouldn't be jumping if it wasn't—unless she was simply remembering the morning's passion—which wouldn't be beyond the possible. Sitting here on a bench in the park, with people passing her by, a snapshot in her pocket of the father who had died without a word to her, and her mother physically less than ten minutes distant but so far out of reach that it broke her heart to think of it, Casey was desperate to connect in a special way with someone.

She looked away, then back, and he was still there. Definitely Jordan.

With the tiniest hitch of her chin, she invited him over.

Pushing off from the fence in a fluid movement, he held her gaze as he approached. She had to tip up her chin when he neared, but she couldn't have looked away if she'd tried. She imagined she saw tentativeness in his eyes. It gave her the courage to smile and say, "I thought that was you. I have a whole empty bench here. Want to sit?"

He joined her, leaving an open space between them. Coming forward, he put his elbows on his kness and let his wrists hang between—and it was hard not to notice those wrists. They were lean but strong and tanned. Gone was the watch with its ratty old band. In its place was a Tag Heuer, not quite a Rolex but handsome, highly fashionable, and far from cheap.

For a minute, he faced out, taking in her view from the bench. Then he turned his eyes back to hers. "You looked sad."

It was a simple statement. She didn't have to respond. But he was there, and she remembered the fullness she'd felt that morning, and it was so far preferable to loneliness that she said, "My mother's sick. She was hit by a car three years ago. She hasn't regained . . . awareness in all that time. She's in a long-term care facility on the Fenway." She patted her cell phone. "I just talked with the nurse. Mom's had some trouble lately. I try to be hopeful," she said with a brief, brave smile, but it was gone in a flash. "I mean, she *has* to wake up. She's only fifty-five, which is too young to die, and I need her. She's the only family I have. But something's changing. I'm afraid . . . she's . . . giving up."

"What do the doctors say?"

"That she's giving up. Maybe she should, if there's no hope."

"Is there none?"

Casey struggled to find an answer. She had fought and fought to hold on to even the smallest bits of hope. Sitting here with Jordan, though, she just didn't know. "Everyone was hopeful at first, right after the accident. Then she passed the three-month mark without waking up, and it wasn't so good. Six months, nine months, a year went by. That was awful, the first anniversary of her accident. Now we've passed the *third* anniversary, and there are times when I feel like I'm holding up the banner of hope all by myself."

"I'm sorry."

She looked out over the Public Garden. "I used to be able to shut it away. This week— I don't know—it's harder."

"Is that because of inheriting the town-house?"

"No." She could be honest—with him, with herself. "Something's changing. The nurses sense it." She added quietly, "So do I. I want to think she's on the verge of waking up. But the odds are against it."

"Were you and she close?"

"In the way of most mothers and daughters."

"Meaning?"

"On and off. I wanted to think we'd be 'on' more as we got older. I really wanted to think that." Looking back at him, she forced a smile. "There you have it—the reason for my sad face."

"It's a beautiful face."

The remark might have been innocent, had what happened that morning never been. But it had been. The look on his face said he remembered it as clearly as she did.

"I was worried it was something else," he said, still with his elbows on his knees. "I was worried you were having second thoughts."

Feeling the heat afresh, she pressed her lips together and shook her head.

He seemed relieved. Releasing a small breath, he sat back against the bench.

Casey let the heat warm her insides. It

filled the emptiness now, just as it had that morning. Tucking away thoughts of Caroline, she watched the world pass. She was momentarily content.

After a time, she said, "Why aren't you married?"

He gave a startled laugh.

She shot him a sharp look. "It's a fair question."

"But blunt, the way you ask it."

"Why aren't you? I know some guys your age who've been married three times."

"So do I. That's why I'm waiting. When it happens with the right woman, it lasts."

"Are your parents still married?"

"Yup." Hooking his elbows over the back of the bench, he stretched out his legs. "Going on forty years."

Casey was envious. "Is your father a gardener, too?" She pictured a tight-knit family, with father and son sharing their love of the land.

Jordan dashed the image with a crisp, "Lord, no. He thinks gardening's for women. He's a cop."

"Wow. There's an extreme. And you didn't want to follow in his footsteps?"

"Nope. Never wanted to be a cop."

"Just a gardener."

"It's a kinder life. You find a weed, you pull it out. Can't do that with humans. Even the bad ones have rights."

"You could say gardening is cleaner in that sense."

"In that sense, yes," he said, and smiled.

Casey caught her breath. It was the first time she had seen him really smile. It lit his face, turning what was handsome into something heart-stopping.

"What?" he asked, still smiling, but distractedly now.

She pressed a hand to her chest, gave a quick headshake, and looked out across the Garden toward the swan boats. After a minute, she asked, "Have you ever been on those?"

"No."

"I have. My mother took me. It's my very first memory of Boston. I've been telling Mom that she needs to hold on so that she and I can take *my* daughter there. If I ever have a daughter." But, of course, having a daughter wasn't the immediate issue. Making Caroline hold on was paramount now.

Casey felt a gnawing inside and gnawed on her lip in response. She didn't know why, but the worry was stronger now—certainly more persistent, popping up again so soon.

"Have you had dinner?" Jordan asked.

She came forward on the bench. "Meg left sandwiches. I had half of one. It's a good thing. I don't think I could eat now."

"Too worried?"

"Mm." She pushed up from the bench. "I have to go." She set off with her hands in her pockets, one on the phone, which was on the picture of Connie.

Jordan was beside her in an instant, matching her pace. When he was still beside her after crossing Beacon, going down Charles, and turning up Chestnut, she realized that he was walking her home.

"You don't have to do this," she said.

He just kept walking, and she didn't argue. Safety wasn't an issue. Nor was independence. She was confident on both scores. What kept her quiet was the attraction. The closer they got to Leeds Court, the more she felt. The closer they got, the more she wanted him again.

When she turned onto the cobblestones that led to the Court, Jordan paused. She stopped and looked back. His eyes met hers in the dusky light.

She retraced those few steps, coming very close. "You don't have to do this," she said again, more softly this time and with such a different meaning.

"I do," he said, also softly, and there was no mistaking the unsteady breath he took. His eyes moved over her face. She felt wanted. More, she felt *needed*. Coming from as solid a man as Jordan appeared to be, it was a heady thing.

She walked into the Court with Jordan beside her. Neither of them betrayed any urgency, but when she reached her front door and tried to fit in the key, her hand shook. Taking the key from her, he did the unlocking, let her inside, followed, and closed the door.

He caught her to him then, and the instant their mouths met, every bit of the sensation that had burned in Casey that morning was back, and it was mutual. They kissed at the door with a deepening involvement of tongues, and touched as they reclined against the stairs. But Casey wanted it slower this time. She wanted to prolong the possession, because she couldn't think of a better way to spend the night.

So she led him up to the room she had

claimed as hers, and there was something about the comfort of a bed that was conducive to lingering, even when the heat between them was high. They kissed, they touched, they tasted. Jordan's shirt came off first, then hers, and the rub of her still-sensitive breasts against his chest, first from under, then over, was heavenly. Piece by piece, the rest of their clothing fell to the floor, and though Casey was as fully aroused as Jordan, there was no instant joining. Rather, they explored each other in ways that they hadn't had the patience for that morning, and it pushed them even higher. When he finally rose up and entered her, she was so close to release that it would have happened anyway. Having him inside, reaching his own climax while she was still throbbing, made it all the more intense.

And that wasn't the end. He didn't even withdraw, but lay there nuzzling her ear, her neck, the hollow between her breasts, the swell of one, then a nipple—and that quickly he was hard again. But, oh, he was good. He knew how to hold back, allowing only that hardness and the quiet sounds deep in his throat show how turned on he was.

Casey loved those sounds, and not only the ones deep in his throat. She loved the way he sucked in a breath when her mouth reached the hollow beneath his ribs, loved the way that breath shook as it left him when her tongue traced the thin arrow of hair beneath his navel. The pleasure she took from these sounds was a conscious one. She might have been proud of herself for arousing him this way, but that wasn't what she felt. Nor was there a sense of power. What she felt—*all* she felt—was the pleasure of knowing the pleasure he felt.

He climaxed first, then brought her there with his hand—again, inside her all the while, something Casey had never experienced. Nor had she ever experienced one bout of lovemaking so soon after the other, and then came a third. This one was more mellow, an eternity of the kind of gentleness that was at the same time firm, fast, and hard. She didn't know how he did that, but it was what she felt. The bottom line was yet another orgasm, this one deeper and even more satisfying than all the ones that had come before it—because what she felt from him had gone past physical to emotional. He made love to her like it mattered.

Like the orgasm, the contentment was deeper this time, too. Exhausted at last, they lay on the bed with their bodies entwined, and Casey was at peace. Thinking about it, listening to the leveling off of his breathing as he drifted to sleep, she imagined that she had landed in a place that was rooted and strong. She didn't know if she could stay there long, but for now it felt really good.

She either dozed or simply zoned out on serenity. When she finally opened her eyes and turned her head, Jordan's face was inches away. His eyes were closed, his features at rest. Studying them, she felt rootedness and strength again, and was inspired.

Careful not to wake him, she eased off the bed, tied on her robe, and tiptoed into the hall. It was a short walk to the other end. Once there, she opened the door only enough to slip through. The room was dark. It was a minute of groping against the wall by the door until she found a switch. It lit a lamp that stood on the table catercorner from the old leather sofa and the overstuffed chair.

Bathed in soft light, the room was less

imposing. It smelled of leather and dark wood, and was actually quite homey. She looked first for Angus, checked on and under every possible perch, even gave the bathroom a quick look inside, but other than a bowl of water, a half-eaten bowl of food, and the litterbox, there was no sign of the cat. So she explored. She opened one armoire and found it filled with the kinds of slacks, sweaters, and blazers that Connie most frequently wore, along with several more formal suits and a tux. She opened the second armoire and found the opposite extreme—a collection of Gore-Tex jackets and pants, fleece pullovers, turtleneck jerseys, and wicking tees of the type that a hiker would wear. Casey would never have pictured Connie in these. Most looked new. Some still had tags from the store.

She thought of the brochures she had found with his canceled checks, applications for trips that had been filled out but never sent. It struck her that Connie might well have had dreams, too, at least some of which had never been realized. She wondered if he had ever had dreams of a relationship with *her*. Since there were no brochures for that, no applications to fill out and leave unmailed, she might never know.

Closing the left armoire door on the sadness of that thought, she opened the right door. There were drawers here. She hesitated for just a minute with her hand at the ready, aware that this was perhaps the most personal space and not sure she wanted to violate it. But if not now, when? she wondered. Besides, she wasn't looking for intimate items. She was looking for a large manila envelope with journal pages inside. If it was here, even hidden under socks, she would see it.

She began opening drawers. They contained socks and boxer shorts, undershirts and handkerchiefs. She found pajamas in one drawer, wool scarves and flannel shirts, neatly folded, in another. She found a drawer filled with loose change, collar stays, and cuff links. She found nothing resembling a large manila envelope.

Closing the armoire door, she went to the table where the lamp stood. Beside the lamp was a stack of professional journals and books. She glanced through, recognized most, picked up two to thumb through later. A lower, smaller shelf was built under the first, but there was no large manila envelope there, either. She went into the bathroom and searched the stack of reading matter on a corner of the tub. Here was vicarious living at its best—*People* magazine, along with *Field and Stream, Outdoors,* and *Adventure.* That was it.

The only thing left to search was the nightstand. Intent on looking there, she emerged from the bathroom—and Angus was there. He'd come out of nowhere to sit straight by the bed and stare at her. She wondered if he had been wandering through the dark house and just returned, or whether he had been here in the room all along, watching her search. He seemed as elusive as Connie's affection.

Whispering his name, she went up to him. She crouched down within arm's reach and held out a hand. Though his nose twitched, his eyes never left hers.

"Is that your bed?" she asked with a glance at the Sherpa ball tucked snugly beside one of the armoires. Its middle was indented. "I'll bet that's comfy and warm."

Angus didn't reply.

"I saw your things in the bathroom. Meg does a good job with the litter. And it looks like there's plenty of food in your bowl. And water beside it."

Angus continued to stare.

She sighed. "Okay. Movin' on. Maybe you know where I might find the next part of *Flirting with Pete.*"

The cat actually blinked. It was a slow blink. Casey recalled her mother's cats blinking as a sign of trust. She found that encouraging.

She raised her hand to touch Angus's head, but he drew back. There was no mistaking *that* message.

She spoke very, very softly. "I want us to be friends, Angus. I can understand that you're missing Connie, and that I don't fit in here. And I don't know what's going to be next week or the week after that. But you won't be left alone. I promise you that. Connie loved you. So can I."

Angus gave her another blink. It was a while in coming, but was ample reward for her sitting there with him. Slowly, she stood. The cat sat directly in front of the nightstand. Not wanting to scare him off, she ever so slowly reached above him and opened the nightstand drawer. Inside was a treasure trove of miscellanea—a pair of glasses, Bic pens with various colors of ink, tiny Post-it pads, and small, thin spiral-bound notebooks. There was a pocket pack of Kleenex and a tube of lip balm. There was a crossword puzzle, torn from a small magazine and half completed. And a microcassette recorder.

She took out the recorder and held it in her hand for a minute, acutely aware that the last person to touch it had been Connie. She had found one like it in his desk. That one had been blank. Trying not to get her hopes up, she pressed PLAY and heard nothing. Pressing STOP, she rewound the tape for several seconds, then let it roll. This time, she heard his voice. It was a familiar sound, one she had heard countless times. As always, it was low; Connie Unger had a way of making his point without raising his voice. But it was even more quiet now. More private. Introspective.

She had known not to expect a personal message. After all, he hadn't left one anywhere else. Still, something touched her when he began to speak. He talked in bits and snatches, about the changing world and the need for psychologists to keep pace. After every few phrases, he began with, "Tell them . . ." She realized that he was composing a speech.

She listened until she reached blank tape. This time, she rewound all the way. The first thing she heard when she pressed PLAY was, "Call Ruth." The phone number followed, as did, quickly, introductory words for his speech, starting with a thank-you to his host. Casey listened through the rest, stopped the tape where Connie had stopped, and returned it to the drawer.

Angus meowed.

"Oh my," she whispered and knelt. "You recognized his voice, too."

Angus meowed more plaintively.

"I know," she cooed. He didn't pull back this time when she raised her hand. She touched the top of his head tentatively at first, then with more conviction, stroking the silky fur there, scratching his ears. All the while, he looked at her, seeming confused.

Seizing the moment, she ran her fingertips down his spine and, when he raised his rump, all the way up his tail. It was a bushy tail, quite long. Raised as it was, its tip was nearly even with the nightstand drawer. When it started to lower, though, it pointed straight at the iron knob that opened the cabinet beneath the drawer.

Casey stroked the cat a minute longer. Then, reaching around him, she opened the cabinet. It held copies of *National Geographic,* all standing, spines out. The only thing breaking the pattern of yellow was a large manila envelope that had been slipped into their midst.

She pulled it out. On the front was a familiar scrawled "C." Pulse racing, she unfolded the clasp and looked in at the wad of typed papers. The briefest glance at the cover page told her what she needed to know.

Sitting on the floor with Angus nearby, she read the pages in the envelope. When she was done, she stayed there and thought about what she had read. Finally, reclasping the envelope, she tucked it to her chest along with the journals she had taken. On impulse, needing comfort of her own, she leaned forward and tried to kiss Angus's head, but apparently that was going one step too far. He drew back, looking on the verge of a hiss.

So she just smiled and whispered, "See

you soon, big guy," and went quietly to the door. With a glance back at the cat, she flipped off the light, slipped quickly out, and ran smack into a large human shape.

Chapter Fourteen

Little Falls

Jenny screamed.

Pete held her by the elbows, steadying her. "Just me, just me."

"I thought you'd left," she cried. She was breathing hard, half afraid to believe because the cold had been so real, so *icy* that it shook her still. But his hands were warm and his eyes warmer. He smelled of the no-nonsense soap she had bought in bulk on her last trip to the mall. And then there were his arms. They drew her in and held her with a conviction that said, "I told you I'd stay, so here I am." But it was the way his face moved against her hair, her temple, her cheek that finally convinced her. He had shaved. The stubble that branded him a traveler was gone, leaving the smoothness of having arrived.

She sank against him, whispering, "Oh God, oh God, oh God," over and over.

"Nope," he hummed, "just me."

She raised her eyes to his, about to tell him what a horrendous time she'd had, when her thoughts started breaking apart. Panic, chill, fear—all dissolving. Desperation gone, surrendering with a sigh.

"Better?" he asked.

She nodded.

He kissed her, so quickly that she didn't have a chance to stiffen.

"Okay?" he asked.

She nodded and he kissed her again, only now she was remembering his earlier kiss, and the yearning she had felt then surged back. It filled her so completely there was no room for fear.

"Kiss me," he whispered, and she did. It was the most natural thing to open her mouth against his, to move it and taste him, and when he said in a moan against her lips, "You do that so good," she believed him. She could feel his response, the rising, the angling to get closer. When his fingers slid down her spine and put pressure on the small of her back, she felt his erection pressed against her. It should have disgusted her. But disgust wasn't what she felt. No, it was curiosity. And a belly-deep ache.

He raised his head. Slowly he released her. She saw his eyes, a deep, deep blue. "It's heart's-desire time again," he said.

"Yours or mine?"

"Yours."

"What would yours be?"

"You know. But I'm trying to learn about priorities. So. Tell me what you'd like."

Same thing you want, Jenny surprised herself by thinking. When the thought embarrassed her, she dropped her gaze. It fell on his belt buckle. She hooked her fingers there and felt his heat.

He grunted. "Think. Your heart's desire. All you've wanted to do in Little Falls but never had the chance."

She didn't have to think for long. "Go out riding." Other couples did that all the time, and *they* didn't have motorcycles.

"That's it?"

She thought for another minute. "Maybe stop for something to eat." Other couples did that, too. Jenny heard Miriam talking about it with AnneMarie and Tyler all the time. The hot place was Giro's, an all-night diner twenty minutes out of town.

"Easy enough," Pete said. "But you'll need to dress warm. It'll be cold on the bike."

"That rules out the quarry, I guess."

He remembered her wish. She could see it in his eyes. "Swimming? Too cool. But we can ride out there and park."

Jenny liked that idea. She carried it with her up to her bedroom, where she scrambled out of her Neat Eats outfit, stripped right down to the skin, and went stark naked down the hall to the bathroom, half hoping Pete would see. The anticipation did things to her body. She was weak-kneed turning on the shower, and while she waited for the water to warm, she touched herself. None of her

fantasies—and there had been hundreds,
no *thousands*—none had gone as far as
this. They had focused on the love, gentleness, and normalcy that she had decided should come before sex, and she
had never had enough of the first to
move on to the last—until now.

She felt feminine. For the very first
time, she felt justified dusting her body
with perfumed powder and slipping into
the low-cut panties and bra in her
drawer. She brushed out her hair, brush-
ing it hard until the curls were less tight.
She felt light-headed.

She supposed that was why she went to
her mother's dresser and dug through the
middle drawer for the small tissue package that was tucked in the pocket of what
had been her mother's favorite blouse.
Inside were a pair of drop earrings, two
large pearls apiece. She fastened them on
and measured their length against the
length of her hair. When her hair came
out longer, she tucked one side behind
her ear. That felt just right.

She pulled on jeans and a large sweater,
and went looking for boots. The closest
she could come to Pete's leather ones

were the tall rubber things that she wore
during mud season. Like everything else
in the house right now, they were spot-
less. She put them on.

She took out the anorak Miriam had
given her several years back. She was going to miss Miriam. Maybe they would
bump into each other out west. Seattle
wasn't all that far from Wyoming.

Pete was waiting by the side door with
a hip to the wall and his ankles crossed.
He straightened, looked her up and
down, and grinned. "You look cool."

She grinned back. "You, too."

"Neat earrings."

She touched the pearls. "They were my
grandmother's. She was the first woman
in the county to go to medical school.
She came back here afterward, even
when people said she was crazy to do it,
but she was dedicated. She wanted to
help the sick. So she opened an office.
Mostly she made house calls."

"The townsfolk must have loved her."

"No. They didn't appreciate her. She
was too different."

"Was she your mother's mother or
your father's mother?"

Jenny tried to decide which would be more believable. In the end, because she had taken the earrings from her mother's drawer, she said, "She was actually my mother's sister, but much older and different from my mother. I always thought of her as my grandmother. She loved me that way. I was ten when she died."

"I'm sorry she wasn't here to help you when things got bad."

So was Jenny, or so the fantasy went. But it wasn't all fantasy. There *had* been an older sister. Jenny had met her once, then built a story around her. Everyone needed a relative like that.

"But if she'd been here," Pete went on, "she would have taken you away, so we would never have met, you and I." He raised the hand that had been tucked by his side. It held two helmets. "You have a choice this time."

Jenny was barely grasping the meaning of his having bought a second one, when he nudged them her way. "Which one?"

No contest. She took the one she had worn before, the one that smelled of him.

Within minutes they were riding down

the road, past the houses of neighbors who had watched Jenny in scorn all those years. *They thought I wasn't worth a dime. They thought I wouldn't go far. They thought I didn't have a prayer in hell of meeting a man who was more worldly and better looking than any of them.* Her head rose a bit with each charge until she wore Pete's helmet proudly and thought with satisfaction, *They should see me now.*

They couldn't, of course. They might hear the motorcycle, but it was whipping by too fast for them to see who was on it even if she hadn't been hidden in a helmet, and, besides, it was foggy and dark. One part of her knew it was chilly, too, but she didn't feel any of that. Excitement kept her warm.

She hugged his middle on the ride through the center of town. At the far end of Main Street, he reversed direction and wove back along side streets, up one and down the next until no street in the three-block-by-three-block grid had been missed. If Jenny didn't know better, she would have thought he wanted to wake anyone sleeping in the apartments over the shops or in the houses between, just as punishment for their unkindness toward her.

But Pete wasn't spiteful, as that tiny part of her wanted to be. He was curious, that was all. She imagined he wanted to see everything about her past one last time before they left, and so did she.

They passed the elementary school, a rectangular structure with peeling paint on all sides and a worn playground in back. Jenny had loved kindergarten there. She had even liked first and second grade. By third grade, though, she had begun to feel odd. She couldn't invite friends over, what with her parents' arguing, and, besides, her father gave them the willies, the way he dropped her off and picked her up, glaring at anyone who came close. So she was left out of after-school and weekend things, and because those things were what everyone talked about *during* school, she was left out of that, too. Because she was left out, she was a perfect target for the boys, who played the kind of tricks on her that Darden would have whipped them for had he known, which would have only made things worse, which was why she never told him. Silent suffering was safer.

"See that open field?" she called to Pete a bit farther on. "That's Town Field. We celebrate holidays there. Cookouts on the Fourth of July. Parades on Memorial Day. Races for the volunteer firemen in the fall and ice scuplture contests in winter."

"Sounds quaint."

Didn't it just, Jenny thought, but she didn't want to sound bitter, didn't want to *be* bitter, not with her time in Little Falls growing short. So she showed Pete where Miriam lived, where her kindergarten teacher lived, even where Chief O'Keefe and his wife lived, though it made her feel uncomfortable. She would have shown him the house where Deputy Dan lived—its garage housed the police office, and it was a real pretty place—but he had a different road map in his mind. Following it, they rode to the VFW hall, parked under the chestnut tree where Jenny had first set eyes on Pete, and sat while the bike idled, gathering strength. Then they roared along Nebanonic Trail once more, up the mountain and down, and out toward the interstate.

Pete took the curve of the up ramp at a heart-pounding angle and, reading Jenny's excitement well, sped ever faster along the highway and through the night. She imagined it would be like this when they left for good. Astride Pete's bike, she could go anywhere, do anything, be anyone.

Too soon he pulled off the highway, but the sense of power stayed. It grew even stronger when, knowing just which roads to take, Pete turned in at Giro's. He parked the bike, fastened their helmets to the handlebars, took her by the hand, and led her inside.

It was Jenny's dream come true. For once, she was one of the gals with one of the guys, sliding into a booth, ordering the same thick, oozy burger they did, munching the same greasy fries, drinking the beer on tap. When Pete fed the jukebox and dragged her to the small dance floor at the end of the bar, she was in seventh heaven. She danced like she had alone in front of her television, danced like others did. When he held her close and started moving in a way that was smooth and sexy, in a way she had never seen, read, or even dreamed about, she was in a heaven way beyond seventh.

"You're so cool," he kept saying, and the more he said it, the more cool she felt. *Easy to hold your head high and keep your shoulders back when someone was looking at you like he wanted to see you. Easy to meet his eyes when they held everything you wanted to see. Easy to smile when he gave you such a sweet glimpse of the rest of your life.*

And it wasn't over when they left the diner. They drove to the quarry, which was nearly deserted by then, and entered through Jenny's special hidden spot. The motorcycle carried them up the gentle path to the far edge of the pitch-black pool. They set their helmets on the ground and changed places, so that she was in front, leaning back. His arms held her there, no questions asked, hands under her anorak, stroking her middle.

"Some people say there's a quarry creature down there," she told him. "They say it came out of the rock when the place was flooded, and lives in the very deepest part."

"So you believe it?" Pete asked.

She thought for a minute, then nodded. "I like thinking it has a whole family down there, so it isn't alone. It's a peaceful creature. It hasn't ever hurt anyone."

"Has anyone ever actually seen it?"

"Some people say so."

"Have you?"

"I'm not sure. I come up here a lot and just sit on the edge and look and look and look at the water. I've imagined the creature so many times. Maybe one of those times was real."

Pete's hands rose until his thumbs brushed the undersides of her breasts.

She closed her eyes. "Hard to believe sometimes, what's real and what isn't." He was cupping her breasts so very lightly that it felt fine. No, it felt better than fine. It felt wonderful. But it wasn't enough.

He helped her turn in the saddle to face him and looped her arms around his neck. This time his hands went under her sweater and found the lace of her bra.

"So *cool*," he whispered. He caught her mouth in a kiss that was shortened only because they were both breathing hard. Then he unhooked the bra and caressed her bare breasts. "Feel good?"

Jenny nodded. It felt *so* good she couldn't have found the words, and even if she had, couldn't have pushed them past her throat. From there on down, everything inside her was swelling, more and more as his hands kneaded and tugged, more and more with the pleasure his eyes held.

"Want to go home?" he asked in a husky whisper.

She gave another quick nod.

Less than a minute later, she was helmeted behind him and they were on their way. This time, Jenny didn't see what they passed. She closed her eyes inside the helmet and concentrated on savoring whatever it was that had taken over her body—because it had been taken over, for sure. It was humming and throbbing, doing things it had never done, making her *think* of doing things she had never done, like rubbing Pete's stomach and slipping her hands lower.

She gasped at what she felt.

He returned her hands to a safer place

and called back a choked, "Keep that up, and we'll go off the road!"

"I'm sorry!"

"Don't be!"

Well, she wasn't. Not really. She was feeling as high as when they had been racing along the highway, or dancing at Giro's, or petting at the quarry. She was feeling like maybe good things really were possible.

He sailed down her street, careened into the driveway, and braked at the very bottom of the side steps, but when he took her hand to lead her inside, she balked. "Bad memories," she said with the shake of her head, and he seemed to understand, because he was the one who made for the pine tree out back and held aside the curtain of boughs for her to enter.

If it was cold, she didn't notice. Her body was so hot that she couldn't get her clothes off fast enough, and then the heat Pete generated took over. He kissed her and touched her until she was begging him to do something, *anything* to end the nagging she felt in her belly. But he wasn't rushing, he said. He wanted her to feel finally what a woman should feel, he said. He wanted her to know she was beautiful and feminine and loved, he said, and if she decided she wasn't ready to have him inside her, that was all right, too, he said.

But she was ready. Nothing about Pete was even remotely like the past. Her body was on fire.

He did it then, pushed inside her until she barely had room to breathe, and when he began to move, she thought she would die. She felt it all, the push and tug of it, vivid, hot, and challenging, until she arched her back and came apart.

"I've never climaxed before," she confessed.

"I'm glad."

"I've never really made *love* before."

He brought her hand to his mouth and kissed her fingers.

They were in the attic, sitting beneath the gable on a makeshift bed of pillows and quilts. A single candle flickered nearby. Pete wore nothing but his jeans, which were zipped but not snapped.

Jenny wore nothing but her pearl earrings and his butter-soft shirt. It was a scene out of a fantasy, like something she might read in *Cosmo*. She felt so normal, so *happy* to be normal, so physically pleased and emotionally full that she wanted to cry.

She touched his face, wide-set eyes and eyebrows, high cheekbones, straight nose, square jaw. She ran her fingers through his hair, which was inky, thick, and stylishly long. She traced the curve of his ear, touched the left lobe where an earring might sit, imagined a tiny diamond there. She marked his collarbone with her thumbs, palmed the firm muscles of his upper arms, let her knuckles graze the hair on his chest.

Then she sighed. "Whatever do you see in me?"

"I told you at the start. You're different."

"I'm not beautiful."

"I think you are."

"I don't have long legs like a model."

"That's okay. Taking all that energy to grow long legs leaves them scrawny everywhere else. Long legs don't turn me on." He unbuttoned the shirt she wore and spread it wide. "This does."

She felt the caress of his eyes, felt herself warm up and start aching all over again. She made a sound that was vaguely his name.

"What do I see in you?" he asked. "I see freshness. Newness. Innocence."

"I'm not innocent. I'm not even decent. I've led an awful life." It bothered her to think how awful. It bothered her that Pete didn't know. But if she told him and he left because of it, she didn't know *what* she would do.

"I've made my own mistakes," he said.

"Not like mine," she assured him.

He was suddenly brash. "Wanna bet? I stole my best friend's sweetheart. How's that for decency?"

Jenny figured there was more to the story. "When?"

"When I left. Everyone was begging me to stay, telling me how much they needed me, how much they *depended* on me, but I could taste freedom and, man, was it sweet. But they kept arguing and begging and reasoning. By that time the need was raging inside, and I couldn't get it out, because the guilt was bad enough without the yelling. I figured I'd show them I wasn't a saint, knock their starry-eyed view right out with a one-two punch. So I took her away with me."

"Did you love her?"

"No," he said without meeting Jenny's eyes.

"What happened then?"

"It lasted a month. I gave her money and sent her back, but it was never the same for her there. She left again, alone that time. I don't know what happened to her after that." He finally looked at Jenny. "I know what happened to me. I moved from place to place and couldn't find peace. It was like I had the mark of Cain on my forehead. I met all the wrong women. Until you. I don't deserve you, Jenny, but I want you anyway. I'm willing to change to keep you. We'll start over together."

Jenny's heart was so full that she was able to say little more than a wishful, "You make it sound easy."

"It has to be, if you want it enough."

Jenny wanted to believe that in the very worst way. "But what if there are other people involved—like that friend and your family? What if they don't want you starting over?"

"They will. Times are hard. They need the help."

"My father will say the same thing. He won't want me to leave."

"The situation is different. Your father doesn't need you the same way. His needs are entirely selfish. But you've been loyal to him all these years. You've put your own interests second to his. Now's *your* time."

"But he's my father."

"You're an adult. You have a right to make choices of your own."

"You don't understand. He won't *let* me leave."

"No, *you* don't understand," Pete insisted. "You aren't *his* to let or *not* let leave. You're your own person. He makes the choices that decide his life. You have a right to make the ones that decide yours."

Lord, how many times she had told herself that. Dan had said it, too, and Reverend Putty, and Miriam.

"What if he disagrees?"

Pete grinned. "I'll help you convince him. Between the two of us, it'll be a cinch." Prayerlike, his hands came down between her breasts. His palms raked her nipples. His mouth followed.

She clutched his head. "I want to start over. I've been wanting to for so long. Only I couldn't."

He worked his way up until his mouth was next to hers. "Me neither, because I kept thinking I could do it alone. But I can't." His eyes went to hers. He looked vulnerable. "You'll leave with me, won't you?"

She caught her breath.

"Marry me? Have my babies?"

She put her hands to her mouth. She couldn't believe what a *gift* he was, offering her everything she had always, always wanted.

"I love you, Jenny."

She paused then, thinking again— still—that he was too good to be true. "Really?"

"Really."

"How can you be sure?"

"I've had lots of relationships. I've never told a woman I loved her before."

"There's so much you don't know about me."

"I know what I need."

"What if there was something so dark it'd curdle your blood?"

"You've heard my dark secret. Yours can't be much worse. Besides, blood doesn't curdle."

"You know what I mean. What if there was?"

"If there was, it'd make me feel less guilty for my own crummy past. It'd help me remember that things have to be different this time. I love you, Jenny."

He sealed the words with a kiss, and she returned it, but that didn't seem enough somehow. She wanted to do something special, something different, something other women in his life might not have had the courage or the know-how or the love to do.

Still kissing him, she urged him to his back. She licked his chin, then his throat. She scraped her teeth down his chest, along the line of hair that tapered toward his navel, and all the while her hands worked at his zipper. By the time her head reached it, she had him free.

He was hot against her lips, smooth to her tongue, musky in a way that cleared her head of the past so completely that nothing could mar the purity of her pleasure—and it was a shock, that pleasure. She had started this for him. It ended up being just as special for her.

And so the night went. They talked, made love, and slept; talked, made love, and slept. Shortly before dawn they climbed out to the roof and watched the sun rise and slowly burn off the fog. With the fog went the chill, and with the chill went prudence. Opening the quilt, they lay nude in the still-pale sun, and once that was done, making love was inevitable.

Some might have said Jenny was thumbing her nose at the town, making love in broad daylight that way. Jenny herself would have said, if asked by someone who had no business asking, that she was simply christening her new slate roof.

In truth, she was celebrating a change in her life. She had never been as happy or as bold, certainly never as sure of herself as she was with Pete. And calm. That, too. Even with Darden coming home the next day.

So she slept deeply, back inside the house now, once the sun had moved higher, and she only awakened when the sound of the doorbell grew insistent.

Chapter Fifteen

Jenny struggled into her nightgown as she ran down the stairs. Holding the neck closed and the fabric bunched away from her breasts, she opened the front door a crack and squinted into the mid-morning light.

Reverend Putty looked to be leaving. He quickly turned around and came back. "Dear God in heaven, I was worried," he said with a sigh. "I've been ringing the bell for ten minutes. I was beginning to think something was very wrong. Normally, I'd have simply assumed that you were off walking or even in town, though I just came from there and I didn't see you, but then Dan asked if I wouldn't remind you about the roof, since I was coming out here anyway, and when no one answered the bell I got to thinking—" He looked upward and crossed himself.

"I was asleep," Jenny said.

"Well, I can see that"—he glanced at his watch—"but it's eleven in the morning. That's nearly half the day gone." He sighed again. "All right, I'll tell Dan to tell Merle that whatever he thought he saw up on that roof earlier was wrong. Here you are, covered head to toe in a prim-enough gown. Merle said you were naked, can you imagine that? 'Naked on the roof in the cold,' he said. I asked Dan. We agreed you'd have to be out of your mind to do something like that."

Jenny yawned.

"Though if anyone has reason to be," Reverend Putty went on, "you do. It's been a rough spell for you, MaryBeth. I was glad to see you at the dance Friday night. After that, I was hoping you'd be at church on Sunday. I wrote my sermon with you in mind. Well, with Darden in mind, actually. It was about God's love and what it means to forgive. I believe some of my people needed to hear it, though I do understand how they feel. They're frightened. Darden was intimidating even before all this. But I think what we have to do now is to lay the past to rest. He paid for his crime. It behooves the rest of us as good Christians to welcome him back."

Jenny wasn't holding her breath for that to happen.

"It was an upbeat sermon. I'm sorry you missed it. If you'd like, I'll print up a copy for you. I have to hand it to that computer. It does come in handy for times like this when someone just can't be there to hear my message. You used to like coming to church, MaryBeth."

"I went because Darden went." He took her with him. She hadn't had a choice. No matter that her mother refused to go, or that Darden's belief in God was questionable. He had wanted the town to see her standing beside him.

"I recall you came even after Darden went away."

"A few times."

"Why did you stop?"

Jenny might have shrugged and looked away. But knowing what lay ahead, she wanted her say. "It was a bad time. I was alone and feeling guilty and sick. I needed someone to tell me I wasn't terrible, but no one in town would do it. I thought that because people were in church, in God's house, they might see me more kindly. *Look* at me more kindly. They didn't. They could've used your sermon back then."

"Try to understand, MaryBeth. They found the situation frightening. They didn't know what to say."

Jenny worked her head around on her neck to ease a kink that sleeping in the attic had left.

"They would like you back."

"Did they tell you that?"

"They nodded through my whole sermon."

Jenny could certainly see it. Reverend Putty's sermons put Darden to sleep all the time.

"I'd like you back, too. You and Darden, both. Perhaps next Sunday? It would be a sign to the town that you're willing to forgive and forget." He bobbed on his toes and looked amused. "Consider this a personal invitation"—he shot another quick look upward—"from You Know Who, via His servant, yours truly. God loves you, MaryBeth."

"Does He?"

"Why, of course."

She wasn't sure she believed that. "I waited for Him to help me. He didn't."

"Oh, He did. He left you alone to work things out for yourself, so that you'd become a stronger person. I can see that you are. Those are beautiful earrings you're wearing. They were your mother's, weren't they? Yes, they were. She wore them on her wedding day. I do believe she said they were a gift from your father. I married them, you know. I've been here that long. They were happy back then. Ahhh, dear. All we can hope now is that she's resting in peace and forgiving Darden." He tipped his head. "You used to look just like her. Maybe not so much anymore. You look quite different, actually."

Jenny felt quite different, actually. "I found someone who loves me. His name's Pete."

"Pete? Pete who? Do I know him?"

"No. He's from out west. You probably

passed him on your way here. He rides a motorcycle."

Reverend Putty scratched his head. "I don't remember passing a motorcycle."

"He was going in to get our breakfast. Coffee and doughnuts." Just like the best of the *Cosmo* men did. She smiled at that. "He's so cool."

The pastor remained puzzled. "I think I would've heard the noise of a motorcycle."

"Not the way he oils his machine," Jenny said.

"Ahh. Well. That's nice. I'm happy for you, MaryBeth. You deserve a good man."

"I'll be leaving with him."

"Leaving Little Falls?"

Jenny nodded.

"Will Darden be going with you?"

"No. This is his home."

"But you're his daughter. You're all he has."

"Yes, but now that you've given your sermon on forgiveness and invited him back to the church, he has you and the flock. Doesn't he?"

* * *

Pete brought back two jumbo cups of coffee and a dozen doughnuts. "I have a sweet tooth," he confessed and proceeded to consume three doughnuts to each one of hers. Jenny might have worried, if his body hadn't been so firm. But she was hungry, too, and there was no mystery why. In no time, the whole dozen doughnuts were gone.

He sat on the rear legs of his chair and patted his belly. "That was good. I don't feel one bit guilty."

Neither did Jenny. But the issue of guilt was a land mine. It lay just below the surface, unseen by the naked eye but ready to explode. "If you did feel guilty, what would you do?"

"Chop wood. Run a couple miles. Back home? Mend fences. By the time my stomach was growling again, the guilt would be gone."

"What about other kinds of guilt? Like about your family."

"I can't turn the clock back and change what I did or didn't do. All I can do is go on."

"Have you forgiven yourself then?"

"That would mean what I did was okay, which it wasn't. But I can move on and learn from mistakes and be different."

"Moving on for you means going back to your family. By being different now you can make up for things you did then. I can't. So what do I do with the guilt?"

"What guilt?"

"Guilt. Doing things. Not doing things." She was skirting that land mine, but coming ever closer. "Don't I owe it to Darden to stay?"

"Do you want to stay?"

"No! *No!* But Darden went to prison for me."

"He went for killing your mother."

"But he did it for me." She wanted to say more, wanted it so badly she could almost taste the words. But a tiny part of her swallowed them back down, afraid still.

"Jenny?"

She looked away.

The front legs of his chair hit the floor seconds before he took her chin and turned her face to his. "I love you, Jenny."

"You don't know me."

"I know enough."

"What if you don't? What if there are things—"

"—that would curdle my blood?"

"I'm serious, Pete."

"So am I. I love you." He pressed his chest. "Right here, where it isn't necessarily rational but where it feels as real as anything else in this world—right here something clenches each time I look at you. Like you're the key. Like you can help me make things right. Okay, it sounds weird. A week ago I didn't know who you were, and maybe, just maybe, if I'd been a day earlier or a day later riding through Little Falls, we wouldn't have met. But I don't believe that. I think we'd have met one way or another. I love you." He made a show of thumping his chest.

Which was how she loved him, she realized, and she knew then that she had to tell him more. Maybe not everything. But certainly more.

So she took his hand and led him upstairs, through her bedroom closet, up the ladder, into the attic. Way at the back under the eaves was a box of newspaper clippings. They covered her mother's death, her father's arrest for the crime, and his trial.

Pete carried the box to the back window and sat down to read.

Jenny crouched in a shadowed front corner and watched him lift out one article after another. She knew each by heart, she had read them so many times, knew just what he was reading when, and read along in her mind. She waited for a look or a sound to show he was as revolted as she was. Her breath came in harsh gasps from the place deep inside where the past festered, and all the while she pressed the same spot on her chest that he had pressed on his, felt the tightening there, the fear, the hope.

Finally he folded the last article, slid the box back under the eaves, and came toward her, and her fear rose and rose and rose. But his face held neither revulsion nor hate. His expression was sad, but tender. It was a miracle, she knew, but the love that she so desperately needed to see was still there.

Settling onto his knees, he pulled her between them. He buried his face in her hair and took the same kind of long, grieving breaths she had just taken. After a bit he sat back on his heels. He kissed her hands, held them to his heart, and said nothing, which was really what Jenny needed most. It was her time to talk. Things that she had locked away so many years ago started spilling out.

"We never got along, my mother and me. We looked just alike—except she was twenty years older—but even when I was just born, with little bits of hair, I looked like her. She was MaryBeth June Clyde, and I was MaryBeth Jennifer Clyde. It was my father's idea to name us the same. She told me that. He was trying to make her happy, only it didn't work, it couldn't work, because I wasn't Ethan. He was born two years before me, but he died before his first birthday. She wanted me to take his place, but I couldn't, so she hated me, and she hated my father."

"Why him?"

"Because he betrayed Ethan by loving me." Jenny shuddered. "Sick, sick, sick."

"Your mother?"

"The whole thing!" Jenny felt Pete's heartbeat traveling up her arm. It was calming, soothing, accepting. It gave her the strength to return to that awful time. "She hated me because he paid attention to me and not to Ethan, but Ethan was dead, only she wouldn't admit it, and when Darden couldn't take her yelling about it anymore, he turned to me, which made her *madder*."

"You were a pawn."

"They all said that, too."

"Who?"

"Lawyers, social service workers, police. They said it wasn't my fault, and they kept apologizing, but *they* weren't the ones being asked all the questions. *They* weren't the ones trying to keep the answers straight. I had to tell them everything over and over."

"Want to do it one last time?"

She did. For Pete. He hadn't run out, but was still there, saying he loved her, crouched whisper-close, holding her hand, keeping her calm, and it felt good, so good to talk after such a long, hard silence, to *share* for the very first time, a little weight taken from her chest with each word she spoke.

"My mother was mad at me because I forgot to pick up her pills on the way home from school. They were sleeping pills. She couldn't get through the night without them. I said I'd go back into town, but she said she needed them *now,* and that I was stupid and selfish, and that I was a witch and had Darden under some kind of spell. She started hitting me."

"With the walking stick."

Jenny moaned and nodded. Yes, with the walking stick.

"What did you do?"

She rubbed her palm against his chest. Even calm, even stronger than she had ever been, even relieved to be speaking at last, the remembering was hard. Her body was all rubber and shakes. But Pete's heart was beating that steady tattoo, and his hands held understanding. Suddenly it was like he had opened a door and a force on the other side was sucking the words from her mouth.

"I backed up and tried to protect my-self, but there wasn't much protecting you could do with a stick like that. She tripped me when I tried to run, and then I was on the floor and couldn't go any-where but against the wall. She just kept yelling and whacking me with that thing, and one part of me knew I deserved it—"

"You didn't deserve it."

Jenny swallowed. "I wasn't what she wanted."

"That wasn't your fault."

"But I made it worse."

"How?"

"By letting my father love me."

"*Letting* him? You were a child, Jenny. Children need love. If they don't get it from one parent, they seek it from an-other. Where was he while she was beat-ing you that day?"

"At work. By the time he got home there was blood all over the place. He got scared."

"So he took the walking stick and hit her. One blow, the papers said."

Jenny remembered the sound of it and winced. She remembered the sight of it, the smell of it, and swallowed down a rising bile. "When people are desperate, when they think they're going to die and then they're afraid they won't, they do things they wouldn't be able to do other times."

"So now he's coming home."

She nodded.

"Are you afraid of him?"

She nodded again.

"Then why are you still here?"

Her eyes begged him to understand this, too. "Because he did it for me. Don't you see? He did it so I could be free. Only I'm not. He told me to wait here for him and keep the house going until he got out. So this is my jail. I can't leave because I owe him, and I need to be punished—"

"For *letting* him? No, Jenny."

Explain, she cried. *Tell him everything. He loves you. He won't leave.*

But she couldn't. Not yet. The risk was too great. "And anyway, where would I go? What place is safe? The only things you ever see in the news are bombings and shootings and rape. I've lived here all my life. I don't know anyone anywhere

else, and even if I did, I don't have
enough money to live alone, and there's
no way I'm going to be finding another
job now that Miriam is closing Neat
Eats. I'm *pathetic!*"

He took her face as he had done other
times, only his hands and eyes were fierce
now. "You aren't pathetic."

She squeezed her eyes shut. "Pathetic
and weak and guilty. None of this would
have happened if it wasn't for me."

"You didn't ask to be born. They made
that decision, then they screwed up your
life."

"Pathetic and weak and guilty."

Pete's hands tightened. "Open your
eyes, Jenny."

She couldn't. She was afraid of what
she would find.

"Open them," he said, but more gently
this time, and his hands weren't so much
holding her face as cradling it, ten separate fingers saying that she was precious
and fragile and was to be protected at all
costs.

She opened her eyes.

"If you were either pathetic or weak,
you'd never have survived the last six

years. It hasn't been easy. No one's helped you out much."

"Dan checks up on me."

"Not his father?"

"No. Just Dan. But that's okay. I like him better."

"Does he ask you over for dinner? Does he drive you to the mall when you need clothes? Does he hold your hand when the nightmares come?"

"Reverend Putty came by a lot."

"Past tense."

"Well, he still comes. Just not as often."

"And likely only when Dan asks him to, am I right? Okay, so there was Miriam. She hired you when no one else would, in return for which you worked your butt off. She didn't lose on the deal, and P.S., she didn't ask you to come with her to Seattle, did she. No, Jenny, you aren't pathetic and weak, and as for guilt, guilt is relative. Taken out of context, most anything sounds bad. Look at the whole. You were only eighteen when your mother died. *Only eighteen.*"

Jenny shuddered. "It's like yesterday sometimes, I can see it so clearly, eyes open, eyes closed, night, day, no matter."

"That's the legacy they left you. Has anyone ever apologized for that?"

No one had. No one at all.

"I didn't think so," Pete said. "Now, you want to tell me that after all that, you owe it to Darden to stay here with him for the rest of your life? Ask me, and you don't even have to stay till he gets back!"

She had argued that one with herself. "I think I should."

"Why?"

"Because it's the right thing. He wanted me to meet him at the prison gate. I said no. I couldn't go there, not even one last time. But I said I'd be here, and if I'm not, well, God, I don't know. It'll be pretty bad anyway. He won't want me to leave."

"Can he make you change your mind?"

"I don't want him to," she wailed. "Nothing good can come of it, nothing good ever did, but he's my father, he's the only one I have so close."

"You have me now. That gives you a choice."

"I know, I know, I know."

"Still you're torn."

"Well, if he's changed, mellowed out, you know, it would be awful if I just said hello and goodbye. But he hasn't changed," she reminded herself and hardened. "I've seen him every month. He hasn't changed one bit. And I can't go back. I can't pick up where we left off. I can't. I *won't*. He's a disgusting man. He doesn't care about anyone's needs but his own. And he's jealous, Pete. I don't know *what* he'll do when I tell him about you."

"Well then," Pete said, straightening his shoulders, firming his jaw, looking ready to take Darden on and not the least bit worried, "that's something to look forward to, I'd say."

Jenny tried not to worry. That didn't mean she didn't check the refrigerator three times Monday afternoon to make sure Darden's four six-packs of Sam Adams were there, or that she didn't repeatedly check the bottles of antacid in the medicine chest against Darden's list to make sure she had bought the right brand and strength, or that she didn't unmake the bed with the silk sheets, jump in the middle, roll around, and then make it over—twice—to make it look like she'd been sleeping there all week.

She still hadn't cleaned out her mother's things. She vowed to do it the next morning, no ifs, ands, or buts.

For now, though, what she wanted most was to spend time with Pete, and that's what she did. They stayed in the attic on their bed of pillows and quilts, sometimes naked, sometimes not, and they made love over and over. Jenny was good at it, actually. She knew positions Pete had never thought of. But he was a quick study. His body had a natural flow, fitting around her, responding to her, spurring her higher and higher. He had more stamina, had *ten times* more stamina than she had thought a man could have.

And that was only the first of her discoveries. She learned how beautiful a man's body could be, how gentle and giving, and that she could take from it for her own pleasure and become something more. She learned about sweet afterglows, one after another after another, and about the kind of self-confidence that let you look into a man's eyes for hours without looking away. She learned that kisses could erase scars. She learned what it was to be loved so deeply and rightly that the dirt of the past was washed away and the future became a thing of promise.

No matter that less than a day remained. No matter that there were short, sharp moments of terror when she thought of what might happen when Darden got home and started talking, and what Pete might do then. No matter that there was the guilt, still—always, the guilt.

For the first time in the whole of her adult life, being with Pete, she was happy.

Midday Tuesday, Jenny set off for town. She wore her usual sweatshirt, sneakers, and jeans, but left her baseball cap home. She was tired of hiding. Her hair was curling up, but it was clean and shiny, a beacon to her mood, which was one of high courage and hope even in spite of the morning's phone calls.

Three times Darden had tried. Three

times she had blocked her ears to the ring of the phone. Oh, she knew it was him. No doubt about that. No one else ever called. But she didn't want to hear his voice. Besides, there was nothing he had to say that couldn't wait.

So now she walked toward the center of town, tall and strong, moving like a woman on a mission. Jenny Clyde was ready to fly. She wanted Little Falls to know it.

Chapter Sixteen

BOSTON

It had been Jordan, of course. Nobody else would be wandering around her house in the middle of the night. He caught her arms to steady her and glanced at what she carried.

"I was visiting with Angus," she explained. "While I was in there, I picked up some things to read." She didn't elaborate, and he didn't ask. He actually didn't say a word, just took her hand and led her back to bed. They didn't make love this time, but simply lay in each other's arms until they fell back to sleep—and it was what Casey needed. If she had left Connie's room feeling alarm on Jenny's behalf, it was soothed by Jordan's presence. Like the garden he had made, he exuded calm. Selfishly, knowing that time was short, she took all the calm he offered.

Sure enough, he was up at dawn's first light to go home.

She stayed in bed a few minutes longer to enjoy his lingering scent. As the warmth of his body faded from the sheets, though, she grew restless. When her thoughts reached the churning point, she bolted up. She showered, made coffee, and carried a mug down the stairs.

This morning, Ruth's paintings gave her pause. Seascapes all, they captured the effect of the sun hitting waves in one, a fishing dock in another, a small island in the third. Casey looked from one work to the next. Each conveyed confidence. More, they all conveyed hope, which was what she clung to as she went on through the office and out the French doors.

The garden's silence was broken only by the sweet calls of the birds that came and went from the feeder. Boston was still groggy this Thursday morning. The sun had barely emerged from the harbor to the east.

Sipping her coffee, Casey wandered along the garden path. When she knelt to study Jordan's impatiens, their upturned little faces studied her back. Standing, she wandered among the white flowers, around the patch of pinks, over to the blues. Jordan had reeled off their names, but she had no idea now which went with what.

No. That wasn't so. Looking closely, she could identify a few. She saw bluebells among the blues, and lilies among the whites. Among the pinks, there was bleeding heart; no mistaking their shape.

Bluebells, lilies, and bleeding heart. She felt quite proud of herself. Jordan hadn't mentioned any of these. They were words from her childhood, names to go with shapes. She wasn't Caroline's daughter for nothing.

Fragrance? Well, that was something else. She couldn't identify the separate scents, but the combined bouquet was sweet, indeed.

Carrying the sweetness with her, she climbed up a tier to the azaleas, which had opened enough to show small apricot-colored flowers. The rhododendrons, too, were more open than they'd been the day before. Their flowers were larger and, she could see now, white.

She moved on to the carpet of trillium under the oak, knelt and touched one of the blooms. The petals were three-pronged,

low but elegant. They did well under deciduous trees, Jordan had said. She glanced at
the maple on the other side of the walk. It,
too, had a blanket of flowers beneath it.
These were different, though. Each bloom
was tiny, far less showy than the trillium, but
there were dozens and dozens of them.
They were blue.

Creeping phlox. The name popped into
her head. Caroline had grown creeping
phlox. Hers had been pink.

Casey straightened. Walking all the way
to the back of the garden, she stood and inhaled the evergreens there—inhaled once,
then again, and again. She lingered amid
the pachysandra, then returned to the lilacs,
put her nose to a cluster, and drew in its
scent.

These moments were peaceful. As soon
as she settled into a patio chair to finish her
coffee, though, a sense of urgency returned.
Jenny Clyde was growing more desperate.
In her way, so was Casey. Her mother was
failing; her father remained elusive; and she
knew that there was more to the story of
Flirting with Pete.

Draining the last of the coffee, she returned to the house. For hope—for good

luck—she touched one of Ruth's paintings as she passed, then went on up the stairs. She had already explored the master bedroom and found the clue it held in this bizarre scavenger hunt. Only the storage cartons remained.

First thing, Casey found books. Some were the work of other psychologists, but most were Connie's. Some cartons contained twenty copies of the same book; these cartons had come straight from the publisher. Other cartons held a mix of his books. Every book she opened had his signature on the title page.

Signed copies, she heard her mother say. *You could sell them for more than the retail price of the book. Why do you need all those copies of the same title?*

She could take one of each title for herself. Then she would have signed copies. Somehow, though, getting a signed copy this way hurt.

Turning away from the cartons, she found the boxes that Jordan had carried here from the office. These contained inactive files. Casey perused them only to see if any were labeled "Clyde." When she found none, she went on to the next box, and when she came up empty with that one too, she went on to the next.

She stopped when Meg called up saying that her nine o'clock client had arrived, but she was back up there at noon. Thanks to a cancellation, she had two hours to spend at her search. She was calculating how much headway she could make in two hours when Meg offered to help. She accepted.

Meg opened and closed cartons. Casey sorted contents. She found more books and more files. She found the original copy of Connie's doctoral dissertation, typed on a typewriter whose "w" wasn't quite right. She found original manuscripts of his books.

"What are you looking for?" Meg asked when, with a grunt of frustration, Casey pushed yet another box her way to close.

"Personal things of his," she said, sitting back on her heels. Original manuscripts were a gold mine. Harvard would love them. Casey didn't need them. "Pictures, letters, scrapbook," she said; these she did need. "A high school yearbook. A large manila envelope with a 'C' on the front. Have you ever seen any of those things?"

"No," Meg said as she dovetailed the top

flaps of the carton. "He never asked for my help when he was working up here." Mirroring Casey, she sat back on her heels. "Are these books all his?"

"Yes."

"Do you like to read?"

"I do."

"Have you read his books?"

"Every one."

Meg asked a timid, "Do you think I should try one?"

"One of these? No. They're academic. Not light reading." Casey turned to the next open carton. "Ahh. A me-box."

"Maine."

"Hmm?"

"M-e stands for Maine," Meg said.

Casey stared at her in astonishment, then laughed at herself. "M-e for Maine. Whoa. That one passed me by."

"Maine was Dr. Unger's thing," Meg said with enthusiasm. "That's what the garden's about. Y'know the back part, with the trillium and the junipers and the hemlocks? He told me once that the smell there reminded him of home, and I could believe it. I grew up in Maine, too." She caught herself fast and said an emphatic, "Actually, I *grew up* in New Hampshire, but I was born in Maine, and the landscaping's the same, one state to the other, unless you go to the coast, which is different because of the salt air and the wind."

"So he re-created that smell here." Casey was appalled—she hadn't made that connection either. "But not at the beginning. Before Jordan started working here, the garden was just grass and weeds."

"But then Dr. Unger got homesick. He told me that once, because sometimes I get homesick, too."

"Did he ever go back to visit?"

"I don't know."

"Do you?"

She shook her head. "There's no one I want to see." Abruptly, she brightened. "Did you ever wish you had dark hair?"

Casey smiled at the sudden shift of topic, but she was quickly distracted as she sifted through the first Maine carton. It, too, was filled with books, but of a different sort. These books were old and well used. Connie had signed his name here, too, but not as the author. He had written a careful, formal, child-to-adolescent *Cornelius B. Unger* on the flyleaf to indicate ownership.

She found *Treasure Island* and *The Swiss Family Robinson*, *Moby Dick* and *Gulliver's Travels*. She found *Hans Brinker, or the Silver Skates*, *The Adventures of Tom Sawyer*, and *The Wind in the Willows*.

"Those are old books," Meg said.

They also looked as though they had been read many times. There was a personal feel to these books. She sensed it keenly. The fact that Connie had saved them suggested they were childhood treasures.

There were more in the box, classics as well. After Casey had looked at each one, she put them back and slid the carton to Meg.

"So, *do* you like your hair?" Meg asked. She was wearing one of the scrunchies Casey had given her. It had lavender shades in it, and looked really pretty with her auburn hair.

"Yes."

"What about your freckles?"

Casey smiled. "I'm okay with them now. I used to hate them."

Meg's eyes went wide. "You did?"

Casey nodded. "Covered them with

makeup before I had any business *wearing* makeup."

"You *did?*" Meg asked in delight.

"Yup." Casey dug into the next box and emerged with more children's books. Same with a third box.

"I guess he really liked to read," Meg remarked. "Why do you think he kept these?"

It was certainly the right question. Casey wished she had a good answer. "Maybe because he loved to read. Or because someone he loved gave them to him. Or because he knew these editions would be valuable one day."

Meg said, "I think he was saving them for grandchildren."

"He doesn't have any grandchildren."

"But he will. Don't you plan to have kids?"

Casey wondered how the man could think of giving books to grandchildren when he wasn't even on speaking terms with his *child*. Same thing with setting up bedrooms for grandchildren. She wondered what kind of fantasy life he had lived, all alone here in his beautiful home.

"Don't you?" Meg asked.

"Don't I what?"

"Plan to have kids?"

"At some point."

"Do you worry about your biological clock?"

"Not yet."

"I do. I want kids."

"Do you have a boyfriend?"

Meg shook her head no. More quietly, with diffidence, she said, "Someday, maybe." She perked up. "Do *you* have a boyfriend?"

Casey thought for a minute. She couldn't call Jordan a boyfriend. She was sleeping with him, though, so he had to be something.

She compromised with an affirmative, "In a manner of speaking. For the time being, at least. But no more hints. My lips are sealed." With a glance at her watch, she reached for another box. "One more of these babies, and then I'm back to work."

That last box contained high school notebooks. They told her Connie had studied chemistry, Latin and French, American history, and art. They did not tell her where he went to high school, though that was the information she wanted. Hard as she looked, she couldn't find the name of the high school or the town—and by then, she had a client waiting, so she had to postpone the search.

Joyce Lewellen came at three. Her face was drawn, her fingers laced, knuckles white. "I'm not sleeping. I'm not eating. I'm just sitting home, walking from one room to the other. It's like right after he died."

"Do you know the judge's decision?" Casey asked.

"No. We get it tomorrow. So here I am, anticipating losing and feeling the same old anger. I can't talk to family, can't talk to friends. I've seen them roll their eyes or give a kind of . . . sigh. They're tired of me talking about it. They don't understand at all what I'm feeling. How can they? They may have loved Norman, but he wasn't part of their daily lives. He wasn't key to their future."

Casey suspected it was more a case of family and friends having lost interest in the fight. They had moved on. So had Joyce's daughters. Joyce was the only one who was running in place, going absolutely nowhere at all.

"Can you get him back?" Casey asked quietly.

"No. I can't. I know that. But winning this case—it'll give me something. It'll end the whole thing."

"Closure."

"Yes. If I win, I get closure."

"And if you don't win?"

"No closure."

"Why not?"

"I'll always wonder why he died."

"What have the doctors said?" Casey asked. She knew the answer, but it didn't hurt to have Joyce say it aloud.

"They said he had a massive reaction to the anesthesia. He'd never had anesthesia before. How was I to know?"

"You? Why would you know? *How* would you know?"

"Someone should have."

"Why you? Why not his mother?"

"How would she know? He'd never had anesthesia before. I just said that."

"Exactly. No one knew that he would react the way he did—not his mother, not him, and certainly not you. On the other hand, you've done everything you could to find an answer to why he died. Regardless of how the judge rules, you can find closure in that."

Joyce looked torn. "What if I can't? I mean, it's one thing to say that there isn't enough evidence to get a jury to convict. But that doesn't mean there isn't *some* evidence. Who's to say that the evidence we have isn't correct? That's why I need a win. I need a definitive decision. 'Not enough evidence' won't do it for me. I need this resolved."

Casey could identify with that. By the time she got back upstairs, it was late afternoon, and, bent on a resolution of her own, she was energized. She guessed that between the two rooms, there were still a dozen boxes she hadn't searched. Alone now, she went at them with a vengeance, pulling, pushing, bending over rather than sitting so that she could more quickly examine the contents of each.

When all was said and done, only one was memorable. The most personal of the cartons, it contained relics of Connie's childhood. There was one crocheted afghan, slightly tattered. There were a pair of tiny brown shoes, badly scuffed. There were several baby pictures, showing Connie in various stages prior to school age. He was a sweet, vulnerable-looking child whose features pulled at her with their familiarity. It was a minute before she realized she saw herself in them.

Likewise, the hair. There was a glassine envelope with a lock the identical color of Casey's. She felt a catch in her throat, a visceral link, when she reached in and sifted that hair between her fingers.

But the monkey got to her even more. It was faded brown and stuffed, with scraggly legs and patchy fur. One clouded eye hung by a thread, the other was missing altogether. It was the sweetest, rattiest thing Casey had ever seen. Lifting it with care, she buried her nose in its sparse little belly. It had the musty smell of age. She guessed that Connie had loved it. Guessed that he had slept with it long after anyone was supposed to know. Guessed that he had given it a life, a name, and a personality, such that to toss it away would have been murder.

That was certainly what she had felt about her stuffed duck. Daffy. Not terribly original, but there you had it. Daffy. Its wings went in different directions, and its beak curved to the side, but she hadn't ever been able to pack it away. Even now, it sat on her dresser back at the condo, its lumpy body propped against a lamp.

Her Daffy had loved her with all his little stuffed heart at that time in her life when she badly wanted two parents. She didn't know what Connie's need had been for this monkey, but she knew that she couldn't put it back in that box. She couldn't even leave it with Angus on Connie's bed.

Carrying it downstairs, she propped it against the pillow in her pale blue room, angled toward the nightstand, where the photograph of Connie lay. That must have been the right thing to do, because the monkey settled in and looked content. That was some solace to Casey, because when it came to learning more about *Flirting with Pete,* she had struck out. In all of the cartons, there had been nothing remotely resembling a large manila envelope with a "C" on the front. She didn't know where else to look.

Discouraged, she headed for the garden, but found herself instead sitting on the carpeted runner that covered the stairs leading down to the office, studying Ruth's paintings. If woodlands were the center of Connie's life, the ocean was the center of hers. Where he favored deep, dark shades of greens, reds, and blues, Ruth's art sparkled with pastels. If ever there was a statement of the difference between two people, these paintings were it. Casey wondered for the umpteenth time what had ever drawn them together.

Ruth's paintings were hopeful and bright, even at dusk in the stairwell's shadow. They were an invitation. She was sorely tempted. But torn.

Thursday nights were for yoga, and Casey needed the class. She skipped it, though, because even more than yoga, she needed to talk with her mother. She figured that Caroline might have a word or two to say on the matter of Ruth.

This night, however, Caroline didn't have a word to say on any matter at all. She was sleeping, perhaps breathing more heavily than normal, though not sounding distressed. Feeling a great big lump in the pit of her stomach, Casey sat by her side, held her bent hand, and studied her face in the dim evening light. She didn't mention

Ruth's name. She didn't have the heart, with everything else Caroline had to fight.

After a while, she called softly, "Mom?" She waited, watched for a blink, a twitch, even the tiniest tic to indicate awareness. "Do you know I'm here, Mom?" She waited, watched, grew frightened. "I need to know what's going on with you. This is starting to make me nervous."

Caroline just lay there, propped on her side with her eyes closed.

Casey leaned closer. "Can you hear me?" she asked in full voice.

She waited a while longer. Caroline remained motionless, breathing in small echoes. In time, unable to deal with the fear, Casey kissed her mother's cheek, stroked her hair, and said, "It's okay, Mom. You're tired. We'll talk next time I come. You'll feel better then. I love you." Her voice broke. She kissed Caroline's cheek once more and pressed her forehead there to absorb Caroline's warmth. She needed that warmth. It had been there for her even when she had sworn off it in the name of independence. She had been shortsighted then. She saw that now. One could need warmth and still be quite independent. Caroline had known that. Through good and bad, she had been loyal and loving. Casey didn't want to lose her.

Fearing that it might happen anyway and not wanting to face that possibility, she gently put her mother's hand on the sheet and backed out of the room.

Friday, in Casey's book, was professional enrichment day, on which, typically, she attended seminars, met with colleagues, read professional journals. On occasion, she went to the beach. Restorative therapy, she called it.

She headed for the beach this Friday morning, but not to play. She needed answers, and Ruth Unger was the only one left who might have them.

She called first, of course. She didn't want to drive all the way to Rockport and find that Ruth wasn't there.

Ruth answered the phone. Casey hung up. Juvenile? Yes. But she had a right to a moment's regression. Her disdain for Ruth went back to her teens, when she had first discovered the woman's existence. Lacking other explanations for how Connie could ignore his daughter, she made Ruth the bad guy.

Ruth had stolen him from Caroline, or so ran the first scenario. Connie had been on the verge of calling Caroline again, when Ruth had stepped right in, turned his head, and pinned him down.

Ruth had poisoned him against Casey, went another scenario. When Connie had expressed an interest in contacting Casey, Ruth had gone into a jealous rage. She wanted him to focus on making *her* pregnant, rather than distracting himself with the product of a one-night stand—who might not even be *his* child, Casey imagined Ruth arguing, because *we* don't know who else Caroline Ellis was seeing at the time.

Casey even imagined that Ruth had gone so far as to snatch letters Connie had written to Casey from the outgoing mail.

In time, the scenarios fell apart. The more Casey learned about the workings of the human mind—and the more she watched Connie—the more she held him responsible for his own behavior.

Not that Ruth was completely off the hook. Casey didn't understand why, particularly after the years passed and they remained childless, she hadn't prodded Connie into making even the smallest gesture toward his only child. Casey didn't understand why she hadn't made the gesture herself—or called Casey to tell her of Connie's death—or why she hadn't contacted her since.

These thoughts simmered in her as she headed north on I-93. They gained heat as she drove northeast on Route 128 and were hot enough when she reached Gloucester for her to consider turning back. But she was out of options. And besides, she reasoned, if she lost her temper and let loose on Ruth, it was nothing Ruth didn't deserve.

Turning onto Route 127, she followed the curve of Cape Ann until she reached Rockport. She knew the way to Ruth's house from the center of town. She had driven it before—oh, not all the way up from Boston just to see Ruth's house, but she had driven past it four, maybe five times in the last dozen years, when she'd been in Rockport anyway, doing the tourist thing. Other than growing more gray from the blow of sea salt, the house hadn't changed much.

It sat at the end of a street with stubby grass and coastal shrubs, a Cape-style home with a large slate roof that slanted up and back from a conventional doorway flanked by windows. Casey parked in front and went up the stone walk. She rang the bell and waited, head down, wondering why in the world she had come, but she was too stubborn to leave.

The door opened.

Casey knew what Ruth looked like. She had seen her at Connie's side during professional dinners, and, more recently, had seen her at the memorial service. On each of these occasions, Casey had thought her conventional looking for an artist. But conventional wasn't the feeling Ruth conveyed now. For one thing, since last week, she had cut her hair from an ear-length bob to a short, feathery cap. What had been a mousy salt-and-pepper shade was now more salt-and-shiny, and what had been a tidy helmet was now windblown. A slim woman, several inches taller than Casey, she wore a soft pale blue shirt that flowed down over a tank top and shorts. Her feet were bare, her toenails orange.

She looked . . . looked so much like what Casey imagined Caroline would have

looked like in another ten years that her
throat grew tight.

Ruth seemed nearly as taken aback as
Casey, but she was the first to recover, and
in the most unexpected way. She broke into
a bright smile that was filled with genuine
warmth. "Casey. I'm *so* pleased." She
reached for Casey's hand. "Come in."

Casey didn't resist. Totally aside from
Ruth's appearance, the last thing she had
expected was that Ruth would be pleased
to see her. That unbalanced her at a time
when she was still trying to deal with the
knot in her throat, and then there was the
house. Inside that Cape-style exterior was a
veritable cavern of tall windows, skylights,
and glass doors leading to a deck that offered no less than three different ocean
views. Here was the artist's home, with an
easel, holding the work-in-progress, set up
at one of the windows, and other canvases
in various stages of completion propped
around.

"I'm *so* pleased," Ruth repeated, still smiling.

Gradually Casey got her bearings enough
to realize that a small part of her was
pleased, too. Ruth was one step removed

from a relative, and she seemed genuinely happy to see Casey.

But Casey couldn't forget the history of this particular near-relative. So she asked a blunt, "Why?"

Ruth's smile faltered, but she remained warm. "Because you're Connie's daughter. Now that he's gone, the sight of you does my heart good."

Casey was suddenly angry again. "Why now that he's gone?"

"Because I miss him." Ruth's smile was gone now, leaving kind features in a serious face. "And because this is long overdue. I've been wanting to meet you for a while."

"Why have you waited?"

Ruth hesitated, then said with care, "Because Connie did not want the contact made."

"Why *not?*" Casey asked. This was why she'd come.

Ruth drew in a long breath. "It's not a simple answer. Will you come sit on the deck?"

Casey would have been perfectly happy getting her answers there by the door, then turning and leaving. But there was something about Ruth's genuineness, and the brightness of her home, and the hope inherent in her art that spoke to Casey. So she let herself be led toward the deck through the living room, first past a large white sectional sofa that formed a U and was flanked by a stone coffee table bearing art books, elegant carvings, and large iron lamps, then past the easel and canvases.

"Would you like a cold drink?" Ruth asked when they were on the deck.

Casey shook her head. Grasping the railing, she faced the sea. The tide was out, leaving a foreground covered with seaweed-strewn rocks. Gulls called to each other as they dove, rose, coasted on air currents. The waves rolled, crashed, and receded in a soothing rhythm.

Through no will of her own, Casey's anger faded.

Ruth came to stand at the railing not far from her side. She, too, looked out. "I was always an ocean person. Connie wasn't. He liked things closer and more contained."

Casey turned her head. "Why?"

Ruth met her gaze. "Security. He didn't trust things that made him feel helpless."

"Where did that come from?"

"You know the answer."

Casey certainly did. "Childhood, only I

don't know a thing about his. I don't even know the name of the town where he grew up."

"Abbott."

"Not Little Falls?" Casey challenged.

"I've never heard of a Little Falls. He came from Abbott."

Abbott. A name so long sought, that simply revealed.

"It's a small town in Maine," Ruth explained, "though I can't tell you much more than that. I never saw the place myself. When we were first married, I used to suggest taking a drive there, but he refused to go back. The years he spent there weren't happy ones."

"Why not?"

Ruth turned troubled eyes to the ocean. It was a long minute before she faced Casey again. "He was always such a private person—didn't want anyone knowing about his past—but he's gone, and you're his flesh and blood. If anyone has reason to know, you do. It's not like there was anything violent or perverted. I used to think there was," she confessed. "I used to imagine some great big awful event that warped him forever."

So had Casey. "And there wasn't?"

"No. No single act of mayhem, just years of hurt. Connie was born puny and bright. Neither trait was appreciated in Abbott. He was the object of derision from the time he was the smallest child—ridiculed, taunted mercilessly, made the butt of jokes. He was withdrawing from people even before he started grade school, and with the pattern established, it became self-perpetuating."

Casey could easily make the transition from the child Ruth described to the man Connie had become. But there was the element of intervention. "What did his parents do?"

"What *could* they do?"

"Sell the farm."

Ruth smiled ruefully. "There was no farm. Not as you and I know it. If his mother grew vegetables or raised chickens, it was to put food on their own table. They lived close to the center of town in a very small house on a very small piece of land. I'm not even sure they owned it. Whatever, they couldn't afford to move away. Money was short, and living in Abbott was cheap."

"Victimizing their child was about *money?*"

"No," Ruth said with care. "It was also about Connie's father, Frank. Frank was a burly, physical type—everything Connie was not. He was *convinced* that if anything could 'cure' Connie of being a sissy, it was the macho culture of Abbott. Clearly, it didn't work. Connie's life was a misery. The only way he could survive was to put up walls."

"What about Connie's mother? How could she stand by and watch that?"

"Not easily, I think. She did have a soft spot for Connie, but she was first and foremost a docile wife. Her husband had firm beliefs, and she wouldn't buck them—and who am I to criticize her for that? I haven't done much different. We call it respecting our spouse's wishes."

Casey didn't think the situations were at all alike. "But Connie was a child. He was suffering. I can't imagine being a mother and not doing anything to help."

"She did help. Very quietly, she did what she could."

"Like what?"

"Encouragement. The father didn't know if Connie should go to college."

"Didn't want him *bettering* himself?" Casey asked, dumbfounded.

"Didn't want him growing even more isolated from what his father considered to be normal, quote unquote, and healthy. When push came to shove, the man might have been okay with Connie's going to U of Maine, because he worked there himself, but Harvard?" She shook her head. "That was Connie's doing. And he didn't do it alone. His mother was behind him, quiet and invisible, but pushing. He won a full scholarship, left Abbott, and never returned."

"Not even to see his parents?"

"His father died right before he left, and his mother moved away. This was all a long, long time ago."

"But indelibly etched," Casey said.

"Yes. Connie never got over it. His personal life was ruled by fear of ridicule and rejection. So he enhanced his professional life. With each degree he earned, each paper he delivered, each book he wrote, he felt justified in distancing himself. His credentials grew into a shield."

Casey saw it clearly. "He became the professor who was so brilliant that his eccentricities were excused. And that, too, became self-perpetuating. The more it happened, the less accessible he was for personal relationships, and without personal relationships, he wasn't open to hurt." Only there was a big piece of the picture missing. "How in the world did he ever come to be with my mother?"

Ruth smiled sadly. "The same way he came to be with me. Hope dies hard. He always desired acceptance. He dreamed of love."

"Don't we all?" Casey countered. "But the rest of us can at least carry on a personal *discussion* with a friend. Not Connie. Yet he had an affair with my mother. So, how did he get past his fear of rejection?"

"He ended the relationship before he could be rejected—at least, that was the case with your mother. In my case, he ended the intimacy. Just withdrew into himself. Or maybe," she said more introspectively, "he was that way all along, only I thought it would be different once we were married. I thought he was just old-fashioned, waiting until marriage to share his deepest, darkest thoughts."

"You thought you could change him."

"No," Ruth corrected patiently. "I thought he was different." She grew introspective again. "But the times were different, too. Back then, we met, dated a little while, decided to get married, and just did it. We made the decision as much on practical matters as love. When I met Connie, he was already a well-respected professor, already published many times over. Yes, he was painfully shy, but I found that endearing. More important, he offered me a financial stability that I wanted." She smiled. "I wanted to paint, but I didn't want to starve while I did it. Also, quite honestly, I didn't want to be bothered while I painted, so the fact that Connie had his own busy professional life appealed to me."

"And love?"

"I loved Connie. The more I learned about him, the more I loved him." She held up a hand. "Yes, I know that sounds strange, but don't you see? Connie was a victim of a childhood that scarred him badly."

"Did he never have therapy for that?"

Ruth shook her head. "An irony, isn't it? He's the doctor who can't hear of being a patient. Had he been a psychiatrist, he might have been forced to have therapy.

But it wasn't required for his degree, and he didn't seek it out on his own."

"It was too threatening."

"Far too threatening. I used to suggest it. Way back, when I didn't know whether to divorce him or just move out, I told him he needed it. I told him he was missing out on good things in life. I offered to see a therapist *with* him." She gave a quick headshake. "*Far* too threatening. So I did move out—and, lo and behold, our relationship improved."

"Connie was less threatened."

"In fairness, I was better, too. My expectations changed. As soon as I accepted him for what he could and could not do, I was fine."

"But . . . living apart from your husband all these years?"

Ruth smiled. "I have friends. I have not been lonely. Besides, you may be too young to understand this, but there are scores of women who would find separate living an ideal situation. I got the best of my husband, along with all the freedom in the world."

"But no kids," Casey pointed out.

Ruth eyed her directly. "I can't have kids. I knew that before I was married."

Casey felt instant remorse. "I'm sorry."

"Things happen for the best. I've had a rich life. I sometimes fantasize about having had a daughter, but we might as easily have been at each other's throats as not. I have nieces and nephews, and now grands of each."

That raised another issue. "In the townhouse, the spare bedrooms upstairs?" Casey asked. "What's their purpose?"

Ruth smiled gently, said quietly, "Dreams. Connie did dream of lots of things. You might not believe this, but many of those dreams revolved around you."

A flash of anger returned. "Why couldn't he pick up the phone?" Casey cried, and in the next breath answered herself. "Fear. Fear of rejection."

"Fear of failure."

Casey suffered from that herself, but she had never guessed it of Connie. "Failure?"

"Fear that he'd be a lousy father. He might not have had therapy, but he did know his limitations."

"And he couldn't get past them?" Casey asked in a last-ditch attempt at criticism—

because her heart had indeed softened. It had softened toward Ruth, who was no longer just a name and a face, but had become very real, very sympathetic, even likable. And it had softened toward Connie.

"No. He couldn't get past them."

"But he knew about me. He knew where I was and what I was doing."

"Yes."

"Did he care?"

"He left you the townhouse. He loved that place, truly loved it. He could have had it sold and given the proceeds to charity, but he gave it to you. So you tell me. Did he care?"

Casey couldn't answer. Her throat was too tight.

Ruth rescued her. "He cared. Believe me. He cared. Connie had feelings just like you and I do. He just expressed them differently. In my case, it was calling me at six in the evening, every single day that we weren't together, to make sure that I was all right. In your case, it was decorating the townhouse in a way he thought you might like. Yes, he did that. In your mother's case, it's the flowers."

"Flowers?"

"He has fresh ones delivered to her room every week."

"No," Casey said. "The nursing home does that."

Slowly, conclusively, Ruth shook her head. And suddenly it made sense. Casey had never seen flowers in the rooms of other long-term patients. Nor would the nurses be remarking on the flowers, as they so often did, if flowers were just another part of the package. Casey had just assumed . . .

Casey had hit a jackpot in her scavenger hunt for learning who Connie was, yet she left Rockport feeling deflated. In learning so much, she had given up a lot. How to be angry at Ruth? She wasn't the enemy. How even to be angry at Connie? He was a victim in his own right.

But Casey needed an enemy. She needed someone to blame for Connie being Connie, for Caroline being unresponsive, for the call earlier that morning, wondering if she had made a decision about the teaching position in Providence—which she had not, she explained, and begged for more time. A definite answer by Monday? Yes, she could do that.

No enemy there. The department had to offer the job to another therapist if Casey turned it down. They were under pressure, too. She couldn't find fault with them.

Who, then, to blame for the ills of the world? Darden Clyde was a fair candidate, and she did have a lead. Abbott, Maine. It might not be Little Falls, but it was a place to start. She planned to do that first thing in the morning.

More immediately, though, there was Jordan. She could be angry at Jordan. He hadn't been in the garden that morning, though it was Friday and he was due. She had done an extra-long yoga routine just in case, but no Jordan, and that worried her. He might have come while she was in Rockport; she knew instinctively that he wouldn't neglect the garden. But *she* was not the garden. She was a thinking, feeling human being with whom he was doing some very intimate things. Yet he hadn't shown up Thursday night—hadn't come by, hadn't called, hadn't held her.

Of course, he had no obligation to do any of those things. They weren't really friends.

She could barely call them lovers. Those very intimate things they did together? Sex. That was all it was. Sex. She knew next to nothing about him.

Suddenly that felt wrong. So she drove straight back to the townhouse, feeling anticipation the closer she got. She was trying to decide whether the anticipation had to do with seeing Jordan or coming home—an amazing thought, *that* one—when she pulled down the back alley into view of the parking space behind the garden. Jordan's Jeep wasn't there.

Disappointed, she took a quick look inside the garden, just in case—and there was definitely a sense of the familiar now. Unable to resist, she went inside and stood in the woodsy part. If she moved in close to the hemlocks so that she saw nothing but green fronds, and if she then inhaled, she might well have been in the midst of a forest; the sensory effect was the same. Nature was a potent drug. God as clinician, she thought with a smile. Divine aromatherapy.

Feeling calmer, she set off on foot for Daisy's Mum, heading for the address that had been printed on the receipts for the checks Connie had written. It was an easy walk past brownstones, lindens, and window-box geraniums, down West Cedar to Revere, then down Revere to the tiny side street just shy of Charles. The store was the only one amid a handful of townhouses, but, even aside from the customers who browsed on the sidewalk, there was no missing it. A long awning stretched over its front windows and doors; it was striped, burgundy and white to complement the brick of the neighboring townhouses, but the crowd of plants that lay under the awning put those townhouses' window boxes to shame. The plants in front, bathed in sun, offered a profusion of flowers in bright yellows, whites, purples, and blues. A handful of other flowering plants hung in the shade of the awning, along with dozens of green plants.

The fragrance of the flowers lured Casey forward. Inside, she found a surprisingly small space with a stone floor and walls, stacks of decorative pots, and a bevy of garden sculptures. The plants here were green; color came from cut flowers that stood, grouped in kind, in tin vases of various sizes and heights. A stone slab marked the checkout counter. Behind it, writing out a sales slip, was a pretty woman wearing a white cotton shirt and jeans—Daisy herself, judging from her sense of command. She looked to be in her mid-forties.

Casey waited her turn without any feeling of impatience. Though the store was a fraction of the size of her own garden, it conveyed the same sense of peace. Plants did that, she decided. They were natural and beautiful. Aside from the poison ivy type, they weren't hurtful as humans could be.

"May I help you?" Daisy asked.

Casey stepped up to the counter. "I'm Casey Ellis, Connie Unger's daughter. Are you Daisy?"

The woman broke into a broad smile. "I am," she said, and held out a hand. "I'm so pleased to meet you. We adored your father." Her smile faded. "I was so sorry to hear about his death. He was a very sweet person."

Casey nodded. "He left me the townhouse. I just wanted to tell you how spectacular the garden is."

Daisy smiled again. "Thank you. That was Jordan's doing."

"Is he here?"

"Now? No. He should be back soon, though. I know that he has to clean up for an appointment at four." She tossed a glance at the ceiling. "His phone's been ringing."

Casey mirrored the tossed glance. "Is that the office?"

"Oh, no. He lives up there."

"Ah."

"It's so much better having someone right here. He answers the phone off-hours and all."

"Ah."

"I believe he was hitting your place after his appointment. Would you like me to leave him a message?"

"Nah," Casey said with a casual shake of her head. "It was nothing important. I'll catch him when he's at the house. I'm glad I stopped by, though. The shop is a delight." She took a business card from the holder by the register. It had the name of the shop drawn in elegant scrollwork. "Really pretty."

Daisy smiled. "Thanks. Stop by again."

"Will do." Casey slipped the card into her pocket and went out the door feeling that the shop, and Daisy, were new friends.

As she headed back toward the townhouse, though, her thoughts turned to Jordan. Funny. She had assumed that her garden was the focus of his day. Naturally, she had wanted to think that. Seeing the flower shop, though, feeling the buzz of activity, hearing Daisy talk about phone calls and appointments, she realized that she was only one of the stops he made in his day. He was a busy man. He had a whole other life that had nothing to do with her garden.

Well, so did she.

She gave him one last chance. When she arrived at the townhouse, though, and found him nowhere in sight, she went inside and put overnight things in her gym bag along with the three installments of *Flirting with Pete*. She spoke softly with Angus for a minute from the door to Connie's room. She told Meg that she might not be back for a day or two. She stopped in at Connie's office for a map.

Then she put her bag in the trunk of the Miata, climbed inside, and headed for Maine.

Chapter Seventeen

The farther Casey drove from Boston, the more urgency she felt. Caroline was laboring for breath again; Casey called en route and learned that. The doctors were monitoring her for signs of infection. In patients like Caroline, infection was one of the major causes of death.

Casey debated turning around and driving back. But she couldn't bear feeling useless—still, yet, again. Besides, if Caroline had taught her anything, it was to act on her beliefs. She might not approve of Casey's cause, but she would approve of Casey's going after it. Connie, conversely, would approve of the cause—at least, the part of it that involved Jenny Clyde.

It wasn't often that Casey had the approval of both of her parents, and this felt right. She couldn't back off now.

So she kept her foot on the gas and the

car headed north. An hour into the drive, she passed through the southeast corner of New Hampshire. By then, she had returned a call to one of her yoga friends, who was concerned when she hadn't shown up at class the night before, and to a client who wanted to reschedule an appointment.

When she entered Maine, the highway opened up. A number of cars turned off at the outlet stores in Kittery, then again at the Ogunquit exits, then again when she hit Portland, but by the time she passed the two-hour mark, even Portland was behind her.

She stopped, filled the car with gas, checked the map, and drove on. By the time she reached Augusta, three hours had passed, she had picked up a new client through a referral, and, phone calls notwithstanding, she was tired of the highway. It was another hour yet, though, before she reached Bangor. At that point, she left the highway, trading speed for interest. The road north now had one lane in each direction. As fate had it, she ended up behind a rusted pickup with Maine plates, going on the slow side of thirty miles an hour.

She ruled out honking as a city thing. She

ruled out passing as suicidal. More wisely, she executed a few deep yoga breaths, paced herself comfortably behind the pickup, and took in the scenery. Pines and firs hugged the sides of the road, greens and blues in such subtle variations that the palette was entirely soothing. She passed the occasional open field with a farmhouse, lean-to, or garage. She passed the occasional little home so neatly tucked into the woods that she wouldn't have seen it had she been driving faster. She passed the occasional lake.

She nearly missed Abbott. Forty minutes off the highway as she cruised at under thirty miles an hour, it was little more than a bump in the road that included a Grange Hall, a post office, and a convenience store. Famished by now, she pulled up in front of the store. Three boys in their late teens, wearing earrings, tattoos, and evil-looking tee shirts, slouched on a bench in front cupping cigarettes in their hands, as though tendrils of smoke, alone, wouldn't give them away.

Casey could identify with rebellion. She had been there herself. But she wouldn't want to tangle with this trio in a dark alley.

She pictured a young Connie, in Ruth's words "puny and brilliant," and couldn't help but think that if the boys in town had been as rough looking in his day, he wouldn't have had a chance.

Trying to look as unassuming as possible, Casey parked the Miata, went up the wood steps, and on into the store. She was relieved to be inside not only because of the boys, but because in addition to shelves of packaged foods, there was a counter with a short-order cook. Climbing onto a stool with a cracked leather seat, she gave a quick glance at the handwritten menu board and ordered macaroni and cheese and a Coke. Being the only customer there, she didn't have long to wait— only as long as it took for the woman to turn to the pots on the burner, scoop up a ladleful of the stuff, and glop it on a plate.

"Just passing through?" she asked when she slid the plate in front of Casey.

The macaroni and cheese was crusted on top. It was comfort food, and Casey felt in need of that. "I don't know," she said, fork in hand. "That depends. I'm looking for information on a family by the name of Unger. They lived here a while back."

The woman put her elbows on the counter and frowned. "Unger? Huh. I've lived here all my life. That's forty-five years. Never heard that name, though."

Casey would have guessed that the woman was older than forty-five. She looked weary in an expansive, worldly way. Prominent lines between her brows and shoulders that sloped steeply suggested that she had borne the weight of big worries for far more than forty-five years.

"You may be too young," Casey said. "I'm guessing that this family left town fifty-five years ago, give or take." She ate a forkful of macaroni and cheese.

"You need to see Dewey Heller. He's seventy, but he's been town clerk for the last hundred years. His office is down back of the Grange Hall. If anyone would remember, he's the one, but he's long gone for the day now."

"Can I go to his house?"

"You could."

Casey waited. When nothing more was forthcoming, she said, "Would you tell me where he lives?"

The woman shook her head. "He'd fire me. He owns this place." She shot a quick glance around. "It was a general store until he hit sixty and lost interest. He doesn't take kindly to pretty people in fancy sports cars. That's a nice one out there. Aren't you worried our boys might decide to take it for a spin?"

Casey swallowed another mouthful of macaroni and cheese. Then she smiled. "I'm a city girl. That car has every antitheft device you've ever heard of and then some. No, that's not a problem. The *problem* is that tomorrow's Saturday. Will your town clerk be in then?"

"Nine to eleven. He takes Monday's off to make up for it."

That appeased Casey, but only briefly. She still had the rest of the day here in Abbott, and couldn't bear the thought of wasting the time. "If I can't talk with the town clerk today, what about the police department?"

"Department?" The woman gave her a wry grin. "Try officer. One. Uh-huh, you could talk with him, but he's young. He's only been in town ten years. It's hard to keep them, when you can't pay them much." She glanced at the door. "Well, give it a try. Here he comes."

The khaki-clad officer was named Buck Thorman. A year or two older than Casey, he was tall, blond, and well built. The cook made the introductions and went to another part of the store. Straddling the stool two down from Casey, Buck asked the kind of questions that cops in small towns could be expected to ask when a stranger showed up.

Casey indulged him. Yes, that was her car. No, she hadn't bought it new. Yes, it had a stick shift. Overdrive, yes. Cassette, no; CD, yes. One-twenty-eight horses, thank you. No, she never drove over eighty.

"So why're you here?" he asked when the important stuff was done.

"I'm tracing my family tree. It includes people by the name of Unger. They lived in Abbott a while back."

"Must have been a big while back. I've never heard of any Ungers."

Casey didn't point out that he hadn't been in town but ten years, which wasn't all *that* big a while back. He was preening now, still straddling the stool but with his back to the counter and his elbows braced there in a way that showed off the breadth of a mus-cled chest. She felt no attraction at all, but she wasn't about to tell him that. She was here for a purpose. If he could assist her, she would let him think what he wanted.

"How about Clydes?" she asked. "Darden Clyde? MaryBeth Clyde?"

He scratched his chin. "Now, that's familiar. Where did I hear that name?"

She held her breath. After a minute, he gave a bewildered shrug. "What about a town called Little Falls?" she asked.

The officer pursed his lips, shook his head. "No Little Falls. I know Duck Ridge, West Hay, and Walker. I know Dornville and Eppick. Little Falls? Nope."

Casey let out a short breath. She was getting tired of dead ends.

"Want a tour of town?" he asked, as though that might ease her disappointment. "Abbott's not a bad place." He leaned closer and said under his breath, "Not very exciting, which is why the good kids leave and we're stuck with the geniuses out front."

"Don't judge a book . . . ," she cautioned. "I was a rebel once. So where do the 'good kids' go?"

He shrugged with his mouth. "Bangor, Augusta, Portland. There's more to do there. More jobs. Me, I'm just paying my dues here, if you get my drift. It's a pretty dry place, never much by the way of interesting crime." He snapped his fingers and ended with his pointer aimed her way. "That's why the name's familiar. Fourteen, fifteen years ago there was a murder involving a pair of Clydes."

Casey's hopes rose. "That's it," she said with enthusiasm. "Husband and wife. Fourteen or fifteen years ago?"

"Don't quote me on that."

"It happened in Little Falls."

Officer Thorman shook his head. "Well, that could be, but there's no Little Falls around here. Maybe it's in another part of the state."

"Do you remember where it happened, from the murder coverage?"

"Nah. I mostly remember the trial, and it would have taken place in Augusta or Portland. I might've paid heed if I'd been older, or if it had involved international stuff, like terrorism. But domestic violence?" He stretched out long, solid legs and gave a long-suffering sigh. "I grew up hearing about domestic violence. It gets boring after a while, whether you're seeing it around you or trying to police it. A couple more years here, then I'm going for the FBI. But hey, tell you what. Let me show you around town, and it'll make my week. Hell, it'll make my *month*."

Casey did want to see Abbott. Her father had grown up here. Casey had no cause to doubt Ruth on that.

Finishing her macaroni and cheese, she poured the Coke into a take-out cup, paid the bill, and, while Thorman warned the trio of boys that if they so much as *touched* the Miata he would bust them for the pot they'd been smoking right there on the bench two days before, she slid into the passenger seat of the cruiser.

Heading off on a side street, he drove her first to the local garage and introduced her around. Next, he drove her past the Laundromat and past an appliance repair shop. Then he drove her past the stone ruins of a large building on the banks of a stream.

"That was the shoe plant," he explained. "I'm told that at one point most everyone in town was connected to it in one way or another."

Casey was intrigued. Pivotal stuff had gone on in these plants.

She imagined that Connie's mother—her grandmother!—had worked here, and felt the twinge of a connection. She might have liked to get out and explore the plant, but Thorman drove right on, this time to the schoolhouse—and she did get out here. She couldn't resist.

"All closed up for the year?" she asked, gesturing him to pull up at the cracked cement walk.

"Closed up for good," he replied. "The kids go to a regional school."

Leaving the cruiser, she wandered around the old frame building and tried to imagine Connie here. Harvard Yard this was not, but that actually made Connie easier to understand. He, too, was a dichotomy—the successful professional versus the shy and lonely child, grown to boy, then to man. She could see Connie here, sitting on the ground at the base of the gnarled gray oak, watching the other kids play.

When she returned to the cruiser, the officer drove her up and down streets that were lined with very old houses and very old trees. Houses and trees were both shabby, though Casey imagined they weren't always that way. The houses were small, sensibly built, and spaced comfortably apart. Those that were larger weren't vertically so. Rather, they were like trains, with additional cars hitched on at the left, the right, or the back.

There were people here and there. Some were old, some young. Some sat on porches, others sat on steps. The occasional child ran across a front yard or climbed over an oversized tire or crate.

Fascinated, Casey made him drive slowly, then directed him over the route a second time. This time she was looking for flowers, peering around to see backyards when there were no flowers in front. If Connie had re-created his native Maine in Boston, those flowers ought to be here. But they weren't. She saw trees and grass. She saw ragged shrubs. She saw rocks and moss and dirt.

Disappointed, she sat back with a sigh. The officer returned her to the Miata.

"How about dinner?" he asked just as she reached for the door handle.

She smiled. As grateful as she was for his time, she didn't want to encourage him. Besides, hadn't he said that the tour would make his week? Dinner wasn't necessary. "Thanks, but that macaroni and cheese filled me up. Besides, I'm exhausted. I have phone calls to make and papers to read, and I need sleep after that. I didn't see a motel here."

He brooded, but just for a minute. Taking the rejection with grace, he said, "Nope. Not here. Not next door in Duck Ridge either."

She waited. He didn't go on. It struck her that this was an Abbott game.

Finally, patiently, she asked, "And the town after that?"

"There's a place there."

"A 'place'?"

"Bed-and-breakfast."

"Can you give me directions?"

What the West Hay House lacked in personality it made up for in quiet, which was just perfect for rereading *Flirting with Pete.* Casey was the only guest. She had her choice of bedrooms. She had her choice of bathrooms. She even had her choice of breakfast muffins. "I only make one kind each morning," the innkeeper explained before she went up to bed, "so you might as well decide."

She chose blueberry, and they were surprisingly large, moist, and good. She took that as a promising sign.

Indeed, it was. Returning to Abbott well before nine the next morning, she explored the town again, this time on her own. She stopped at the school again and walked through the playground. She stopped at the ruins of the shoe plant and wandered among the stones. Then she drove to the residential area. More people were visible today, doing Saturday chores, tending to their houses, their lawns, their cars. Her own car didn't pass unnoticed; many eyes turned her way.

She smiled, nodded, and didn't let herself be rushed as she drove slowly up and down the streets, imagining which house had been Connie's. The one she settled on was a small frame house painted yellow with white trim. The paint was faded both there and on the picket fence out front, and the yard had a neglected look. But there was a rocking chair on the porch. She imagined her grandmother rocking there. The woman would be petite, like Casey. She would have white hair, a wrinkled face, and a gentle smile. She would be wearing a flowered dress and a white apron, and she would smell of homemade bread. Anadama bread.

Whoa. Casey didn't know where *that* had come from. She didn't consciously remember having ever had anadama bread, but she must have. She had a vision of cornmeal and molasses. Anadama bread, like macaroni and cheese, was comfort food. So, for that matter, were grandmothers— which told her where *she* was at, just then.

Feeling lonely, she returned to the center of town and parked at a spot where the cell phone reception was strongest. She accessed her messages. There were a bunch from her friends, none of which she returned because she didn't want to have to explain where she was and why. More important, the nursing home hadn't called.

Satisfied by that, she drove to the Grange Hall shortly before nine, continued on around to the door in the back, and parked the Miata beside a classic station wagon just as Dewey Heller was turning the CLOSED sign to OPEN. He smiled and waved her in.

"That's some station wagon," she said with an admiring smile. She might not remember anadama bread, but old cars she did. "My mom had one like it years ago."

"Bet hers didn't have wood on the sides."

"Sure did," Casey said with pride.

"Bet hers wasn't as old as mine. Mine was built in forty-seven, and we didn't call them station wagons back then. They were beach wagons—not that I ever shuttled folks back and forth to the beach, but I did shuttle them to the train station, so when they started calling them station wagons, it fit. I was just over getting coffee at the store. Donna told me I'd be having a visitor. She said you're looking for Ungers. Well, that'd be Frank and Mary and their son, Cornelius. Poor choice of a name for a child, even back then. Anyone could see he was a frail little thing. He needed a solid name like . . . like *Rock*."

Casey was so pleased to have found someone who knew her father's name that she smiled. "Rock wouldn't fit who he became."

"What'd he become?"

"A famous psychologist. He died a month ago. I'm here partly to see if there's any famly left."

"Nope. There wasn't much to start with once the father died, just the mother, and she's long gone. What's the rest?"

Casey was confused.

"You said 'partly,' " the old man reminded her. "What's the rest?"

But Casey couldn't move on yet. "Tell me about the mother. What did she look like?"

"She was a pretty thing, small with long, long hair that might've been a bit redder than yours. She was—" Busty, he gestured. "O' course, all the women looked"—he repeated the gesture—"what with the aprons they wore back then."

"Was she nice?"

"Nice enough."

"Did she work at the shoe plant?"

"They all did. What's the rest?" he repeated.

She smiled in a way that begged him to indulge her a bit longer. "Did they have *any* family here—even extended family, cousins and such?"

"None that I knew of. So what's the rest?"

Casey gave in. "I'm trying to find Little Falls."

It was the old man's turn to sigh, only his was one of pleasure and came with a smile. "Little Falls. Haven't heard it called Little Falls in a while. That'd be Walker."

"Walker?" she repeated in an excited

whisper. It was real then. If Little Falls existed, Jenny Clyde existed, too.

"It's about thirty miles on up the road," Dewey Heller went on. "Little Falls was its first name, not because there's a waterfall there, 'cause there isn't, but because the Little family was the ones founding the town, and those founders threw a big shindig every year when the trees turned red and orange and such. Around the time of the Depression, folks felt they needed a bigger name, if you know what I mean, so they voted, and it was official. Walker. Thing is, the locals clung to Little Falls for the longest time. Then came zip codes and area codes and what-have-yous, and it was Walker more and more. A few of the locals still call it Little Falls. Ask me, Little Falls has more character as a town name than Walker." He scrunched up his face. "Walker. Kinda . . . blaahh, don't you think?"

Casey didn't think it was *blaahh* at all. She didn't care what it was called as long as it was real.

Elated, she said her goodbyes and headed north again. She didn't mind that thirty miles took fifty minutes driving on that two-lane road, because she was close, so close to finding Jenny Clyde, and she had done it through sheer persistence. Connie would have been proud.

WALKER TOWN LINE, read the sign. She slowed a bit, wanting to take in everything she passed. The houses here were as old as in Abbott, but slightly larger and better kept. Same with the yards. Some had flowers; others had lawns. In both instances, care was clearly taken.

Wanting to hear and smell as well as see, she turned the AC off and opened the window. *Flirting with Pete* was fresh in her mind. She figured she would know pretty quickly if this was the right town.

She grew more alert when the houses began coming closer together, and when she caught sight of a street sign that read WEST MAIN, her pulse quickened. Jenny Clyde lived on West Main. Assuming the journal was based on fact, Casey might well have already passed the house.

Resisting the temptation to drive back to see, she continued on and was rewarded the instant she reached the center of town. Turning onto Main Street, she found it exactly as the journal described it. Green awnings with white lettering ran over the stores. The green was slightly faded and the white not as clean as the journal depicted, which suggested that some time had passed since the "urban renewal" Jenny had mentioned.

Lining one side of the street were a hardware store, a drugstore, a newspaper office, and a Dunkin' Donuts. In the journal, the Dunkin' Donuts had been a five-and-dime and a bakery, but the change was plausible, Casey thought.

Lining the other side of the street were a grocery store, a garden center, a luncheonette, a yogurt shop, and a secondhand clothing store. Here, too, some things were changed—namely the yogurt shop in place of an ice-cream shop, and the secondhand clothing store in place of Miss Jane's. The change from ice cream to yogurt was consistent with the times, and as for Miss Jane's, the owner hadn't been nice to Jenny. Casey decided it would be poetic justice if she had gone out of business.

Cars were parked angled in along the street. She pulled into a free space. It happened to be in front of the newspaper office.

WALKER CITIZEN read the white lettering on the green awning above the front windows and door. Casey decided this was a good place to start.

Leaving the car, she went inside. There were three desks. A young woman sat behind a computer terminal at the first. The second had neither a computer nor a person, though it had two telephones and many slips of paper. The third desk, in a position of supervision at the back of the room, was larger than the first two so that it rose a bit above. It did have a computer, but Casey immediately focused on the man there. He was thin and, despite a receding hairline, oddly adolescent looking. She knew just who he was. Oh yes, she did.

Walking right up to his desk, she extended a hand. "I'm Casey Ellis, and you must be Dudley Wright the Third."

Dudley stood, tall and gangly, and gave her a toothy grin. "I am."

She glanced at the plaque on the desk. "Editor in chief?" she teased. "You're too young to be that."

His grin turned cocky. "I was named editor in chief when I was thirty-two."

If the journal was to be believed, he had

wanted to be editor in chief at thirty. "Thirty-two?" she echoed. "That is remarkable. A friend of mine was named editor in chief of her local paper at twenty-nine. Now, *there* was a brilliant journalist," she added, because a little needling didn't hurt. This man hadn't been particularly understanding of Jenny, either. Jenny had said he was twenty-six. "How old are you now?"

"Thirty-three," he said and, deflated somewhat, sat back down. "How can I help you?"

Seven years, if the journal was to be believed—seven years had passed since Jenny had written her story. "I'm looking for Jenny Clyde—uh, MaryBeth," Casey corrected herself.

"Don't bother. She's gone."

"Gone where?"

"Dead."

Casey gasped. "No."

"Yes."

"Are you *sure?*"

His smile was smug. "I wrote the obituary myself."

Casey was stunned. She had imagined Jenny might be fictitious. She had never imagined that she was dead. It didn't make sense, not with Connie's note. *She's kin.* Present tense. *How to help?* Future implied.

Connie had asked for her help, but there was no helping someone who was dead. There had to be a mistake. She would have to dig deeper. Jenny was her cause.

Dudley Wright III seemed to take strength from her upset. Sitting back in his chair, he laced his fingers over a concave middle. "Fact is, she drowned. Right here in the quarry."

"That can't be," Casey said. Jenny had gone to the quarry with Pete. It was a magical place. She had been happy there. Casey couldn't imagine how Jenny could have gone from happiness to hopelessness so quickly.

Well, she could imagine it. She had sensed the desperation in the journal. And surely there were pages that Casey hadn't yet found. At least, she assumed there were more pages. The story wasn't done.

"What can I tell you," the newspaperman said. It wasn't an offer.

Casey came up with alternatives. Knowing how uncaring the town had been, Jenny might simply have up and moved away, leaving behind people who wanted to believe she was gone for good. Dead was certainly gone for good. The townsfolk might tell themselves that. Drowning in the quarry could be their explanation for a disappearance.

"And Darden Clyde?" she asked.

"Oh, he's here. Still giving people the heebie-jeebies. He's got another woman now. She moved right in with her two kids. No one seems to know if they ever married, but she must fill some need of his, because he's kept her around. But he's changed since MaryBeth drowned. He was difficult before. You didn't want to look at him crossways. Now it's worse. He's mean and impossible."

Casey couldn't imagine why any woman would subject herself and her children to a man like that. But the situation wasn't unique. She had worked with any number of women who took abuse of all kinds from their men and didn't have the wherewithal to leave.

"Does he have relatives here?" she asked. Darden's relatives might be *her* relatives.

"Not any that'll admit to it."

"Then there are some?" She held her breath.

"No. I was being funny. No relatives."

Relieved, she let out the breath. Much as she hungered for relatives, she didn't want any who were connected to Darden.

There were questions to ask—like when and how Jenny had died—but Casey wanted the death confirmed first. So she said, "Thank you. You've been a help," and set off for the door.

"Why are you asking about the Clydes?" Dudley called. He was on his feet again.

Casey returned to his desk Along the way, she drew a brand-new business card from her shoulder bag. She passed it to him. "I'm a psychotherapist. I've read about Mary-Beth. I wanted to talk with her."

"Read about her where?"

"There was all that coverage of the trial," she said, thinking of the clippings in Jenny's attic. It didn't answer his question, but he didn't seem to notice.

"You could visit the graveyard and talk to her all you want. Darden's made a little shrine there." He studied the card. "You're from Boston? I've been to Boston. Can't deal with the traffic, though. Psychotherapy? Are you writing a book?"

"Maybe," Casey said, because Dudley

struck her as the type to be impressed by that. "It depends on what I learn."

She waited for him to say something— stood there, inviting him to take back the earlier words and confess that Jenny wasn't really dead. When the silence dragged on, she lost patience. "You have my card. If you think of anything, I'd appreciate it if you'd give me a call."

Desperate to talk with someone else— anyone else—she walked back between the desks, went outside, and crossed the street.

The luncheonette was a sweet thing with a counter, booths, and, at eleven in the morning, a surprising number of people. Taking a stool at the counter, Casey ordered coffee. A mug of it was before her in an instant, but even in that short time, she had spotted the plate in front of the woman on her left. "That omelet looks fabulous," she said. "What's in it?"

The waitress answered for the woman. "Corned beef hash and Monterey Jack cheese. Can I get you one?"

"Um, yes," Casey decided. She wasn't sure how much she could eat, wondering if Jenny was really dead, but she figured that if she fit in with the locals a little, she might get more honesty from them.

"It *is* fabulous," confirmed the woman on her left. She was young, blond, and attractively rumpled in jeans and a sleeveless flannel shirt. An infant slept in a car seat by her foot. "If you're just passing through and want a taste of Walker, a hash-and-Jack omelet will do you well. Where're you from?"

"Boston. Do you live here?"

"All my life."

"How old's the baby?" Casey asked, smiling at the bundle in pink.

"Four months. She's a good napper for now, but if she's anything like my others, I won't be able to do this much longer. Nice to have a quiet brunch, y'know? Where are you headed?"

"Here. I'm looking for MaryBeth Clyde."

The woman's brows went up in instant recognition. "MaryBeth?"

"The daughter," Casey specified, because Jenny's mother was MaryBeth, too.

"Oh dear. MaryBeth's been dead—" She called to the waitress, "Lizzie, how long since MaryBeth Clyde died?"

"Seven years," said a man on Casey's

right, who had been talking with a friend until then. "She drowned seven years ago."

Seven years ago? "Are you sure?" Casey asked.

The waitress confirmed it. "It was seven years ago. She died in the quarry."

"Was she swimming?"

"She jumped," said the man.

Casey felt a shooting pain. She was thinking of the desperation she had sensed in Jenny when the woman on her left said, "They don't really know she jumped. No one saw. They found her clothes up on top, so they assumed that's what she did."

"Could you blame her?" asked the waitress. "Darden was out of prison, and a meaner so-and-so you've never met in your life."

"Now, now, Lizzie," said the man two stools to the right of Casey. "Did Darden ever hurt you?"

"He never leaves a tip," Lizzie declared. "Walks in here like it's his right to be served and begrudges us the cost of the food."

"Ach, he's not that bad. I talk with him now and again. He had a rough time with a wife like that, so he did what he had to, and he paid the price. Then the girl kills herself the minute he gets home? Not good."

"Did she leave a note?" Casey asked, not yet ready to accept that Jenny was dead. She recalled the last few lines of the journal. *Jenny Clyde was ready to fly.* But that was an expression. Surely she hadn't meant it literally. Casey had interpreted it to mean, simply, that she was taking off, leaving town, escaping her father.

"No note," said Lizzie, and turned back to the pass-through window.

"No body either," said the woman on Casey's left.

"What?" Casey asked.

"They never found a body," said the man on her right.

"Well, then, she's still alive," Casey decided.

"Nuh-uh," the man two stools over insisted. "The quarry swallows them up. She's not the first one disappeared. It's legend."

The waitress delivered Casey's omelet. Casey wasn't sure she could eat it. Her mind was moving along the lines of the town of Walker, not caring if Jenny died or not, failing to look very far. "Did they do a search?"

"As much as they could," said the man on her right. Looking over his shoulder, he called to a man in one of the booths, "Martin, you were in on the search for MaryBeth Clyde, weren't you?"

"The daughter? Sure was. We looked all over, down to the bottom of the quarry, through the woods. The old Buick was there in the woods, but the girl was gone."

Casey looked back. "How can there not be a body?"

"Easy," said the man beside her. "It could've been one of two things. Day before she died there'd been a good rain, and that was on top of a wet summer, so the river was flowing good. Her body could've washed right over the rim of the quarry and been carried down through the rapids and on into the big lake where it'd never be found. The big lake's more'n a hundred feet deep at some points. Or, the quarry creature could have gotten her. Swallowed her right down."

Jenny Clyde had believed in the quarry creature.

"Is there a chance," Casey asked, "that

she just left her clothes up top and walked away?"

"I don't know how she'd have done that," called the man in the booth. "Y'see, there were footprints just her size there at the top of the quarry. They went right to the edge and then no more. If she'd left her clothes and walked off, there would've been foot-prints in the other direction."

"What about being carried in the water a while and *then* walking out and away?" Casey asked.

"She'd have been found," said the man on her right. "She wasn't the kind who would just fit into any old crowd. She was odd looking."

"Not odd looking," scolded the waitress. "Just *visible,* with all that red hair and those freckles."

"There are ways to disguise those things," Casey argued. "What if she let people think she was dead, while a friend took her way far away?"

"She didn't have any friends," scoffed the man on her right.

"She had a boyfriend," Casey said.

"She did not," he drawled.

"His name was Pete," Casey insisted.

The waitress clicked her tongue. "Pete. The guy on a motorcycle. I do remember that. Only no one met him. No one saw him. No one ever heard the bike."

Casey had a sudden thought. It had to do with a woman who was desperate and a man who was too good to be true.

The woman on her left distracted her. "Do you really think she's still alive?"

"Yes," Casey said impulsively.

"Then you need to talk with Edmund O'Keefe. He's the chief of police. He was there."

"Edmund? Not Dan?" Dan O'Keefe was the one in the journal.

"Edmund's the father. Dan's the nicer of the two, but he's gone."

Casey pulled back. "Gone?" If it was another alleged death, she didn't want to know.

"Quit, swore off law enforcement, left town," clarified the man on her right, letting Casey relax.

"Too bad," mused the man two stools over. "Dan was the best. Big loss, his leaving. Good luck with the chief, little lady. He's tough."

Chapter Eighteen

The police station was located in the garage of a small house on a side street off Main. The house was white with pale blue shutters. It had a small porch, and no rocker, but there were rose bushes out front. They were actually quite beautiful, if a bit leggy and lean.

Pulling in beside a cruiser, Casey crossed the pebbled driveway to the side door of the garage. A vine climbed the walls here—not quite the wisteria on her own pergola, but something pretty and green—an ivy, she would bet.

Opening the screen, she went inside. The place was quiet. Maps were tacked on one side of the wall, "wanted" posters on another. There were two doors, one of which, at least, she figured led to a holding room of some sort. Behind the lone desk, a young man was reading the paper. He set it down when she came in, but said nothing.

"Hi," she said brightly. "I don't think you're Edmund O'Keefe."

"No. I'm his deputy. Can I help you?"

Casey guessed that seven years ago, when the drowning had allegedly taken place, this young man hadn't been old enough to vote, much less serve as a police officer. "I think I need the chief. It's kind of personal," she added more softly, even in a bit of a conspiratorial tone, because second-guessing the outcome of a suicide investigation conducted by the chief of police was personal indeed.

"Personal?" repeated the deputy. "Well, he's gone home for lunch. If it's personal, you could go there. Know where he lives?"

Casey scratched her forehead. "Uh, I think I remember . . . *which* street is it?"

"Go back to Main, turn left for two blocks, then right. They just repainted the house, so you may not recognize it. It isn't blue anymore. It's taupe. Taupe. There's a new one. Dot is still trying to decide if she likes it, so tell her how pretty it looks."

"I will," Casey said with a smile, and left before the deputy could ask any questions.

In no time, she was back on Main Street. Turning left, she drove for two blocks, then turned right. The newly taupe house had cream-colored shutters and trim, and was the first one on the left. It was a Victorian. Casey thought it looked quite handsome.

Parking by the berm, she went up the cement walk, up four wood steps, and across the porch. The rocker here was a two-seater that swung from a frame of its own.

Peering through the screen, she called, "Hello?" She had to call again before an attractive woman appeared. Early sixtyish, she wore jeans and an ironed blouse, had dark hair, wide-set eyes, and fine features. She opened the screen door with a smile. "Hello."

Casey liked her looks and her lack of pretense. "Hi. I'm Casey Ellis. I'm a pyschotherapist looking for information on MaryBeth Clyde, the daughter. I understand that your husband led the investigation into her death. I was wondering if he'd be willing to talk with me. I've come at a bad time, I know. You're having lunch. But I've driven up from Boston, and probably should be heading back before long."

"Boston?" Dot said, brightening even

more. "We have a son in Boston." More softly, she added, "He's an artist. My husband doesn't love that, but I'm pretty proud."

Casey liked her all the more. "I've always been in awe of artists. My mother was something of one."

"Oh? What did she do?"

Casey might have given a hurried answer and moved on, if she hadn't sensed that the woman was genuinely interested. "She wove all sorts of things. Her specialty was Angora fur. She raised the rabbits, harvested their fur, dyed it, spun it, and wove it."

"Angora is from rabbits? Funny, I'd have said it was from goats. Or sheep."

"Rabbits," Casey confirmed with a smile, but the smile quickly faded. "They're sweet little things. It took me a while, but I found a weaver in the Midwest who had other Angoras and was willing to drive out for these."

Concerned now, Dot asked, "Did your mother die suddenly?"

"She was in an accident three years ago. She's still alive, but only in a way. She isn't aware."

"I'm *so* sorry. That must be devastating for you."

Casey took a breath, swallowed, forced a smile. "It's almost a relief to focus on other things, even MaryBeth Clyde's disappearance."

"Most around here would call it a suicide," Dot cautioned. "My husband certainly would." She gestured. "Come in. Please. He's eaten enough of his lunch. How about you? Can I get you a ham sandwich?"

She shook her head. "You're kind to offer, but I had an omelet at the luncheonette not long ago. I'm fine, thanks." She was barely into the front hall when a man came from the back of the house. He was tall, with thick gray hair and sun-lined skin. He wore khaki pants and a short-sleeved white shirt. Casey saw neither a badge nor a gun.

"Ed, this is Casey Ellis," Dot said. "She wants—"

"I know what she wants," he interrupted in a voice that was gravelly and deep. He stopped with his feet slightly apart and put his hands on his hips. "She wants information on MaryBeth Clyde, but there isn't much that wasn't in the report. It was a suicide. The. End."

Casey was fearing that the interview was over before it had begun, when Dot took her elbow and guided her right past the police chief and into the parlor. It was a pretty room, sunny and stylish in the way of the woman of the house. Both had a country feel—simple and straightforward, with charm and a quiet intelligence. In the woman, that intelligence took the form of sensitivity. In the room, it took the form of art that hung on the walls, elegant frames holding family pictures, current best-selling biographies on lamp tables, and exquisite needlepoint pillows on chairs.

Casey lifted one of the latter. It was a floral design drawn with artistic license. "Did you do this?"

"I stitched it. My son did the design for me."

Casey looked at a pair of paintings high above the hearth. A diptych, they captured a farm in a snowstorm. They had the same freehand feel as the pillow. "He did those also?"

"Yes." In a stronger voice, clearly meant for her husband, she said, "He's become quite successful. His work is being shown in galleries in Boston and New York. He makes a handsome living at it, which is more than most artists can say."

"She didn't come to hear about Dan," Edmund said as he joined them.

"No," Dot replied patiently, "she came to ask about MaryBeth Clyde, but Dan felt for the girl, so it's perfectly appropriate to talk about Dan."

Casey was confused. "Dan is the artist? I assumed there were other sons."

"No other sons," Dot said. "Two daughters, but only Dan."

Casey glanced at the frames that held family photos. Even from a distance, she could see there were grandchildren.

Dot was with her here, too. "Five grandchildren to date from the girls. Dan has yet to meet his dream girl."

"He's a bleeding heart," scoffed the father. "He was too compassionate to be a cop. You have to make tough decisions sometimes."

That brought Casey back to her cause. "Like knowing when to call off an investigation?"

"Why is it," cautioned the chief of police, "I'm getting the feeling you disagree with my conclusion? You know, it wasn't just me.

There were others involved—even my son, the bleeding heart. He was right up there sayin' it was suicide, pure and simple."

Suicide was *not* pure and simple. Casey was in a profession that knew that. She was also experienced enough in that profession to know that a woman who was as desperate as Jenny Clyde might, indeed, kill herself.

But Casey was desperate, too. Her father had asked her to help Jenny. She couldn't do that if Jenny was dead. Granted, she hadn't read the ending of *Flirting with Pete,* didn't even know if there *were* any more pages of it.

Ed O'Keefe hadn't moved. "What makes you think she isn't dead?"

"Nothing," Casey said, easing up. "I just wondered about the lack of a body. I know about the river, and I know about the quarry creature. But isn't it possible that MaryBeth climbed out of the water and got away?"

"Where would she go?" the chief asked. "She had no friends. She had no money. She had no experience outside of Walker."

"Would she have gone with Miriam Goodman?"

He crossed his arms on his chest. "First

off, Miriam was right here in town when MaryBeth disappeared. She didn't move west until several weeks later. So I know what you're thinking. You're thinking that she went somewhere else and then met up with Miriam later?" He shook his head. "I checked it out. Darden made me. He was thinking the same thing you are. Loony man." The last was muttered under his breath.

Casey tried a different angle. "Supposing, just supposing she was still alive; were there any other relatives she might go live with?"

"No."

"Any she might have contacted in the years since she disappeared?"

"No."

"No boyfriend?"

"No."

"Any follow-up of any kind?"

"Only Miriam. I told you, I only did that because Darden nagged. Why do you want to know all this anyway? Are you writing a book?"

Had it not been for Dot O'Keefe standing right there, she might have given the same answer she had given the newspaperman. But she couldn't lie in front of Dot. "No," she said quietly. "No book. I read a case study. That's all."

She regretted having said that when the police chief dropped his arms. "What case study?"

"Maybe not a case study. A journal. It could have been fiction, too." Discouraged, she looked at the diptych above the hearth. Snow and all, it was a positive thing, because the farmhouse was a misty red lure, beckoning in the storm. "Probably fiction," she murmured, approaching the hearth. Her eye fell on the smaller framed family photos that stood on the stone mantel beneath the diptych. One was of a daughter, her husband, and two kids. Another was of the other daughter, her husband, and three kids. There was a photo of all of them, plus Dot and Edmund, plus what might have been other relatives. And there was one showing both daughters, Dot and Ed, and a man Casey assumed was the son, Dan.

She gasped. "Omigod." She pressed her chest. "Omigod!"

Dot came to her side. "What is it?"

It was Jordan. Her gardener. The man who had worked for Connie for seven years. Who often seemed too wise to be only a gardener. Who hadn't found his dream girl yet. Whose father was a cop. Whose last name was nowhere in Connie's files. Just Daisy's Mum.

"Omigod," she cried again, involuntarily this time because she had thought of something else, and in its wake her mind was racing, trying to connect the dots, trying to grasp the ramifications.

"Is something wrong?" Dot asked.

Casey managed a feeble, "Uh, no. Not wrong. He just looks like someone I know."

The proud mother smiled at the picture. "Handsome guy, isn't he?"

Casey couldn't get to her car fast enough. After just a minute of fishing in her overnight bag, she pulled from the pocket of yesterday's slacks the business card she had stuffed there when she was leaving Daisy's Mum. At the time, she had admired the logo but merely glanced at the rest. Now, driving away from the taupe Victorian with its pretty cream shutters, holding the steering wheel for dear life with the card propped between her forefinger and the leather, she looked more closely. At the bottom were a phone number and the name of the proprietor.

D. O'Keefe. No red flag yesterday. There were scores of O'Keefes in the Boston phone book. She had also assumed that the D was for Daisy. Oh boy, had she assumed wrong.

She had assumed that Dan was for Daniel. Wrong there, too. And what else had she assumed wrong?

Dozens of possibilities crossed her mind as she drove south, and the slowness of the first stretch of road didn't help. She accessed more voice mail from friends and talked with the nursing home. She was increasingly impatient, too annoyed to wait passively behind leisurely Saturday drivers, so, eyes on the road the whole time, she did honk and pass a couple of cars on that two-lane road, then many more once she hit the highway. She wanted to be back in Boston, and she wanted to be there *now*.

Four and a half endless hours after she left the O'Keefes, she crossed the Tobin Bridge and entered Boston. It was late afternoon. Traffic slowed her some, but she held a course for Beacon Hill, and *not* for the townhouse. She went straight to Daisy's Mum, squeezed the Miata into a small parking spot, and strode across the street.

The shop was closed for the day, but she had expected that. She was far more interested in the townhouse doors on either side. One said OWENS on the doorplate, so she went to the other.

O'KEEFE, the plate read. Furious by now, she rang the bell, then waited with her hands on her hips, her head bowed, and her mouth tight.

"Yes?" came a voice through the intercom. Not *a* voice. *His* voice.

"It's me," she said. "Let me up."

There was only the briefest pause, but it was long enough to tell her he recognized her voice, too. The buzzer rang; the door clicked open. Within seconds, she was running up a flight of stone steps old enough to be worn uneven at the center.

He stood with his hands on his hips in an open doorway on the second floor. Backlit, he looked larger and more imposing than ever. The closer she got, the more detail she saw. He wore a tee shirt and shorts. His jaw was shadowed, his hair messed, his feet bare.

She stopped one step shy of the landing, struck by how handsome he truly was. His mother was right about that. Not that Casey had ever thought otherwise. Handsome, sexy, expert at gardening, expert at making love—that was Jordan. He was also agitated, if the set of his mouth meant anything.

She didn't know what *he* had to be agitated about. *She* was the one who'd been taken for a fool.

Needled by that thought, she mounted the last step and marched right up to him. "I've just had a fascinating day in a town called Walker," she said. "I drove around, saw the sights, had a fabulous hash-and-Jack omelet at the luncheonette. I had an even better visit with your parents."

"I know," he informed her tightly. "I just got a call."

Refusing to be intimidated by what was clearly annoyance on his part, she barreled on. "They kept talking about their son Dan, but I didn't make the connection until I saw a photo on the mantel. You let *me* think you were a gardener."

"I am a gardener."

"You sure looked it—scruffy beard, torn jeans, crusty boots. Disreputable—that's what I thought you were. You didn't tell me you were a cop."

"I'm not a cop."

"You were," she charged. "I asked, and you denied it."

"You asked if I'd ever *wanted* to be one," he corrected. "I answered no, and that's the truth. I hated every minute of it. Why were you in Walker?"

"Enlightenment," she said. "You're a 'bleeding heart,' to quote your dad. Too soft. So you tried to help Jenny Clyde. You encouraged her to leave town before her father got out of prison, only she didn't have the courage for that. So she stayed, and something awful happened."

A muscle moved in his jaw. "You saw the journal."

"I saw the journal. I wasn't sure it was real, but I needed it to be, because my father had asked for my help with Jenny, and I wanted to please him. It was the first time he'd ever asked me for anything. *Anything*. But the pages I had stopped short of the end, so I went looking. Little Falls isn't on maps anymore. It took me a while to find it. You couldn't have told me?"

He held up a hand. "Hold on. You didn't ask."

"You were the *gardener*," she cried, feeling betrayed by that on top of everything else. "I wasn't supposed to ask you about Jenny Clyde. I assumed that the pages I saw were confidential."

"If that's so, why were you up asking people in Walker?"

"I didn't tell them what I'd read. I wanted to locate her, that's all."

"Who'd you ask?"

"Does it matter?"

"Sure does. I need to know who you saw and what you said."

He did sound like a cop now. Only he wasn't one, not anymore. And Casey needed her own answers first. "Is Jenny dead?"

"Were you asking that up there?"

"They all think she's dead," Casey said by way of an answer.

Jordan inhaled, rolling his right shoulder. When he blew out the breath, his annoyance seemed to go with it. He pushed a hand through his hair and left it at the back of his neck. "Oh, Casey," he said on a note of despair. "Did you have to race on up there?"

His tone took away some of her steam. "Yes," she said in defense of the trip. "I didn't know how else to get answers."

He rubbed the shoulder he had been rolling moments before. "But you didn't get them. You just stirred up trouble."

"No, I didn't," she argued, puzzled. "I asked questions, then I left."

His smile was grim. "Clearly, you've never lived in a small town. The call I just got was from my dad, and it wasn't only to say that you'd been to the house. Word's spreading already. I'd wager that by morning, most everyone in Walker will know you were there, and why."

"I was only asking questions."

"You were raising doubts. Whenever there's a violent death with no body to show for it, there's doubt. Jenny's death had been put to rest. Now you've resurrected it."

Had he yelled, she might have argued more. But the sensible tone he used was hard to fight. With caution now, she asked, "And what's the harm in that?"

Jordan studied her for a minute. Then he

hitched his head toward the room behind him and said with resignation, "Come in. You can read it for yourself."

She went forward. As soon as he closed the door behind her, he set off for another room. The one she was in was large, minimalist in decor but attractive and clean. She saw no paintings—not on the wall, not on easels. Aside from the art books stacked on a simple wood table, there was no evidence that he was interested in painting, much less had painted the pieces she had seen in his parents' home.

Casey swallowed. She wrapped her arms around her middle. She didn't have to be told to know that he owned this place, just as he owned the shop downstairs. On this turf, he exuded command. She struggled to process the fact that her bad-boy gardener was a man of greater skill and smarts than she had initially thought.

And she had aimed to shock Connie by having an affair with him? What a joke *that* was! Except the joke was on her. Connie would not have been shocked. Far from it. Hadn't he asked, through his lawyer, that she retain the gardener? An argument could therefore be made that Connie had actually fixed them up.

She found that thought humiliating. She didn't dwell on it, though, because Jordan returned to the living room carrying a large manila envelope. When he reached her, he held it out.

"This is what you're missing, I believe."

Chapter Nineteen

Little Falls

Head held high, Jenny fairly floated along the side of the road, moving through air so clear it sparkled. The fog that had spent the night in town had dispersed with the sun, giving her an unobstructed view of all she passed, and she put it to good use. Her eyes searched out the people she usually avoided. They found Angie Booth and her two mongrels, all three startled into silence by her smile. Likewise Hester Johnson and her sister, who froze in the act of removing the mail from the box that stood by their rusty hinged gate. Nick Farina stared without saying a word and that gave Jenny pause, but only until she thought of Pete. Then she smiled at Nick, too.

She found herself humming. It was one of the songs she and Pete had danced to at Giro's. She strode on in time to the beat.

Merle Little's car approached from ahead, passed her, then slowed. She imagined Merle was stunned by her grin, but she didn't look back. Instead, she smiled at Essie Bunch, who stopped sweeping her veranda to watch her pass, and though Jenny couldn't actually see the Websters, the Cleegs, or Myra Ellenbogen, she smiled in the direction of the television sounds coming from their homes and fancied they were amazed.

She turned the corner onto Main Street, where the same people had parked the same cars at the same angle they always did. She walked under those deep green awnings with large white letters, past the same people sitting once again on the same wood benches.

Old habits died hard for her, too, though. All of them staring at her at such close range made her nervous. But today she didn't lower her head, and she refused to look away. After a second of remembering the woman Pete had helped her find inside herself, she met their eyes and smiled.

She continued on to the last side street, turned right, then turned in at the Neat Eats sign. Miriam was in the big kitchen stuffing cannoli with a pastry cone. She looked up. Her hands were suspended for several bars of a hard-driving country song before she punched an elbow at the radio switch, killing the sound.

"Jenny, you look different again, and it isn't just the hair." She set down the cone. "Today's the day Darden comes home, isn't it? You seem calm. Even . . . happy?"

Jenny was. Oh, she was. What she had been dreading for so long was here, and things were nowhere near as bleak as she had thought they would be. Choices. They were the key. She had choices now. "I wanted to tell you before you heard from someone else. I'm leaving Little Falls."

"No way."

Jenny grinned. "I am. With Pete. Remember I told you about him?"

"You bet I do. He's the guy with the leather jacket and boots. The biker. Jenny, uh, how much do you know about him?"

Jenny drew a little heart in the confectioners' sugar that dusted the edge of the table. "Enough. And he's not a biker, not like you think. He has a motorcycle, but there's no gang. He's the nicest person I've ever met. He brings me things and takes me places. We went to Giro's Sunday night."

"Hey, so did I. When were you there?"

"Late. Around midnight."

"No way. I was there from eleven to one. I'd have seen you."

"Well, it might have been one-thirty. I don't remember, we did so much that night." Memory of it made her blush.

Miriam glanced at the window. "Is he outside?"

"No. He's back home, getting ready."

"But I want to meet him."

Jenny wasn't taking any chances. Pete was her savior. He was her pride and joy, her heart's desire. She wasn't having anyone meet him and find fault just because he was hers.

So, politely, she said, "There isn't time. We're leaving tonight."

"*Tonight.* Oh, wow!" More cautiously, "Does your father know?"

Jenny was back to drawing in the sugar, an arrow through the heart this time. "Not yet. But we'll wait to see him before we go." She made a mess of the arrow's feathers and erased it all. It didn't matter. She didn't need to draw pictures. She had the real thing etched inside. "So, anyway, I wanted to let you know I won't be coming to work anymore."

"That's okay. Like I told you, it's slowing down fast."

"I wanted to thank you. You've been nice."

Miriam pouted. She wiped her hands on her apron and gave Jenny as much of a hug as she could without smudging her with powder. Then she held her back. "Where are you going?"

"To his family's ranch in Wyoming. Maybe if you're driving around there, you'll come see me."

"What's the name of the ranch?"

"South Fork." When Miriam looked

skeptical, she explained, "It's at a fork in the road, just south of Montana."

"Ahh. Well, that sounds exciting. Good luck. Hey, listen, if you want me to write a recommendation, I will. I'll say what a good worker you've been."

"Oh, I won't be working. Pete has money, and besides, I'll be busy on the ranch."

Miriam gave her hand a floury squeeze. "I'm glad for you. It's good you're leaving. You need a new start. I hope everything works out with your guy, Pete."

"Pete?" Dan O'Keefe asked. He had a hand up holding open the screen door of the room in his garage that housed the Little Falls Police. The outside of the door was framed by ivy. It made the place a little more approachable. "That the same one Reverend Putty told me about yesterday?"

Jenny looked past him to the desk, bookshelves, file cabinets, and electronic equipment crammed into too small a space. She refused to let his doubtful tone wreck her good mood. "He's taking me back to Wyoming with him. We're only staying here until Darden gets home."

"He's coming in on the bus?"

"Uh-huh."

"The six-twelve?" Dan pushed the door open wider and gestured her in with the hitch of his chin. "Let's talk about this."

Jenny's good cheer did falter then. The police office held memories she didn't care to revisit. She hadn't planned on going inside. It was bad enough to look in at the place through a pretty ivy frame.

But Dan had always treated her better than most. She wanted him to see that she was calm now, that she knew what she was doing and wasn't afraid. She wanted him to see she was happy.

He brushed dust from the seat of the wood chair across from the desk, and settled on the desk's corner.

She stood behind the wood chair with her fingers curled over its top.

"Don't want to sit?"

She shook her head, shrugged, smiled an apology.

"We were rough on you, huh? You seemed older than eighteen back then. Hard to remember you weren't. Does Darden know you're leaving?"

"Not yet."

"Does he know about Pete?"

"Not yet."

"He won't be happy."

Jenny felt whispers of the old panic. But that old panic came from confusion and guilt, as much as fear. Now she had Pete to help with the fear, and while there was still guilt, the confusion was gone. She wasn't staying with Darden. She wasn't living that way. Pete had given her a choice. She knew what she had to do.

The whispers died away. She stood straighter, took a deep breath, and said with a smile, "I told him I'd be here when he got back, so I will be. But then I'm leaving. He's been in jail six years. Well, so have I. He's getting out, so I am. He wants to come back here, I want to leave. I'm twenty-four. I have a right to decide what I want to do with the rest of my life."

"No need to convince me," Dan said.

"I'm the one who's been telling you to leave. I only wish you'd done it sooner— got more of a head start on him."

Jenny wasn't worried. "He won't find me."

"Well, he's not allowed to leave the state without permission. That's a rule of his parole." He flexed his shoulder, like it was sore. "Of course, he might do it anyway, but if he does, they'll go after him. Want to give me an idea where you'll be, so I can alert the authorities if there's a problem?"

She shook her head. "You'll be the first one Darden asks."

"I'd never tell him. You know I'm on your side." His brows went up. "You think he'll torture me to make me tell?" He chuckled. "I'm taller and stronger than he is. Besides, I'm the law. He won't hurt me."

"People do crazy things when they're desperate."

"Darden's not that crazy."

"He's a mean man. You said it yourself. Anyway," she said with a burst of renewed excitement, "we'll be riding for a while, Pete and me. It might be weeks before we get to his place."

"Maybe I ought to meet him, this Pete. Then I could vouch for him if Darden starts yelling that you've been taken against your will. Is he around?"

It was eleven-thirty. Pete might be sleeping. Or showering. Or doing his laundry. Jenny had offered to do it for him, but he had refused. He said it was luxury enough having a washer and dryer to use after days on the road, and that he wasn't having her be his slave. He had even taken the last of *her* things to wash along with his. The last time anyone had washed anything for her, she had been nine.

"Rides a motorcycle?" Dan asked with a teasing grin. "Seems to me there was a time when you wanted one of those yourself. Not too long ago—what was it, three, four years since Nick Farina's grandson rode one into town? Old Nick was fit to be tied. Hated the sound, hated the looks. You, you'd stop and drool every time you passed. Old Nick hated that, too. He nearly had a heart attack when the grandson considered selling the bike to you. I think Nick would've moved rather than see and hear that machine every day. Strange, he hasn't complained about your Pete's."

Jenny smiled. "When you go fast enough, no one sees or hears."

"I've never heard *that*, Jenny Clyde." Dan studied her in the way he had of telling her he knew a whole lot about a whole lot—and briefly, so briefly, she wanted to hug him for being kinder than most. But she didn't know how he would take to that, and then the urge passed.

He rubbed his shoulder again, frowning now. "I worry about you. Reverend Putty says you're lying around in your night-gown all day."

Jenny's smile turned coy. "Reverend Putty's wrong. I only put the nightgown on when he came." She remained behind the chair only long enough to see that Dan got her drift, then she went to the door. "I have to go. I just wanted to say goodbye. I'm sorry if my leaving's going to make more work for you."

"For me?"

"With Darden."

"I'll handle Darden."

She nodded, gave him one last big smile, and was gone.

By the time she reached the school, it was 11:50 and warm. She pulled off her sweatshirt and tied it around her waist, then sat down at the end of the stone wall edging the playground and smiled her way through ten minutes' worth of the earliest of her childhood memories. No matter that they were part real, part made-up. People needed happy memories, just like they needed adoring grandmothers and aunts.

At twelve sharp, the bell rang. Joey Battle was one of the last children out of the school. He came stumbling down the steps in heated argument with another boy, who gave him a mighty shove and ran off. Joey was scrambling up off the ground, looking murderous and ready to give chase, when he saw Jenny. By the time he was heading her way, the murderous look had mellowed to one of hurt.

She fell into step beside him, lifting his baseball cap up so she could see his eyes. "What was that about?"

"He called me a mutant."

"Being a mutant isn't so bad if it means you're different from *him*. He's a bully. I could tell."

"The kids like him more than they like me."

"They don't like him. They're afraid of him."

"I wish they were afraid of me."

"No, you don't. You want them to like you. They will."

"When?"

"When you start liking them. It's catching."

He kicked an acorn out of the way. "Did the kids like you?"

"Some did."

"Because you liked them?"

"Yes."

"So why don't they like you now?"

"Maybe," she said, "it's because they're afraid of me."

"I'm not afraid of you."

That was one of the reasons, even apart from their looks, why they were friends. She wished she could take him with her, but she couldn't. She wished she could ease things for him here, but she couldn't do that either. All she could do was to hope that he would remember her as someone who loved him—surrogate mother, aunt, sister, whatever *he* chose to pretend—and smile at the memory sometimes.

She scratched the top of the cap that hid the short wisps of red hair that were all Selena had left of his curls. Her hand had no sooner lowered when Joey's fingers found it and slipped inside. Immediately, she felt emotion tugging at her heart.

"How come you're here?" he asked.

"I have to say goodbye. I'm going away."

His eyes flew to hers. "Where are you going?"

"To Wyoming."

"When'll you be back?" It was almost more of an accusation than a question.

She couldn't tell him the truth. Feeling a twinge of guilt and more than a little sadness, she said, "Not for a while."

"*When?*"

How to explain to a child?

"I don't want you going away," he cried.

The tug on her heart grew sharper. "That's 'cause we're pals."

"Why are you going?"

"I have to."

"Why?"

"Because I met a man—"

Joey tore his hand from hers and raced off. But her legs were longer than his. She caught up fast.

"That *always* happens," he cried when she stopped him. "First Mama, now you."

"No."

"Yes."

"No." Jenny crouched down and held him still. "*No.* It's not the same with me. But I can't stay here, Joey. My father's coming back."

"So? You said he didn't kill your mother."

"He didn't. But he did other things. Does other things. I can't stay."

"Take me with you."

"I can't."

"Why not?"

"Because I *can't.*"

"Why not?" he yelled.

She pulled him close and held him, just

as she would a child of her own, and in that brief instant, she allowed the pain of leaving to wash through her. Her throat tightened. Her eyes filled with tears. She felt more sad than she would have dreamed possible, and suddenly deathly scared.

It was a while before she was able to whisper, "I wish I could explain, but you're too young, and anyway, I don't have the words."

"Is Wyoming far?"

"Yes."

"Will you ever be back?"

She hesitated, then breathed a quiet, "No."

"I'll *never* see you again?"

She held him back so that she could see his face, his freckled, dirt-smudged face now streaked with tears. "You will. Just not here."

"Where?"

"Somewhere else."

"Where?"

"I don't know."

"So how do you know you'll see me at all?"

Jenny thought of Pete and how he had

come along just when she was out of hope, and she felt a sudden conviction. Quietly, she said, "Because I do."

He seemed to be holding his breath. "Are you sure?"

She nodded. Then smiled. "It'll be a surprise. You won't be expecting me, then, boom—there I'll be. Honest. That's how it'll happen."

"Maybe next year?"

"Maybe."

"Or when I'm big?"

"Who knows." She brushed her thumbs over his cheeks to wipe away the tears.

His eyes suddenly lit. "When it happens, will you take me to Chuck E. Cheese?"

She nodded.

"O-*kay*," he said, grinning. Then he danced away. "I gotta go."

Jenny watched him run off down the street, taking with him a tiny piece of her heart. The pain of it was sharp and swift, and curbed only by the fiercest of wills. Then, letting herself think only good thoughts, she set off for the store.

She bought potatoes, carrots, and stew

meat. She bought tapioca. She bought Rice Krispies and marshmallows. She splurged and bought ready-made subs for Pete and her to have for lunch. Then she splurged on two more for the fridge. For good measure, she tossed in a bag of pretzels.

"Looks like you're having a party," said Mary McKane as she tallied the bill.

"Maybe," Jenny said with a smile, sweeping the bag into her arms.

Thoughts of following Pete to the ends of the earth kept the smile on her face through most of the walk home. It was only when the house came into sight, still in the distance, down the road, that she felt a qualm.

She walked faster. The qualm grew. She switched the bag to her other side and started to trot. She was practically running by the time she turned in at the driveway and saw the motorcycle, there, beside the garage—and even then she didn't feel better until she walked into the kitchen and saw Pete at the stove. She sagged against the wall in relief.

One look and he knew. "You thought I'd left," he chided as he relieved her of her bag, "but I won't. I've told you. I'm not leaving without you. Why won't you believe that?"

"Because sometimes I still can't believe you're real."

"Do I look real?"

"Yes."

He put her hand to his heart. "Do I feel real?"

She felt it pulsing. She nodded.

"Well?"

Tell him, Jenny. I can't. *Tell him everything.* I can't risk it. *He loves you.* But does he love me enough?

She covered her face with a hand. He pulled it away, drew her against him, and said into the sweaty warmth of her wild red hair, "I made hot chocolate to make up for sleeping through breakfast, but now it's warm outside. You feel like you could use something cool."

"Hot chocolate's my favorite drink."

"I figured that," he said with the kind of grin that turned her knees to soup and her mind to slush. "You have three big tins of it in the cupboard."

"I'll have some now."

"You're not too hot?"

She shook her head, sat down at the table, and imagined snow falling outside while she waited for her drink.

In the first months after the death of Jenny's mother, Jenny had lived mainly in the kitchen, the spare room upstairs, and the attic. Dan had someone clean the blood from the living room, but she couldn't bear being there, and as for the bedrooms, they held a horror all their own. It was two full years into Darden's incarceration before she slept in her own room again, and then, only after she had been ousted from the spare room by a raccoon, and *then,* only after she had scrubbed the bedroom top to bottom.

Six years later, she still avoided the living room. The bedroom that her parents had shared was dusted twice a year. She kept the door shut the rest of the time.

Tuesday afternoon, she opened it wide, dragged in the cartons that had been waiting in the garage, and filled them with armloads of her mother's things. She didn't fold anything, didn't stop to look at anything or reminisce. She closed one full carton and turned to the next, closed that carton when it was full and turned to the next, and all the while she cursed Darden for not wanting to do this himself, for not *caring* to do it as a way of saying goodbye to his wife.

He was punishing Jenny, of course. She knew that. He was playing another of his little mind games meant to keep her guilt alive, and it succeeded to a point. Even rushing, even refusing to look at a single blouse, slip, or skirt, even in spite of her long talks with Pete and the resolutions she had made, she felt guilt and pain and regret.

Then it stopped. Her mind rebelled and shut down. Guilt, pain, regret—she packed them away with the last of her mother's things, closed the carton, and walked out.

The tub was filled with lilac-scented bubbles. They rose high above the water in a cumulus field broken only by Jenny's head and knees. She had her eyes closed until she heard Pete at the door.

"Hi," he said.

She smiled shyly, because he was all man and still so new to her.

"Doin' okay?"

She nodded. "Feeling strange."

"Sad about leaving?"

"A little. Weird, huh?"

"No. This place has been the whole of your life." He came to sit on the edge of the tub and found her fingers in the foam. "You wouldn't be human if you didn't feel sad."

"What time is it?"

"Five. The stew's nearly done. So that's his favorite meal?"

It was. Stew, and tapioca pudding, and Rice Krispies treats, and beer. "If I hate him, why do I care?"

"Because you're kind. This is the first home-cooked meal he'll have had in more than six years."

"I'm not kind. I'm just buttering him up. He'll be mad when I tell him I'm leaving. It may get ugly."

"Ugly I can handle, as long as we're outta here by midnight. That's when the bike turns into a pumpkin."

She grinned. "Midnight. Okay. I'll remember."

He caught the last word with his mouth and gave it the kind of thorough tasting that had Jenny clutching his shoulder. Pulling back, he started taking off his clothes. By the time he was naked, Jenny had made room for him in the tub. It was another minute before he had her arranged on his lap, no time before he was inside her, and not much more before Jenny felt the crescendo of tiny explosions in her deepest, sweetest heart.

Previews of coming attractions, she thought and held the image along with a smile through lingering kisses, climbing out, and drying. The smile faded when she pulled on the flowered dress Darden had sent, and was completely gone by the time Pete walked her outside.

"Won't you change your mind and let me come?" he asked.

When she shook her head, she felt the springy shiver of less than half the hair Darden was expecting to find. He wasn't going to like that at all. "I have to go by myself."

"I could drive you. Be your chauffeur."

If only, she thought and headed for the garage. "I have to go alone."

"But you don't have a license."

"I know how to drive." She had been starting the Buick and turning it around once a month for the last six-plus years. Sometimes she had even driven it away. Oh, yes, she knew how to drive. Maybe not well. But going into town was forward, and forward was easy.

"What if someone stops you?"

"Who would? Anyone who sees me will call the police station, but the chief will be home having dinner and Dan'll be in town watching for the bus."

"Did he tell you that?"

"No. But I know Dan."

And she was glad that he would be there. She didn't know what Darden would do when he saw her hair.

Jenny knew he wouldn't beat her. That wasn't his style. Rather, he would prey on her weakness, would poke her guilt back to life and prod it until it had swollen to ten times its normal size, until it was so oppressive she couldn't breathe, until she was willing to do anything, *anything* to make it shrink.

If that happened, she might lose her resolve.

She whirled around and clutched Pete's shoulders. "You have to be here when we get back, promise me, *promise* me, Pete?"

He crossed his heart.

She might have asked it a dozen times and still not been reassured, not for lack of faith in Pete, but for fear of Darden. But she had to leave. It would not do at all to be late.

So she climbed into the Buick, turned the key, and pressed its aged engine to life. Moments later, she was weaving down the road and into town.

Chapter Twenty

It shouldn't have been dark at 6:12, but the clouds had been gathering over the heat all afternoon and were piled so thick that the lowering sun was lost. What remained was a stifling gloom.

Jenny heard the bus first, a warning rumble coming from over the rise. She could almost smell the diesel and dirt before they became reality when the bulky vehicle rolled into town. Hissing and whining, the bus pulled in ahead of the Buick. As Jenny watched, its door swung open.

Nothing happened at first. Jenny stared at that door, stared without blinking while she struggled to breathe. Every imaginable glitch preventing Darden's return raced through her mind, every imaginable complication that might keep him from walking off that bus had been prayed for. *Please, God, let him go somewhere else.* She didn't care where, as long as it wasn't near her.

Then he appeared, and her heart twisted. He wore the slacks and sweater she had taken him on her last visit, and carried a small duffel containing his personal effects. He took one step down, then the next, and hit the ground staring at her, looking none too steady and far older than his fifty-seven years. She wondered if he was sick, or if being free had simply shaken him up.

For sure, *she* wasn't being shaken up by freedom. She was embracing it with open arms. All she had to do was survive that stare.

"Hi, Daddy." She covered the small distance to where he stood, kissed him on the cheek, and took his bag. "How was the ride?"

He continued to stare. Behind him, the door unfolded and shut and the bus wheezed off. Even then he didn't move. He looked stunned.

"Where's your hair?" he finally asked in a strangled voice.

An accident at work, she could say. Burned in the flare of a broken gas range. Close call, she could say. Lucky she escaped with her *life,* she could say.

"I cut it," she said.

"But I like it long. I want to see it long. I want to *feel* it long. MaryBeth," he whined, "what the hell did ya cut it for?"

She had hurt her arm, she could say. She hadn't been able to wash or comb long hair, so she had cut it, she could say. Her arm was better now. Thank you.

"I hated it long," she said. "I always . . . did." Her voice withered at the end, Darden's glare was that frightening.

"So that's my welcome home? That's what I get for sitting more'n six years in the can? That's what I get for dreaming night after stinkin' night of your hair? How could you *do* that to me, baby? I *loved* that hair long."

The guilt, oh, the guilt. *Stay calm. He's my father. No matter. He can't make you do anything you don't want to do. He'll try. You knew he would, but you're not a child anymore.*

"It's only hair, Daddy."

"You cut it right before I got home, knowing how I felt, knowing I wanted it long. You did it to hurt me."

"No." But she had.

"Hey, Darden," said Dan O'Keefe, coming out of the dark, "how's it going?"

Darden faced Jenny for a long moment before acknowledging Dan with a curt, "Not bad."

Jenny looked hard at Dan, begging him, *begging* him with a flurry of brainwaves not to say a word about her leaving or, worse, about Pete. She would tell Darden herself when the time was right.

"So you're out," Dan said.

"Looks that way."

"MaryBeth's done a real good job keeping the house up for you. You ought to be proud of her, doing it alone. I got a call from your parole officer the other day. He says you're thinking of getting the business going again."

Darden shrugged. "I don't know how much moving there is to do. I don't know how people'll feel about hiring an ex-con to do it. Keys in the car, Mary-

Beth? It's startin' to spit." He walked to the driver's side of the Buick.

Dan took the duffel from Jenny and tossed it into the backseat, then closed the door once she slid in. She didn't have to look at him to hear him think: *Call me if there's a problem, Jenny, call me whenever, and I'll do what I can.*

But he couldn't help. With Darden back, no one could.

Darden gunned the engine, swung a U-turn, and sped back through town. By the time they got home, the sprinkle had turned to a steady rain. He pulled into the garage, climbed out, and caught Jenny's hand just as she was about to make a run for the house.

"Come 'ere, baby," he said, pulling her close. "Give Daddy a hug."

Jenny tried to pretend it was innocent, that it was the kind of hugs fathers gave daughters all the time. She wrapped her arms around him and squeezed, and ignored the feel of his mouth on her neck and the way his body curved to fit her, but she couldn't bear it for more than a second, couldn't *bear* it, so she gasped, cried, "Omigod!" and tried to pull away. "The stew'll burn. I have to go."

His arms held. "I need this more than food."

"But I worked so *hard*, Daddy." She wriggled away one body part at a time. "I knew you'd hate my hair, so I worked hard to make dinner right. Please, don't make me spoil it, *please?*"

He let her go. She forced a smile, but it vanished the second she hit the rain. She raced to the house and, ignoring her wet clothes, busied herself at the stove.

Pete was in the attic, packing the last of their things. Her mind's eye saw him there, waiting like they had agreed, letting her talk to Darden one last time. But he was listening, she knew that. He had an ear to the floor in just the spot where the voices from below carried up. He would be down in an instant if Darden tried anything. He would be down, anyway, when it was time.

She clung to that thought.

Darden dropped the duffel on the floor. He grabbed the dish towel from the bar on the oven door and mopped rain from his face and neck. Jenny took it from him in exchange for a beer. "Your favorite. Welcome home."

He put the bottle to his mouth and tipped back his head. The beer glugged past his Adam's apple again, and again, and again. By the time he righted his head, the bottle was empty.

He opened the refrigerator and pulled out a second one. "What a shitty day. First the bus, then your hair, then Dan O'Keefe watching me. I've been watched more in the last six years than in all the ones before that taken together." He slipped an arm around her waist and nuzzled her ear. "The only one I want to be watched by now is you, y'hear, Mary-Beth?"

She tried to take a breath, choked, and began to cough. It was a while before she could stop. She wiped at her nose and her eyes. "I don't feel so good," she whispered.

"That's 'cause your dress got wet. Go change. You must have something else that's nice."

Jenny had the dress she had bought at Miss Jane's. She ran up the stairs to her room, tore off the despicable flowered one, and fumbled wildly in her closet for the other.

"Pete?" she whispered toward the attic. "Are you there?"

"God, yes." He had the hatch up and looked none too pleased. "I don't like this, Jenny. I'm done up here. I'm coming down."

"No."

"You can introduce me, we'll tell him we're leaving, then we're gone. He can help himself to the stew."

"No! I owe him this. Please. Just dinner."

"Who are you talking to, baby?" Darden called.

She whirled around, clutching Miss Jane's dress to her chest. "Not talking. Taking breaths. Breaths."

He came into the room. "We could lie down a little, you and me."

"No, oh no, I'm fine. I want to give you dinner. It's ready."

He reached out and tugged at the dress.

She knew that hungry look and held tighter to the fabric.

"Let go, MaryBeth."

"Dinner," she begged.

"Let me see. Just for a minute."

Still she resisted. That was when he said her name in a harder voice, a voice that told her he would have his way if he had to tie her down to do it, that the more she fought, the more exciting she was, that "seeing" would be the least of it if she didn't give in.

She released the dress, bowed her head, and, like old times, sent her mind off to that special place where the pain and the shame couldn't reach. Only her mind wouldn't stay there this time. It came right back to the bedroom and Darden with a desperation that made her stomach churn. A scream gathered at the back of her throat and threatened to shatter the night.

Stay calm. She listened to the rain on the slate roof. *Stay calm. The choice is made.*

"I need my dress," she said.

He handed it over. "I don't know what's wrong with you. I love you, baby. I love to look at you and touch you. Okay, so it's been a while, but you used to like it."

"I *never* liked it," she muttered into the

folds of the dress. The fabric had barely fallen past her hips when she hurried by Darden and ran down the stairs.

Her hands shook while stirring the stew and dishing it out. She tried to cheer herself by thinking of Pete, of Wyoming, of freedom, of love. But it was hard with Darden in the room. He had a way of sucking out the good in a place and leaving nothing but bad. Even this dress—so long coveted, so special, the first thing Pete had ever seen her wear—was soiled now. She would never wear it again.

"Why aren't you eating?" Darden asked. He was on his third beer and starting to sweat.

Jenny couldn't have swallowed food if her life depended on it. "My stomach's upset. Is the stew okay?"

"It's fine. Just fine. You always were a good cook, MaryBeth, a damn sight better one than your ma, I gotta say."

"She taught me."

"She never made anything like this."

"She did. I remember."

"And I don't? Believe you me, I know what that woman could and could not do. She couldn't cook, she couldn't think of no one but herself, and she couldn't fuck worth beans. You can do all those things, baby."

Jenny scraped back her chair and went to the stove. She gave the stew a venomous stir, took the whole pot to the table, and refilled Darden's plate. She pushed the basket of warm rolls closer. Beyond it, she set a dish of still-warm tapioca pudding and several square Rice Krispies treats, ready and waiting.

From the far end of the table, she said, "I'm leaving, Daddy."

Darden looked up and made a face. "Leaving what?"

"Here."

He sighed. "Some things never change. Ten times a week when you were little, you said you were leaving. Running away, you said then. Come on, baby, come on. It's time to grow up."

"I have. That's why I'm leaving."

He sat back in his chair and stared at her.

Once, she would have shrunk from that stare. Now she thought of her choices and stared right back.

He pushed a hand through his hair. It had gotten thinner in the time he was away. "MaryBeth, baby, don't do this to me now. You're what I lived for in jail. Don't start in with threats."

"I'm leaving."

"Shut up, MaryBeth."

"I'm leaving tonight."

He sighed again. "Okay. Where are you going this time?"

Jenny was past the point of caring if he pretended she was a child. "It doesn't matter where. I just wanted you to know."

"You're right, it doesn't matter where. I'll find you wherever. I'll come after you and bring you right back."

"No you won't."

He frowned at her then. "What's wrong with you?"

"I can't do it. I can't take it anymore."

"Take what? My love, I'm your father. Most girls'd give their right arm to be loved like you are."

Jenny didn't think so.

He came toward her, moving quickly. "Now stop it! You'll do or take whatever I say. You're mine, *mine,* MaryBeth. I made one fuckin' big sacrifice for you. You're not running out on me now."

Pete suddenly filled the door behind Darden, motioning her to come. Jenny saw him there. But she couldn't leave yet. She had to make Darden understand, had to give him one last chance. She owed it to him and to herself. "I can't stay, Daddy. What we do isn't right. It's sick."

"Sick that I love you? Sick that I live for you? Sick that I told them I was the one hit your ma, when it was you all along?"

Jenny gasped. Spoken aloud, the words were like knives. They cut her up inside and made her bleed through all the old crusted scabs.

She shot Pete another quick look. Her eyes had filled with tears by the time they returned to Darden. "It was self-defense! She would have killed me if I hadn't stopped her!"

"Hitting her once would have stopped her. Once, and she'd have gotten away with a concussion. You hit her *five times*."

"I didn't know," Jenny sobbed, "didn't know I was doing it, I was so scared." Her shoulders were slumped, her arms hung limp. No amount of wishful thinking could change the raw truth. "I hurt so bad all over, and she kept coming at me just like she'd been doing for days and days and *days,* so I hit her until she didn't move."

"You killed her, MaryBeth."

Jenny wrapped her arms over her head. "I know, don't you think I know?"

"Want me to tell the chief about that? Or Dan? Huh? You want that, Mary-Beth?"

Her arms fell away, her head came up. "I wanted to tell him when it happened, only you wouldn't let me! You made me sit here and tell stories, and feel guilty because you were in jail, and feel *angry* because you were in jail when I wanted to be there, because I didn't know I could do something like kill someone, and I didn't know what *else* I could do, and it scared me so I couldn't think straight, and *still* you wouldn't let me confess."

Darden moved closer still. "I was trying to save your hide! You'd never have made it in jail. They'd have raped you a hundred times over and left you filthy and diseased. Hell, I wouldn't a even wanted to touch you then. So I spared you that and did six friggin' years myself, and this is what I get—you're *leaving*?"

Jenny fancied Pete was thinking of tackling Darden, he looked that angry. Then he caught Jenny's eye and the anger eased. He hitched his chin toward the door.

She backed that way. "I'm leaving," she told Darden again. She simply couldn't live with what he wanted.

Still he argued, "I took the fall for you. I was punished for a crime I didn't commit."

"You did so commit a crime!" she screamed. "You committed a whole lot of them! Over and over!"

"So I was punished. Shouldn't you be punished, too?"

"I have been. *Have* been. For years and years, in ways you can't begin to imagine. But I'm tired of it, Daddy." She backed farther away.

"You *owe* me!"

Shaking her head, Jenny took another step. "I kept the house going. I turned the car around. I waited till you got home and made you the supper you wanted, and I kept telling myself I owed you, but I don't, I *don't* owe you more than that. If it wasn't for your touching me, she wouldn't have beat me, and if she hadn't done that, she wouldn't be dead. She was my mother. You made her hate me!"

"She was a jealous bitch!"

"She was your *wife!* You were supposed to do those things to *her,* not to me. Why couldn't you have loved her a little? That was all she wanted."

"She wanted Ethan."

"She needed you."

"Well, she sure as hell doesn't need me now, but I need you, MaryBeth. You're here, and you're alive." He stopped and looked at her, smiling. "You got the best of her, y'know, even with your hair short."

Jenny knew then that there would be no reprieve. She could talk all she wanted, but he wouldn't hear what she said, not one word. "I'm leaving now," she said as calmly as she could.

He started around the table. "Think I

won't be able to find you? Don't kid
yourself. I'll follow you to *hell* and bring
you back." He pointed to her chair. "So
get your ass back over here, and save
both of us the trouble."

She started to cry again, large gulps of
pain, because it was all so pathetically
simple. "Why can't you leave me alone?"
she begged. "That's all I want. Just *leave
me alone*."

"Or what? You'll kill me like you killed
her? No way, baby. I can protect myself.
But threaten me again, and I'll tell. So
help me God, I will. Hell, if you leave
here, you're no good to me anyway. It'd
be no sweat off my back if they did lock
you up then."

"It doesn't matter."

"It will once they cuff you and strip
you and stick you in a cell."

"They won't. I'm leaving. I have Pete
now. He's taking me away."

"Pete?" Darden sneered. "Who the
hell's Pete? You're not going anywhere
with anyone named Pete."

"That's where you're wrong," Pete said
in a booming voice.

Darden went right on. "You're not going anywhere with any man but me. You're mine. *Mine.* Besides, what man's gonna want *you?* You got your daddy's mark all over you, baby. What man's gonna take you when he knows all you've done?"

"*I'm* taking her," Pete vowed as he crossed the kitchen. He opened the door and spoke quietly, gently. "Come on, Jenny. He's not worth your tears."

Jenny slipped out.

"Get back here!" Darden roared, but she was already running through the pitch-black rain toward the garage. As soon as she reached it, the motorcycle pulled alongside. She hopped on the back and clung to Pete as he gunned the engine. The machine fishtailed on the wet stones, then shot forward just as Darden ran into its path.

There was a thud and a hideous sound—scream or curse, Jenny didn't know which—and it nearly sent her right off the road, but she couldn't stop or even look back. The choice was made. There was no last hope for change, no going back. She was committed.

The enormity of it had her breathing

in harsh sobs at first. But the dark of night was a cushiony comfort, as was the rain, which cleansed, and there was Pete, mostly Pete, who had heard the worst and stayed with her. Every few breaths, he took a hand from the handlebars and rubbed her fingers, touched her arm, or reached back to tug her closer.

The rain gentled as they passed through the center of town. By the time they reached the other side, it had washed away her tears and become little more than mist, and a warm one at that. She smiled when she recognized the road Pete took, and was pleased, so pleased. He remembered her dream.

He parked the bike in their old hiding spot and helped her off. Taking her hand, he led her through a maze of pine, hemlock, and spruce to the very top of the quarry. There, from a platform of newly bathed dirt, they looked out over the pool.

It was theirs alone. If humans had been there earlier that day, all signs had been washed away. The air smelled of earth and wet leaves. The woods sang softly of leftover rain dripping from bough to bough to mossy bed. The quarry pool was glassy, save for raindrop circles here and there.

Pete laced his fingers through hers. "So fresh here. A beginning. Are you with me, Jenny love?"

Her throat went tight, but she smiled and nodded.

"Know I love you?" he asked.

She nodded again.

His voice grew husky. "This was what brought me through here, y'know. To find you and take you home." He kissed her softly.

Jenny buried her face in his shoulder so that he wouldn't see she was crying again. But he knew. He rubbed her back and pressed her close and whispered gentle, soothing words while, one by one, she wept away her last tiny ties to the past. Finally, with a sniffle and a long, ragged breath, she smiled. When she lifted her head, it was to see his love and know she had made the right choice.

His gaze shifted to the quarry pool. She followed it just in time to see the clouds mirrored in the water shift, then part, exposing a sweet crescent moon.

Let's swim with the moon, she thought and looked up at Pete. *Can we?*

He grinned. *Don't know why not. It's warm enough. It's your dream.*

They peeled off clothes that were already wet. Jenny folded hers in a neat pile and would have done the same for Pete's if he hadn't grabbed her hand and drawn her up. He wove his fingers into her hair until the heels of his hands framed her cheeks.

You are the sweetest, purest, prettiest woman, Jenny Clyde. Come swim with the moon and me.

She ran her hands up his body. Standing on tiptoe, she held his face as he held hers. Eyes wide in anticipation, she nodded.

He positioned himself on the very edge of the platform, a precious vision in Jenny's mind. His body was sculpted, long and lean, dark hair, fair skin, all man. Moonlight glittered in his hair and his eyes, and lit the tiny diamond stud that he had put in his ear for her, just as surely as he had placed the crescent moon overhead.

He stood with his toes curled over, held

his arms out for balance, lowered them to his sides. Then, in a motion so graceful as to take Jenny's breath, he soared up, over, and down. He entered the water with barely a splash, and surfaced moments later to gesture Jenny along.

She stood on the very edge of the precipice with her toes curled over, held her arms out for balance, lowered them to her sides. Then she paused. She couldn't duplicate his grace, but this was no time to worry about what she would look like, where she would land, and what pain she might feel. She had come this far; there was no turning back.

Below, Pete was waiting, smiling, with the light of that crescent moon rippling around him and his arms open wide.

She took a deep breath, bent her knees for the gentlest of boosts, and left the platform on a prayer. Incredibly, the prayer was answered. Her body rose in a perfect arc, descended in a sleek silver line, and slipped neatly into the water, not an arm's length from Pete.

She came back up along his body, surfaced to his applause and a hug, then, led by his hand, dove again. He took her deep, in and around blocks of granite lit by the moon that shimmered on the surface high above. They chased their shadows and each other, and found a sweet playmate in the quarry monster, then shot to the surface with a burst of air and laughter, and clung to each other through bobbing kisses.

Next dive's the one, Pete finally gasped. His eyes were expectant, his smile divine. *Are you ready?*

His face was a stained-glass vision in the night—new places, new people, new love—she saw them all there. Plus kindness and gentleness. And friendship and fairness. And hope.

Was she ready? She took a last look around the quarry, raised her eyes in a silent farewell to the tallest of the evergreen boughs and the moon's sweet smile. Then, etching these in her heart as the best of one life, she looked at Pete and nodded.

Chapter Twenty-one

BOSTON

Heartsick, Casey stared at the last page of the journal before finally setting it down with the others on her lap. But she could not get the last image out of her mind. She remained at the quarry in Little Falls—and unaware of the leather chair where she sat, or the cup of tea that Jordan had made her that waited now on the rattan coffee table alongside a half-eaten slice of pizza, unaware of Jordan himself, sitting halfway down the long sofa diagonal to her chair.

From the quarry, she mentally reran earlier installments of the journal, picking out things like the haircut that Pete had evened up but that hadn't been even at all when Miriam had done repairs, the tray of hors d'oeuvres that Pete had devoured but that Jenny had carried intact to work the next morning, the motorcycle that no one in town had heard, and the visit to Giro's that no one had seen. She recalled the man in the diner talking about a single set of footprints up there at the top of the quarry by Jenny Clyde's clothes.

The pieces fell into place. She raised stricken eyes to Jordan's. "There was no Pete." The psychotherapist in her knew it; the woman couldn't argue. Pete had been too good to be true. Literally. "Jenny Clyde was delusional. She was so desperate for love that she conjured him up. He was her savior. He gave her the courage to leave Darden, leave Little Falls, leave life. She made him real, so that committing suicide became a palatable option." Feeling the bleakness of it, she took a shuddering breath and sat back.

Jordan rose. He didn't leave the room this time, simply went to an oak sideboard that stood against a wall and returned with a handful of pages. "But you were right to question what really happened. She didn't die," he said, and offered her the pages.

Fearful, Casey held his gaze. She wanted to hope, but only one image came. That image had Jenny Clyde in a rehab center much like Caroline, disabled for life after the fall from the top of the quarry.

"Take it," he urged gently.

She had no choice. Not knowing would be worse than anything on paper. Putting the pages on her lap, she began to read.

The call came at three in the morning. Dan O'Keefe rushed into his uniform and drove out to the Clyde house, not because Darden Clyde demanded it or because it was Dan's job, though both were true, but because he was worried about Jenny. . . .

The pages described how Dan had found Jenny in the woods, bundled her up, and driven her to a place far from Little Falls, where she would be safe—leaving everyone in town, most importantly Darden, believing she was dead.

The reading didn't take long. It left Casey first with relief that Jenny had lived and was physically intact, then with admiration for Jordan. It also left her with a slew of new questions.

Her eyes found his. He was still seated on the sofa, where he had remained, patiently, she realized, for the entire time she had been reading, save short breaks to bring her food and drink.

"Your friend was a therapist?" she asked.

"Yes. He works at the Munsey Institute. It's a private mental hospital in Vermont. He met me halfway, took Jenny, and returned to the hospital."

Casey was familiar with Munsey. She also knew that the cost of private hospitals often exceeded insurance coverage, and wondered if Jordan had saved Jenny there, too. "Did you pay?"

"No. I would have, I felt that guilty. I let Jenny down, just like the rest of the town. But the hospital always takes in a few patients for free. Jenny was one of the lucky ones. She needed a place like that if she was to have a chance to recover. It was safe. The doors were locked. Ironically, where most patients there saw themselves as being locked in, Jenny saw those locks as keeping Darden out. Her greatest fear, still, is his coming after her."

"She can't still be there," Casey said, because the days of endless hospitalizations, even for suicidal patients, were long gone.

"No. She stayed for three months. She

had intensive one-on-one therapy, and when she was stable, they added group therapy to the schedule. She's a bright woman. She's a *strong* woman. She came along really well. Like I said, fear of Darden has been the hardest part of her recovery."

"If the fear remains, how could she handle leaving the hospital?" Casey asked.

He smiled gently. "I wish I could say there was a great psychotherapeutic break-through, but the change was pretty circum-stantial. I sent local papers to the hospital, so she was able to read about her death and the funeral that Darden put on. Time passed, and he didn't come after her. That gave her courage. Then she changed her looks."

Casey took in a sharp breath. "I *liked* her looks," she said, though the words were no sooner out when the therapist took over. "But she didn't. She must have felt they were a beacon. Covering up all that red with hair dye would be easy. But the freckles?"

"Dermatologists have remarkable tech-niques at their disposal. Her freckles aren't completely gone, but the shadows that re-main are easily covered with makeup. And the scars on her legs are visible only if you go looking for them. She felt better when those things were done. When she was discharged from the hospital, she went to a halfway house not far from there. She continued seeing her therapist and worked part-time at a diner. It was the perfect job for her. She was in the kitchen cooking, so she wasn't visible to the public. By the end of the year, when Darden hadn't come after her, she was ready to move on."

"Where did she go?"

Wearing an indulgent look and a small, expectant smile, Jordan sat back.

It took Casey all of one minute to come up with the answer. Then she put a hand to her chest and cried a soft, astonished, "Meg?"

He nodded. "Jenny thought Meg Ryan was cute and lovable and funny, all the things she wanted to be, so she chose that name."

"Meg? *My* Meg?" Right under her nose, and she hadn't guessed. But it made total sense—hair so dark and auburn that it could have been dyed, skin that was pale, even the limited scope of Meg Henry's world and the simplicity of her enthusiasm. There was her jumpiness at sudden sounds, and the poker she had been carrying that first day. She hadn't been cleaning the fire-place—she had been frightened that Darden had found her out. And *then* there were the questions Meg asked, questions that came a bit too fast, seemed a bit too odd. *Did you ever wish you had dark hair? Do you like your freckles? Do you worry about your biological clock? Do you have a boyfriend?* Meg Henry wasn't all that much more so-cially adept than Jenny Clyde.

"My Meg," Casey repeated, embarrassed that she hadn't seen then what seemed so obvious now. "But she hasn't been my Meg for long," she reasoned aloud. "Before me, she was Connie's Meg. Clearly, Connie knew who she was."

"Yes."

"Did he hire her for that reason?"

"Yes. His longtime maid was retiring. Jenny knew how to cook, and she knew how to clean. He liked the idea of having her close."

"Because she's kin," Casey said, and ad-dressed another piece of the puzzle. "What's the connection?"

"Your great-grandparents," Jordan an-swered. "Their name was Blinn, and they were from Aroostook County, way north in Maine."

"Blinn? As in Cornelius B.?"

Jordan nodded. "The senior Blinns had two daughters, Mary and June. The daughters were separated in age by more than a dozen years, and were never close. Mary was the older. She married Frank Unger, moved to Abbott, and gave birth to Connie. Years later, June married a local boy, Howard Picot, and gave birth to Jenny's mother, MaryBeth. That made Connie and MaryBeth Picot first cousins. MaryBeth met Darden Clyde at a county fair, moved to Walker to marry him, and gave birth to Ethan, who died, and then to Jenny." He took a breath, let it out. "That makes you and Jenny second cousins."

Casey might have had trouble repeating the lineage, but she got the key points. Connie and MaryBeth Clyde were first cousins. Casey and Jenny were second cousins. Casey and *Meg* were second cousins. Amazing.

"But Connie was a visible guy," she said. "Didn't it occur to Darden that Jenny might take refuge with him?"

Jordan was quietly apologetic. "Connie

might have been visible in your circles, but in Walker? They didn't know the name Unger, and they didn't know psychology. Besides, Darden thought Jenny was dead."

Thought. Past tense. Casey didn't want to think she might have changed that.

Setting the possibility of it aside for now, she said, "Connie hired Jenny, knowing she was his cousin. Did you come to work for him before or after that?"

"Before."

"You got him to hire her?"

"I told him about her. He hired her himself."

"How did he come to hire *you*?"

"Daisy's Mum had been doing his plants for a while. I recognized his name on the roster and started doing the work there myself."

"Why would *you* recognize the name, and not Darden?"

Jordan's smile was dry. "I was a cop, and the son of a cop. I grew up hearing the kinds of background information most people never hear. When MaryBeth died and the trial took place, family names were the kind of trivia that we busied ourselves with. So I knew who and what Connie was. Then, when I came here and met him, he and I clicked."

"Did he know where you were from and what your connection was to Jenny?"

"I told him. He was comfortable with it."

"And you own the shop," she said, unable to keep a thread of accusation from her voice.

Jordan nodded. "I bought it when I moved here."

"From Daisy?"

"She wanted to work there without the responsibility of ownership."

"You didn't tell me you owned it."

"You didn't ask."

No. She hadn't asked. "Why did you buy it?"

"Because I love plants. Because I wanted a steady source of income. Because I needed to put down roots somewhere. Beacon Hill was a good place. Daisy's Mum was a good fit."

"But you're an artist. I saw your work at your parents' house." She didn't tell him she thought it was wonderful. She was still peeved to have been kept so completely in the dark. "How can you do both?"

"I plant by day and paint by night."

"Where do you paint?"

"I have a studio upstairs."

"And you sell your things?" In galleries in Boston and New York, his mother said.

"I also do illustrating."

"Illustrating?"

"Of plants, for things like Audubon publications."

Casey was thoroughly impressed. "Why didn't you tell me you painted?"

"You didn't ask."

"Did you have to parade as a *gardener?*"

"I *am* a gardener," he said without apology. "I love planting things and helping them grow."

Casey had a sudden awareness. "The police station in Walker. All those vines. And the roses near the house. You did those!"

He turned hesitant. "The roses aren't dead?"

"Not at all. The ivy could probably use a pruning." When he seemed relieved, she asked, "Haven't you gone home to look?"

"Not lately." He sat back, the image of resignation. "You met my dad. What do you think?"

Casey smiled. "I adore your mom."

"That isn't what I asked."

Diplomatically, she said, "I think that you and your dad are very different people."

"That's for sure. He wouldn't be pleased if he knew my part in Jenny's escape."

"Not even all these years later?"

"No. He's a by-the-rules kind of guy."

"But Jenny escaped Darden. Wouldn't he appreciate that?"

Jordan gave a doubtful shrug.

"Did you write the journal?" Casey asked.

"No. Connie did."

"Connie." She hadn't suspected that. "When? Why?"

"When Jenny—Meg—came to work for him, she was still edgy and unsure. He wanted to help her without actually treating her as a client, so he encouraged her to write out her story, but she wasn't a writer. She couldn't fill blank pages. So Connie agreed to do the writing himself if she told him her thoughts. She got into that. Connie may have held the pen, but the words are mostly hers."

"But you worked with Connie on the section about you."

"Yes."

"Did he ever consider having it published?"

"No. He considered it confidential. It was therapeutic for Jenny. Once the whole thing was down on paper, she could let it go."

Casey understood that. Journaling had come into vogue as a therapeutic tool for just that reason. Still, she was disappointed thinking about the letter C and the note Connie had scrawled. If he had written the journal himself, they might have been notes to himself.

"Did he mean for me to see the journal?" she asked now.

"He never mentioned it to me. But if he left it in his desk, I'd say he did. Connie didn't do things by chance."

"He died by chance," Casey pointed out. "He didn't plan that. He didn't have advance warning. It was a sudden, massive heart attack. There was no history of heart problems."

Coming forward, Jordan put his elbows on his knees, linked his hands, and smiled sadly. "There was, Casey. He had a mild heart attack before I ever knew him, and he hadn't been feeling well in the months before his death. Ruth knew, although I doubt anyone else did. He put up a good front, then kind of sagged when he got home. I saw him at home, so I knew. He sensed what was coming. He left his affairs neatly arranged."

Casey felt an odd relief. She did want to think that he had deliberately left the beginning of the journal in his desk drawer for her to find. That did, though, remind her of Jordan's concern when she had shown up there earlier that evening. Connie had written, *How to help?*

She sighed. In a cautious voice, she asked, "Have I messed up bad?"

Jordan didn't answer—which, as far as she was concerned, was an affirmation loud and clear.

"Meg's in danger?"

He shrugged. "Don't know. Darden's living with another woman now. Maybe he won't care."

"Fat chance," Casey declared. "Pathological people don't just let go. He'll come after her if only to let her know that he's still in charge. He'll stalk her. He'll lurk in the shadows. He'll intimidate her to the point that all the progress she's made will be reversed." *She's kin. How to help?* "She told me she lives on the flat of the hill. Is it a safe place?"

"There's no doorman, but the front door is locked."

"Well, that's lovely," Casey muttered sarcastically. "He just has to wait nearby until someone else opens the door, then slip in with a smile, saying he's visiting his daughter. No one'll suspect that a man his age is a threat. Aeeeyyyy."

"He won't get to Meg's place unless he learns her name. Meg Henry means nothing to him."

"Casey Ellis does. I introduced myself by name any number of times. I said I was from Boston."

"The phone book will give him the address of your condo, but there's nothing to connect the condo with the townhouse, and the townhouse is where Meg works."

Casey swallowed. She squeezed her eyes shut in a telling way.

Jordan understood. "Ah, Christ," he murmured.

Without opening her eyes, Casey said, "I gave my business card to the editor of the newspaper. It's my brand-*new* business card, the one I just did up at Kinko's with the address of my brand-new office." She opened her eyes and wailed softly, "I was trying to help. I didn't know where Little Falls was, so I went looking, and I didn't know Jenny was supposed to have died"— she stared hard at Jordan—"because I hadn't been *privy* to the last set of pages."

"Hey, it's not *my* fault. I didn't know he was leaving *any* pages for you to see. When he gave the last chapters to me, I assumed he was breaking the journal up for safe-keeping. He never told me I was holding them for you."

"And I didn't ask what you had and what you knew," Casey droned. Bending forward, she pressed her face to her knees. "I wanted to help—I mean, *really* wanted to help. He'd never asked me for anything be-fore. I wanted to do it right." Sitting up again, she gave Jordan a dismal look. "I have a way of messing things up. I act with-out thinking. We're talking mega-impulsive. There I was, up in that luncheonette, asking in a big loud voice how they could be sure Jenny was dead if there was no body. I sug-gested she might have been carried down-stream, gotten out, and walked away. I asked who might have given her haven. When *they* asked if I thought she was still alive, I said yes in my big loud confident voice. So where does that leave us?"

"On alert," Jordan replied.

"Maybe no one will tell Darden," she said hopefully, but his expression told her otherwise.

"Talk of your visit will spread around town, but so will talk of Darden going on the warpath. If my dad hears that, he'll call."

"Does your father know Jenny's alive?"

"No. But he knows she was the reason I left. He'll put two and two together—the timing and all—and he'll call. For whatever faults I found with his style of law enforcement, I never questioned his smarts."

"Then we just wait?"

"Not much else to do right now."

"Do we tell Jenny?"

He thought about that for a minute. "Not yet. There's no sense in frightening her."

"She'll hate me."

"No. She adores you. Right from the beginning, she was telling me how smart and sweet and *beautiful* you are." He paused. "I didn't argue with her."

Casey felt a melting inside. When he looked at her that way, sexy and knowing, he was her gardener again. But now she knew he was much more—entrepreneur, artist, savior of Jenny Clyde. Casey needed time to process it all.

She looked away. Seconds later, she glanced at her watch. It was nearly eight, still light outside Jordan's window, but growing mellow as the sun lowered. She felt a sudden urge to be in her garden. She needed the comfort it would give her.

But she couldn't get herself to go home yet. Another urge was even stronger.

Rising, she said quietly, "I have to visit my mom."

Jordan was just as quickly on his feet. "I'll take you."

"No need. My car's right outside."

"So's mine."

"But what if someone calls to warn you about Darden?"

He pulled a cell phone from his pocket. It was smaller and far more high-tech than hers.

"Ah," she said. "I should have guessed. Do you always carry that?"

He nodded.

She thought of the times they had stood so close that clothing was pressed to near nothing. "I never felt it," she remarked.

He stared at her. *You were too busy feeling other things,* she could all but hear him say.

With a growing warmth on her cheeks, she turned toward the door.

Jordan guided her down the stairs and out a back door to the Jeep. Part of her wanted to ask if he didn't have a luxury car stashed away along with all of his other secrets. The other part of her, though, was content with the Jeep. Entrepreneur, artist, gardener—it fit him.

He negotiated the traffic skillfully, knowing just where he was going. When he pulled up in front of the nursing home without a word of direction from her, she said, "Do you deliver the flowers from Connie yourself?"

"Sometimes. But I've never met your mother, if that's what you're asking."

It was. Casey was thinking back to the discussion they'd had on a bench in the Public Garden, when she had first told him about Caroline. He had been genuinely sympathetic. He had asked appropriate questions. Nothing he'd said would have been inconsistent with his knowing Caroline's situation. He might have indeed put those flowers on Caroline's dresser himself, even talked with her, and still his questions would have been apt.

Casey opened the door and slid out of the Jeep. When she turned back to thank him for the ride, he was already rounding the car. Putting a light hand at her back, he guided her to the steps, and she didn't object. She had been here many times with friends when Caroline had first been injured. The closest of Caroline's Providence friends still came from time to time, and Brianna still came with her once in a while. But once in a while wasn't now, and Brianna wasn't Jordan. When she was with someone, a link to the living world, the ache inside her wasn't so bad.

Casey smiled at the woman at the front desk and continued up the stairs with Jordan by her side. She waved at the night nurse on the third floor, and went on down the hall. When she paused on the threshold of her mother's room, it had nothing to do with Jordan being with her, and everything to do with the IV drip, the oxygen tube, and the heart monitor. These were new.

"Oh God," she whispered softly.

"When did you talk with the doctor last?" he asked.

"This afternoon while I was driving back from Maine. Seeing it's something different, though."

"Should I wait outside?"

She shook her head no. She wanted him with her. The hollow inside would be *devastating* if she was alone.

Caroline had her back to the door. Casey rounded the bed, switching on the small bureau lamp as she went. It illuminated a sweet bouquet of apricot roses. She touched them to show Jordan that she appreciated them, then went the rest of the way to be by her mother's side. She kissed Caroline, but it was a minute before she was able to work her mother's free hand out from under the sheet. It felt cooler than usual. Sitting on the edge of the bed, Casey warmed it against the knot in her throat.

Swallowing down the knot, she forced a brightness into her voice that she didn't feel. Caroline's eyes were still half open, which meant she hadn't settled in to sleep for the night. "Hey, Mom. How're you doing?" When Caroline didn't respond, she said on a hopeful note, "You've given the doctors a scare. But the IV must be doing the trick. Your breathing's no worse." It was no better either—a low rasp through faintly parted lips—but Casey continued to keep her voice light. "I brought you a guest. He's a friend of mine." She tacked on a whispered, "I think," and glanced up at Jordan.

He hunkered down by the side of the bed so that he might be in Caroline's line of sight. "Definitely. Hi, Ms. Ellis."

"Caroline," Casey corrected.

"Caroline."

"College graduation was the cutoff point. After that, she wouldn't respond to my friends unless they called her by her first name. She wanted to be considered their friend, too. Didn't you, Mom?" When Caroline offered nothing more than that low rasp in and out, Casey scolded, "You have to say hello back."

After a prolonged silence, Casey let out a breath of her own. Heartbreak collided with frustration, producing a spark of annoyance. "Jordan worked for Connie. He designed the garden at the townhouse. It's spectacular, Mom. So's the art on Connie's walls. His wife, Ruth, did a lot of it. She has a place in Rockport. I drove up there on Friday. She's a very nice person."

"Casey," Jordan warned quietly.

She ignored him. "And then there's Abbott. That's the name of the town where Connie grew up. I was there this morning. Omigod, was it only this morning? I feel like an eon has passed since then. It was a hoot, Mom. I didn't know which house was his, but I saw ones that might have been. I saw the ruins of the old shoe factory where his mother probably worked. And I saw where he went to school. It's closed up now. The kids are bused."

Casey felt Jordan staring at her. She glared back. "What? Is this wrong, Jordan? I've spent the last three years saying all sorts of sweet and positive things, and it hasn't helped. Maybe this will." She returned to Caroline. "Besides, you probably recognize me more this way, right, Mom? I was always challenging you. I was contrary more often than not. Jordan, here, is a more pleasing person."

"My dad would argue with that," Jordan said, dragging a chair forward. "He couldn't stand me." He sat in the chair.

"Just because you're a 'bleeding heart'?"

"The term he usually used was 'sissy.'"

"Excuse me?" Casey said, because she

couldn't imagine a man any less sissyish than Jordan.

"From way back when I was a kid, that was what he called me."

"Why?"

"Because I liked to draw. Because I was happy working in the garden. These were not things that spelled M-A-N in his book." He added a cynical, "So I gave him what he wanted."

She heard anger in Jordan's voice. This was no stating of fact, as he'd previously done. He was telling her what he felt inside, and it intrigued her. "Which was?"

"I played football. Beefed up the muscles, beefed up the attitude. I was a local hero. I was the talk of the town. I was the one all the girls wanted to date."

She waited. "And?"

"I dated as many as I could, played one off against the other. A total ladies' man. Part of me loved it."

"The other part?"

"Hated myself. I knew how shallow the whole thing was. I hurt my shoulder in my senior year—oh, I didn't do it deliberately, but I wasn't sorry it happened."

"Oh my," Casey whispered, finding another clue that she'd missed. "Dan's shoulder. Your scars. His ached when he was tense. You rub yours."

"My posture changes when I'm tense. The shoulder feels stress."

"What happened to the girls?"

"When the football was done? They hung around for a while. When I moved back to Walker, they fell to the wayside."

"Why did you?"

"Move back? Two reasons. It was a cheap place to live while I built a portfolio. And my mother begged me to come home. My sisters had all married and left town—"

"And there's *another* thing," Casey broke in. "You didn't tell me you had *sisters*."

"You didn't ask," he reminded her. "It was clear you didn't want to know anything personal. You loved the sex because it was anonymous and therefore dangerous, and because you wanted to shock Connie."

She was vaguely aware of her mother lying there beside them. More, though, she was aware of the bitterness in Jordan's voice. And he was right. Anonymity, danger, shock—they were a turn-on indeed, but they didn't tell the whole story. "It didn't feel anonymous," she confessed. "The whole garden thing didn't. There was a connection the first time I saw it." More quietly, she added, "The first time I saw you."

Eyes locked with his, she felt the connection still. It was stronger now and just new enough to frighten her. "Finish your story," she said to ease the fear. "About Walker. About working with your dad. How'd that come about, if you two didn't get along?"

"I needed money, and my dad needed help. I figured I could do it for a couple of years."

"Did you really hate it?"

He looked down at his hands. When he looked up again, his voice was calmer. "Not all the time. The people in Walker are good folk. There's definitely a sense of belonging. As boring as cruising around town could be, there was always someone who'd wave or smile or gesture you over and give you a bag of homegrown tomatoes. What I hated was the law enforcement stuff—locking up drunks, enforcing restraining orders, hunting down underage kids who'd stolen smokes from the general store. Those kids bothered me the most. They were begging for attention, begging for someone to show a little interest in them, but my father didn't see it that way. He saw the problem as a lack of discipline and the solution as a night in the slammer. 'Book 'em, Dan-O,' he'd say, like he was a TV star, like these kids even knew the phrase!" He took a tight breath. "So I booked 'em, but then I made a point to talk with them as much as I could. Hence, I was a 'bleeding heart.' "

Casey was thinking that "bleeding heart" was better than "sissy," when she recalled what Ruth had told her about Connie. "My father had a similar experience with his father."

"I know. We shared that."

"You told him about you and your dad?"

"He asked."

"And he told you about him and his dad?"

"I asked."

Casey felt a moment's jealousy, but Jordan eased it. "He couldn't have said those things to you, Casey. He wouldn't have risked looking weak in your eyes. Me, I was nothing. He didn't care how he looked. Besides, once I told him my story, he knew I'd understand his."

She nodded and looked back at her mother. "Are you taking all this in, Mom?" she asked, but got only that low raspy sound in return. She jiggled Caroline's hand against her neck. "You're eavesdropping on pretty riveting stuff." She glanced at the IV bottle, which continued its slow drip, and at the oxygen tube, which lay inert, and at the heart monitor, which beeped ever so softly and steadily.

So, what do you think, Mom? she mused silently. *Does he have potential?*

Caroline would surely say he did. She would like his looks. She would like his vulnerable side. She would like the fact that he was an artist.

What about the Connie connection? Casey wondered, but she figured that Caroline would be too impressed with Jordan to care that Connie had been the one to hire him. Caroline would be thinking that Jordan was head and shoulders above Casey's other beaus.

But he lied to me, Casey might argue and amend that in the next breath. *Well, maybe he didn't lie, but he let a misconception stand. The dark and brooding gardener? That big macho act? What does that say about his character?*

Caroline would say, insightfully, that Jordan had portrayed himself as being all brawn, because he had grown up believing that machismo was more appealing to women than turpentine and oils. The message in *that,* Caroline might add, was that he had done what he did to impress Casey, which meant that he liked her.

Of course he likes me. The sex is great.

Caroline would roll her eyes. She would tell Casey to grow up, and inform her that love wasn't only about sex, for which Casey had no comeback at all. She didn't think this was about love. It was way, way, way too soon.

Confused and discouraged, she looked over at Jordan. "We ought to go."

Casey didn't even stop for her car, but let Jordan drive her straight to the townhouse. They went in the back garden gate, and for the longest time she just stood there in the dark, drawing in the smell of the woods. It had a healing quality. She welcomed its comfort.

Jordan remained by the gate. Looking back, she sensed his hesitance. So she returned to him, but there was no seductive little body slide this time, no purring or sweet taunts. She wasn't angry at him. Oh, yes, he might have told her from the start who he was. But he hadn't lied. He was her gardener. That was what she had needed him to be.

And she needed him to be something different now. She slid a hand into his and asked softly, "Spend the night?"

"As what?" he asked back, suggesting that the role-playing had changed for him, too.

"You," she said and prayed he wouldn't ask more questions, because she didn't have any more answers.

He didn't ask. Instead, he drew up her hand, kissed her knuckles, put an arm around her shoulder, and set off for the house.

It was a long time before they fell asleep, but Casey wasn't concerned. Sundays were for sleeping in. Totally aside from the absorption of lovemaking, which didn't allow for worrying about Caroline or Jenny or Darden, there was the luxury of being in bed with someone she cared about. Casey thought about this when she awoke briefly at six and nestled into the cup of Jordan's body. Her last thought before falling back to sleep was that she could stay this way until noon.

Fate, however, didn't allow that.

Chapter Twenty-two

First came Angus. When he leapt up onto the bed, Casey came awake with a start. Calming quickly, she wondered if she could sit up and pet him without scaring him off. In that instant, though, he only had eyes for Jordan. Wading through the pile of covers, he climbed gracefully over Jordan's chest to the side away from Casey, turned, and crouched. Not quite satisfied, he extended a single paw over Jordan's ribs. Then, regal, possessive, even defiant, he squared his head and stared at her.

"Oh boy," she murmured, and might have gone on to say something about male buddies, if a phone hadn't rung. Caroline? Her eyes flew to the nightstand, heart pounding for the second time in as many minutes.

But the ringing phone was Jordan's. Barely opening his eyes, he stretched an arm up and over Angus to retrieve it. His thumb connected the call. "Yeah," he said. Within seconds, he was wide awake. "When? . . . What did he say?"

His eyes met Casey's. She couldn't make out the words coming from the other end, but there was no mistaking irritation.

"Yeah. I know her," Jordan said, looking at her now with chagrin. "She might have learned some of that from me. . . . No, I didn't send her there. Why would I have done that? . . . She did *not* know I was your son. There are tons of O'Keefes in Boston." Propping himself up on an elbow, he listened and said, "She probably connected Jordan and Dan at the end and was embarrassed. That was my fault, not hers. What else did Darden say? . . . He didn't make any threats? . . . Fine. Let him curse me. He's hated me since the night Jenny hit him. I'd rather he demonize me than take off looking for her." He listened, sighed. "Hold on, Dad. It was an innocent comment. Jenny's dead and buried. You gotta tell Darden that. The last face I want to see at my door is his. . . . Will you know if he leaves town? . . . Can you *check*? . . . Yes, I'd appreciate that. . . . Sure. . . . Yeah."

Ending the call, he lay back down and rested the phone on his stomach.

Angus had removed his paw and was sitting up, but he continued to stare at Casey.

"Jenny's dead and buried," Jordan murmured in self-justification. "Meg's alive and well."

"Is Darden making noise?" Casey asked, feeling both guilt and dread.

"Yup. He told Dad he wouldn't put it past me to have spirited Jenny out of town and squirreled her somewhere."

"Did he say he was going looking for her?"

"No. But that doesn't mean he won't."

"If he's obsessed, he won't let go."

"Tell me," Jordan said dryly.

"Should we tell Meg?"

He thought about that for a minute. "Not yet. He won't know how to find her. He'll come after me first, then you."

"Me?"

"He has your name. Probably got it in the luncheonette. Your number's in the phone book."

"For the condo."

"We pray."

Casey clutched the sheet to her chest and sat up. "I'm sorry."

He studied her with what looked like exasperation. Then, incredibly, his face softened with a gentle smile. "I know you are. You didn't make this problem. If any one of us—Connie, me, even Meg—had known to fill you in before you visited Walker, you would've held back. But you didn't know. I can fault your act, but not your intent." Wrapping a hand around the back of her neck, he drew her head down to his chest. Long fingers worked their way through her hair, combing, stroking, soothing.

Casey closed her eyes. The last time anyone had done this for her, it was her mother's soothing hands and Casey had been too young to know how old she was. Between Caroline's condition and Darden's threat, relaxation should have been impossible. But Jordan was superseding all that. What he was doing was heaven.

She purred her satisfaction, then whispered, "Is Angus still staring?"

"Yup," he whispered back.

"Does this bode ill?"

"Nah. He's in here, isn't he? Seems to me,

as recently as last week he wouldn't leave Connie's room."

"He's a good cat."

"It's a good house."

Casey took a deep breath. "A friend of a friend wants to buy."

"You can't sell."

"Why not?"

"Because I love the garden. Someone else may not want me to tend it."

"Is that what you are, a tender?"

"Tender's a sissy word. I'm a gardener."

"You're a painter." She loved saying that. It was still a surprise.

"I couldn't be one without the other."

"Not because of the money."

"No. The inspiration."

She was thinking that she understood that completely, when the sound of the doorbell broke into her thoughts. Angus was off the bed in a shot. Heart pounding, she bolted up. "Who is that?" she asked as she jumped out of bed.

Jordan was on his feet and pulling on his khaki shorts. "My car's outside. That makes me nervous."

She reached for her robe. "Would Darden know that car?"

"Sure would." He zipped. "I've driven it to Walker." He fiddled with the button at the waist. "Not in a while. But Darden wouldn't forget."

Casey pushed her arms into the robe. "And if he did have this address—"

"—my car here would confirm his suspicions," Jordan finished and made for the hall.

She followed, tying the belt of the robe as she ran. "It can't be Darden. He was talking with your dad in Walker just a little while ago."

Jordan trotted down the stairs. "It was last night that he talked with my dad. Late. Dad tried calling me at home and figured I was out. It didn't occur to him to try my cell number until Mom mentioned it this morning."

Casey ran down after him, praying that it wasn't Darden at the door. If the man came to Boston and found Jenny, his appearance would wreak havoc in her life. She was Meg now. She felt safe. To have that safety shattered would be tragic, and it would all be Casey's fault. She would have *really* let Connie down then.

Jordan strode through the foyer. Putting

one hand on the door, he looked through the sidelight.

Stopping several feet behind him, Casey held her breath.

Jordan blew his own out with a sputtered half-laugh and stepped back. "I believe it's for you," he said with a hint of chagrin.

Puzzled, she glanced through the sidelight. At the same time that she saw Jenna, Brianna, and Joy, they saw her. But they had also seen Jordan. They were looking alternately astonished, excited, and amused, pointing at the doorknob, telling her to open up.

She looked at Jordan. "Are you ready for this?"

"Would I ever be?" he asked, and reached for the knob. He pulled the door open, then stood with remarkable dignity while Casey's friends looked him over, talking all the while.

"Couldn't find a parking space in the Court," Brianna announced.

"Had to park on West Cedar," added Jenna.

"Good thing we didn't give up," Joy declared.

Brianna murmured, "Why, Casey, you little

devil." Her eyes remained on Jordan. "And I was worried?"

"You've been avoiding us," scolded Jenna, but she, too, was looking at Jordan.

Same with Joy, who chided, "Not returning calls."

"Don't I recognize this man?" It was Brianna again, singing the question, because she certainly did recognize the man.

"Don't *I?*" asked Jenna, though her tone was more puzzled than teasing.

All three waited, looking expectantly at Jordan.

Casey gave a resigned sigh. "Ladies, this is Jordan O'Keefe. Jordan, left to right, please meet Jenna, Brianna, and Joy, my best friends."

Jordan nodded to each, then, fully composed, said, "I'm sorry. If I'd known you were coming, I'd have dressed."

Jenna chuckled. Joy snickered. Brianna eyed him askance and cooed, "Excuse me, but didn't I see you working in the garden out back last week?"

"That's not where I saw him," Jenna said with a look of dawning. "It was at an art show—"

"He's an artist," Casey confirmed. "And he's my gardener."

"And obviously something else, too," put in Joy. Her gaze was on the button of Jordan's shorts, which had never quite gotten fastened in his haste to get to the door.

Brianna turned to Casey with barely suppressed glee. "I'm sorry. I would really like to dwell on the nature of your relationship with the gardener who is an artist, but this is my moment and I'm taking it." She stuck out a hand. It was her left one, and it wore a beautiful new diamond ring.

Casey gasped loudly. "Brianna! Omigod! You did it!" She gave Brianna a tight hug, then held her back to look at the ring. "It's magnificent." She hugged her again. "I'm proud of you."

Brianna was beaming. "So am I."

"When did you get it?"

"Friday night. I'd have told you sooner, if you'd answered your calls."

Jordan broke in, scratching the back of his head in a sheepish gesture, "Uh, this is where I make my exit, ladies." The implication was that he had been responsible for Casey's unanswered calls. It was a perfect alibi, saving Casey from having to mention Maine. "Congratulations, Brianna," he said.

"Oh, don't leave," Brianna cried. "We're celebrating!" As she spoke, Joy produced a bottle of champagne, and Jenna a large bakery bag. "If Casey has orange juice, we have Sunday brunch. It may not be as good as the one Meg made, but we can pretend."

At that very moment, as though conjured up by the sound of her name, Casey saw Meg as she turned in from West Cedar. Her head was bowed. From the distance, she looked lonely, even dejected.

Casey felt a new soft spot inside. Meg was her cousin. Her *cousin*.

"Okay, guys," she ordered her friends, including Jordan in the group, "you all go inside. I'm going to talk to Meg and see what we can do." Cinching her robe tighter—and not caring one whit that it was all she was wearing—she ran barefoot down the steps and along the sidewalk.

Meg looked up. Stopping short, she broke into a smile that transformed her face into something quite pretty.

Casey smiled back as she neared Meg. "I know that I'm making a total fool of myself running barefoot down the street in my bathrobe, but my friends just got here. Brianna's engaged! Isn't that *wild?*" She slipped an arm through Meg's and ushered her toward the townhouse. "You could *not* have come at a better time. Can we do an impromptu celebration? They brought champagne and something from a bakery, but you're the one who knows if we have orange juice and, after that, what we have in the fridge to scrounge up. Can you help?"

Though Meg continued to smile, Casey thought she looked a little pale. It struck her that she was simply wearing less makeup. Looking for them now, she could see the faded dots where vivid freckles had once been.

"I can help," Meg said eagerly.

With their arms still linked, Casey put her head close. It was easy; they were much the same height. "But I have to warn you," she said in the way of a woman-to-woman conspiracy, "Jordan's here."

"Jordan?"

"He spent the night."

"Spent . . . the night?"

Lips pressed together to suppress a smile, Casey met her gaze.

When understanding dawned, Meg's eyes lit. "You and Jordan?"

"Don't you think he's gorgeous?"

"Yeah, but he's . . . *Jordan*."

Casey knew exactly where Meg was coming from. She, on the other hand, came from a different place.

"Precisely," she said, guiding Meg up the stairs and into the townhouse.

Within half an hour, Jordan had added a shirt to his shorts, Casey had put on cutoffs and a camisole, and Meg was serving a full breakfast for five on the table in the garden in the sun. The rhododendrons were nearly in full flower, the lilies taller, the verbena richly purple and broader. Wherever the fragrance came from, it was appropriately festive in honor of Brianna.

They were just digging into huevos rancheros when Jordan's phone rang. Casey's eyes flew to his, but he had already gotten up from the table. He answered the phone as he walked toward the office. Making sure to smile for Meg's sake, she glanced regularly in his direction. When he ended the call and caught her gaze, she joined him there.

"That was my father," he said quietly. "Darden's car is gone."

Casey's heart sank. "What does 'gone' mean?"

"Not in the garage, not in the driveway, not in the parking lot of the church or anywhere else around town."

Casey moaned. "How long has it been gone?"

"They don't know. Darden could have taken off after he called Dad last night. Or he could have left early this morning." He punched out another number. "Boston cop," he murmured to Casey, then said into the phone, "Hey, John. Jordan O'Keefe here. Remember that situation you and I hoped would never crop up?. . . Yeah. Afraid so."

Casey saw another Jordan then. Listening to his half of the conversation, she heard the consummate professional at work. Cool and levelheaded, he gave the detective on the other end as much factual information as he had on Darden, his car, and its plates. He gave the addresses of Casey's condo in the Back Bay and his own on the hill, since both were in the phone book, and Darden might head there. He gave the address of the townhouse on Leeds Court, saying that it wouldn't hurt to have a cruiser pass by from time to time, just in case. He also gave the address of Meg's apartment on the flat of the hill, but with the caveat that it was simply an FYI thing.

"Darden doesn't know the name Meg Henry," he said as much to himself as to Casey when he ended the call, "and, anyway, her phone number's unlisted. He won't know where she lives unless he spots her on the street and follows her home."

"She looks different now."

"Not that different," Jordan said with regret.

"Why's he driving a Chevy, and not the Buick?"

"The Buick died long ago. The Chevy belongs to the woman he lives with. Her name's Sharon Davies."

"And she really has T-O-U-G-H on the plates?"

"That's what Dad said."

"If she's tough, what's she doing with Darden?"

"He has a house. Talk has it that she was

moving from town to town with her two kids, staying wherever she could, spending as little money as she could. When she moved in with Darden, the deal was that she would do the cooking and cleaning in exchange for a solid roof over her head."

"Does she know where Darden went?"

"Looks like she's with him."

"What about the kids?"

"They're at the house, but they don't know a thing. They can't say when Darden left. They were both sleeping."

"She left her kids alone?"

"They're old enough. The daughter's sixteen, the boy's eleven."

Casey tried to be positive. "It could be an innocent little trip," she said, but she didn't believe it any more than Jordan did, judging from the look on his face. So she quickly added, "Should I take Meg away?"

"Nah. That'd be more upsetting to her. Besides, Darden wouldn't know to come here. He didn't know who or what Connie was. If he had, he would have shown up here long ago. For now, she's safest with us."

* * *

Brianna, Jenna, and Joy were gone by noon. Casey walked them to their car on West Cedar. When she returned, she found Jordan on the sidewalk talking with Jeff and Emily Eisner, and it only made sense to invite them into the house and out to the garden. There was food left. Jeff and Emily were hungry. Jordan wanted seconds, and Casey wasn't averse to having more herself.

Meg was delighted, because she clearly liked Emily. They knew each other from Emily's visits to Connie, and talked easily. Neither Emily nor Jeff talked down to her. To the contrary, they almost seemed protective—praising her baked French toast, thanking her warmly when she came around with the carafe to refill coffee cups, chatting with her about local shopkeepers.

Casey noticed this. But she also noticed how comfortable Jordan was, even more so than when Brianna, Jenna, and Joy had been there. Then he had remained on the periphery of the girl talk that centered on Brianna's engagement, but with Emily and Jeff he was in his element. This was the social side of Jordan that Casey had never seen. He was totally adept.

She was thinking about that, nursing a

last cup of coffee, when the Eisners gave their thanks and left. Jordan walked them back through the house and returned with the Sunday paper. Casey watched him approach. He put the paper on the table, sifted out the front page, and sat down. It was a minute before he realized she was staring at him.

He set the paper down and arched his brows in a silent question, *What?*

"Emily whispered *the* most interesting thing in my ear when they were leaving," Casey said sweetly. "I told her how pleased I was to have Jeff and her as neighbors, and *she* said how grateful she was to *you* for going over there and suggesting she drop by when I was so down last week. *That* was manipulative, Jordan."

He didn't answer, just sat there with a small smile on his face.

"I should be furious," she said.

Still he didn't speak.

"So why aren't I?" she asked.

"Because," he said quite correctly, "you know my heart was in the right place."

She did know that. Regardless of the ways in which he might have misled her, she had never sensed an ounce of malice. Mischief?

Yes. Her gardener had been laconic by design. Had he been less so, he would have given himself away. He was knowledgeable and articulate. He was insightful. He had known that Emily Eisner was what Casey had needed that day, though he'd had no way of knowing about the piano bench.

It struck her as she sat looking at him now, though, that Caroline was right. Scruffy beard, torn tee shirt, worn jeans, unlaced boots—like taciturnity, they were part of the macho image he was conditioned to play where women were concerned.

"Anything else on your mind?" he asked gently.

Thinking that he didn't need to put on a macho image, when he was masculinity at its best even without, she shook her head.

Then she thought again. "Yes." She glanced around at sun-strewn paths and flowers growing more lush by the day. "How can I feel content, at a time like this?" It was an ominous time, a time of waiting, and Darden was only part of the problem. There was Caroline. Yes, Casey felt little catches inside when she thought of either one of them, but the panic she might have felt was in control.

By way of answer, Jordan sank lower in his chair, stretched out his legs, and grinned lazily.

It was the garden, he was saying. The garden was an oasis, an escape from the woes of the world. And no, she couldn't sell it. She understood that now. Her condo in the Back Bay couldn't hold a candle to this. Nor, truth be told, could the farm in Rhode Island. That farm had been Caroline. This townhouse with its magic garden was Casey. This was where she was meant to be.

She sensed that Connie was pleased with her realization, and that pleased her in turn.

Still Jordan grinned. Oh, he was saying more, all right. He was saying that *he* was here, and that made a difference. He was right. But she wasn't admitting it.

The Sunday morning sounds of birds and a city moving at half-speed were suddenly broken by the honk of a horn. A second honk followed, then a third, a fourth, and on—and not in the way of a car alarm. These honks were irregular, man-made, jarring, and angry. They came from the front of the Court.

Casey's eyes met Jordan's.

Laziness gone in a flash, he was out of the chair, loping down the stone path to the door.

She was fast on his heels. "Dudley wouldn't have been so stupid."

Jordan took the stairs two at a time. "Sure he would. He'd love to take credit for sparking a story."

Casey ran faster to keep up, down the hall and through the front foyer. Jordan pulled the door open just as she came alongside.

A dented Chevy sat half on the cobblestones, half on the curb that circled the center grove of trees. It faced in the opposite direction of the rest of the cars, with the driver's door at a space between parked cars, smack in front of Casey's walk. She didn't have to look at the license plate to know that the irate driver was Darden Clyde.

"Go back inside," Jordan told her as he started down the steps.

Ignoring his warning, Casey followed him right down. They reached the front gate as Darden emerged from the car.

"There's no *fuckin'* place to park here," he yelled, advancing on Jordan. "Okay, O'Keefe, where is she?"

"Who?" Jordan asked. Standing with his

shoulders straight and his feet slightly apart, he was large and immovable enough so that even Casey had to stand behind.

"My daughter," Darden bellowed, red in the face.

Casey watched the man with a morbid fascination. Had she not known what he had done to Jenny, she might have thought him good-looking. Despite thinning hair, his features were even and his eyes a striking blue. But she did know what he had done. That gave everything about him a predatory look.

"You buried your daughter," Jordan said.

"With no body in that grave, and then comes a woman yesterday," he shot Casey a hateful glance, "shooting her mouth off about MaryBeth not being dead, and suddenly here *you* are at the house of that very woman. You left town right after MaryBeth disappeared. There's a connection."

"MaryBeth is gone, Darden. Dead."

Casey couldn't argue with that. MaryBeth was dead. So was Jenny. But Meg was alive and somewhere behind her in the house.

"What'd you do, O'Keefe?" Darden seethed, chin forward, nostrils flared. "Smell something good back there in Walker and take her away for yourself? Pete? There was no Pete. Pete was *you*. But she's mine. D'you hear? She's mine. You can't have her. I've come to take her back."

"You're totally wrong about this," Jordan said in a firm voice. "You'd do best to turn around and go back home."

"Not until I get my daughter." Suddenly his eyes flipped up a notch, past Jordan, and a malevolent gleam entered his eye. "Well, well, well. All three at the same address. Isn't *this* interesting."

Casey turned. Meg stood at the open front door, staring wide-eyed at Darden. She looked frozen in fear.

Casey ran back up the steps and put herself between Meg and Darden's view. As softly and gently as she could, given the fear she felt herself, she said, "Don't speak to him. You don't have to say a word."

"Lousy hair color, MaryBeth," Darden taunted, "but it could be purple and I'd still recognize you. I don't know what your game is this time, but you're not getting away with it."

Casey turned so that her back was flush to Meg. She held Meg's hands behind her. Darden hadn't moved from his car; Jordan was still blocking the path. But Casey could see other movement in the Court. Attracted by the ruckus, neighbors had begun to appear—the lawyer, Gregory Dunn, Jeff and Emily, several others that Casey knew by sight but not name. Some were simply curious and watched; a few moved cautiously forward.

One of the latter, the lawyer, had a cell phone to his ear. Casey prayed he was calling the police.

But Darden was one step ahead. With an evil smile, he drew a revolver from his pocket and aimed it at Jordan. Still smiling, he called out to Meg, "Is this what it's come to, MaryBeth? Do I have to kill for your sake for real this time?"

Casey was horrified. In her periphery, she saw the neighbors who had approached now backing off.

When Meg whimpered behind her, Casey held her hands tighter. She knew Jordan didn't have a gun—she might have missed a cell phone in his pocket, but not a gun—which meant that he was in serious danger. She was trying to decide whether he had a chance of rushing Darden without getting shot, when a new movement caught her eye. Someone had slipped out of the car right behind Darden—a woman. She wore a tight, sleeveless blouse, was buxom though not fat, and had short, bleached-blond hair and a hard look.

It was Sharon Davies. Casey knew this without a doubt.

"Drop the gun, Darden," she said in a voice that was as hard as her looks.

"Stay out of this," Darden muttered without even looking back.

"Drop the *gun*," she repeated.

Darden kept the gun trained on Jordan.

"Drop it," Jordan ordered. "Probation violation is one thing, assault with a dangerous weapon is something else entirely. Don't make things worse for yourself."

"Make things *worse*?" Darden hollered, though Jordan was only a few feet away. "She's mine. I want her. If I can't have her, I got nothing to lose. I've rotted for years because of her." He was clearly festering. "I got *nothing* to lose."

Sirens sounded in the distance. Jordan extended a hand. "Give me the gun," he urged softly.

"When hell freezes over," Darden growled.

Grasping the gun with both hands now, he took up the slack on the trigger.

A third hand grabbed for the gun. Casey had barely realized that it was Sharon's when Darden half turned. There was a struggle. Jordan lunged at Darden. A shot rang out.

Meg and Casey both screamed. Casey would have run to Jordan if Meg hadn't started to shake—and if common sense hadn't told her to keep both of them away from that gun. Turning, she held Meg tightly, while she looked, anguished, over her shoulder at Jordan. He was sprawled on the pavement with Darden beneath him. After several seconds, though, she saw him move.

Not so Sharon Davies. She was frozen in place, Darden's gun in her hand. Eyes wide, she stared at his lifeless form.

Jordan pushed himself to his knees. He studied the man for another minute. He searched for a pulse, then looked at Sharon. "He's dead."

Meg gave a small cry. Casey didn't know if it was a cry of grief or relief. She didn't feel the latter herself until Jordan rose to his feet.

Sharon seemed dazed. She met Jordan's gaze with a start. When he held out a hand, she released the gun—and suddenly she looked more haunted than hard. "What he did to MaryBeth?" she said in a quavering voice. "I always heard the rumors. But I told myself it wasn't true, not even when my own daughter said he was touching her in bad ways. She's a wild girl. I figured she'd heard the rumors, too, and was only trying to make trouble. But listening to Darden just now, it all came clear. He raped my daughter. I'm sure he did. She was right. She was right all along. For what he did to her—for what he did to MaryBeth—he deserved to die."

The sirens were coming closer.

Meg was a mass of shakes, but when Casey tried to guide her back into the house, she held her ground with startling strength. So Casey tried to shield her from the sight of Darden, but she wouldn't have that either. She craned her neck until she could see her father, whose unseeing eyes might well have been looking right back.

Casey continued to hold her. Knowing Meg's past, knowing all that Darden had done to her and what it had driven her to do, she imagined that Meg feared Darden would bound right up from the stones and attack. "It's all right," she said softly. "It's all right. He can't hurt you."

"I dream this," Meg murmured, sounding on the verge of panic. "I dream it all the time. He won't let it go. He just won't."

Jordan joined them in time to say, "He has, Meg. He's dead. It's over for good this time. He can't hurt you anymore."

Casey slipped an arm around him, but only had time to trade him a grateful look before a police cruiser turned into the Court with its lights flashing. It stopped with a jolt. Two officers emerged at a crouch, guns drawn. Two others ran in from West Cedar, doing the same. Jordan went to join them.

Jeff and Emily passed him on their way up the steps. Emily put a hand on Meg's back. "Are you okay?"

Meg swallowed hard, tore her eyes from her father, and gave a convulsive nod.

Casey kept an arm around her. "She'll be fine," she said, and repeated the assurance when others of the neighbors cautiously approached. One thing was clear: they all knew and liked Meg.

"She baby-sat when our grandchild came

to visit. We wouldn't have trusted anyone else," one vowed. Another said, "She walked our dog when my father had a stroke and we had to rush home to Pough-keepsie on the spur of the moment."

"Meg made chicken soup for my wife when she was sick," said Greggory Dunn. "It was the only thing she could eat."

"It was Miriam's recipe," Meg murmured, and looked unsurely at Casey.

Casey smiled and nodded, acknowledg-ing that she knew the story. "Miriam was a good person," she said, and felt Meg relax just a bit.

Minutes later, Meg looked toward the street again. "Can I go down and see him?"

"Are you sure you want that?"

Meg nodded.

Casey understood her need for closure. As despicable a person as Darden Clyde was, he was Meg's flesh and blood. Meg had spent far more time with him than Casey had ever spent with Connie—yet here Casey was, living in Connie's town-house, visiting Connie's hometown, seeking out Connie's wife, tracking down Jenny and Pete. All this was a form of closure, too.

That said, there were other reasons why

Casey wanted to help Meg. Gratitude was one—Casey appreciated all that Meg had done for Connie. Compassion was another—Casey ached at what Meg had experienced growing up, and wanted to help make things better now. Yet another was a growing affection—Meg was eminently likable, in her innocent, agreeable way. And then—the kicker—they were cousins. Casey suspected she would forever feel protective of Meg, and that wasn't a bad thing.

Holding her arm, Casey led her down the stairs.

A pair of EMTs had already arrived and done enough of an examination to deem Darden beyond help. Having covered the upper half of his body, they were talking with one of the policemen. The other three, along with Jordan and Gregory, were with Sharon Davies. The lawyer was talking, using terms like "necessity defense" and "defense of another." Casey caught enough of it to understand that since Sharon had shot Darden to stop him from shooting someone else, she would never be charged with his death.

Slipping her arm free of Casey's, Meg

went to her father's body. She knelt, pulled back the sheet with a shaky hand, sat back on her heels. "I haven't seen him in seven years," she told Casey in a small voice.

"You had no choice."

"He loved me."

"Yes."

"Too much."

Casey was surprised that Meg could put it so well, given the storm of emotion she had to feel at that moment.

"Maybe it's better this way?" Meg asked.

"I think so," Casey said. She couldn't imagine another scenario in which Darden knew where Jenny was and would leave her alone. His need for her had become an obsession that wasn't about to ease on its own. Death was the only scenario in which Jenny's fear ended for good. Jenny had known that seven years ago. It had taken this long, with an unexpected twist, for it to come to pass.

"Do you believe in ghosts?" Meg asked Casey, still looking at Darden.

Casey was about to say no, which was surely what Meg needed to hear. But she hesitated. She had felt Connie's presence more than once. She could even argue that Angus carried a bit of Connie's spirit.

Meg looked up at her. "Will he hang around here and haunt me?"

She sounded so frightened that Casey said a conclusive, "No. We'll make sure of that, you and I." The EMTs returned. She took Meg by the arms and gently led her away from the body. "He's dead," she repeated, close by her ear. This was exposure therapy at its most opportune. "You've seen it right here with your own two eyes. Is he yelling at you now?"

"No."

"Is he scowling at you?"

"No."

"Is he touching you?"

"No."

"He was an angry, unhappy man. Maybe now he'll find peace."

Meg's eyes were bright with tears. "I'd like that. I don't want him angry and unhappy. He was my father."

The police had questions, and there were arrangements to be made for returning Darden to Walker for burial. Meg decided—

wisely, for her emotional well-being, Casey thought—that Jenny should remain dead. She had no desire to return to Walker. She was Meg now, and she liked her life.

The official story, as told to Edmund O'Keefe by Jordan in a phone call later that afternoon, was that, overcome with suspicion, Darden had come after Jordan with a gun, there had been a struggle, and Darden had been shot.

Sharon was the only one from Walker who had seen Jenny, but she empathized strongly enough with Jenny's situation to keep her name out of it. In so doing, of course, she also kept her own daughter's name out of the story, which was an important factor.

By late afternoon, the Court had been cleared. Casey and Jordan returned to the garden and insisted that Meg stay with them there. It was a peaceful place, separate even from what had happened in the front of the townhouse. There was hope here. There was growth here. Jordan pointed that out, freely naming the flowers this time. He showed Casey the hydrangea buds, the early peonies, and the last of the sweet woodruff. He explained that the heliotrope would bloom in tight little clusters through most of the summer, that the agapanthus and viburnum, both white, were excellent as cut flowers, that the bluebells would soon go dormant and that he would plant petunias in their place. He told her which plants were perennials, how they bloomed fresh each year, the same in some ways but different in others. He knelt by the gardenias, seeming especially fond of those. They were just at the start of their bloom, yet their fragrance was rich.

Listening to him talk, Casey was charmed. She followed him from flower to flower, while the birds flew in and out, and the bees flitted around. The fountain trickled endlessly in a steady, soothing stream.

Meg didn't say much, nor did she sit still for long. She was jumpy, out of her chair at the slightest noise. She calmed when Jordan gave her little chores to do, such as deadheading the rhododendrons, removing lilac blossoms that were past their prime, and pulling the beginnings of weeds from between the stones on the path. She was clearly happiest when she was active. Idleness allowed her to remember and to worry.

Casey identified with that. When she was busy, she didn't dwell on Caroline's condition. So, after Jordan's lesson, she spent a while doing paperwork for insurance claims and, when that was done, went inside to phone the next batch of her clients and tell them that her office had moved.

She was about to return to the garden when Jordan sauntered inside, bringing a warmth into the cool room. He had a pencil behind his ear and a hand behind his back. He seemed pleased with himself.

She gave him a puzzled little smile.

The hidden hand came forward and put a paper napkin on the desk. On it was a pencil sketch of a gardenia blossom, like those starting to open outside. No, she realized, lifting the napkin in amazement. It was more than a gardenia. Embedded in the petals were Casey's own features, so subtly placed but true-to-life that she was stunned. Eyes, nose, mouth—he had captured them all, even the shape of her face in the heart of the flower, rimmed by her hair, wildly curling round and about the elegant spray of the petals.

So simply drawn, so beautiful. She flattened the sketch to her thudding heart. "I'm going to frame this."

His cheeks grew red. "Don't frame it. It's just a fun little thing. I wanted to make you smile."

"You're very talented," she said, and felt a moment's awe. "Artist. Gardener. Savior. I haven't thanked you for rescuing me from my latest blunder."

"What blunder?"

"Rushing to Walker. Giving my business card to Dudley Wright. Bringing Darden here."

"Was that a blunder?"

"It sure would have been if you'd been killed. It sure would have been if *Meg* had been killed."

Leaning across the desk, he curved long fingers around her neck. "Hey, neither of those things happened. What happened," he said as his smile turned admiring, "is that you forced the issue. By going up there, you brought things to a head. Meg's free now. So, apparently, is Sharon Davies's daughter. You did good, Casey Ellis. Connie would have been proud."

The warmth inside Casey swelled. He

hadn't had to say that. He certainly hadn't had to say it with such conviction. But he seemed to know that it was what she needed most to hear. She could love a man capable of that kind of caring, could love him in a heartbeat.

That realization was jarring in its suddenness. But Casey couldn't shed it. It settled inside her—nestled there, germinated and grew—giving her cause for thought as afternoon became evening. Shortly before nine, when the nursing home phoned to say that Caroline was seizing again, Casey couldn't have turned anywhere else.

Chapter Twenty-three

Casey hadn't been so jittery since the first days after the accident, when Caroline had hovered between life and death. This wasn't much different, a stubborn little voice in her said. Caroline had always managed to pull through. Contrary to the doctors' expectations, she had stayed alive for three long years. A few more wouldn't hurt. A few more, and a cure might be found—a miracle waker-upper, a breakthrough brain-damage mender, something, *anything*.

Casey didn't want to be frightened. She certainly hadn't given up hope. But all the stubborn little voices in the world couldn't soothe her as they used to. The violence of Darden's death earlier that day hadn't helped.

Jordan drove. Casey sat in the passenger's seat. Meg slipped into the back before either of them could suggest she stay at the townhouse—not that Casey would have suggested it anyway. She was filled with a sense of dread, but it was different from the hollowness she had lived with these three years. Having people with her seemed to help.

They rode in silence and were quickly at the Fenway. Casey was met at the third-floor desk by the doctor on call. He was somber.

"Frankly, I'm amazed she's still with us," he said in a hushed voice as they walked quickly down the hall. "These seizures are stronger than the ones she's had. We have your do-not-resuscitate order, so we didn't take any invasive action, but we did sedate her. The seizure ended, though it took a far larger dose this time. That brings an additional danger."

Casey had an inkling of that. She knew enough about medicine and its effects. Still she had to ask. "What danger?"

"Her system is slowing down on its own. If we slow it down too much with medication, she dies."

"But if you don't stop the seizures, she dies anyway."

"Yes. And with a struggle. We call that a

'bad' death. We'd much prefer that she be comfortable. Then it's a 'good' death."

"Hence the sedative."

"Yes."

Ann Holmes was with Caroline, bringing Casey a small measure of solace. Of all of the nurses, she was the one Casey trusted most. As they entered the room, she was adjusting one of two drips that hung from the IV pole. The oxygen tube was in place. The heart monitor beeped.

Caroline's breathing was loud and coarse, but she looked much as she always did at night—on her back now, with her eyes closed, her mouth slightly open, and her hands fixed on the sheets. The only signs of a recent disturbance were her hair and the bedding, both of which were mussed.

Going to the far side of the bed, Casey smoothed wisps of still-beautiful silver hair behind Caroline's ear. Taking her mother's hand, she pressed it to her heart. She didn't speak. Her throat was thick with emotion.

"She's had a rough time of it," Ann said softly.

Casey nodded.

"Nurses sense things," Ann went on in that same low and gentle voice. "We can't tell you how or why, but, even aside from physical changes, we know when a patient like Caroline is making a statement. You need to help her, Casey. You need to let her know it's okay."

Casey's heart clenched.

"She's ready," Ann whispered.

"I'm not," Casey whispered back. She had been warned of this moment. She had been walked through the ways in which patients approached death, the things they did, the things they needed—and she would have been ready for it all, had it happened within a month or two of the accident. But when Caroline didn't die, Casey had grown complacent. She told herself that recovery would simply take time. She had gotten used to living with hope.

Now Ann was saying it was time to let go. They had definitely reached a different place. How to accept that?

"Is she sleeping?" Meg whispered from close by Casey's shoulder.

Casey cleared her throat. Quietly she replied, "In her way."

"Does she know you're here?"

"Mmm," Casey hedged, then, without

looking at Ann, admitted, "I'm not sure. Probably not."

"Why is she making that noise?"

Casey darted a look at Jordan. He stood at the foot of the bed, a solid comfort. Taking strength from that, she told Meg, "There's stuff that gets in the way of her breathing. She doesn't have the strength to clear it, so it just stays there."

"Is she in pain?"

"No."

"I'm glad." Meg was quiet for several minutes, then added, "She's very pretty."

Casey smiled. Throat knotting again, she nodded in agreement. Caroline was indeed very pretty. She would always be so in Casey's mind.

Taking her mother's hand, she gently extended the wrist and straightened the slender fingers, one, then the next, and the next. Interlacing them with her own, she turned Caroline's hand over. In the process, she got a look at the underside of her arm. It was darker in color than the top.

She looked in alarm at Ann, who said, "It's a circulatory thing." What she didn't say was that it was not a good sign, but the regret on her face sent the message—and, besides, Casey had known what it meant. Well beyond what she'd been told at the start, she had read most everything there was to read about complications and signs and prognoses of people in Caroline's condition.

Everything was pointing one way. Casey's heart was heavy with that admission. She rubbed Caroline's arm, thinking it might help with the "circulatory thing," knowing it wouldn't, needing to do it anyway.

"Will she wake up?" Meg asked.

Casey wanted to say yes. Desperately, she did. But she couldn't get the word out.

Jordan shifted position, drawing Casey's eye. He made a tiny movement, asking if she wanted him to take Meg out to the hall. Casey gave a quick shake of her head. She didn't mind having Meg there. Like Jordan, Meg was a reminder of her life now. That reminder helped ground her in reality. It was probably what she needed most.

"I hope she'll wake up," she finally told Meg, "but it's not looking good."

It didn't look any better two hours later. Caroline's breathing had grown even louder. No sooner had the doctor suctioned out fluid than it was replaced by more. Her head was already elevated; they raised it again, with negligible effect. Likewise, none of Casey's arm rubbing, face touching, and soft talking appeared to make a difference.

She had never been more frustrated. Watching Caroline mark time, as she'd done these three long years, had been hard, but sitting helplessly by while she deteriorated was an absolute agony.

Meg was dozing in a chair. Jordan stood near Casey, who sat on the bed by Caroline's side.

"Maybe you ought to take Meg home," she suggested softly. "She needs sleep. So do you."

"And you."

Smiling sadly, Casey looked at Caroline. "It was like this right after the accident, hours and hours of just sitting here, waiting for something to happen. I'd sleep on and off in the chair. I could do that now, too. I hate to leave her alone."

"They'll call you if she takes another turn."

"I know. But I'm still ten minutes away. I was closer at the condo." She gave a disbelieving half-laugh. "Two weeks ago, the condo was home. How could everything have changed so fast?"

He didn't answer, simply slipped a hand in hers. She touched her cheek to his shoulder for the sheer comfort of it.

Then an idea hit. Catching her breath, she righted her head. "Oh. *Wow*." She looked up at Jordan. "All these months I kept thinking that if Mom improved, I'd find a way to move her home with me. I barely had room then. Now I do. I want to show her the townhouse."

"She can't see it," he reminded her gently.

But the thought had taken root. "Maybe not, but what's the harm? She's been lying here for three years. Maybe that's the trouble. Maybe she needs a change of scenery to show her there's still a world out there. There's plenty of room at the townhouse. She'll be just as comfortable there as she is here. For what it's costing here, she can have a live-in nurse there." Her mind was filling with possibility. "I'll be able to see Mom between clients. I'll be right there if anything happens. I'll feel like I'm *doing* something." She had another thought. This one brought a small smile. "Isn't it a kind of poetic justice? Connie gave me the townhouse, but he never gave her a thing. I think it would be fitting and proper for her to see the place. To stay there. To use it."

"Would she want that?" he asked quietly.

"If she doesn't," Casey challenged defiantly, "let her open her eyes and tell me."

The move took place early the next morning. An ambulance brought Caroline to Beacon Hill, where she was met by Casey and Jordan, Meg, and a private nurse. In no time, Caroline was settled in Connie's big sleigh bed. Casey wouldn't have put her anywhere else.

Angus appeared to agree. After hiding behind the draperies until the flurry of activity was done, he ventured out and ever so cautiously approached the bed. He leapt onto it and sniffed his way up one side of Caroline and down the other. Then, seeming not at all bothered that she wasn't Connie, he curled into a ball at her feet and went to sleep.

That was the good news.

The bad news was that Caroline gave no sign of being aware of the move. If she shifted her eyes, it wasn't in response to any stimulus. Her hands lay inert. She didn't even cough, just continued rattling on with each breath.

Casey blamed her lack of awareness of the move on heavy sedation, but she didn't dare ask the nurse to cut it back. Nor did she ask the doctor, when he stopped by at noon. The alternative was seizures, he would say. None of them wanted that, least of all Casey. She wasn't tempting fate. She was tired of doing that.

Besides, her emotions had taken an interesting turn. The triumph she had expected to experience bringing Caroline into Connie's home never materialized. In its place was an odd contentment. What Casey felt—absurd as it sounded—was a sense of peace.

The move was right. She knew it in her soul. In bringing Caroline here, there was a closing of the circle in Casey's own life.

She was still frightened, but the fear was controlled, enough so that she was actually able to see clients—not only see, but counsel them well. Yes, a stranger might call her cold and unfeeling, working while her mother lay unresponsive in a bedroom upstairs. But a stranger hadn't worn Casey's shoes for the last three years.

Ahh, but there were strangers who had. Casey was one of many thousands holding vigil for loved ones who had been in comatose states for extended periods of time. Having talked with a few and read the stories of others, she knew that survival for those who watched and waited required a nominal return to normalcy. Just as Casey couldn't possibly have spent every minute of the last three years at Caroline's side, she couldn't do it now. Nor did she think her mother would want it. Caroline was a doer. She would respect Casey for respecting the needs of her clients.

One of those clients was Joyce Lewellen, but it was a different Joyce who came in from the waiting room. This Joyce had color on her cheeks and a bounce in her step. She looked as though a great weight had been lifted from her shoulders.

"Well?" Casey invited with an anticipatory smile as they took their usual seats.

"We lost," Joyce said.

Casey had expected to hear of a win. Her smile was erased by surprise.

"The judge ruled against us," Joyce explained, "but the weirdest thing happened. I wanted to win. You know how badly I wanted that. I didn't sleep last Thursday night. I was a mess, waiting in the lawyer's office for the decision to arrive. When it came, he read it himself, then he read it to me. Then he put the paper down on the desk. And . . . just like that . . . it was over. I mean, all the things you'd been telling me ran through my mind, and suddenly they made sense. I tried. No one can say I didn't. I tried to find someone responsible for Norman's death. And I couldn't. The doctors did try to save him. Okay, maybe they should have guessed that he might react adversely to the anesthesia. Maybe something in Norman's medical history should have given them a hint. But it didn't, and after the fact they did what they could to save him. I'm not saying I'm happy. Norman's still dead. The girls are still without him, and I'm still alone. But I'm content with the judge's decision. I took it as far as I could. Win or lose, I tried."

Content. Casey had used the same word to describe how she felt about having her mother here with her in Connie's house. Her situation wasn't any happier than Joyce's.

Caroline was still in a vegetative state. But Casey had *done* something in bringing Caroline here. Just as Joyce had *done* something in pursuing the lawsuit.

"You were feeling helpless after Norman's death," Casey said, which was how she'd been feeling herself.

"Very. Our marriage wasn't perfect. I've told you about that. But he was good to me, and he certainly was good to the girls. I felt I owed it to him to try."

"You were very angry last week."

"I know."

"Do you feel angry now?"

"You told me to let it go."

So Casey had. Thinking about that, she left her seat, went to the desk, and took two butterscotch candies from the drawer. She gave one to Joyce and unwrapped her own as she settled back into her chair. She slipped it into her mouth and folded the paper. Looking at Joyce again, she gently repeated the question. "Do you feel angry now?"

Joyce thought about the question this time. "If I try, I could get myself worked up. But the bubble burst, and I feel relieved. If I could bring Norman back, I would, but I can't. If I could find someone at fault for his death, I would, but I can't. I was there during the hearing. The judge seemed intelligent, and he seemed fair. Now he's made his decision. He took it out of my hands."

Casey envied Joyce. She wished *she* had a judge to take things out of her hands— someone to issue a decision in writing saying, definitively, that Caroline's time had come. Caroline was withdrawing from her. The question was whether it was time to let go.

Caroline was never alone. When Casey wasn't with her, the nurse was by her side, and when the nurse took breaks, Meg was there, sitting on the side of the bed, holding Caroline's hand and singing softly. By mid-afternoon, Brianna had stopped by. Then Jenna and Joy and others of Casey's friends came. Then two members of her yoga class. Then several of Caroline's friends from Providence. Then Emily.

Jordan was in and out through the day. At one point, when Casey remarked wistfully that she would have liked to carry Caroline to the garden, he took things in his own hands and brought the garden to Caroline. He filled vases with viburnum and sweet woodruff, with bluebells, lilacs, and lilies. He brought the first of the peonies; he brought sweet William and bleeding heart. By late afternoon, Caroline's room was nearly as gay with fragrance as the garden itself.

Early evening found Casey alone with Caroline, marveling at it all, when a soft knock came at the open bedroom door. Ruth Unger stood on the far side of the threshold, looking far less confident than she had in her own house the Friday before, clearly unsure of her welcome, clearly respecting the bounds of that threshold.

Casey was startled. She might have hesitated—might have reminded herself that Caroline might not want Connie's wife anywhere *near*—had Casey not spent that little time with Ruth three days before. Against her better judgment, she had liked Ruth then. And now she was touched.

With a tentative smile, she gestured her into the room.

"I wasn't sure . . . ," Ruth began, trailing off when she neared the bed and looked at Caroline. She seemed truly grieved.

"How did you know she was here?" Casey asked.

"I call the nursing home every Monday."

Casey hadn't known that. No one at the nursing home had told her. Of course, she hadn't asked. "Why . . . do you call?"

"To see how she is," Ruth explained, her eyes still on Caroline. "I didn't trust that Connie could pick up the phone and make the call, but I felt he ought to know if there was a change."

"Were the flowers your doing, too?"

"No. He did that himself." She paused, gave a diffident smile. "Of all the times I imagined bumping into your mother on the street, I never pictured we would meet like this."

"Why would it matter?" Casey asked, though without bitterness. Much as she wanted to, she couldn't feel anger toward Ruth. "You got Connie."

"Yes. I did. And he loved me in his way. But she was part of his life."

"One night. That's all."

"One night, one daughter," Ruth corrected with a small smile, and here, too, Casey was touched. Ruth had no cause to make Casey feel good. Yet, she had done it on Friday and was doing it now.

"Well," Casey said softly, and let it go.

"I saw Jordan downstairs," Ruth said. "I'm glad he's here."

"You know Jordan?"

"Yes. Jordan and I have something in common, and it's not Connie."

Casey was a minute in following, but she finally did. "Art."

"We kept seeing each other at shows, even before we realized that we shared this other connection. He's far more talented than I am, of course."

"He would probably argue with that."

"That's because he's a gentleman," Ruth said, then continued, "I brought dinner. Coq au vin. Meg is heating it up."

"That was *very* sweet of you."

"I wish there were more I could do."

"This is helpful—the thought and all. I truly appreciate it."

"If there's anything else, I'd like you to call and ask."

Casey smiled. "I will," she said, meaning it.

Ruth nodded. She continued to study Caroline for another minute. Then she gave

Casey's shoulder a light rub. "Let me know how she does?"

Caroline's breathing worsened. When the nurse rolled her onto her side, Casey was there, helping hold her body, urging her to cough up what was clogging her airways. "Come on, Mom. You can do it. Do it for me."

But Caroline didn't respond. When they propped her in a half-seated position, the rasping was as bad as ever. The phrase "death rattle" kept coming to Casey's mind. Each time it did, she pushed it away. But each time it returned.

Even Meg heard the change. She stood against the side of the bed opposite Casey, while her eyes focused on Caroline. "It's like she's trying to tell you something, only you can't hear her, so she's speaking louder and louder. What is she trying to say?"

Casey feared that she knew. Leaning close, she begged, "Talk to me, Mom. Tell me what you're feeling." When she heard nothing, she pushed the issue. "We always used to talk, you and I. Remember how we did—not even so much before the accident, but after? You talked to me, Mom. I could hear you clear as day. You were thinking your thoughts, and I heard them."

"Could anyone else hear her?" Meg asked.

Casey smiled sadly. "No. But no one else knew her well enough to be able to think her thoughts."

"If you were thinking her thoughts, were they real?"

Casey was taken aback. She stood straighter. If getting a handle on reality was the goal, Meg had certainly asked the right question—which was humbling for Casey, a dose of reality in its own right. Meg was no therapist, indeed had no formal education beyond high school. But she had lived through an emotional crisis and intensive therapy, and emerged a fully functional human being. That earned her a certain credibility.

Suddenly Casey was curious. "Tell me about Pete," she asked.

Meg looked surprised, but only for a minute. "What . . . should I say?"

"Was he real?"

"In my mind, yes. *Real* real? No."

"Had you grown up with imaginary friends?"

Meg shook her head.

"Were you aware when you first saw him that you'd made him up?"

She seemed to grapple with the question. When she finally answered, it was with an element of unease. "I want to say I was. That way I won't sound so crazy."

"Meg, I carry on conversations with my mother," Casey confessed brashly. "Is that much different?"

"It is," Meg maintained. "You don't act on what you imagine."

"I have. I planned us a trip once. I booked space for us on a cruise to Alaska."

Meg looked appeased. "The whole time Pete was with me, I thought he was real. I did. I just didn't know if he would *stay*. I used to think I'd come home and find him gone. I couldn't believe that he would really want me."

Casey had read all this in the journal. "When did you realize that you'd made him up?"

Meg considered her answer. "I used to think it was when I was at the hospital. When I first got there, I was kind of on the fence. Sometimes I believed he would come and get me. Other times, I knew he wouldn't. Couldn't."

Casey sensed there was more to her answer. She waited.

Finally, in a small voice, Meg said, "When was the first time I thought that maybe he was all my imagination? It was when I climbed out of the quarry and hid in the woods. I mean," she said with sudden animation, even angst, "we were supposed to go somewhere good together. He was leading me there. I kept diving and diving, only I wouldn't stay down."

"Did you think he might have drowned?"

"No. Oh, no. Pete wouldn't drown. He was strong. He was a good swimmer." Self-conscious of the outburst, she gave Casey a sheepish smile. "Well, I imagined he was. But then he didn't come back up to the surface to get me. I started getting tired, and he wasn't there to help me stay underwater, and I couldn't do it on my own. When I climbed out of the pool, he didn't come. And then I just felt alone, like I'd always been."

Casey thought about the last few times she'd tried to talk with Caroline, when her mother hadn't responded. She had felt alone then, too. Thinking about being alone now, though, she didn't feel as acute a pain. "Did you feel alone at the hospital?"

"At first I did. I didn't know anyone. But they were all really nice. They wanted to help. I'd never had people wanting to help me before. Well, I had. There was Miriam. But she wasn't like Pete."

"Do you ever think you see Pete now? In stores? On the street?"

"How could I? He doesn't exist. I made him up, because I needed him so bad."

"Do you miss him?"

She started to shake her head, then stopped. Looking sheepish again, she said, "Sometimes. He loved me."

Casey felt a stab of compassion. Impulsively, she rounded the bed and gave Meg a hug. "Other people love you, now. You're a very lovable person."

"You know what I mean," Meg murmured.

Casey did. She had read *Flirting with Pete.* The kind of love Jenny had found in her Pete was something else.

"But it was a game," Meg said softly. "I know that."

Casey held her back and studied her face. Yet again she wore less makeup; her freckles were pale but distinct. Likewise, with the auburn rinse wearing off, her hair was becoming a more natural shade of red.

"A mind game," Meg went on, meeting her gaze more surely. "I needed someone to take me away. I didn't want to live if I had to be with Darden. I was desperate, so I played games. That's what I learned at the hospital."

"Do you believe it?"

She considered that. "I do. Don't you?"

Casey nodded. She knew about games that the mind played. They were called psychoses. Some were brief, others prolonged. Some were debilitating, others not so. Jenny's psychosis developed in response to a marked stressor, namely Darden's imminent return from prison and the horror that would wreak on her life. Once removed from that situation, she had been successfully treated.

"Is that how you feel, when you hear your mother speak?" Meg asked.

Casey gave her a blank look.

"Desperate?" Meg added. "Like you need to play a mind game?"

* * *

Casey sat cross-legged on the bed in the dark. She was dressed for bed, but she hadn't slept more than a few minutes. It was one in the morning. She had sent the night nurse down to the kitchen and was watching Caroline alone.

No, not alone. Angus was with her, curled up by Caroline's feet. He seemed to have staked a claim to the spot, and hadn't moved far from it since she had arrived.

Jordan came barefoot across the carpet. "Hey," he whispered, lightly grazing her neck with the back of his hand. It was a brief gesture, incredibly tender, surprisingly reassuring. "Couldn't sleep?"

She smiled, shook her head, reached for his hand.

He stood studying Caroline. "Her breathing sounds . . ."

"Bad." Casey couldn't delude herself.

He drew her hand to his mouth, kissed it, then flattened it on his chest and held it there. "What are you afraid of?" he asked quietly. "What's bothering you most?"

Casey didn't have to think for long. She had been asking herself the same question all night. "Being alone. Having no backup in life. I didn't always agree with her, but I always knew she was there. She's my mother. I'm not sure you get the same kind of unconditional love in your life from anyone but a mother. I've had clients who've never had that, and it haunts them. I've had clients who had it and lost it at too young an age. Here I am at thirty-four. I should be grateful for having had her all these years. Why am I so greedy to want more?"

"You said it. She's your mother. It's a unique relationship."

"She loved me even through the bad times. She loved me when I was at my most unlovable."

Jordan smiled. "I can't imagine you being unlovable."

"Trust me. I was. I was bratty. I was rebellious. I was totally obnoxious at times."

"She must have known why. It's easy to put up with things when you know the why of them."

"It's the unconditional-love thing. I was her only daughter. She had lots of friends, but only one daughter."

"You're using the past tense."

Casey hadn't planned it. The words had just come out that way. She watched Caroline's face to see if she had noticed, too.

Of course, she hadn't. Her eyes were closed, her life's energy focused on breathing, on dragging air in and pushing it out, an increasing struggle, a plea.

A plea. Casey felt it.

Meg's words echoed in her mind. *It's like she's trying to tell you something, only you can't hear her, so she's speaking louder and louder. What is she trying to say?*

Ann Holmes's words followed. *You need to help her, Casey. You need to let her know it's okay.*

"Is it okay?" Casey whispered.

She was looking at Caroline, but it was Jordan who answered. "Using the past tense? If you've used it, it's okay. You're the one who counts, Casey."

"No," Casey said. "This isn't about me. It's about her." But as soon as the words were out, she knew they weren't true. Caroline was beyond differentiating verb tenses. What mattered now, selfish as it sounded, was Casey's own coming to terms with that. Her use of the past tense, after all this time adhering so carefully to present and future, meant something.

The subconscious often knew things first.

But Casey's conscious self wasn't far behind. Sitting there in the dark, she had the sudden understanding that her life had come together. Loose ends were connecting, needs were being met. She had resolved things in her mind between her parents, had found a special lover in Jordan, a blood relative in Meg, and an unexpected friend in Ruth. The townhouse was working for her. So was practicing solo. She had friends who loved her and colleagues who respected her. She had a garden that was an oasis in stormy times and pure bliss in calm ones.

What are you afraid of? Jordan asked. *What's bothering you most?*

Being alone, she had answered without pause.

It struck her now, though, that she wasn't alone. If she hadn't seen that before, the last few days had shown it to her. She was surrounded by people she cared about deeply and who cared deeply about her. She had a very rich life.

Alone? Alone was a term that she had come to use simply because she'd grown up in a single-parent home. But she had never been alone. Not really. Had she been her own client, she might have suggested—

gently and nonconfrontationally—that she had used "alone" as an excuse for misbehavior, anger, even self-pity.

She didn't feel any of those things now. Sitting here with Caroline and Jordan, she felt peaceful. Anger was gone. Bitterness was gone. So was fear.

Her mother would say she had finally grown up. And perhaps that was what Caroline had been waiting for, why she had hung on these three long years, living a life that was no life at all. She had been waiting for Casey to find that inner peace on her own, had given her time and space, which was very much the way Caroline had raised her. Casey had been a strong-willed child. She'd had a mind of her own, had needed to make her own mistakes and find her own answers. Now she had. Caroline had given her the time to do that. It was a final gift.

Jordan kissed the top of her head. "I'll keep the bed warm," he said, startlingly attuned to her thoughts and needs. "Call me if you want me."

Casey choked up. She suspected the sudden swell of emotion had as much to do with her feelings for him as with what she had to do now. Unable to speak, she nodded silently. Her heart was full as she watched him leave the room.

Eyes filled with tears, she returned to Caroline. "He's something, isn't he?" she managed to ask through a smile. Then, "See?" she teased. "You can't argue. If he were one of my earlier guys, you'd be telling me that I haven't known him very long and that I should be cautious. But he's a keeper, don't you think?"

She brought Caroline's hand to her mouth, kissed it, and tucked it under her chin. Her throat ached with emotion, but she forced words out. They couldn't wait. It was time.

"Mom?" she whispered. "I need you to listen to what I have to say. This is really important." She paused to wipe at the tears that trickled down her cheek. In the time it took to sniff back others, she felt a tiny remnant of fear. Once the words were out, she couldn't take them back. But this was the right thing to do. She knew it in her heart.

"It's okay, Mom," she said ever so gently. "You can let go. I'm okay. I really am okay. You can let go now. You can leave."

Hugging Caroline's hand, she cried softly. But there was more to be said. She sniffled again and recomposed herself. "I want you to be happy. I don't want you to suffer more than you have to. You've fought so hard, but you're tired, and I can't fault you for that. This has gone on too long. Let's make it a good death." Her voice rose to a wail on the last, and again she wept softly. It was another minute before she managed to continue, her voice hoarse. "If you've prolonged this for my sake, I'm sorry." She took a broken breath. "No. Actually, I'm not sorry. Three years ago, I wasn't ready. But I am now. You made it easier." She went on more brightly. "I'm glad you met Jordan. He's the one, Mom. I really think he is. Have you ever heard me say that before? No, you haven't. But he's only one of the things that's right with my life." She gave a small, mildly hysterical laugh. "I mean, did I think that things were *wrong* with my life? No. But now that the pieces are all falling into place, things are so *right*." Her voice wavered, tears starting again. "I want things to . . . to be right for you, too. I want you peaceful. You deserve that. I love you so much."

Sobbing quietly, she pulled a tissue from the box on the nightstand and pressed it to her nose. She didn't immediately speak when she regained control this time. Rather, she noticed Angus. No longer curled in a ball, he was sitting up now, large green eyes on Caroline. Her own eyes followed. Caroline was breathing more easily.

Her first thought was that she was imagining it. So she listened with a more objective ear. It gave her the same hopeful report.

Casey had no delusions. Gone were visions of Caroline recovering. Reality had quenched that hope. A new one had arisen, though. It had to do with dying in peace.

Convinced from this quieter breathing that she was saying the things Caroline needed to hear, Casey went on. Her voice was nasal now, thick with tears. "You were an incredible mother. I think I knew that deep down, even when I hated you. But you always did the right thing, Mom, even when that meant standing back and letting me mess up and then make amends. Even now. You hung on for me. I think you knew Connie died. You took a turn for the worse then. Still you hung on. But it's okay," her voice trembled, rose, broke. "It's . . . okay to go, to let . . . go."

Crying again, rocking back and forth ever so slightly, she pressed Caroline's hand hard to her mouth. She didn't try to stop the tears. This was the last physical support her mother would ever give her, and she took it greedily. The scent of eucalyptus was fading. She breathed the last of it in.

In time the weeping ebbed. Gently, she stroked Caroline's forehead, her cheek, her hair. "It's okay," she whispered. "I'm okay. I mean, you can never be dead as long as I'm around. I'm *you* in so many ways. I never saw it. Never wanted to see it. I wanted to be independent and do things my way, but my way was pretty often your way. Especially lately." She actually smiled. "You'll always be with me, Mom. Kind of like Jordan's perennials. Every year, something'll bloom in my life to remind me of you. It'll always be different, never the same, but it'll be good. Love lasts."

Having said that, Casey was content. Suddenly exhausted, she lay down with Caroline, held her close, kept her warm, and put her ear to her mother's heart until there was no beat left to hear.

Summer in the garden was a time of ripening. The birches filled out, the hemlocks grew taller, maple and oak leaves deepened to a richer green, junipers to a sea green-blue. Less chirpy now that the mating season was done, the birds were raising their young. As the weeks passed, those fledglings joined their parents pecking at seeds in the feeder. Bees hovered over the rhododendron, and when those blooms passed, the gardenias, and when those passed, the hydrangea. Butterflies flitted into the garden from time to time, beautiful to see, too quickly gone.

Casey's practice thrived—just seemed to proliferate right along with Jordan's impatiens. She didn't know if it was her own reputation catching on, word passed on the sly by the likes of Emmett Walsh, or simply the cachet of having an office on Beacon Hill.

But her schedule filled. After a month in Connie's office, she felt she had been there forever. Apparently, so did Angus. Once he ventured from the master bedroom, he became her shadow. Oh, he was stealthy about it at first, keeping his distance, moving with silent dignity. But by the time the hostas in the garden had raised elegant purple spikes, he was curling right up to her thigh during client sessions. If he was indeed the spirit of Connie, she couldn't complain.

Nor could she complain about Jordan. He helped her bury Caroline and live through the grief, and he kept her garden growing, always with a new bloom to succeed one that withered as summer progressed. Just as ferns grew to replace trillium, petunias took the place of sweet william, periwinkle spread, and lupine bloomed regal and tall, so Casey's relationship with Jordan evolved. She didn't rush it. After having been impulsive for much of her life, she needed time. With her mother gone now, and her father before that, she was the adult in the family. Loving Jordan had been a sudden thing, come on her at a precarious time. She wanted her life to settle and see if that love would take root.

Jordan could not have been more attuned to her needs. In life, as in lovemaking, his timing was faultless. He knew when to introduce her to his art, and when to introduce her to his friends. He knew when to take her to plant flowers at Caroline's grave, when to suggest that they go to Rockport to visit with Ruth, and when to drive her to Amherst to meet a thirteen-year-old boy with bright red hair.

Joey Battle. Casey knew him on sight. He was living with a married couple, friends of Jordan's, and attending a small private school that did as much nurturing of the soul as the mind. Jordan picked up the tab.

"Well, I couldn't let him stay in Walker," he argued, seeming embarrassed when Casey was awed by what he had done. "I didn't help Jenny when I should have. I wasn't making the same mistake twice."

Casey loved him all the more for that. And then, there was even more to love him for. Come August, he drove her up to spend time with his parents in Walker. His mother had been to Boston several times prior to that, and she and Casey had grown close, but this was the first time in a while that Jordan had seen his father. He swore he wouldn't have had the courage to go if Casey hadn't been with him, and she almost believed him. His father intimidated him—she could see it the instant they came together.

Jordan was a strong man. He knew who he was and what he wanted in life. Yet his father had the power to make him grow silent, evade questions, be defensive. That certainly didn't weaken him in Casey's eyes. Even if she hadn't known by profession what he was feeling, she would have identified with it personally. She had been there. She was *still* there, wanting her parents' approval, needing to think she was making them proud. Parents held a remarkable power over their children. It didn't matter how old those children grew, or how distant in their everyday lives. They received messages from their parents from the moment of birth. Those messages were nearly as deeply etched on the psyche as hair, eyes, and height in the genes.

Jordan did grow more confident as the visit progressed, particularly when his sisters and their families arrived. They were delighted to see him and doted on Casey. For Casey, who had never known family beyond Caroline, it was an exciting day.

But the excitement wasn't done. The morning after that family gathering, Jordan drove her yet another hour north to a quiet, tidy little town. After passing through a modest town center, they turned onto a narrow, tree-lined side street and pulled up at a small frame house that was yellow with mossy green shutters and was surrounded by hemlocks and pines, junipers and yews, and, in gently defined beds, many of the same flowers Casey had on Beacon Hill. A pebbled front walk cut through those beds. It led to three wooden steps and a wraparound porch. A pair of rocking chairs sat on the porch. An elderly woman rocked in one.

Casey shot Jordan a quizzical look, but he didn't say a word. Rather, he rounded the Jeep, took her hand, and led her up the walk.

The woman on the porch stopped rocking. She had white hair and a wrinkled face, wore a flowered dress and a white apron, and looked nearly as puzzled as Casey. But she seemed familiar, oh so familiar.

Casey's heart began to race.

The woman didn't take her eyes off her. Those eyes were blue, Casey saw as she climbed the steps with Jordan—faded with age, but blue nonetheless. Blue eyes, white hair that might have had a reddish tint in her youth, a gentle smile that might actually have been loving, if Casey had been prone to fancy—which, of course, she was.

The woman extended a trembling hand to Casey, at the same time that Jordan said softly, "This is Mary Blinn Unger. Your grandmother. Age ninety-six."

Fall in the garden was glorious as only falls in New England could be. The maple turned orange, the birches yellow, the oak red. Black-eyed Susans multiplied, asters opened with splashes of pink, and viburnum produced berries. The vines that wove through the pergola, up the brick walls, and against the potting shed turned into tapestries of oranges, reds, and browns.

Slender in a stunning white gown, with a garland of ivy in her hair, Casey walked from the house, up the stone path, to the wooded spot where Jordan stood with the minister. Brianna and Joy had preceded her as her bridesmaids, as had Meg as her maid of honor, looking absolutely beautiful now with naturally red hair, artfully groomed.

Casey walked alone, but she wasn't alone in any sense of the word. Friends and family-to-be filled the garden on both sides. Caroline's spirit was as strong as if she were right there at the head of the walk. Likewise, Connie. His office would never be filled, his garden flourishing, and his cat adoring of Casey if he didn't approve of this match.

Jordan waited, so handsome that it took her breath, so focused on her and only her that it brought tears to her eyes. There were truly times when, like Jenny with her Pete, Casey wondered if he was real. She didn't need to pinch herself to be sure, though. All she had to do was to turn her head, look around, call his name, and he was there.

Snow fell before the end of November. It coated the few leaves that still clung to the trees, blanketed evergreens that had already shrunk into themselves for the winter, and carpeted the garden path. Much as Casey loved spending time outside, she was ready for the change. Winter meant staying indoors, with a blazing fire, hot mulled cider, and Jordan. It was a time for settling in as husband and wife, and seeing to the fine points of merging their lives.

Jordan sold his condo, moved his office to one of the spare bedrooms and his studio to the cupola, and tutored Casey in critiquing his work. Casey sold her condo, gave Meg as much furniture as her apartment would hold, sold the rest, and opened her first ever joint bank account.

By the time snowdrops had pushed their pristine white heads from the thawing ground, and the crocuses opened petals of yellow, purple, and pink, it was late March, and Casey was showing.

By the time June arrived with its dogwood blossoms, its wisteria, and the leafing out of the maple, birches, and oak, she was large, indeed.

By the time she gave birth in early August, the garden was as fertile and rich as she felt herself.

That Casey's life took on the rhythm of the garden was only fitting. Both of her parents had loved flowers and trees, as did her husband. And Casey herself? The garden grounded her. It kept her head clear and her mind focused on what was real and what was not. It gave her hope in moments of worry, and ease in moments of stress. It bore witness to the perennial nature of birth.

When their daughter celebrated her first birthday there among the flowers on a sunny summer day the following August, she wore a delicate wreath of daisies in her baby-soft strawberry blond hair, ate cake with chocolate frosting and ice cream with a wooden spoon, and fell on her face toddling after a butterfly.

Her father scooped her up and nuzzled her stomach as he carried her to Casey, who kissed the boo-boo until she was laughing again.

Life was good.